THIS FAR, NO FURTHER

JOHN WESSEL

Island
BOOKS

ISLAND BOOKS
Published by
Dell Publishing
a division of
Bantam Doubleday Dell Publishing Group, Inc.
1540 Broadway
New York, New York 10036

ISBN: 0-440-22490-X

Reprinted by arrangement with Simon & Schuster

Printed in the United States of America

Published simultaneously in Canada

November 1997

10   9   8   7   6   5   4   3   2   1

OPM

for Susan   for waiting

ACKNOWLEDGMENTS

For some reason a number of people took a chance on an unpublished author. . . .

I was fortunate to have Molly Friedrich as both agent and audience during the early drafts. Her judgment of the book's worth meant a great deal to me. Much of it was written with her (and Sheri Holman, her assistant) in mind as my ideal readers. I hope that never changes.

I was equally blessed to have Bob Mecoy as an editor, especially in the later drafts, guiding the book to publication. From our first conversation it was clear that he believed in the book and understood what I was trying to do, even when my attempts fell short of the mark. Thanks also to Carolyn Reidy, Michael Korda, and everyone at Simon & Schuster. For early support I'm grateful to *Cincinnati Magazine*; the Mercantile Library of Cincinnati; and the Santa Barbara Writers Conference.

Sue Grafton was the first to see anything of value in these pages, the first to care that they might be made better. She treated a rank amateur as a fellow writer, which is quite extraordinary. I will never forget her genuine interest in the characters, her kindness, her encouragement.

Finally, my deepest gratitude goes to my friend Barbara Ritchken, who listened to my nightmares with endless patience, and then showed me how to end them. This book is the result.

In the middle of the journey of our life
  I found myself astray in a dark wood. . . .
        —Dante's *Inferno*

Man, man I'm just scared of living. It's killing me.
        —Mickey Spillane, *The Deep*

Behold, I show you a mystery;
  We shall not all sleep, but we shall all be changed.
        —I Corinthians 15:51

PART ONE

ELENYA

ONE

He hits you? I didn't know he hits you," Donnie Wilson says, professional concern in his voice, the best sincerity money can buy. "Why in God's name—"

"Different things. If something's not perfect—see these lines below my eyes? He wants to burn them off. Like setting brush fires. The week before it was cellulite. Remember cellulite?" She shakes her head. Even barefoot in a plain black slip Elenya Rosenberg is sensory overload. Her dark red hair is cut very short. The skin on both arms is a soft brown and lightly freckled. Her face is pale, her eyes light amber. And then there's the rainbow of black-and-blue marks under both arms, across her back, inside her thighs, within the untanned triangles on each breast.

"Last month Stephen decides one of my hips is slightly fuller than the other. So that's all he can see now, he says, whenever I'm naked. Which isn't often. This imbalance. I'm no longer symmetrical."

"Reluctant fat." I wrap the Burberry I found in Donnie's executive washroom around Elenya's shoulders. Her own coat's probably salvageable and the black pumps cleaned up okay, but her dress is another matter. The late shift janitor could only give me Spic and Span, and I'm not sure Donna Karan originals are drip-dry. "That's what they call cellulite now. According to Oprah. Reluctant fat."

"You should have told us," Donnie says, waving me away—I'm supposed to wait in the corner. From the look he gives me you'd think it was me that threw up on his new pinky ring. "Really, Elenya. There are procedures to follow in situations such as this. We could have protected you somehow, done something—"

"Like what, Donald?" She sets a highball glass on the carpet. It's rimmed with dried Alka-Seltzer, like salt on a margarita. "Tell me. Please. About my situation."

"I don't know exactly. *Something.*" Donnie's not much for details; he's a Big Picture Guy now and looks the part—three-piece gray pinstripes, red power tie, a white shirt struggling to contain his tree stump of a neck. I think he's been hitting the tanning bed. The weather's brutally cold again tonight—a typical Chicago February—but Donnie's skin has that crisp bronze sheen that comes from spending lunch hours vacationing in the Caribbean.

"Gosh, you're just so reassuring," Elenya says softly. She sits back in her chair, crosses her legs. The trench coat barely covers her knees. "Maybe you could introduce your hippie friend here—did you tell me his name was Harlan? Harry?"

"Harding," I say, pushing my hair back. She nods. I haven't been called a hippie since high school. I probably do need a haircut. And I could have dressed better. My Levi's are worn through at the knees. I forgot my belt. My boots are scuffed. But Donnie just called me a couple of hours ago, interrupting my afternoon nap.

"She wants to meet you, buddy," he'd said then, his voice hollow from the ether of his car phone. "Why,

I have no fucking idea. Just remember to keep your goddamned mouth shut. This is my dog-and-pony show. I've already got her brain-dead lawyer to deal with. And for Christ's sake don't show up until after seven. Because I'm not buying your fucking dinner."

I shake her hand—surprisingly warm given her clothing and dotted with freckles like tiny four-leaf clovers—then retreat to my corner seat. It's drafty back here. And there's a teak minibar keeping Donnie's mineral water properly chilled. It's turning on and off every two seconds and driving me nuts. He hasn't offered me any water but that's okay. I'm trying to cut down.

"You're concerned about the money," Donnie says to Elenya. He leans against a bookcase filled with golfing figures. "This is perfectly understandable. What *you* have to understand is that these things take time. You have to be patient. We just found out about this last week. And really, Elenya—I mean, my God, let's be frank here for just a moment, if we may—if your husband didn't even tell *you* about the two million in Swiss funds—after twenty-two years of marriage—"

"Twenty-three," she says. "I don't know, Donald. It must have slipped his mind." She pulls the topcoat tighter around her. Whenever the jazz CD on Donnie's stereo turns moody it's drowned out by a nasty Siberian Express whipping around our Schaumburg office tower. The last prediction I heard was minus fifteen and falling; too cold even for more snow. It's chilly in here tonight; none of us are very comfortable.

But then this office wasn't designed to be functional. The chairs we're perched on are leather straps stretched over flat black steel, rickety as cheap lawn furniture but numbered and signed by a trendy River North artist. They're arranged around a coffee table the size of the black monolith in *2001*. Donnie's new desk—a narrow slab of Italian marble barely wide enough for a phone—has no drawers.

It's a vice president's corner office. Donnie's new promotion has landed him on the tenth floor of Schaumburg Associates, a suburban firm handling corporate security. I myself work from the living room of my Lakeview apartment, a third floor walkup above a Greek restaurant. Clients like Elenya Rosenberg rarely make the three-story climb. The moussaka and souvlaki smells baked into the walls can be deterring.

I lost my PI license ten years ago—the state board has this picky rule about convicted felons—and since then most of the work I do is runoff from other PIs. It's legwork mostly, cases they consider dead ends, clients they find too annoying. More and more I've been doing odd jobs and errands for Donnie; things he prefers keeping informal, off the books. "There are things we do," Donnie sometimes says, "that we don't do."

Lately that's meant following Dr. Stephen Rosenberg on a Grand Tour of exciting northern Indiana. Stephen's a professor at my alma mater, the University of Chicago—a tenured, highly respected cosmetic surgeon at the Medical Center—who spends his Wednesdays indulging a fondness bordering on obsession for small towns, cheap motels, a blonde nurse named Lucy Williams. It's not exactly white–collar crime, and the boys at Schaumburg Associates don't like getting their hands too dirty.

Exactly how Donnie got involved with the Rosenbergs isn't clear to me—Donnie hasn't said and I don't like asking too many questions. It's what endears me to the Donnie Wilsons of the world. There's a standing offer for me to work out here full-time but I can't see that happening. Not that I'm exactly overwhelmed with work. But whenever I'm westbound on the Eisenhower I feel like I'm heading the wrong way.

"Everyone in overseas finance is working on this," Donnie says, making the racquetball conversation I had with a guy from First Chicago sound like we convened the World Bank, "absolutely the entire section, top-notch men. And Elenya, believe me, the Swiss are not unreasonable about these things. So perhaps your lawyer—Warren Frost? Yes?—should coordinate this next phase. Because I really don't see what's to be gained by continuing this surveillance. I really don't." Donnie sits behind his desk, folds his hands on the marble top, nods sympathetically. He could be reading a will. "I understand Mr. Frost is out of town for a few days. My advice? When he returns you retain a Geneva firm to consult. Build a paper trail. Shake the tree until something falls. And have a little faith in the system."

I'm charmed by this soothing lawyerly talk. Because this is the same Donnie Wilson who grew up with me on the South Side and paid his Catholic school tuition stealing tenspeeds from the church lot. This Donnie ran numbers for the ward boss and once told me he'd helped fix the Special Olympics. "The special people weren't so special today, you know?" he'd confided, counting his money, ones and fives plucked from a crowd of tourists. "The slow learners weren't so slow. And some of the gimps were ringers. Threw the spread way off." Only in Chicago. He won a bundle on the wheelchair races.

Elenya Rosenberg doesn't seem as charmed.

"I don't believe this," she says. "Warren was right. You're dropping me."

"Nobody's dropping you," Donnie says, frowning.

"We'll certainly be around for further consultations. But we've gone as far as we can reasonably go." I catch him sneaking a look at his Rolex—I think he has Blackhawks tickets. "Despite what Mr. Frost may think," he says, "there are limits—"

"I didn't see any limits in the photographs you showed me," Elenya says. "Are you telling me those pictures—two shopping-bags-ful, I think you said you had—aren't sufficient?"

"For a divorce, sure. A sixty–forty split. The house, the Porsche—let him keep the Le Sabre; who needs it—am I right? Half the stocks and mutuals. The summer place in New Buffalo. Everything we agreed on." Donnie loosens his tie just a bit. He's still not used to wearing Brooks Brothers this late in the day. "But for two million in Swiss cheese even the IRS doesn't know about? Probably not, no. For that you'd need—well, I don't know—something else."

"Like what?" she persists.

Donnie sighs. He has no wish to spell this out. It's not vice presidential. Once again, I'm impressed. By now, the old Donnie would be explaining how easily Stephen could be set up. He'd be scribbling hookers' names and pager numbers on the back of a *Racing Form*, selecting the Madison Street gutter where Stephen would wake up sans pants, wallet, some important university document. The MCAT results of the entire incoming freshman class, for example. The new Donnie keeps his distance, takes the high road.

The new Donnie turns to me, thankful there's someone else around to take the low road. He busies himself behind me, straightening the Chamber of Commerce service awards on his wall.

Time to leave my corner. I scoot my chair a little

closer to the coffee table, push my hair back, smooth
the wrinkles from my Maroons alumni sweatshirt, Class
of '76. I should have worn some cologne. Except I
don't own any. My clothes probably smell like gyros. I
make a mental note: *buy cologne.*

"No judge will attach a lien to something that
doesn't officially exist," I explain. "Your banking
records don't have any unexplained deposits. No
transfer payments. We can't trace the money." She's
heard this before but seems intensely interested, her
eyes very bright—I doubt if it's my presentation. I
don't think the ouzo's worn off yet. "You'll have to
settle privately with Stephen. Before you get to court.
Make your own arrangements about splitting the
money. For example—your lawyer, Mr. Frost, could
probably set this up—Stephen could transfer whatever
amount you agree on to a different Swiss account, one
in your name—".

"Why would he want to do that?" she says.

"Well, he wouldn't want to," I say, "you're right,
Mrs. Rosenberg—"

"Call me Elenya," she says. "Please."

"He wouldn't *want* to, Elenya. He'd have to be persuaded. Gently persuaded. That it was in his best
interest to do this thing. Everybody's best interest,
really—"

"Meaning what?" she says.

I'm not sure how far to go with this. "Meaning
we'd need more than adultery. His medical practice and
tenure would have to be jeopardized. Put at risk." I
pause, feeling Donnie's eyes on the back of my neck.
"He'd have to feel threatened."

"You're talking about blackmail," she says simply.
I like this woman.

"Not blackmail," Donnie says, frowning. "No need to use that word—"

"You want to frighten him," she says to me. "Correct? And you want to have something on him that would absolutely ruin him."

"That would be nice," I agree.

"I really don't think that word's appropriate," Donnie says, shaking his head.

"I'm sorry, Donald. What word would you prefer?" she says, looking at him as if he'd just walked in the room. "Extortion? Because this certainly sounds like blackmail to me. If we may be frank here for just a damn moment."

Donnie's flashing me a look I'm familiar with—*this far, no further*—so I retreat to my corner. The facade of suburban gentility is slipping a bit, the First Ward intensity returning to his eyes.

She reaches for her purse, fingers fumbling on the carpet until she looks up and sees me watching her. I look away. She's forty-three; I know this because of the copy of her driver's license Donnie gave me, along with a clipping from the *Trib*, some charity function she'd hosted for the hospital's Women's Board. Neither picture does her justice. She's three years older than Donnie, who's six months and two days older than me. Somehow I'm the only one in the room with age lines on my face.

"The rest room was which way?" Elenya says, standing a bit too quickly; one hand grips the top of her chair. For the first time I notice her fingers are trembling. "I don't think I can deal with any more of this tonight. Maybe another time—"

"End of the hall, next floor down," Donnie says, already reaching for a phone to call her a cab. Probably figures he can still make the third period. Such are the joys of his day. But Elenya takes one wobbly step and falters. The ouzo's kicking in again, another aftershock. One hand covers her mouth. I'm afraid she'll pass out, so I take her straight to Donnie's executive washroom. I'm beginning to think that's why I'm here.

The stalls are solid walnut, better wood than anything in my apartment. They're both polished like heirlooms. Elenya selects door number two. It's a tight fit but we can both just squeeze inside. It smells like Clorox. We kneel on the limestone tile. The porcelain toilet bowl shines like milk glass.

These humbling occasions always remind me of confession: Dear God, please believe me, I won't do this again. Her contractions come in cycles. I wipe the sweat from her face with a paper towel, dry her lips with my handkerchief. At one point she leans her forehead against my palm, rocks slowly. She seems very small. The coat covers her like a shroud. Her body shudders violently.

When it passes she sits back against the wall. Her knees are as red as her eyes. "God," she says, still breathing hard. "You get older. You forget how much it hurts to throw up."

"Would you like some water?"

"Please," she says, nodding. I let the water run cold, which isn't easy; the taps turn on and off automatically. I have to dance back and forth, accompanied by Bread, Air Supply, Seals and Crofts—the living dead of seventies soft-rock. *Diamond Girl/You sure do shine.*

The bathroom's bigger than mine at home and better stocked; I find aspirin, Dramamine, paper cups.

An exhaust fan hums overhead. For the ninth or tenth time today I search for my watch, which I lost last night. "I don't usually drink," Elenya says, her voice hoarse. She takes two aspirin tablets, sips the water. "Maybe you can tell."

"You had a rough day."

"I did, didn't I?" she says. "You wouldn't have a mint or something, would you? My breath must be disgusting and I don't know where my purse went to." It's drying in one of the sinks. Let's hope Vuitton bags are waterproof.

I give up my last stick of Juicy Fruit; the ultimate sacrifice. Elenya refolds the gum wrapper neatly, like origami, places it gently on the floor next to her bare legs; an action I find endearing.

"This isn't me," she says, chewing gum. "I really don't drink, not even wine. A little on special occasions. Birthdays—last year Stephen took me to Ambria— that's it, really—"

"I know."

"But I'm at this really horrible sports bar tonight with Donald casually telling me about this money my husband has—which I've never even seen—after showing me all these pictures of Stephen with Lucy and some teenage slut doing *things* I've never seen—"

"I know, I know."

"—when I notice these three men at the next table—friends of Donald's, consultants I'm probably paying for, CPAs, tax lawyers—who should be there to *help me*—and they're passing something back and forth under the table. Giggling like fourth-graders. With me *right there*. This ugly picture. While they eat cheeseburgers, and drink beer, and watch some basketball game that's on about five hundred TVs—and I just suddenly realize: the divorce won't be the end of it. It will simply never end. Never."

"It's over now, Elenya."

She cocks a finger, sends the gum wrapper scooting across the tile floor. "It will never be over, Harding. Because I'm a dinner story now. An anecdote. The kind men tell each other in bars—the stupid, sorry bitch who settled for a house with a second mortgage and a Porsche with bad brakes while her husband's on an island somewhere with some twenty-two-year-old *shiksa* blonde—"

"So you ordered ouzo?"

"So I sent my herb tea back, yeah, and ordered ouzo. But it didn't help. Half a bottle—I couldn't even feel it, I was so numb. Until Donald brought me back here to sign his stupid paperwork—*then* it hit me, *wham,* like a roller coaster when I was a girl. Even the licorice taste. And you saw the results." Her dress is hanging by a small window I've cracked. It's dripping on the floor like a faucet with a bad washer. "Funny how something like that—how something tastes, can remind you—Why are you staring?" she says.

"I'm not," I say but she's right, I am staring—at the ginger-colored bruise on her left shoulder, which reminds me of my own childhood, and bruises just like that one on my mother's arm. For years while I was growing up I assumed she'd hurt herself doing housework. *Don't assume,* she told me later. *Just don't assume you know.*

"I'm sorry, Harding," Elenya says, "really sorry about all this mess—"

"You don't have anything to apologize for. It's easy to understand. Hell, just the CPAs would be enough to make me nauseous."

"You're very sweet," she says, her voice still rough. She pats the floor. "Do you think you could sit down, just for a minute? My feet are freezing."

I hesitate, thinking of Donnie and his Blackhawks tickets. It must be nearly the third period; I think the Red Wings are in town. And there's my own social life to consider: *Destroy All Monsters!* is on late-night TV. "We should get back—"

"Not just yet," she says. "Please."

Before I close the narrow window and pull the drapes closed—they're hanging from a wooden rod that matches the stalls—I look outside. It's clear and very cold; still no snow. The view from the tenth floor is as scenic as Schaumburg ever gets: bare trees in whitewashed planters meet yellow speedbumps. The pretty blue and red dots in the distance aren't a Seurat painting, just brake lights on the tollway.

Ten floors below me a battered pickup waits for someone, mindlessly circling piles of last night's snow, a skater doing compulsory exercises. The truck must have an oil problem. Exhaust blankets the blacktop like fog at a Kiss concert.

I close the window tight, fix the decorative wooden blinds, draw the little ruffled curtains. I've never been in a bathroom so cozy.

When I sit Elenya leans her head against my left shoulder, slides small white toes under my jeans. The tile floor is cool and smells of limes. I'm not sure how she's comfortable—I'm not—but neither of us moves. It's like a first date.

"We were friends once, you know," she says quietly. "At least, I thought we were friends."

"Who?"

"Lucy. When she first worked in Stephen's office,

before she switched to Psych; eight, nine years ago. We'd have lunch together sometimes, a little Middle Eastern place on 53rd Street. I don't think it's there anymore. And she sent me birthday cards. It might have started then, the affair—"

"That long ago?"

"Not the whole time. They must have gotten back together."

"You must have known—"

"I *heard* things. Hyde Park's just a small town, you know. And hospitals are even worse. You hear gossip—at least you think it's gossip, at the start anyway. So you try not to hear. After a while, you just try not to think about it." The building begins to shut down for the night and the lights dim. The Fifth Dimension's cut off mid-song. *One Less Bell to Answer.* "Listen, I need to ask you something. This other girl last night. Not Lucy. The young one—"

"Yes?"

"Was she screaming? You can't tell on the pictures. Or the cassette. I mean, she's yelling, he's yelling, everybody's yelling, but was she screaming?"

"I don't think so," I say carefully. "Not exactly, no."

"How old was she?"

"I don't know."

"Was she underage?"

"I wasn't checking IDs, Elenya."

"Well, where did she come from? Room service?"

I don't feel much like talking about this. The girl came from left field. "I'm not sure where she came from," I admit. "The weather made things difficult."

What I leave out is that I lost her husband not once but twice last night. The storm was brutal; roads and businesses shutting down behind me all the way south. I-65 reopened around six. I'd slept in my clothes, wrapped in blankets, a Coleman space heater filling my dreams with kerosene hallucinations. A convoy of diesels climbing onto the highway was my alarm clock, rattling the metal ribs on the floor of the truck, pushing me half-awake into a snowbank; at least the sun was up. The glare was blinding. The parking lot was empty. The Buick was gone. So was the girl.

"She's just so young," Elenya says softly.

"Yes."

"She could be a student of his—"

"I don't think so."

"But you don't *know*. Can't the motel clerks or somebody tell you something? Did you talk to them?"

"There wasn't anyone to ask."

She nods, yawning; I yawn too; it's contagious. Her eyes are heavy. All that's keeping her awake is a painful curiosity; the weight of the day.

"We don't even know her name," she says.

For the first time I notice how she sometimes holds her hands, gripping her fingers; rubbing the skin as though smoothing out a pattern. Some of the joints seem red, maybe swollen. With all the marks on her arms and legs it's easy to miss.

"Elenya, are you sure you really want to know all this?"

"Yes. Of course." She seems surprised. "Why? You wouldn't?"

"Probably not."

"I don't believe that," she says, fighting off another yawn. Her head nods against my sleeve.

"I'm just not sure it helps anything. But maybe I've been outside too many motel rooms."

"Are you married?" she says.

"No."

"Ever been?"

"No."

"Ahh," she says, nodding, curling against me. "The wisdom of the amateur."

This last is a whisper. Her eyes close. The long day finally ends. Lipstick and makeup—and husband—are long gone. She's sick, sweaty, battered and bruised and wrapped in a borrowed raincoat. It doesn't much matter. She looks beautiful, smells wonderful. I think her husband must be crazy.

I think of the tiny space she must take up in bed.

When I gently move her, changing my position, her left arm falls to her side. A crumpled paper falls from her relaxed hand. She nuzzles against me, whispers something under her breath. It's one of the prints my friend Allison made for me this morning—a group shot, Stephen, Lucy, the girl. One of the more explicit, it's a unique double penetration. The girl's tethered to the bed with stainless steel chains.

The picture's squeezed together, compacted into a tight warm ball, covered with fingerprints. I wonder at its small size as I pry it open. Something hard is at its center.

Inside the photograph I find a wedding ring.

How long has she had it crushed so fiercely in her fist?

TWO

have trouble sleeping. Maybe it's a guilty conscience. *Was she screaming?* I wake early, call my friend Alison. She's not keen on spending a Friday afternoon on the Indiana tollway. But she agrees to make some phone calls for me, and maybe ask around the university, and before long she's telling me to pick her up at noon. She has tai chi at nine, movement at ten, breathing at eleven. And she's swamped with work—it's quarter rush at Hyde Park Photo Supplies. Every idiot with an SLR has vacation pictures.

My kitchen's cold this morning. I boil some water in a saucepan, rinse out the green stuff subletting my Cubs mug. The instant coffee's from a store that left the neighborhood a decade ago. These flavor crystals do not exactly burst into life.

Sugar would help; so would creamer. I don't have either one but I waste a good five minutes looking. I do find cans of deviled ham and Dinty Moore stew. No expiration dates, they're good for forty, fifty years. The closest thing to creamer is a bag of flour. A white moth flies out, shaking its wings; a pale phoenix. The flour looks like creamer. I stir in a spoonful.

What I'm avoiding with this process is dealing with the photograph that's sitting before me on the kitchen table, the one that Elenya Rosenberg clutched like a rosary last night. I left a Janson's *History of Art* on it overnight but it's just as wrinkled now as when it fell from Elenya's hand.

I take the photo and my coffee into the living room and raise the shades. It's very sunny this morning, an arctic brightness. The digital sign on the bank across the street is frozen at two degrees. Too cold for snow. Traffic on Broadway is slow. Steam rises from gratings, manholes, exhaust pipes, commuters running for the #36 bus. My windows are framed with ice, inside and out.

There are records everywhere. Alison gave me a program for cataloging LPs on a Mac I inherited along with a spit sink and miles of floss from the deceased dentist who was the previous tenant. It's a project that will outlive both me and the Mac. Meanwhile Patti Smith's *Wave* has been in the tape deck so long the outer shell is lost in the sofa cushions. It plays while I shower and shave and then more or less put the same clothes back on. That's my outer shell.

Here I go and I don't know why
I spin so ceaselessly

I hold the photo to the light. It's not pleasant to look at. Lucy looks drugged; Stephen slightly manic. But then he's got a lot on his mind—a wife at home; two women with him in the motel room; yet another woman—her name's "Lola" this week—on the phone, an 800 sex number. When I described this scene to Donnie yesterday he just shrugged. "It's a Wednesday; he's a doctor, Harding. It's his day off, right? Some guys play golf." Donnie wanted two sets of pictures, an audiotape, Lola's number.

We were in Donnie's office; my first stop after the long drive from Indiana. Donnie's Sonyphones were tucked beneath his chin like a doctor's stethoscope. The batteries in my Walkman were dying a slow death and I was on auxiliary power myself. Every time I closed my eyes I started dreaming.

"Not pleasant," he agreed. "But we already knew he was a bastard."

"You don't think it's enough."

"The sadism, that he's an unfaithful prick? No."

"What about some kind of drug frame?"

"Was he on something different last night?"

"Coke. Lucy likes Ecstasy, Special K. But he's got lots of pills in his black bag—uppers mostly, anti-psychotics, synthetics. Phenobarb. I can't always tell when he takes those. There's always something new."

"And syringes."

"Sure."

"Did you see him inject the girl?"

"No."

"Did you see him strike the girl?"

"With his hands? No."

"Meaning what?"

"Meaning he and Lucy are a fun couple, fully acces-sorized. Canes, rods, thrashers. Modern munching. Some of it hurts and some of it doesn't."

And sometimes I can't tell.

"How do we know what he carries in his bag?" Donnie said, curious.

"We looked." Alison planted the bug inside the bag's felt lining while Rosenberg was making rounds; it might have been the only time in her life she'd worn white. She looked very professional. And she'd found more than pills that day—handcuffs, leather restraints, piercing needles, rings. Some of it Alison had to explain to me, so I could explain it to Donnie Wilson, so he could explain it to Elenya's lawyer, Frost. How

Rosenberg would explain it to his interns if they looked in the bag was a mystery.

"Is the girl underage? Fourteen maybe? Tell me she's fourteen."

"I think she's legal."

"We're fucked, then," Donnie said. "And you're off the clock, Harding."

"So start a new clock."

"I told you, it's over. If I'd known he was gonna start fooling around with somebody else I wouldn't have hired you—"

"You mean somebody like this girl. Somebody this young. I'm not that fragile, Donnie. Okay? I won't break."

But I know what he's thinking: you broke once already, big-time. And forget that Hemingway shit about being stronger in the broken places. The truth is those places snap like twigs the first time they're tested.

"You're not a social worker," he said. "You get too close."

"I couldn't be further away."

In the pictures I showed Donnie—like the one here in my apartment—the girl's face is blurred. But her body's in perfect focus. There's not much doubt about what I was concentrating on.

My answering machine's under the couch, and while I drink a cup of coffee that's treading the fine line between espresso and canned gravy, I replay the latest pleas from creditors. Some are more creative than others. One begins by telling me I've won a fabulous Florida vacation and need only appear at this address on the West Side and ask for Sal . . .

I fast-forward to a familiar high-pitched voice—my landlord, Minas, owner of Athena Gyros below me. I'm a little behind on my rent. Minas doesn't sound happy. His message ends with the sound of a cleaver hitting a cutting board. My one idea for breakfast—borrowing eggs and Greek coffee—is probably out.

The last message is better: a thank-you from the Wilshires—the only other client I've had lately—for finding their daughter Carol, a Mundelein College student who disappeared midterm. Carol was majoring in religious studies—what they call prenun at Mundelein— and her family, accustomed to tabloid TV, naturally assumed she'd been abducted by a serial killer. I get a lot of referrals from serial killers.

I thought I'd find Carol shacked up with a guitar player in Wicker Park—that happens with intensive prenun studies—but where I finally found her was in a Ringling Brothers clown school outside the Quad Cities area. It was a first for me, meeting someone who'd actually run away with the circus. I found Carol at a petting zoo near Kmart, sweeping up after rabbits and chickens, leading a brown pony around a track for a group of birthday kids wearing party hats. Face painted, she was having a great time. "You have to follow your bliss," she told me. Carol's bliss was in Decatur. In its own way it was more mysterious than being abducted by a serial killer.

But that case was the exception. When I first started out in this business it was just Donnie Wilson and me with two cheap metal desks, no clients, and half a dozen rats in a storefront on South Paulina. Back then, I had the naive idea that finding someone's missing daughter or spouse would reunite a loving family, heal a wound.

It happens. The Wilshires are proof of that. Down-

state girls—and boys—turning tricks in Uptown sometimes return to happy families on Walton Mountain.
But you soon learn there are often very good reasons
why mothers disappear, children run away. It's not
always much fun dragging them back.

Angela Martinez helped me learn that.

I spent six months looking for Angela. It was
my own case—I still had a license—and I used every
contact I had to find her. It didn't help. She outwitted
me at every turn—changed names, hair color, friends.
She disappeared every time I got close to her. She was
a fifteen-year-old cheerleader from Springfield and I
couldn't catch her. It was embarrassing.

I came to dread the weekly reports I made to her
father, Eduardo Martinez. He listened patiently each
week to my explanations on a speakerphone in his den,
ice cubes tinkling in a glass. When my explanations
were done, he reimbursed my expenses by certified
check. He had lots of money—his business was auto
parts—and even more patience. Don't stop, he said
each week. You'll find her. His voice held no accent, no
expression. The mother never spoke.

I never did find her. She found me. She showed up
on my doorstep one day, tired of running—which
shows how alone she must have felt. She had nothing—
just the clothes on her back, a couple dollars in change,
and two copper bracelets wide as the bands that tie you
to the electric chair.

I helped her into a drug clinic, helped her kick,
which she must have mistaken for kindness. She
begged me not to tell her father where she was. She said
he wasn't looking for her as much as chasing her, something he'd been doing since she was seven. Chasing
her, and catching her.

He caught her again. This time, I helped. I stopped my reports, stopped cashing the checks. It wasn't enough. I told her I'd protect her. I lied. When he came after us in broad daylight—we were crossing Cottage Grove Avenue near the university's tennis courts—I was slow to react. If he'd had a gun, she'd be dead. But he only had a knife. So she's only disfigured.

She still wakes me up sometimes, just before my alarm. I still have one of the bracelets. I carry it around sometimes in my coat, a reminder of Angela's lesson. There are a lot of real nightmares in this world to run from.

Alison is waiting for me outside her store on 55th Street. She climbs into my 4Runner, stores a black duffel bag under her seat, slams the door so hard the dust on my dash jumps into the air. My feet are just beginning to warm up, so of course she turns down the heat. She likes the cold.

"Where's Felicia today?" I ask about her store manager.

"Barrington."

"What's she doing there?"

"A wedding shower we shot last week," Alison says. She pushes her long black hair behind her ears. "The bride's mother thinks her skin tone doesn't look right."

"The bride's?"

"The mother's. Says we made her look 'pasty.' So we have to reshoot the entire book. Seventy-five guests. And they have to rewrap every piece of Wedgwood. Not to mention the toasters."

We head south listening to Slayer—"Cream with a

death wish," Alison says, providing context. She's twenty-seven but younger in her musical tastes. Her black paratrooper boots are propped on the dash. I forget sometimes how tall she is. She's dressed in Modern Gothick; tight black jeans, an oversized black sweater that hangs below her rear, a black Swatch, black earrings, black handbag, a black pendant I gave her hanging between the curve of her breasts alongside a tattoo of a small black butterfly. Her eyes are hidden behind the black prescription Ray-Bans she wears indoors and out—she gets migraines. White socks.

We met in the pain clinic at University Hospital—I have a back problem—while an intern with shaking fingers was injecting a Demerol and Cafergot speedball into her rear. I was in the next cubicle, throwing up. Love at first sight.

"How was your breathing class?" I say.

"Tantric. I'm becoming Princess of the Goths."

"How can movement and breathing be Gothic exactly?"

"You don't get it, Harding. If I do it, then it's Gothic."

"So if you're watching the Three Stooges it's Gothic?"

"Right."

"And if I'm watching them?"

"If you're watching them, it's childish."

I'm impressed. This is a very formidable personal philosophy.

There isn't much traffic once we leave the city, the usual crush at Merrillville but south of that we fly. I-65's clear and dry, a relief after the mess Wednesday night when this whole area was buried under two feet of snow. I saw one or two salt trucks Wednesday, enterprising farmers with plows fixed to their John Deeres, but not much else. Unless there's a big Purdue game in West Lafayette there's not a great deal of urgency out here about snow removal.

An hour south of Chicago we leave the expressway.

"How did everyone like the pictures I did for you?" Alison says.

"Loved 'em." We're on county roads now, flat but twisting; some still icy. The Toyota's sliding each time I downshift. So much for four-wheel drive. Slayer gives way to Joy Division, a definite drop in intensity.

"Something you might suggest—close-ups of Rosenberg's genitals would make nice Christmas cards. A service of Hyde Park Photo."

"You're always thinking, Alison."

"It's called marketing. Which frankly you could use a bit more of. Couldn't you run an ad or something in the Yellow Pages?"

"Under what? 'Unlicensed Private Investigators'?"

"I could put together a clip-art Sherlock Holmes for you. I give great copy."

"Truth in advertising, Alison. Holmes doesn't work for me anymore. He couldn't pass the drug test. Nasty crack habit."

"Yeah, well. Who needs him. Right?" She snaps a new lens on her camera, frames a passing car as though sighting a deer with a .22. "We're on the case now. Whatever in hell the case is. So Rosenberg likes young girls. So what?"

"I don't know."

"I mean, who doesn't?"

"Alison—"

"So what are we looking for?"

"I'm not sure, Alison. Something I missed."

"Well, that could take all day, Harding," she says, digging in my coat pockets for gum. Her face is next to mine. She smells good. She smells like Alison. "Knowing you, that could take months, maybe years. *Light* years. You remember that squiggly mark for infinity . . ."

The Hoosier BudgetCourts sits closer to State Route 2 than the interstate, which may affect its occupancy rate. There's a 76 truck stop close enough to serve as its restaurant. The rest of the area's flat Midwestern farmland. The nearest towns are Lowell, Hebron, and my personal favorite—Dinwiddie, Indiana.

We leave the 4Runner where I left it Wednesday, behind a shuttered Dairy Queen, and walk across the motel parking lot, slippery enough to double as a skating rink. No one's shoveled or put down any salt. After two days both my footprints and Rosenberg's are fossilized in the snow. There are other tire tracks now, but those from Rosenberg's Buick are still clearly distinguishable, leading to the access road, and I-65.

"I don't think they do much convention business here," Alison says. "I don't know. It's just a wild guess." She zips up her short black bomber, pulls on thin leather gloves, sketches tic-tac-toe in the frost covering the front office windows. Everything's paneled in knotty pine—walls, doors, ceilings, even the cigarette machine. There's no clerk in sight. The door's locked. A wave of snow curls just below the vacancy sign painted permanently on the glass.

Alison knocks the snow from her boots. "This is exciting. I'm very glad you dragged me out here for this. Should I get a shot of you scowling, trying to open the front door?"

"Try the bell again." We hear it ringing in short

sharp bursts. I was hoping to get a look at the registry, talk to the night clerk, find out when Rosenberg left for Chicago. I know he was back on campus for morning rounds. But I fell asleep around two. I don't know where he dropped the girl.

The truck stop on the next hill isn't much busier than the motel. Half a dozen cars have invented their own parking spaces in the grid of the snow. There's a car by itself at the edge of the lot. It's facing us, headlights still weakly on, a dead-battery statistic about to happen. The line of fellow mourners at Sears waiting for DieHards has lately stretched into the parking lot.

Alison scratches ice from a corner of the window, exposing the silver-gray ribbon of an alarm system. It's primitive but I don't feel like fighting it.

"I want to check the room at least," I say. "Nineteen. The bridal suite."

"Are you sure this place is even open, Harding?"

"It was open Wednesday night."

"Maybe the storm forced them off the road," she says, walking with me. We're following a path the storm created with drifting snow, trying to avoid the slippery spots. The years of dance and tai chi have given Alison's movements a graceful ease. "That's what happened to me Wednesday night coming back from this gallery opening in Milwaukee—when they closed I-94 I spent two hours in Stuckey's with Seventh-Day Adventists, Christian Scientists—you need any literature?"

"No, I'm good."

We walk to the other side of the building. The parking lot's empty, the snow unmarked except for dog tracks. Just beyond the lot is what's left of the BudgetCourts' playground. The rusty swing set I used for cover Wednesday night sits exposed now in the glare. The seats are missing and chains swing wildly in the wind.

"Remember *Hellraiser*?" Alison says, batting the chains at me. She's getting bored. There's a tripod in her canvas bag and one of her better Nikons but unless you like arctic landscapes there isn't much to shoot.

Wednesday night there was even less activity—the gas station on the next ridge had even shut down. I'd gotten a late start, driven through a snowblind haze and several panic attacks on the Skyway until I picked up Rosenberg's trail from a bug on his rear bumper. It was very dark out here. A dozen pairs of yellow eyes watched me from the ridge, parking lights of eighteen-wheelers circled like covered wagons against the storm. The motel looked like a glacier floe pushed through the cornfields.

The past few weeks Rosenberg has led me all over the state—south as far as Crawfordsville; east to South Bend and Fort Wayne—but nowhere quite as isolated as this. Or rundown. I ruined two pairs of boots that night and now I see why. The motel's septic tank must be backing up. Runoff sewage is seeping through the ice, warm, stringy as seaweed, making the ground a licorice snow cone.

My crow's nest Wednesday night was the top of the slide. Room nineteen's window was like a dirty drive-in movie. To see past the drapes I had to lock my boots in the slide's handles and lean out like a wind-surfer. The first time I did this my watch slid from my wrist into the bubbling muck and traced a perfect plumb line, disappearing without a trace. Lucy Williams sat on the bed watching Astaire and Rogers on a small black-and-white. It looked like *Flying Down to Rio*. Her face was rubbed dull from fatigue and Quaaludes and X.

She'd worked a double at the hospital, a triple here. The bed sagged around her.

I watched as she undressed herself, unhooking her black bra and displaying her profile; turning slowly sideways in a way that was beginning to creep into my daily thoughts. One of the enhancements had perhaps been done on a bad day. Saline settled in two perfect circles when she stretched, raising her arms above her head, swaying back and forth in a sleepy dance different from the one Ginger was attempting.

Elenya had said she thought the affair, recently revived, had started years ago—that might explain the curious nature of their relationship, more predictable than passionate. You could tell they knew each other very well. It was harder to tell how much they liked each other. Especially Rosenberg—he treated her badly. Donnie thought it was just drugs, that Rosenberg was little more than her supplier. I wasn't so sure.

"Are you kidding?" Donnie said. "You think she *likes* the stuff he does to her?"

"I think she likes *him*," I said. "I don't pretend to understand the rest of it."

There were lots of drugs, of course—Lucy was smoking something now, white heroin maybe. The new stuff's pure enough to do that. You could see her struggling to keep up with the pleasure unfolding in her body. Rosenberg was working the phone—barking at his secretary, his nurses, someone named Elizabeth. The man has too much energy. The signal drifted unevenly from his medical bag to a small booster amp in my truck, to my wireless headphones. While he spoke, a curled phone cord was double-dutching against his stiff cock. And the girl? The surprising third member of the triad?

She must have been hidden behind the drapes. When she appeared she was dressed for a nasty gym class with sweatbands on both wrists, matching Jockeys, and satin basketball shorts tugged down low on her rear. Underneath, she wore a leather halter and split-crotch G-string, silver chains connecting her nipple clamps. Her Nike cross-trainers provided traction when Rosenberg started pushing against her hips with two hands and something much more insistent.

The screams and cries were hers and hard to read. She wasn't being restrained that I could see. Which could mean nothing. The wireless headphones I was using weren't made for this. They read Astaire's tap dancing as percussion and boosted that over the midrange orders Rosenberg was barking as he moved to the bed, leaned forward on Lucy's abdomen, forced open her mouth. Her lips were bright red. Beneath a crinoline petticoat Lucy's strap-on rubber cock was smeared with an oily yellow lubricant, so was the corkscrew probe in her right hand. Her leather harness was double-tied; her legs were chained to the bed, bright silver circles trailing to each hook on a red rubber sheet. These were familiar sights.

What was new was the girl.

Her performance was first-rate. I thought so. Rosenberg thought so too. He was inspired, if a little manic from vacuuming up yet another line. Coke's supposed to slow you down a bit but you'd never know it from Rosenberg. I could see the rest of the girl's clothes now, tossed aside on the floor. A long red coat curled around her like a skirt beneath a Christmas tree. Both the girl's hands were free but white-knuckled, wrapped around tiny white anklet socks, the kind with rows of red hearts across the top. She struggled for a better position, spread her legs further, bent forward, shifted her weight. Other than the screams and cries she never spoke. No one used her name. The clamps that pinched her nipples were shaped like clover. Yellow stains dotted her rear like faded daffodils.

I think it was the socks that reminded me of Angela. The two girls didn't really look all that much alike. But the socks broke my heart. It was enough for me to consider leaving my cover to drag Rosenberg through the glass, across the black snow.

But that would ruin the surveillance. Donnie wouldn't be happy. Rosenberg would move his money even further away. And who would a local sheriff believe—an unlicensed PI with a record or a respected surgeon? I've had some experience with small-town law enforcement, none of it pleasant. So I finished what there was to drink in the truck and then returned to the jungle gym with a handful of pills—red, blue, green, some speckled like bird's eggs—I stayed with the primary colors and swallowed three capsules.

So much snow was falling that I could only catch bits and pieces of the tableau—an arm here, a knee, an extended leg. A face, startled and frightened. A pornographic snowdome. Jethro Tull suddenly boomed so loud I had to jerk off the headphones and watch the rest in silence. The girl's brown eyes, meeting mine, were upside down, her mouth wide open. A warmth gradually spread across my face. I had two rolls of film. We finished together.

"I had Rosenberg as an advisor once," Alison says, opening room nineteen with her Discover card. The wood around the frame is frayed as soft as the balsa on a model airplane. "Third year, when I was majoring in biochem, still considering med school. He seemed all right at the time. Kept his eyes above my chest. Didn't expose himself, leap over the desk at me or anything."

"Well, that's all you can hope for," I say. The hinges groan from the cold. Alison puts her dark Ray-Bans away, fits plain wire-rim glasses carefully around her ears. It's the first time today I've seen her green eyes. She puts her Discover card neatly back in its slot in her wallet.

"I can't believe you still don't have a credit card," she says.

"I had several. A nice man from the bank repossessed them. Watch your step, okay?"

The room is pitch black before us.

I fumble for the light but nothing happens. The wallpaper's so greasy my fingers slip off the switch. I can't see a damn thing.

Alison tells me to wait—she's kneeling on the ice, rummaging through her bag for a flash. Her store logo—a black figure with an old-fashioned view camera and tripod—is on everything; the bags, the cameras, the back of the developed prints. She says it's Julia Cameron but to me it looks like Alison. Did Mrs. Cameron wear black jeans?

"He's a fat-sucker, right?" she says.

"I've got one of his brochures in the truck—'Classically Sculptured Rhinoplastic Enhancements/Obagi Facial Rejuvenation.' "

"He fixes noses."

"Big-time. You should see his tax returns." Something's beginning to drift out toward us, a smell familiar from childhood: house-training puppies, sloppy-sweet.

"You met his wife yet?" Alison says.

"Uh-huh."

"How was she?"

"She seems okay," I say.

"He was smart to specialize," Alison says, getting up, brushing the snow from her jeans. A light meter dangles around her neck. "The money used to be in boob jobs, but that silicone's scary shit, Harding. Nobody dies from noses."

Then the wind shifts, pulling the stale air from room nineteen outside as if into a vacuum. I'm now very glad I skipped breakfast. As it is, my morning coffee nearly comes back up. Alison turns away briefly, squinting from the glare.

The heat and the smell pass over us like shock waves.

"This," Alison says, moving quickly past me, "is why I'm not having kids."

I hear voices. Maybe we should have knocked, but Alison's already in the room. It's a false alarm—the voices come from a clock radio and there's no one behind the closed bathroom door. Of course, by then Alison has kicked it open so hard a divot of wood flies past my ear.

"Can't be too careful," she says with a shrug. She's Chicago-born, raised to expect the worst. But mostly I think she just loves to kick.

I open the closets, look around inside and out. Nobody home. Room nineteen's a mess but deserted. Whatever happened here, we missed it. It feels like a crime scene without a body.

We take off our coats, draw the blackout drapes, open the casement windows as far as they'll go. The smell is overwhelming. "Jesus," Alison says. "Indulge your senses."

I lean outside, breathe cold air until my sinuses ache. The sky is cloudless. From here the swing set looks naked and vulnerable in the sunlight. They were probably too busy in here to notice me. And everything looks different from this side of the lens. I see footprints I hadn't noticed before running to the Dumpster— probably maintenance or garbage men.

My new boots—my third pair in as many days— squish like rubber thongs with each step. They're waterproof but even Gore-Tex can't protect you from this kind of shower. The rug's dark enough to hide the stains but the padding and mat must be wet right down to the floorboards. A strong ammonia smell rises from the area around the bed. The carpet there is wet enough to grow rice.

"You ready for lunch?" Alison says, chewing gum. She begins methodically photographing the room.

The heat's been on high for two days. It didn't dry the rugs but it did congeal all the blood and shit and body fluids on the bedspread into a relief map, like the plaster of paris kind you made in school with dark burgundy lakes, carmel-colored mountains, yellow rivers. Old feather pillows minus their cases have been stacked on the floor. And over the bed, smeared across the white vinyl headboard like a scatological Rothko, are three thick horizontal lines, in three slightly different shades of brown.

For a moment I wonder if I have the right room. Nothing connects with anything I saw Wednesday night. And Rosenberg's performances are so tightly scripted any improvisation is surprising. I'm usually asleep by the second time he comes. The girl simply increased the mathematical possibilities. At least, that's what I'd thought.

"Can you handle some constructive criticism?" Alison says. "Your photographs don't really convey— how should I put it—the *texture* of the physical landscape."

"No kidding."

I go through each part of the room. The dresser's cheap pine, scarred with black cigarette burns. All four drawers are lined with curling Con-Tact paper and brown roach eggs. It stands against a stucco wall with swirling plaster, like stale vanilla icing. The desk is also pine, the only thing in the room that matches. There's a leatherette binder—three-ringed and empty—labeled "Guest Services" sitting on top. Since the phone's the same one I saw Wednesday I assume it works. I avoid the cord. The lamps beside the queen-sized bed are made from bowling pins, a wide seven-ten split.

In the back of the closet, behind a row of hangers, there are two flannel robes draped on hooks, their pockets stuffed with mothballs. The naphthalene smell is surprisingly strong. When I run my hand across the top shelf I find a Good News Bible and a Rotary directory covered with thick gritty dust. A large brown spider runs across my hand and then rappels down the wall like a Ranger on maneuvers.

The waste cans by the desk and bed are stuffed with South Suburban *Tribs* and *People* magazines, beer cans, Twinkie wrappers, Lotto tickets. Everything seems weeks old. Maybe Housekeeping needs a quorum of guests before they show up. The waste can in the bathroom's more interesting. It's the kind you'd find in a store or office, locked in the wall with a Kleenex dispenser. In fact, the lock's better than the one on the front door. I roll up my sleeve and dig through garbage layered like a geological timeline—matted Kleenex,

Kotex, razor blades, water-stained *TV Guides* interspersed like folds in the strata.

Alison sits on the edge of the tub, taking my picture. Her glasses keep fogging up from the humidity. It's like a terrarium in here. Moss and lime green barnacles are growing from cracks in the grouting. I take her glasses and wipe them on my shirt but they fog right back up.

"I need some help with the bed," I say. "Try not to get blood on your skin. And watch out for the white stuff on the brown stuff—I think it's worms or maggots. The white stuff, that is."

"What's the brown stuff?"

"Don't ask."

"Harding, you really know how to show a girl a good time," Alison says.

We push the top mattress on its side with our boots, lift the box springs—still dry—to check the floor beneath. Nothing. That was deceptively simple; there's no easy way to examine the bedcovers. I finally pull the fitted sheet from all four corners and just drag everything toward the window. The ridges and patterns split and crumble. In some places the fabric's saturated; still wet and pulpy. In others it's dry, chalky. I root through it all with my bare fingers—I didn't bring any rubber gloves—hoping to find God knows what—the girl's student ID? A curious combination of smells rises the more I burrow; some human, some chemical. My mouth and throat gradually become dry, my eyes itchy. By the time I'm in the bathroom washing up my skin is beginning to burn.

My thoughts drift back to Wednesday night, while I slept in my truck; last night at Donnie's office. Someone else was out here. Someone was very busy while I slept.

Alison leans against the door frame, arms folded. Both little bars of motel Ivory are unwrapped; soap's lathered past my elbows.

"It must have been some party," she says. "Maybe they had Harry Connick, Jr. in from the motel lounge."

"Did any of that stuff get on your skin?"

She shakes her head.

"You're sure?"

"I'm sure," she says. She pulls her sweater over her head and unsnaps her boots. There's a skull and cross-bones and the logo of some death-metal band across her T-shirt. "Harding, how did you miss all this?"

"It must have happened after two, Alison. Or yesterday. I can't tell how long any of this has been here."

"You'd need anthropologists for that, Harding, carbon dating. Get the guys working on the Shroud of Turin. What happened at two? That's when they left?"

"That's when I fell asleep."

"Good, sound detective work," she says, nodding. "Glad to see you're still stressing the fundamentals."

"Give me a break, Alison. They've been doing the same exact shit for three months. How was I supposed to know this week would turn into a Fellini movie?"

"You think the girl's a student of his?"

"I don't know. She wasn't exactly wearing school colors. But something about this—all this, everything here in nineteen—it's just all wrong."

"Why?" she says, rubbing my arms dry with a towel. "They had a special guest at the party this week. So they decided to break out the hats and noisemakers."

"This is serious fetish material, Alison. I've met people into stuff like this. Water sports. Chocolate treats."

"You're hanging with the wrong crowd, Harding."

"Rosenberg and his buddies are neat freaks, Alison. Upper-income. Not frat boys or rock stars. You know? They don't trash the Chippendale. They put down plastic. Rubber sheets. And they shower afterward. In this dump you'd have to stand in the sink and take a sponge bath." It's hard to picture Rosenberg leaving anything like this behind.

"What did Donnie Wilson expect you to find today?" she says, washing her face and arms in cold water.

"I'm not working for Wilson."

"You're doing this yourself? On your own time?" She shakes her head, smiling at me. "Harding, Harding . . ."

"What's that supposed to mean?"

"You're not messing with Rosenberg's wife, are you?" she says.

"What in the world makes you say that?"

"You have that look," she says.

"Alison," I say, taking her arm. "Don't tell me you're jealous."

"I'm not jealous," she says. "I've seen her around campus. She's cute, but she's not my type."

While the truck warms up we listen to Patti Smith, my reward for this wasted afternoon. If I was eighteen I'd have a Patti Smith poster on my wall. Since I'm forty I have to be content with the picture on her cassette, which is the size of a postage stamp.

Alison likes Patti Smith too but her reward's a migraine, triggered by the smells in nineteen. It's coming on fast. She changes to her darkest pair of glasses, slouches in her seat. Her forehead's feverish to the touch.

"Which side of your face?" I say. We swing onto the access road.

"Left," she says. "Will you please not worry about it?"

Pissed at myself for causing her headache I don't even notice the Dumpster fifty yards or so up the road. Alison does. She grabs my arm so excitedly we nearly swerve off the road. Maybe it's the migraine, but when an attack starts everything she can see might as well be under a spotlight. Somehow she notices the black plastic bag sitting on top of a dozen other black plastic bags; the one that—curiously—doesn't have any snow on it.

"I'm psychic," she says. "Booga-Booga."

Of course it's on top. The sheets of cardboard that are steps up the recycled mountain have been rained on and refrozen so many times they break off like glass. Bits of brunch—orange rinds, coffee grounds, chicken parts—are scattered all the way up. And beer cans— several dozen—each crushed and folded. You can still smell the alcohol.

"Let me," Alison says. She has treads on her boots like tires on an eighteen-wheeler. "We don't want you falling. Your back's bad enough. Those old bones take a long time to heal." She's there in two long steps and tosses it down. Nested inside is yet another bag, this one even more interesting: a pillow case—from nineteen?—tied and double-knotted at one end around a red box of Tide.

Stuffed into the box—maybe instead of the towels they used to give away—are a putty knife and a can of spackle, soft as cold cream despite subzero temperatures. What intrigues me are the price stickers on everything. The Tide's from Merrillville Finer Foods. The spackle's from Hyde Park Hardware.

Alison watches my growing interest with a knowing eye.

"Here," she says, handing over her Discover card. "Watch out for splinters."

"Five minutes, no longer," I say, taking my flashlight from the truck. "I promise. I know your head must be throbbing."

She waves me away, curls up on the back seat.

The laundry room isn't far from nineteen. Dryer vents trailing rust marks down the brick wall give away its location. And I don't need a credit card to get in; gold, platinum, whatever. The lock pops when I lean my weight against the doorjamb. But I'm confused. There aren't any footprints here. Not outside, anyway.

Inside's a different matter. It's not a big room. A row of lockers, an industrial dryer. Two Kenmore washers that sit astride a stationary tub. A greasy film that attracts dust covers everything, including the rolled linoleum. So it's not hard to see the footprints on the floor. They come from a door on the far side of the room. Then they go back. They don't go outside.

It's my own fault. I'd forgotten the service corridor, running behind the rooms. Every motel has one, and it would naturally lead here. The mess on the bed must have distracted me. Or maybe I'm just getting sloppy.

The metal lockers are full of laundry soap; familiar one-word expletives—Bold, Fab, Gain, Cheer. I'm wondering who does the maintenance around here;

when was the last time this place was used; what kind of guest would stay here; can anyone really combine fabric softener with detergent and still get your clothes clean.

The service door isn't locked. I hang my coat on a rolling laundry rack and step into the corridor. There must be lights but I can't find them. I turn on the flashlight and wait just a minute for my eyes to get accustomed to the dark. I'm standing at the intersection of two narrow pathways. I realize I must be at the building's corner. I look both ways like a good pedestrian, then head left toward room nineteen. The mud is damp enough to take prints. This place needs dehumidifiers, badly. Every ten or fifteen feet I pass room numbers scratched in the drywall, like shuttered subway stations.

When I get to nineteen I can see wooden plugs and hinges in the wall, the outline of a small door. When I push, thin shafts of light fall into the corridor. When I push harder the door swings into the room. The flannel robes drop to the floor. Without the robes—and the mothballs in their pockets—the awful stench of nineteen begins to drift back to me.

I follow the footprints further down the passageway. Bolted to the outside wall is a sump pump, planted in the damp ground with a copper drainage pipe. The pump's disconnected, its black cord curled like a snake in the mud; when I wipe the grounded plug on my jeans and then hook it back up the pump rumbles to life, water rushing upward past my face. Something else was wired up here recently. Scattered at the pump's base are small ends of wire—blue, green, yellow—copper screws, plastic connectors.

The footprints—they overlap too much in this tight

space to tell much about them—continue ten feet further. Then they stop, just before the end of the passageway, at a spot where the wall looks worked on. I edge my way down. It's probably my imagination but the corridor feels like it's growing narrower, even more airless. And the further I go, the wetter it gets. Maybe I've crossed the water table.

Someone's been busy, all right. There's a web of footprints here in the clay. The drywall's been patched recently, a hurried, amateurish job. Without wire or mesh support it's already caving in. When I hit it with the back of my arm it gives way easily. The hole's about the size of a basketball. I roll up my shirtsleeve and reach down through cobwebs and plaster. I touch bottom but the bottom moves with my touch.

My arm nearly comes right through the drywall. But I retrieve my trophy, pulling it up through the hole. It's oddly shaped, with sharp edges. I shine my flashlight into the hole. I can't see anything else, but the walls are coming alive with rustling, scratching noises—field mice, I tell myself. Let's just keep moving here.

It's a relief to backtrack out the corridor and the laundry room, and return to the bright sunlight. I make one quick search for my watch, using a tree branch to stir up the muck beneath the swing set. It was an alumni watch with my class year on the back, which means it was a cheap Timex with a forty-dollar engraving fee. The more I stir the black sludge the more I feel I can live without it.

The clock in the truck's dash says it's nearly four. Alison's sitting in the back seat, rubbing her face, a look of pain in her eyes. I need to get her home. I really didn't need to bring her, but I like her company. And the truth is, the more interested she gets in one of these jobs, the more I see the deal through her eyes—and the more I see myself through her eyes. The view's much better that way.

My eyes are good enough to notice the car still on the ridge, its lights still on, facing us like a patient predator.

"Let me have your camera bag," I say. "Or just give me the telephoto lens. Did you take something for the pain?"

She shakes her head no. I reach inside the glove compartment, where there's a smuggler's Bible for the discerning tourist: a hollowed *Fodor's Midwest* with Percodan, Fiorinal, Tuinal, Ritalin, assorted yellows, blues, and reds. For longer trips, blotter acid on an auto club TripTik. Most of it's pretty old. I don't travel much anymore.

Alison sticks with aspirin, swallowed dry. She watches as I focus the lens on a red Grand Am, exhaust trailing from its rear. Someone big is sitting behind the wheel with someone else in the passenger seat. Both faces are obscured by sun visors and a glare on the windshield. I've seen a light blue pickup here and there lately—outside Donnie's the other night, for example—but I don't recall a Grand Am tagging along before.

"What's the matter?" she says.

"Nothing. Some guy with his lights on." Illinois plates. But that's not unusual around here. I copy the number on an old lottery ticket in my pocket. Maybe I'll win something.

Then I empty my real prize on the floor mat: another pillow case—stained with blood—tied the same way at the top; containing a curious assortment of relics: pornographic magazines, the kind for swinging couples, with personal ads and explicit black and white pictures; a cracked Beta videotape, white leader spilling from its takeup reel; a plastic mustard bottle, with four syringes rubberbanded around it like booster rockets. A half-empty roll of Saran Wrap. All of it tied together with coarse scratchy rope.

And oddest of all—and somehow most unsettling—an aluminum caulking gun with a serrated trigger. The label on its barrel is the same as the spackle, Hyde Park Hardware. They must have been having a sale. When I pick the gun up it slices a two-inch fold of skin from my palm.

"Are we on some sort of treasure hunt?" Alison says, getting the first-aid kit out. She bandages my hand, wiping it first with iodine swabs. "Hold still, will you? And quit flinching. Jesus, what a baby. When was your last tetanus shot?"

I'm not sure. And what about rabies? My index finger has two small teeth marks. As I drive to I-65 and then north toward home I notice the Grand Am's gone. If Alison weren't sick I'd stop in the truck stop, ask around. But I want to get her home.

"What the hell happened down here, Harding?" Her eyes are closed.

"I'm not sure," I say. I'm wiping blood and some sort of yellow paste on my jeans. It doesn't smell exactly like mustard. And it burns like hell.

THREE

Around ten P.M. I stop at the Belmont Cove
for dinner. My pager beeps twice before I
even get a menu. The pay phone at the
Cove is in the back kitchen, just above a
stationary tub full of live crawfish. While I make my
calls I'm watching two men in hairnets work a deep-
fryer. As far as I can tell everything on the Cove's
menu—chicken, hush puppies, shrimp, turnovers, ice
cream—comes from the same wire basket, the same vat
of espresso-colored oil.

The crawfish are hanging around, waiting to be
boiled alive. I know the feeling. One of the Jamaican
cooks, Jonnie, likes to surprise me by sneaking up and
dropping one down my pants. It's a tossup which of us
is more excited, me or the crawfish.

I can barely read the number, the battery's so low.
It's the first time in months that I've carried a pager.
Getting it out of my sock drawer made me feel like
Jimmy Stewart strapping on the six-guns after years of
farming.

"Alison? You paged me?" I thought she'd be in
bed, sleeping off the migraine.

"A minor success," she says, sounding weary. "I
remembered your negatives from Wednesday were still
in my darkroom. So I printed one up featuring our mys-

tery tramp front and center and showed it around the Women's Center."

"You did? Isn't Rosenberg in that picture?"

"Parts of him," she says. "Don't worry. I was discreet. You can't see his face. But maybe I should have cropped it a bit more. Some of the girls nearly fainted. They lead sheltered lives."

"Did you get a name before you were thrown out?"

"The consensus was, yes, her name's Nora or Noreen; they think she's staying at I-House. At least they've seen her in the dining room."

"Big deal," I say. "Half the campus eats there. Sunday nights there's practically no place else to eat."

"Exactly. So I shlepped over there for dinner myself and talked to Esther at the front desk."

"Any luck?"

"The halibut was very dry," Alison says. "My advice is, stick with the fruit plate."

"Any luck with Esther?"

"Esther at the front desk says a Nora Taylor lives there—"

"You showed her the picture?"

"No. Esther at the front desk would not have appreciated it. You have to pick your spots, Harding."

"I leave that to you. I don't suppose Nora was home. You weren't able to just go up and talk to her directly?"

"Hasn't been in all day. Esther at the front desk thinks Nora's biochem. I could hang around Kent, go to Life Sciences, check with the department secretary. If you want more I'll have to hack into the university computer. They change the password daily. Not that that's much of a problem. I know a girl in the comp center—"

"All that gets us is her academic record, Alison. Life of the mind. We're more interested in life of the body."

"Get your mind out of the gutter, dear," she says.

"Can't we get inside her room?"

"I wouldn't suggest it. For one thing, I don't have a valid ID anymore. And it's a student residence. This is Hyde Park, Harding. There's one cop to buzz you through, another to sign you in, two or three more upstairs. Maybe one in Nora's bathtub. You forget how paranoid they get about security."

"I'm remembering."

"I did manage one bit of mischief. When Esther left the front desk I grabbed a message from Nora's mail slot. 'Don't forget the party Sunday night.' Signed 'Robin.' It's been sitting there a couple days, though, so it might mean nothing. Maybe everybody in the dorm got one."

"I don't suppose Esther knows Robin."

"She might, who knows? By then, she was outside cleaning up the jar of corn relish some idiot dropped on the front steps. Even the cops were out there helping her. Those mason jars explode like grenades."

"Alison, I'm touched. You love your grand-mother's corn relish. And you sacrificed an entire jar for me."

"Don't worry, I'll bill you. Grandma will bill you. How's your hand? Did you try adding ketchup and some relish with the mustard?"

"It wasn't much of a cut. How's your head?"

"Splitting. You owe me time and a half for this one, Harding. It was like Love Canal in there today. I felt like the Toxic Avenger. If I'm on a respirator at forty it'll be entirely your fault."

"Don't worry, Alison. I'll pull the plug."

Peter Tosh comes on the radio. Everyone's jamming. Jonnie brings me coffee the same color as the oil in the vat. It smells a bit like chicken. I get a crawfish down my shirt, two in my pants.

My friend Boone doesn't hear very well in one ear, it has something to do with an accident he had in his childhood, a fall he took in the bathtub—how that would affect your hearing, I don't know. Maybe he got water in his brain. He belongs to an academic type known as Semi-Genius Without Dissertation; very common in Hyde Park, where grocery baggers are often Renaissance scholars working on the ninth draft of their proposal, the way waiters in L.A. are really actors or screenwriters. Boone lives on campus but, thanks to Donnie, works part-time in the labs at Schaumburg Associates. Boone's field is physics but he has master's in both chemistry and engineering. I drove out there earlier tonight hoping he could run a few tests for me—quietly, after hours.

But before Boone and I can get much further than hello Donnie Wilson cuts in, tells Boone to get off the line. Donnie's working late. Boone is in the basement lab ten floors below but Donnie likes keeping tabs on things; he always has.

Right now he's wondering what in the hell I'm doing.

"The Graveyard's overworked, Harding. You've got no business using lab-rats like Boone for your own shit. And the Rosenberg case is finished. You're off the clock, remember?" I can picture him pacing around the office with the cordless phone, a drink in his other hand.

Probably not mineral water tonight. He keeps a bottle of Dewar's locked away in the sideboard.

It was Donnie who named the basement labs the Graveyard. He calls the media center the War Room and his old office on eight the Bunker. In fact, each room in his corporate high rise is hospital-white, as funky as Disneyland. The names remind me of little boys building a treehouse.

"This is absolutely my last motherfucking domestic," he says. "I swear to God. Every single time they come in meek and mild, saying they just want what's fair. Then you show them pictures of hubby with his prick hanging out—big surprise, right?—and suddenly everything changes. Now they don't just want the house, they want each and every single fucking thing in the house, down to the curtain rods, the doorknobs, the fucking *shine* on the doorknobs. It's greed, nothing but greed. And fucking coldhearted revenge. I'm sick to death of it, buddy."

"And?"

"And frankly," he says, "I don't see any way of squeezing another nickel out of her."

"I can see how it's eating away at you. But I might have found something interesting today. I'm following up on the girl. If she's a student and he's really hurting her we can take Rosenberg down—he'll bend right over, you know he will. Hell, Donnie, you used to do this sort of thing for relaxation."

"Not anymore, Harding. Who are you working for here?"

"I'm just looking around."

"Because you're not working for me." He pauses. The line crackles with static and a series of short sharp clicks—is somebody else listening to this?

"Forget the girl," Donnie says. "You hear me? The girl's got nothing to do with nothing."

"And your client Mrs. Rosenberg?"

"*Former* client, Harding. This was your last Wednesday night. And she sure as hell doesn't need you to get a divorce."

"So if I stumble on this two million bucks you won't want a cut?"

"You won't see a dime of that," Donnie says.

"Is that what the lawyer, Warren Frost, thinks?"

"Frost. Jesus, Harding, do yourself a favor. Don't listen to Frost. The bastard's drinking again. It's this Rosenberg bitch. You should have seen his hands shaking last week before he left town."

"It might have been the cold."

"I bet he's away at some clinic, taking the cure. For all I know he's fucking her, too. He sounds like a god-damned teenager whenever he talks about her. Babbling on and on. Believe me, he's borderline, he's this close to going overboard—"

"I can't see your hands, Donnie."

"Very, very close."

He reads from some financial report he's commis-sioned—very hush-hush, even Elenya hasn't seen it—concerning Rosenberg's Geneva account. It's thirty-five pages, he says, single-spaced—he flips through it near the phone so I can appreciate its length.

International banking experts. Tons of footnotes. Cross-references from Zurich to Tokyo. The kind of thing the boys at First Chicago drool over. The sum-mary? Page thirty-six, just one line: No Fucking Way.

"End of story," Donnie says, slamming the phone with a loud click that rings in my ears.

"How does he do that?" Boone says, coming back

on our party line. "Make that kind of noise hanging up a cordless phone? Jeez."

"Does Donnie do that often? Break in like that?"

"Not really," Boone says. "He had an in-house monitor installed on certain lines, supposedly for security but I think he's just getting bored up there in the ozone, sitting in on meetings all day."

Boone sees Donnie more than I do these days. All three of us used to go drinking together. That was years ago, before I went to prison, before Donnie changed area codes.

The cook brings me more coffee. I've given up on eating dinner. I tell Jonnie to fix me a chicken basket to go. Extra Crispy. No crawfish.

"What's the story on the stuff I left you?"

"It's not pretty. The needles had liquid cocaine and benzedrine; there's traces of an antipsychotic, probably Thorazine, but those kinds of compounds break down, and this isn't exactly the FBI Crime Lab."

"Did you screen the tape?"

"No, I just dusted it, tried to put it back together. It's Beta, man. I gave my Beta machine to Goodwill and they weren't real happy taking it."

"What about the pillowcase?"

"Everyone's favorite couple, dried semen and blood. I hope this wasn't your party, Harding. The blood's two different types—A and O. Definitely not safe sex. The Surgeon General wouldn't approve."

"And the mustard bottle?"

"French's Extra Spicy, not a favorite of mine personally. Too many additives. Yellow dye, artificial flavoring. I prefer Dijon. Just a hint of white wine—"

"That's it?"

"Not quite. I found something else everywhere—

the pillowcase, the syringe, even the trigger on the caulking gun. I can't isolate it. It looks like some kind of acid."

"What kind of acid?"

"Industrial solvent maybe, something for cleaning; refinishing. I knew a fisherman used acid like this to clean mudders. You know, river carp. Nasty, ugly fish. Worse than alewives."

"What about doctors?"

"They're more into fly-fishing, aren't they?"

"I mean would they have it around for something—"

"Who knows," he says. "Diluted maybe. Probably not at the concentration you gave me."

"I thought it was mixed with the mustard."

"Oil and water. Suspended, not dissolved—remember high school chemistry?"

"What if it was put on your skin?"

"You'd lose your tattoos."

"No, really."

"Serious tissue damage. Second- or third-degree burns. Possible bleeding with impaired clotting."

The smells from room nineteen come rushing back. So do the yellow stains I saw Wednesday night. I thought it was just lubricant—they come in all kinds of flavors these days; cherry red, banana yellow. Now I wish I'd gone with Alison to look for Nora.

And I wish I'd skipped the pills I dropped and stayed awake all night Wednesday night.

"Any ideas on why he'd use it in mustard?"

"Would he have to hide it?"

"No."

"I have a couple of ideas but they're not pleasant."

"Let's hear them."

"One would be that long-term the mustard acts as a

catalyst. Maybe with heat or a third ingredient present the acid breaks down into something even worse. I'd need more time to play with it to answer that."

"What else?"

"If he was injecting this stuff intravenously—"

"I don't think he was doing that."

"Good. It would probably kill you. Where'd you get this shit anyway?"

"I can't tell you; not yet." The line clicks again. Either I'm getting paranoid or the lab's got call-waiting. "Listen, Boone, do me a favor, all right? Don't leave this at the lab. Take it home tonight, and I'll try to pick it up in a couple days."

"No rush. I'll put it in my bedroom. No one's been there for years, believe me."

"Boone—this acid. What about putting it on a woman. During sex."

"What do you mean. Directly on her skin? Wouldn't advise it. Stick to Aqua Lube. Or this new shit, 2-7 Glyde. Comes highly recommended from the bears in the band."

"Directly on her pussy."

"Christ, Harding, you've got a sick puppy on your hands. It would hurt like hell, like salt on an open wound. You don't need a medical degree to know that."

"She'd let you know it—"

"If she was conscious, yeah. She'd be screaming bloody murder."

I get home around eleven. There's one message on my machine, from Alison. I think she recorded it before I talked to her at the Cove. "I had a great time, Harding," she says, then pauses. "I miss you." My TV joins me for a late snack of cold chicken and Southern Comfort. I take the bottle into the bedroom, watch the Friday night traffic on Broadway. Even in this cold there's a bit of rough trade on the corner. Cadillacs and Lincolns drive slowly by, circle the block, then pull over to negotiate. The bars and adult bookstores across the street have bright neon signs reflected in my windows. I fall asleep around midnight, still dressed, all the lights on.

Around two-thirty someone starts pounding on my front door. I pad in bare feet to the living room. My back hurts.

"Someone to see you," Minas says, already half-way down the stairs. "A woman. Says she has appointment." He shrugs. He clearly doesn't believe it either.

"Alison?"

"Not Alison."

Minas has closed the restaurant. He has his eight-tracks of Greek music cranked up, Pine-Sol drying on the floor. The chairs are on the tables, all but one; a front table where Elenya Rosenberg sits watching the clubs and gay bars emptying out onto Broadway, a different kind of reverse commute. Couples walk home in the cold. Minas is behind the counter, large silver mittens on both hands, waiting for the broiler to cool. He shrugs at me again. "She's waiting for you," he says, amused. Not many people wait for me anymore.

"Elenya?" I say, approaching her. "Are you all right?"

"I needed an aspirin," she says, turning halfway, her profile framed against the window. She's still wrapped in her fur coat. A handful of photos are spread on the table. "Do you have any? And some cold water?

And do you think if I gave Zorba here a great deal of money he'd turn down the balalaikas?"

"Come upstairs," I say, touching her shoulder lightly. I still remember the bruises. "It's a lot quieter. Lots of aspirin, lots of cold water."

"No balalaikas?"

"None. I promise." She starts to stand, then sits down.

"Do you believe in astrology?" I shake my head. "I Ching? Tarot cards?"

"Just the Easter Bunny."

"But you can read these," she says. "Anyone could. This one—where he's coming on her face—is the sign of Change. See? And this one—see how her eyes are closed in pain, her body doubled over—could be the card of Death." Her own eyes close, the color leaves her cheeks.

I help her up, distracted by the photos. What I see in the Tarot is Elenya Rosenberg needing help, getting a different husband.

"Maybe you should check," she says, "make sure no one's out there—"

"Following you? Did you see someone?" She shakes her head. I look through the glass but I don't see anything unusual. It's North Broadway on a Friday night. It's hard sorting the strange from the unusual.

"If you want I'll take a look around."

She says no. Minas watches us, waiting. "Should I lock up?"

"Lock up," I say.

We go through the back of the dark restaurant, past crates of produce, then up the inside steps to the third floor. The forty-watt bulb in the stairwell flickers like a candle. Elenya walks slowly, her mink dragging on every step. "My hat . . ." she says. "My gloves." I don't see them downstairs; they must be in her car.

It's only when we're in my apartment and I'm helping her off with her coat that I notice the nasty bruise on her left cheek. I'm blind as a bat.

"I may throw up," she says. "I'm not certain."

"Here. Sit down." She's wearing a short black dress, a string of pearls, carrying a small clutch purse. She must have black dresses the way Alison has jeans. "Are you dizzy?" I say, shoving old clothes and record albums onto the floor.

She shakes her head no. She sits on the edge of the couch. I don't recognize the look on her face. But I don't know her all that well.

I bring her the aspirin. She takes one, then another. All her movements are slow and deliberate. Maybe she's afraid the couch will fall apart.

"Do you need coffee?" I say. "Because I can run downstairs. Minas usually has some left—"

"No, please."

"Or I could run to the all-night place on Sheridan. It won't take a minute."

"No. Stay here, Harding," she says softly. "Please."

She's on something; I can't tell what. At first I think she's avoiding my eyes. Then I realize she's still trying to keep the bruised side of her face hidden.

"You still have records?" she says, flipping through a stack of albums. "T. Rex, Lena Horne, the Sex Pistols, *Oliver*—"

"They're a little out of order."

"Ours are in a landfill somewhere. We have CDs now."

"I'm a vinyl junkie. Elenya—"

"Stephen plays music in surgery—Bach, Handel,

Vivaldi—it helps him relax, he says. While he cuts things. Snip, snip." She makes a scissors motion near her nose. "God, you've got the James Gang—you're getting old, just like me. That was our first date; the James Gang, and The Who. At the Auditorium Theatre, when they used to still have rock groups. Our first date."

"Both those groups?" It's hard to picture her listening to the James Gang. "Your ears must have really rung after that."

"For days," she says, giving me her first smile of the night. It dies quickly. "I wore a long paisley dress, that I bought just for the date. Wooden sandals. You weren't supposed to get dressed up then, remember? Girls couldn't wear stockings. Even on first dates. And it was summer. And my legs were so awfully white . . ."

"Would you like some music on now?"

"No," she says, her voice empty. "The quiet's nice."

Other than the quiet and the aspirin and the water I don't have much to offer her. She says that's all she needs—aspirin, water, and maybe a bathrobe. "I can't go home, Harding," she says. "Not tonight. Tomorrow maybe . . ." Her voice trails off. "I seem to be very tired," she says.

The pajamas I find her are clean if a little stale, which I apologize for; I sleep in my underwear. "So do I," she says, holding out her arms like an army recruit for the pajamas, robe, slippers I give her.

While she's in the bathroom changing I clean the bedroom by throwing everything into the closet. The door barely closes. I get some old sheets and a blanket and make up a bed for myself on the couch.

When she comes out, fumbling with the buttons on

her pajamas, she looks distracted. For a second I'm not sure she knows where she is.

"Elenya?" I say. "Do you need to call anyone?"

"What?" She turns, slippers squeaking on the hardwood floor, focusing on me. She might be a child sleeping over at a stranger's house.

"Do you need to call anyone?"

"There's no one to call," she says. Her tone suggests this is a new discovery. When she walks down the hall to the bedroom, pajama arms flopping back and forth below her hands, the terrycloth robe trails behind her like a wedding train.

"What about a friend?" I say.

"All my friends have husbands," she says. "And families. I don't want to disturb them this late. Why? Can't I stay here?"

"No, no. I just thought—" I stop. I don't know what I thought.

I follow her to the bedroom. I expect her to crash but she's got something on her mind.

"Harding—what we talked about, the other night." She's standing by the bed, holding on to the headboard. "I've been worrying."

"About what?"

"I wouldn't want you doing anything . . . risky. Or dangerous."

"I almost never do."

"Just for me, I mean, or this money that they found. Since I never really had it I never really lost it. Right?"

"That's one way of looking at it, sure."

"It makes me angry sometimes, to think of *him* having it. But I'll be fine. I'll have plenty to live on. I'm not greedy. And I wouldn't want you doing something crazy."

"Well, all right then. I won't."

She nods, finally sitting down. She's doing that thing with her hands again; rubbing the joints of both fingers; moving them back and forth. It must be arthritis but she's only forty-three.

"Something where you might end up back in prison," she says.

"I don't remember telling you I ever was—"

"Warren told me. He said you're a man with a past. Which I thought sounded exciting. If he was trying to warn me it had the opposite effect."

"Your lawyer told you?" I wasn't aware Warren Frost had followed my career so closely. "What did he say?"

"Just about the girl you were protecting. That she got hurt."

"Yes," I say. "She did." That's one way of putting it. "What else did he tell you?"

"He said you killed someone. Someone named Patner. But the one you were chasing—was his name Martins?"

"Martinez. It was self-defense, Elenya. Martinez was the girl's father, he sent this guy Patner after me—it was a long time ago."

"That's how you lost your license? And hurt your back?"

I nod.

"How long were you in prison?"

"Eighteen months." It's been a while since anyone's asked me questions so directly. But it's all right.

"Did you ever catch him? The father, the one you were chasing?"

"If I'd caught him, Elenya, I'd still be in prison."

I pull down the shades so the morning sun won't bother her. She lays the robe and slippers neatly on a chair and gets under the covers, pulling them to her neck.

"I left my car on the street," she says. "A red Porsche. I don't remember where. Will they tow it?"

"They might," I say. "In the morning anyway. Where are your keys?"

"In my purse."

Her purse is buried in the couch. I get the keys and just slip on some gym shoes and a jacket, thinking it will just take a minute. I go out the back door.

It's so cold now that the air is nearly unbreathable. I hold my jacket sleeve over my mouth. The wooden treads of the back stairs creak and groan as if they might shatter. Walking through the alley I barely leave prints, so thick and hard is the snow, never plowed, just packed down by garbage trucks from Streets and Sanitation. It might still be here on opening day. The three A.M. windchill burns my cheeks.

The Porsche's parked at a meter by the restaurant's side windows. Minas is still cleaning his broiler. Out here it's sub-zero but Minas is stripped to his shorts, sweating, cursing, swigging Greek wine from the bottle. No wonder he can't understand his tenants' complaints about cold radiators. He talks about getting an attack dog but a scene like this would scare most prowlers away. It's scaring me, I know that. He's singing or maybe talking to himself. I can't tell which. As window displays go it beats Field's at Christmas. I rap on the glass and wave. He shrugs.

I get the Porsche started after three or four tries and wait for it to warm up. At these temperatures the oil must be like molasses. I'm looking for the lights switch—this thing has a dashboard like an F-16—knocking CDs and brown bottles onto my lap when headlights from the Jewel lot across the street fill the Porsche with light, showing me briefly, from the plastic containers in each hand, that Elenya likes Yanni and Halcion, not a bad combination. No wonder she's sleepy.

It's a blue pickup again, the driver hidden behind unbalanced brights dancing like theater spots. After pulling from the lot he zooms south to Cornelia, cutting the corner so sharply he takes a newspaper box with him.

I'd take the same route but the Porsche's windshield wipers click on and cruise control kicks in before I can find the lights. The truck's gone. I put the pills and Yanni back on a shelf under the dash, and that's when I see a crumpled white envelope lying between Elenya's leather gloves, as though her hands were still holding it, won't let go. There's a gold cross on a thin chain. A punch card from the Indiana tollway. And a shiny letter opener with a very sharp tip that I just avoid. I turn it around so it points in.

I'd probably ignore it—I'm very cold, and other people's mail is never as interesting as you might think—except for some kind of bright red lettering across the front. I turn on the interior light, spread the envelope out on the seat. It's the size of a greeting card. But not much of a greeting—the red lettering is lipstick that comes off on my fingers like blood. And the word scrawled across the white envelope is simply "CUNT."

I pull the Porsche around the corner, ten feet or so into the alley, and sit with the motor idling, the interior light off. I turn the radio on, listen to some overnight DJ playing oldies and taking requests. I wait—oh, thirty, maybe thirty-five seconds—before turning the light back on and opening the envelope.

It's a card, all right, a birthday card, with a cake on the front and two messages inside; one generic and printed by the manufacturer, another more personal, typed in red.

Happy Birthday!

>A simple thought!
>From me to you
>Here's hoping birthday wishes
>All come true!

Dear bitch: You have a mole inside your right thigh A birthmark on your ass. You disgust him. You disgust me. You middle-aged disgusting meno-pausal dried-up cunt. He does me in your own fucking house. Skip your little class sometime and watch. HE BELONGS TO ME.

When I fuck him do you think he says your name?

Free verse. There's no signature. I sit for a minute, wasting gas.

My mind is racing faster than the engine. I'm think-ing about that bruise on Elenya's cheek, reading the card again several times. The DJ—Rockin' Randy—tries warming us up by playing the Beach Boys. Surfer angst. Not much surfing on Broadway tonight.

I park the Porsche in the alley by my truck and head up the back steps. I turn off all the back lights—the porch, the kitchen, the dining room. The bathroom light is still on. The bedroom light is off, the door half open. When I turn on the hall light I can see Elenya turning sideways under the covers, flipping her pajama bottoms on top of the bedspread.

I turn off the hall light.

"Thanks, Harding," she says, a sleepy voice from the darkness.

"Sure, no problem. It's parked around back."

"I mean for everything. Tonight, the other night. Everything. For not asking questions."

"Of course," I say, pausing a second. "I hope you can sleep."

I leave the bathroom light on, in case she gets sick. Or needs more water. I set the bottle of aspirin by the sink. Halcion—if that's what was in that bottle—can sneak up on you just like ouzo. I stay dressed, even the cold gym shoes. I'm not very sleepy, and I want to be ready, though for what, I don't know. The time is frozen on the bank's sign across the street. The temperature's still frozen at two degrees. I think that's optimistic.

Steam is finally filling the radiators, here and in the bathroom; the pipes complain, kicking and screaming. There's a fight outside somewhere. Voices like threads of memory rise from the street, competing for my attention. There are always voices out there. You don't have to listen.

How long will the wind blow?
Until I die

I lie on the couch in the dark, watching the neon lights dance on my ceiling.

FOUR

"I'll need money," I tell Warren Frost.

It's ten degrees but Frost's jacket is open. His face is red. His rusting Impala crowds a sleek gray Lexus. Most of the Loop attorneys I know love expensive cars but Frost spends discretionary income on antifreeze. There's a sterling silver flask of rum in a shoulder holster, cases of Chivas and French grape strapped in like kids in car seats.

I'm getting hungry. This was supposed to be an early lunch. I left a message on Frost's machine at five this morning—I never did get to sleep—and the reply was okay, eleven-thirty, this address near O'Hare. Instead of lunch it's a typical Chicago meeting—two guys in long-term parking. All we're missing is a body in the trunk of the Impala.

"How much?" he says.

"A thousand to start."

He laughs. "I can hire an army for that."

"Good. Hire one. Try to get them inside Rosenberg's faculty offices, past his secretary. Inside the medical building on Woodlawn. Inside his house."

He considers this, kicking a black chunk of road ice from the Impala's frame. Then he pops the trunk, spins four wingnuts holding down the jack. Beneath the spare there's a roll of fifties like a small head of cabbage.

"You're not really going inside his house," he says.
I shrug.

"Let's start with six," he says, peeling the bills off.
"Any more, you'll give me indigestion. Already I have
an upset stomach. Donnie says what you're doing
should make me very very nervous."

"That's why Donnie won't do it."

"Which only makes me more nervous, Harding.
The man's usually a pit bull whenever he smells more
than three figures."

"The pit bull's a vice president now, Warren. I
think they neuter them or something when they get
above the fifth floor. Take that new office of his. It's not
often neighborhood guys like Donnie go minimalist."

He hands me the flask. I'm not sure how—the flask
has been under his arm, after all—but the rum's nearly
as cold as the wind whipping around the Impala.

I've known Frost vaguely for years—anyone who
hangs around the Daley Center runs into him, either in
court or the men's room—but I can't remember ever
dealing with him directly. You see him on the news
sometimes, advising a client, a phony smile and an outstretched hand fighting off a photographer's flash.

How he ended up advising Elenya Rosenberg I
have no idea.

"Why so fast, Harding?" he says. "Why tomorrow
night? It's her birthday, for Christ's sake—"

"Because that's when I want to do it." I haven't
told him about the card. I haven't told him much of anything, which makes us about equal. "If it doesn't work
out maybe they'll invite us in for cake and ice cream."

He says nothing for a minute or two. I wonder if he
takes this much time buying furniture.

"You look tired," he says finally. "Run-down." I

doubt if he's worried about my health. It's more the concern of an insurance agent writing a policy; protecting an investment. "And your eyes are red."

"Your eyes don't look so great either, Frost." I look for a mirror, settling for the chrome on the Impala. Not so bad. Most of the people I know look tired. Somehow having nothing much to do requires more and more effort.

"I'd like to be there," he says. "In fact, I insist on it."

I shrug. If he stays out of the way it shouldn't matter. I doubt he'll be much help. Hauling a single crate of documents to my trunk makes him winded, brings the rum to his forehead in a line of sweat. Frost has enough documentation here for the Warren Commission. Computer printouts, statistical abstracts— trying to track Stephen's money. I can't imagine using any of it.

"The report on overseas finance and probate law was put together by a couple of interns from Northwestern," he says. "I'd wait an hour to go into the water after that one. But you know what they say. Follow the money." My eyes follow a page torn from an old yearbook fluttering onto the snow—Lucy Williams in white uniform and starched cap, Loyola School of Nursing. More innocent days. I can barely recognize her in clothes.

I recognize someone else in this class picture, though—a male nurse I saw once or twice walking Lucy home after work. He's easy to spot—the only male in Lucy's class. Big even then in a bearish way, now he's mid-thirties with an earnest expression and neatly combed black hair. Once, after seeing Lucy safely inside her building, he came close enough to my 4Runner to get a look at my face and seemed relieved at what he found—not a reaction I often encounter. I feigned sleep. He kept walking.

"There should be a corkscrew below the dash," Frost says. I think we're breaking out the wine but he uses it to scrape his windshield. He wants a real drink.

We drive a mile or so into Du Page County, where the zoning breaks down and you get tract houses and strip malls on the same parcel of land, light industry around the next bend. We park on the street. Frost never feeds a meter, a status symbol of sorts in Chicago. We cross against traffic. Frost walks with both hands in his pockets nervously fingering change.

"You ever call one of those sex numbers?" he says.

"Not really."

"How do you know you're not talking to some housewife in Des Plaines, ironing in her kitchen, laughing at you?"

"That's a different number, Warren."

The Wedge Inn sits between a dying dim sum restaurant and a store selling ceiling fans. It's a neighborhood place with linoleum floors, glass-block windows, Old Style on tap. It doesn't smell real good but most bars don't this early in the day.

I've never noticed this strip of stores or the bar but I'm not surprised Frost knows about it. He clearly has every package store and four A.M. license for three counties on a mental Rolodex. He greets a guy at the door, talks briefly with one or two regulars, shaking hands, back-slapping like a precinct captain—and then hands his flask to Jamie, the woman tending bar. Jamie refills it automatically, like a canteen at the last water hole. And she has a special smile for Frost when she brings us our drinks.

I ask Jamie if she has a phone I could use.

"In the back, honey. By the john. Just watch your feet—we got a little drainage problem this morning."

I sidestep the puddles and feed a quarter into an old rotary phone. The call's completed, costing me my quarter but yielding little—a university operator transfers me to International House. An operator there waits ten or twelve rings before telling me no one in Nora's room is picking up. The next quarter's my last, and the call's long-distance—Springfield—but luckily a friend of mine named Zekman takes pity and accepts the charges. I used to know a guy in the CPD who'd do this for me but he got tired of being a cop. He runs a fishing charter now somewhere in Florida. I get postcards from him sometimes; the kind with huge alligators or the World's Tallest Ball of String.

"It belongs to a Swann," Zekman says.

"At Brookfield or Lincoln Park?"

"No, that's his name, Harding. A doctor, too. Sort of, anyways. A bone-cruncher. But it's red-flagged, your Grand Am." That doesn't mean it's stolen, just that the cops would like to know where it is. Usually that means an expired registration. He gives me an address—Lawndale and 89th—which I know very well. I've got an aunt buried there—dead center in Evergreen Cemetery. Nice landscaping, though maybe not the best place to start a medical practice. No wonder the expired registration notices were never delivered. Former owner? "Another bone-cruncher, Harding—Sawyer, DC." Another address, this one more convincing. I write all this down in a notebook I bought at Walgreens, along with a matching Bic pen. I'm turning into a regular detective.

"Where'd you see it?" Zekman says. "This ghost car."

"A truck stop, in Indiana."

"No kidding. Truck stops have good food some-times. What were they serving, chicken-fried steak? Biscuits and gravy?"

"I didn't really study the menu." Zekman dreams of opening a restaurant. He sits in his office at the DMV reading franchise agreements, *Cooking for Fifty*. Every-body wants to be somewhere else.

Frost watches me come back to the table.

"You have someone in mind to help you?" he says. Our table's small and wobbly—maybe Frost likes it because it's close to the bar. Or it could be his regular table but then something tells me every table in the place is Frost's regular table. There's an Old Style sign over the bar blinking on and off like a broken traffic signal in his bifocals.

"Yes," I say. "I do."

"What's his name?"

I grab a handful of pretzels. "You don't know him," I say.

"Wonderful. I'm just supposed to trust you?"

"That's the way it works, Warren. What did you want to do, run a credit check on him?"

"It couldn't be any worse than the one I ran on you," he says, waving at Jamie for another round. I'm on my first Old Style, which is my limit. Frost is drinking single-malt Scotch like ice tea. I guess it's working. His eyes are beginning to get shiny. "I got your life story in my office on little three-by-five cards. My paralegals are very thorough."

"No kidding. Maybe they can do my taxes for me."

You can always tell a serious drinker by how he sits in his chair. The amateur leans back as if he had all the time in the world. He allows his beer to get a little warm. Frost sits forward with both hands wrapped around his glass. You'd need the Jaws of Life to get it away from him.

"I'm doing this for Elenya," Frost says. "You understand? Because I don't know what else to do. You saw her, right? At Donnie's?"

"Yeah, Warren. I saw her." I go to the bar for some change. No Patti Smith on the jukebox at the Wedge Inn. I punch up the next best thing—Patsy Cline. Jamie gives me a thumbs-up. Kindred souls. I dial my home number and get my machine. Elenya, if she's still there, doesn't pick up. I'm not sure what I'd ask her if she did. I have no real idea what's happening Sunday night, just a feeling that I should be there. For Elenya or the girl, Nora. Or both.

To do what? To prevent what? I don't know.

I carry some peanuts back to the table.

"I don't usually do this sort of thing," Frost says.

"Sure, Warren. That's why you use your spare tire as a money market fund."

"I didn't notice you having a crisis of conscience when I gave you the bills."

"I'll hate myself later," I say. Patsy Cline is walkin' after midnight. "What can you tell me about Elenya's husband, the Nose King?"

"You're kidding. You've been following him for three months. You have to ask me?"

"All I know about are his Wednesday nights. Up to now it's just been Lucy Williams, a little kinky sex. Nothing you wouldn't find in your average porno flick. Then last week they picked up some girl. It got a little rough."

"So?" he says.

"So I'm wondering if he does this often."

"Like tomorrow night, for instance?" he says.

"Donnie only hired me for Wednesdays. Sunday nights is uncharted territory, Christopher Columbus time. We could fall right off the face of the fucking earth, so I'd like a little background."

"There's not much to tell," Frost says. "Rosenberg's surgical practice is a cash cow—more patients than he can handle. He sees some in the hospital, some at the Woodlawn office. He teaches in the med school. He has to do *some* research, of course, only because the university demands it. Probably less since he's made tenure. What else? He likes to garden. He has a mistress. And he beats up his wife."

"There, you see?" I say. "I had no idea he liked to garden. What kind of research exactly?"

"Nothing very important," Frost says munching peanuts.

"Meaning you have no idea, right? Is he popular with the other faculty?"

"Harding, you went to school there, not me."

Like a lot of Northwestern grads Frost is defensive about Chicago.

"That was twenty years ago."

"Yes, well. You know how science at Chicago is. It hasn't changed. Pure research, unsullied by the real world, is the only kind they admire," Frost says. "Unless you win the Nobel. God forbid you do something with some kind of practical use."

"Maybe they learned how dangerous that can be in 1945."

"You mean Fermi, Szilard, men like that? Rosenberg's just a nose-cutter, Harding. He's not in that class. The research he does is probably whether to use Extra Strength Puffs or Scotties."

"Where's he do the research?"

"Someplace called Kent."

"A chemistry lab? Why would he be over there?"

"Who knows? Who cares?"

Another of my selections *Seven Year Ache*, Rosanne Cash—kicks in. Jamie smiles. The old guys at the bar are this close to dancing.

"Have you ever talked with Elenya about Stephen?" I say.

"What do you mean? About what?"

"About what he does. With Lucy, and now this girl."

"Not in specifics. Not until Donnie showed us the photos. That kind of forced the issue."

"Why'd she file now?"

He shrugs.

"Because I can't see her putting up with the abuse—"

"The hitting? I think that's relatively new," Frost says. "Just the last year or so. You're right; she's too strong a woman to take it for very long."

"So when did she start talking about divorce?"

"I'm not sure. Wait—I remember talking to her around Thanksgiving, or was it Halloween—last fall sometime. But it was just talk. She came to my office, asked about settlement. Hypothetically."

"Why'd she come to you? You're the family friend?"

"Something like that."

I wait a second, but Frost clearly doesn't wish to explain this any further.

"What about other girlfriends? Do you know of any besides Lucy?"

He shakes his head.

"A woman named Robin? Ever hear her name mentioned?"

Frost says no.

"Nora Taylor?"

"Where are you getting these names?"

"Do you have a copy of his daily schedule? Where he goes, who his friends are—"

"I can't believe I'm hiring you," Frost says. "You know less about this than I do."

"The other night Elenya mentioned being afraid someone was following her. Did she ever tell you that?"

"No. Now look, I really need to know your man's name, Harding," he says, crossing back to this like a good lawyer on redirect. "Something of his background."

"Like whether he's a Mason?"

"Like whether he was with you that other time, when things didn't go so well." His eyes meet my stare. "When you lost your license. That happened in Hyde Park too, didn't it? The first part anyway."

I'm not angry. In fact, I'm impressed by how long it's taken him to get around to this. Like a lot of drunks he's very light on his feet.

"You'll meet him tomorrow night," I say. "Try to contain yourself."

"He wasn't there that other time? If I have a paralegal slog through the court records—ten, eleven years ago, South Cottage Grove—wasn't that where it happened? Or at least where they found her? Pretty badly cut, wasn't she, on the stomach? And arms? Would I find this other man's name?"

"Shut up, Warren. Don't push it."

"What was the girl's name again—Andrea?"

"Angela." He knows her damn name.

"That's right. Angela Martinez. Whatever became

of her? When she got out of Billings and then the physical rehab at RIC—did you two kids keep in touch?"

"We're not exactly pen pals," I say, looking for Jamie myself now. No more Old Style, though; I'm upgrading to straight whiskey. "Why don't you just drop it, Warren, okay? It was a long time ago. And I thought we were talking about Elenya, remember?"

He thinks better of continuing this after seeing the look on my face. I take note: it only requires five doubles, a half-pint of rum, and the threat of physical violence to shut him up. He orders another drink; I've lost track of how many he's had. But it hasn't affected him one bit. His hands never shake. He has the constitution of the professional alcoholic. He's married to the stuff.

As for me, I haven't gone to bed yet, so the boilermakers Jamie starts setting up for me could be considered just a nightcap. That's the theory anyway. My fists, and my nerves, relax somewhat. Old Style actually becomes drinkable after three or four whiskeys. There is a pleasing anesthetic effect to the combination. Especially with the jukebox now playing Mickey & Sylvia. *Love Is Strange*.

"Vacation pictures?" Jamie says, looking over Frost's shoulder—he's thumbing through the photos I took of Rosenberg and Lucy. If you flip them fast it's like a silent movie. "Somebody had a good time."

"Club Med," I say.

"Sure," Jamie says to me, smiling. "You don't get that kind of service in the Dells anymore."

FIVE

Saturday night passes in a buzz. I sleep off the effects of the Wedge Inn facedown on my couch, waking at three in the morning. Elenya's gone. The Porsche's gone. I'm not sure when either of them left.

I walk to a twenty-four-hour Jewel and buy the Sunday papers and beer and some actual food, even an orange or two. A kid making a pyramid out of cans of green beans points me toward the aspirin. My lucky night—the Large Econo-Size comes with a throwaway watch and a nifty slogan: *Time to Feel Better*. Walking home on Broadway I pass Selected Works, a used bookstore I often frequent, looking for movie books on zombies or Japanese monsters; a watch cat sleeps in the window. Godzilla's on alert somewhere in Tokyo. Everyone's on some kind of vigil tonight. I check my new watch against the store's clock. It's already two minutes slow.

My answering machine is a medley of conflicting voices: Alison warily agreeing to help; Frost confirming the rendezvous spot; Donnie warning me he won't be there as backup so I'd better watch my fucking back with Frost. Boone whispering the acid's really just phenol, something plastic surgeons use for face peels. And Elenya—the first time I've heard her voice since Friday—saying she's back home in Kenwood, don't worry, things will work out. Her voice is a whisper. I play that message twice.

The weather changes Sunday afternoon. The extreme cold backs off. But by early evening weathermen are breaking into talk radio with warnings of another storm. The temperature's been dancing around freezing all day. Something's coming. There might be snow, there might be hail and sleet. The world might end. Heavier accumulations near the lake, of course. Doppler radar forecasts segue into readings from Revelations.

It grows dark early. I put an extra slicker and rain gear in my truck, wear my rough paratrooper coat and insulated boots; clip a portable CB radio to my belt. I'm ready for anything the night throws at me. Freezing rain turns to sleet as I drive south on Lake Shore Drive. By the time I reach Hyde Park it's turned to snow.

On 47th Street my pager goes off, barely two blocks from Rosenberg's house—I make a quick U-turn and find a phone outside a liquor store. A bored cashier with purple hair watches me through the glass. The number's not one I recognize. Neither is the voice.

"—need to see you right away," a woman's saying. The wind and traffic and a breathless urgency interfere with my understanding her plea—"the Chamberlain dining room, I guess—someone gave me your name— oh God I forgot to tell you *my* name, it's Robin—*please I need to see you, I need your help*—" The line goes dead. I stand there waiting for someone—the operator, the cashier, the Stage Manager from *Our Town*— to explain everything I've just heard. All I get's a dial tone.

* * *

Chamberlain is part of a large dorm called Burton-Judson, a Fort Apache–like outpost on the edge of the campus—I know because I lived there as a freshman. Why Robin would assume that I know makes me uneasy. So does the timbre of fear in her voice, one of the most difficult things to counterfeit.

The front gate's closed. Everyone this late must pass customs. I don't have an ID or much of a story and five minutes with a female security guard gets me nothing but an offer to call the residence head and a glance at a mail slot—empty—with the name Robin Connor typed below. Room thirty-five, third floor.

But there's a library next door, and a guard more used to absent-minded law students forgetting their IDs—the libraries outdraw the bars in Hyde Park, even on weekends. The first guy to combine the two—a research library with a four A.M. license—will make a fortune at the University of Chicago.

The guard gives me a temporary pass which I quickly abuse, following a study group from the stacks to the basement, where a connecting tunnel leads back to Burton-Judson. In five minutes I'm outside the dining hall but it's an empty accomplishment; the place is locked for the night and very dark. There's no one around, inside or out.

I'm running short on time. Alison's waiting for me; so is Frost. I don't want to miss Elenya's birthday party. So I cross the small quadrangle to Chamberlain House and wait in the dark until the door opens and I can get inside, seeing as I do that the female guard has left her post, probably to phone me in. I run to the third floor.

It's a coed dorm now; different than in my day. The

door to Robin's room is open just a crack. I knock lightly, pushing the door open—the room's dark; the switch doesn't work. And it's a mess. Jeans and books and papers are scattered on the floor. A tall kid with long hair taps me on the shoulder. He smells like grass. "You a friend of Robin's?"

I don't have time to answer; I can hear the sirens. I was an idiot to show my face—more of an idiot not to wear gloves. As if to make penance I use the back stairs and a different door and go a block out of my way returning to my truck. It's snowing heavier now. The squad cars slide a bit, passing me on my way north.

I get to Greenwood Avenue a few minutes late, without much chance to catch my breath. A yellow Kharmann-Ghia sitting at the end of the block flashes its lights and pulls alongside me.

"Tell me again why I'm doing this?" Alison says, winding down her window. Dots of snow begin sticking to her black hair.

"Because you're good and true of heart."

"Really? That can't be it."

"Because a fellow sister's in trouble."

"Much better, Harding. But, given this weather, not enough."

"Because I'm paying you two hundred dollars."

"Good," she says, nodding, chewing gum. "That should do it. I just needed a little positive reinforcement. You want to come over later? *Day of the Dead* is on Cinemax." Alison has cable. She knows my weakness for zombies.

I tell her briefly about my page and what happened tonight at the dorm.

"The mysterious Robin," she says. "Maybe that card I found wasn't just junk mail after all. You want me to check over there too? At BJ?"

"Tomorrow. Tonight, stay with Nora. If she's even there—"

"Somebody at I-House thinks she's back," she says, rubbing her cheek and temple; another migraine. Blood rushing the wrong way. "At least her mail's been picked up. I don't think anyone's seen her."

"You have the portable CB on channel seven?"

"You betcha." She starts to leave, then notices the camera on my dash. "Not the Leica again, Harding. I must have given you that ten, twelve years ago. It's an antique."

"It has sentimental value."

"That's what the word antique means, Harding," she says, smiling.

She winds up her window, gives me the peace sign, drives south toward campus.

At this time of year the mansions in Kenwood hide their age well. Some look like winter palaces. Of course, when the snow melts in spring they'll look more like failed nobility; lawns gone to seed, rusting gutters, shingles replaced like a patchwork quilt.

Rosenberg's castle dominates its corner lot. Four floors, two stone towers. After a century of different masters and their hasty additions to the manor the design is now almost cubist; gables and balconies jutting in all directions; four front doors. Its facade shifts as you circle the grounds.

Frost is right on time. He arrives on foot. His Impala is somewhere on 47th Street. That's the benefit of a car like that—park it anywhere. Leave the keys in the ignition.

"Where's your other man?" he says. He's wearing a cute felt hat, creased in the middle, one small feather on the side. I can't decide if it's early Sinatra or late Robin Hood.

"Watching I-House," I say.

"Why?"

"That's where we think Nora lives."

"Who the hell is Nora?"

"The girl in the pictures," I say. "Remember the pictures?"

"You hired one guy," Frost says, pushing his hat back, "and you've got him sitting outside a girls' dorm? I'm more and more glad I only gave you the six."

Greenwood Avenue seems deserted tonight. A driveway two doors down leads to a coach house. I take point. The gate's locked but the fence is ornamental. I wait but Frost surprises me and climbs it easily. We cut through a greenhouse to the rear of the main house. A dog barks somewhere. Despite the snow it looks like there's going to be a moon.

Once or twice Frost slips and ends up in the snow. He's dressed for the office, and his shiny black Florsheims have no traction. For the first time I realize his topcoat's the one I gave Elenya. I wonder if it still smells like her. I wonder when she gave it back.

"Have you talked to Elenya today?" I say. We're both staring at the house.

"I couldn't reach her."

We stop behind a row of shrubs at the edge of the property. The snow has drifted heavily here. I have a zoom lens that doesn't fit the Leica. Frost has a small pair of opera glasses.

Up close, the house is huge, half a city block. There's a side parlor with large bay windows not far from us. It must have been an addition. It sits in the yard like a screened-in porch. The windows are brightly lit against the darkness, the shades partly up. I check my new watch: eight-thirty.

Two figures stand in the shadow of a fireplace. The man wears a dark blue bathrobe. The other figure, much shorter, wears a man's long oxford shirt. The tails go nearly to her knees. When she raises her arms her small bunched rear peeks out. She's wearing panty hose and glossy red spiked heels.

The lights are dimmed a bit. The glow from the fireplace fills the room like amber glass.

"Is that Nora?" Frost says. I can smell the dark rum on his breath.

"I can't tell. We'll have to get closer."

"But it's Rosenberg, right?"

"I think so."

"We should have brought some equipment," Frost says.

"Like what?"

"I don't know. Detective equipment."

"We're fine. You're wearing a trench coat."

"Pull your other man, Harding. We can use him better here."

"Not yet."

"Rosenberg's in his goddamn bathrobe. He's not going out. With three of us we could cover the house better. There's no reason to keep him at I-House—"

"Where do you suppose Elenya is?"

"Who knows? This place is like Sam Simeon. She

could be on the next block. The next fucking zip code. Pull your man—"

"Will you relax? I said not yet."

"I'm paying for this fiasco."

"Yes, but I'm running this fiasco. It's my fiasco. Okay?"

Frost grunts something like acceptance. I look up just in time to see the woman's bare back as she drops the oxford shirt. If it's Nora she's changed her hairstyle. I need to see her face but I may have lost my best chance—she slides over the sofa's top velvet cushion, red shoes pointing to the ceiling.

Rosenberg moves to the sofa.

"Can you work this?" I say, giving Frost the Leica. He nods. "If you circle around the house you'll come up on their blind side. Shoot through that other window and you may have enough light." I drape the Leica's strap around his neck like an Olympic medal. At least he has something to do. That's all we want, right? Some sort of purpose, no matter how meaningless? He cuts across the driveway and disappears. It's a relief to be rid of him.

Where is Elenya tonight? Is she even here for her birthday?

I keep getting my feet caught in dead vines and branches, postmortem artifacts from summers past. I'm in some sort of garden. Seed packets with pictures of marigolds and cucumbers are frozen with the mulch. The snow's studded with tomato stakes like course markers in a downhill slalom. I pick my way carefully through the course.

I walk to the edge of the woodpile. Even without the zoom I can tell it's not the girl I saw in the motel. She's on her stomach, her rear a boyish inverted

V. I watch, passive. Rosenberg pushes the boyish figure down, going for the secondary target—Christ, he's got her face buried in the upholstery. Let her breathe, bastard.

Without bugs or a directional mike the show unfolds like an old 16mm skinflick, a peepshow loop. Somehow that makes it more erotic. So does the fact it's Rosenberg's own home, not some crummy motel. I don't have a camera. There's no reason to watch. Despite myself, as angry as I get watching Rosenberg relentlessly fuck this girl, I can feel with disgust my own cock grow hard, pressed against the stacked wood.

"Harding." Frost is nearly under the window I sent him to, trying to stand on an old wooden storm door buried in the ground. He's too close. There's no real cover but he's hidden in shadows; the only light comes from the windows and a weak yellow bulb over the garage. The moon never showed. Frost is motioning for me to follow his path—he sees something interesting in the far bay window. He still has the camera.

"What."

"Look, look." He's waving frantically, teetering on the top edge of the storm door as though riding a surfboard. "Come over here."

I barely take a step. Two things happen almost at once: I see there's someone else in the room, another woman just behind the drapes, now moving forward, her hands tied—

And suddenly, it's daylight again.

Frost must have gotten too close. Either that or Rosenberg wired that storm door. There's a loud click, an auto-switch thrown somewhere over the garage. Wiring and hardware frozen all winter groans to life. Powerful spots on the gutter directly above me jump to life, flood the side yard with light. Stalactites of ice drop from the roof.

Frost and I both move away from that first flash, which takes us backward around the rear of the house. A dog inside the house is barking. My eyes are a storm of white spots. Someone yanks the shutters closed as I trip and fall backward into the snow. When I get to my feet I start running. I should let Frost lead since he's just done this but he's moving slower and I'm not waiting.

We leave the yard, making a wide circle, and stumble through a white gazebo, then some type of solarium, a large wooden deck made from green pine. I'm yelling for Frost. I can't find the rear of the fucking place. And I'm running for the darkness always just ahead.

But the house's perimeter is endless, and motion detectors keep kicking in the trigger spots on gables, downspouts, dormers, trees. They're always a half-step behind us, switching on like bright bulbs on a circuit board. Finally Frost pulls me with him through an empty carport. By the time we're back on the street and running up Greenwood for the Toyota the house and grounds are lit like a NASA launch.

"You still have the camera?" I say, out of breath. I haven't run like that since the 440 in high school track. My hands fumble with the keys in the ignition.

"Just get us the fuck out of here, okay? Before every cop on the South Side shows up. I'll buy you a new camera." He's right. It's no time to argue. Porch lights are going on everywhere on the block. Neighbors hurry out on their front steps, down coats thrown over their bathrobes. I catch glimpses of it in my rearview but mostly I'm concentrating on not bouncing off the parked cars lining the street.

I drive as fast as the weather allows. Hyde Park is a maze of one-way streets and cul-de-sacs. Since I'm not obeying the rules that works to our advantage. We go the wrong way on Blackstone while a campus cop heads toward Greenwood. Unfortunately my Toyota 4Runner is made more for off-road adventures than urban alleys—it's sometimes a tight fit. A vacant garage that I back into off Dorchester nearly takes the paint off my door.

But we're lucky. The flashing blue lights seem always to be on the next block. The sirens doppler away from us.

"Do you get the feeling Rosenberg likes his privacy?"

"That's just Hyde Park, Harding." He's watching the sky.

"You're worried about snow?"

"I'm looking for choppers."

I drive through Washington Park and park on a corner just past the El. Now that the adrenaline rush of the chase is over I'm tempted to turn around and go back. Frost thinks it's a rest stop. He takes a long swig from his flask, then hands it to me. His hands are shaking. No more rum tonight. This is straight Johnnie Walker Black. It burns my throat but I'm not complaining. I take another sip.

"You dropped the camera, didn't you?"

"Harding, I'll buy you a new camera." He doesn't know the serial number and a pair of carved initials inside a tiny heart can lead anyone curious enough directly to Alison, and then to me. How could he know?

But that's only a small part of my motivation for taking a bus or a cab or just walking back to that house on Greenwood Avenue.

I got one brief look through that window before Frost tripped the alarm. I want another. All I have now is a half dozen quick cuts compressed into a split-second montage. What I can recall are the robe being pulled roughly from this woman emerging from the drapes, the man's hands moving past red welts and bruises—there was no black slip to hide them—back to the figure on the couch, now displaying a fearsome scar that curved across the lower back. Stephen removing Velcro ties from two slender wrists. The figure on the couch bent and submissive. Elenya's screams being lost in the alarms.

And tools I assumed were for the fireplace—*don't assume; don't ever assume*—pulled halfway toward the couch, glowing red.

Frost notices for the first time where we're parked. He locks his door. "Maybe we should get going," he says nervously.

"We're going back," I say, putting the truck in gear.

"What? Are you crazy?"

"Maybe but we're going back." But we both jump when my radio wakes up, crackling with static and feedback. Alison, in a harsh fierce whisper, is urgently repeating my name.

SIX

It takes me a few minutes to find her.

Driving down Ellis in a stream of traffic I see Alison outside her car, staring up at a row of gray buildings. I'm riding the tail of an oversized Pontiac with no room to pass. Alison's car door is blowing back and forth in the wind, making the interior lights flash like strobes with each gust. She doesn't answer my calls on the radio.

And I don't think she sees me. I'm still a block away when she slams the car door and sprints alone to the front of the building.

The Pontiac turns at 56th Street so I hit the gas and skip the stop sign at 57th, fish-tailing onto the sidewalk in front of the bookstore. A low stone fence—a planter on the pedestrian mall—stops us, shattering our headlights. I can feel something wet on my face. When I wipe my forehead my hand comes away crimson red. The windshield's shattered like a spiderweb.

What is she running for?

Frost jumps out first and goes to her car.

"Nothing," he yells, looking inside. My door's jammed. It takes me a couple of minutes to get out and cut through the passage to Kent.

She's on the top step, pulling open the heavy brown doors.

"Alison," I call. She turns, not knowing who called. I recognize the look on her face. I haven't seen it often.

"What's happening? Alison—"

"Get your gun," she says. Her black hair's wet from the snow. When I get closer I see she's torn her pants with grass stains; one knee is bleeding. A patch of leather's torn from her jacket like flayed skin. Her glasses are covered with sleet. Her eyes are wild.

I just reach the first step.

"Wait a minute. Alison—"

"Move!"

Then she's inside. Frost is behind me, yelling my name. I hesitate just long enough for her to disappear. I notice lights going on and off on the second floor.

There's nothing in the glove compartment of my truck except faded maps and tire gauges, packets of ketchup, old menus, drugs. I run back to Alison's car, and find a crowbar in the spare tire well.

The wind's howling now. It seems to rock the little car.

"What should we do?" Frost says.

"Find a phone. Call 911."

"They'll trace it—"

"Just do it, all right? And then go down to the hospital ER—there's usually a cop there."

I check under the front seat and find an ice scraper. I stuff it in my back pocket.

I'm back at Kent in less than a minute. But by then the second floor is as dark as the rest of the building.

There's a heavy set of outer doors, four steps, then another set of doors, also open. The lobby is dark except for a faint glow from glass display cases on each of three walls. The air's stuffy; it smells like chemicals. I wait a minute for my eyes to adjust to the dark. I haven't been in this building in years. But after being in Chamberlain it almost feels like I'm back in school.

There is a labyrinth of rooms but only three doors. It's the lady or the tiger time. I check the door to my left. Someone told me years ago that they'll expect you to go right. Just percentages. May as well keep them on your side. I listen at each door, feeling all the while that someone's just behind me. The building's old enough to have a life of its own. I flinch at each of its arthritic groans. But everything on this floor is locked.

The stars are to my right. They're heavy slabs of stone and the stairwell is an echo chamber. There's no way to do this quietly. The glass cases I pass are filled with posted answers to the latest chemistry midterm; formulas, equations, drawings of chemical compounds. Those mysteries are solved anyway.

I can hear someone moving in the corridor above me. I can't distinguish his direction. But it's better to just assume he's coming at me. I grip the crowbar tighter, move toward the stairs.

The light from the lobby fades with each step. The second-floor landing is a different degree of darkness, one without shadows or orientation. I don't see or hear anyone. I walk back and forth checking doors. I could just be walking in circles. I feel newly blinded.

The darkness is disorienting. I finally find a door that's open. It seems quiet inside. I open the door with the tip of the crowbar; it swings smoothly, like a heavy bank vault, perfectly balanced.

I'm in a short, dark hallway. But light is bleeding

from somewhere; I can see just enough to decide the office to my right is empty. I'm pointing at every shadow—chairs, bookcases, floor lamps—as though the crowbar's a semiautomatic. Anyone seeing me first would have a clear shot. If they didn't die laughing first.

Still, most people don't shoot very well. It's harder to hit a moving human target than you'd think from watching TV. And if I can get close enough with the damned bar they won't get a second chance.

A door slams behind me. I can hear sirens now, but this time they sound good. Are those voices coming from the lower floors? I can't tell.

But I move forward, because at the end of the long hallway another door stands half-open, a triangle of light flooding the corridor, and that's where I find Alison. She lies curled on one side. Her right hand's tucked under her left arm, holding her waist. There's a slashing cut going right through her leather coat, across her abdomen. Purple blood pools by her knee.

"You're all right," I tell her, touching her cheek. Her eyes are closed, but she's breathing. Her face is pale. I'm afraid she's going into shock so I try raising her legs.

"There's an ambulance coming. Alison? Can you hear me? You'll be all right. Hang on. They missed the artery."

But it looks like too much blood for the cut, and when I roll her over she groans and opens her eyes. Another red mark soaks the inside of her arm. The letter opener I saw in Elenya's Porsche is caught in the threads of her jacket.

"We fucked up," she says. Then the worst. When I push against the door something pushes back. Nora's body is nude, her legs folded over into an impossible position. The heavy work station looks like a sacrificial altar. The floor's slippery with blood.

In the rear of the room Lucy Williams sits propped like a mannequin. Her eyes open and close. She looks at me without much interest. Beside her near a sink she's neatly laid her coat and hat, like folded laundry.

"Did you bring your camera?" she says. Her eyes are blank. Her hands, folded on her knee, leave crimson marks on her white stockings. Then her hands relax and drop to her sides. She slumps against the wall.

Police sirens are screaming outside the building, flashing blue lights filling the windows. I remove my coat and put it under Alison's head, wiping blood from her cheek and mouth but when a burly cop kicks the hall door open and yells at me to freeze I'm afraid she's gone.

PART TWO
COSMETIC PROCEDURES

SEVEN

We're on the 57th Street Beach at daybreak.

Steam rises from an icy Lake
Michigan. The skyline behind us is
bathed in fog and mist. A typical Chicago morning, full
of harsh beauty, violent death. Black water laps at the
frozen sand.

"Stay in the car, Harding," Jimmy Reilly says to
me. He kicks the door closed and heads out onto the
beach. Reilly's a detective in CPD Violent Crimes. An
older cop named Keegan—Reilly's partner—hitches up
Sansabelt pants nearly as pockmarked as his face; sets
off for the sergeant in charge. There are a dozen uniforms out there now. Four squad cars have pulled off
the shoulder nearly onto the sand, their headlights
shining cross-eyed like klieg lights at a carnival. Traffic
on the Drive slows behind us, gapers craning their
necks for a glimpse of the sideshow.

It's been a long night at the fair. I have souvenirs and
prizes I could have done without; they cling like cheap
cotton candy. A paramedic with shaky hands and a
Revlon tweezers picked glass from my scalp; swathed
the cut with red antiseptic—it no longer hurts but the
dried blood and bandages remain taped to my temple—

Red-Cross stigmata. And there's a bruise on my left shoulder that doesn't hurt but which I rub compulsively, trying to erase something more memory and pattern than pain—the cops that streamed through the door at Kent yelled *face down right now asshole* and when I wouldn't leave Alison fast enough they threw me hard against the wall, jamming my shoulder. Then they took me next door while uniforms searched the building, looking for souvenirs of their own. By the time we left—hours later—Alison's body was gone, replaced by crime scene markings already bleeding into the rug. That was my last souvenir, purchased at great expense. *We fucked up Harding.*

A sergeant patted me down for weapons but didn't cuff me or check my clothes—no one could decide if I was a suspect or a witness. Before they could make up their minds I emptied my own pockets—Percs, footballs—with any luck I'd overdose. I didn't much care.

They ran me through Forensics, mostly for show; kept my coat and shirt and boots; took turns tearing apart what little I'd given them but didn't charge me. Then they left me alone in a bare interrogation room with a cup of cold coffee and a portable Panasonic cassette player.

The tape must have been dubbed from a reel-to-reel; it was full of the stuttering rhythms and clipped words common to old voice-activated recorders. There was a lot of tape hiss and ambient noise but not enough to obscure the identity of one of the participants. I didn't recognize the woman; her voice was soft, with the slight Southern accent you often hear along the North Shore. The man's voice was buried in the mix but by now I could pick Rosenberg's nasal wheeze out of the Mormon Tabernacle Choir.

The woman spoke first.

"—I just asked you Stephen *politely* what happened New Year's why you have to get so
excited I really don't understand—"

"—nothing happened. I told you nothing happened.
Let's just do this shall we and go home—"

"—*God* it feels gross—"

"—you didn't mind the harness. Or the sling. Or
the bridle—you liked the goddamned bridle
just fine—"

"—that was leather and a few strings—this one's
clammy and it covers my entire face and call
me crazy baby but I have this thing about
breathing—"

"—you'll breathe you'll breathe just fine long as
you don't *panic*—"

"—*wait a minute, Stephen, no*—"

"—like this, double it back, over your ears—"

"—not so tight, please, please—"

"—pull your hair back . . ."

"—*Jesus Christ Stephen all right*—what's the rush
baby I'm not *going* anywhere strapped in like
this you may as well just *slow down* for once—"

"—keep your voice down will you? Or I'll tighten
it more—"

"—*God* I was only expressing an *interest* in your
holidays—can't we even have a *conversation*—"

"—they were merry, all right? The holidays? The
holidays were fucking merry—"

"—*stop please that really hurts*—"

The tape lasted twenty minutes or so. I didn't care.
I sat there in my T-shirt and jeans and bare feet,

drinking the cold coffee; a captive audience. Three hours after taking the drugs I was stone cold sober, still waiting for something, anything to kick in. Nothing was working. Everything in the building was beginning to have Alison's name or face on it.

I wanted to see her, wherever they'd taken her; to talk to the coroner, go to the morgue—they said they'd see, they were busy, shut up. A rookie uniform so green his shoes were shined unplugged the recorder and walked me back upstairs to a cluttered office Violent Crimes used on the night shift. He told me to sit tight. "And don't mess with the phones or the paperwork on Detective Reilly's desk," he said. "He's very picky." I nodded—the paperwork was arranged about the way newspapers line a birdcage. I was offered more coffee and a "Just Say No" sweatshirt; I shook my head. I wasn't cold, just numb.

Keegan returned first, carrying coffee cups filled to the brim with vending machine InstaBrew; dog-eared files tucked under growing rings of Right Guard sweat. He was much older than Reilly, with a loud plaid jacket he seemed eager to shed, a Marine's clipped haircut, a pocketsaver stuffed with Bics. He wore the sleeves of his short-sleeved shirt folded above his biceps like a high school gym teacher.

"Doesn't anybody just watch Mr. Magoo and sing carols and drink eggnog anymore?" Keegan said. Reilly came in, yawning. "Honest to God, Reilly—am I the only one not getting laid on Christmas?"

"As if the day should make a difference," Reilly said, punching Eject on the Panasonic so hard the cassette flopped like a fish and landed at my feet. The label was full of penciled letters—"S.R./E.M., S&M, B&D, CBT/NT, GS/BS, FF," half a dozen more I couldn't decipher; enough hieroglyphics to line a pyramid.

"We got shit from this crime scene," Reilly said to me. He seemed resigned to the fact. "This is the crime scene from hell. No signs of a struggle. A body in a hallway, slipped on a knife. Another one inside the room, stuffed behind the door, slipped on a knife thirty, thirty-five times. Blood on the rug and linoleum; blood on the nurse and both victims—no blood on the lab stations, no blood on the walls. No bloody fingerprints. *Our* lab's backed up till early next century so whose blood it is exactly I don't know. And the place is a god-damn college classroom—when the Mobile Unit finishes dusting they'll have nine hundred different sets of prints to match."

"That'll be fun all right," Keegan said, stirring his coffee with a blue Bic. Whisps of ink swirled on the surface like oil spills. "Getting those kids to agree to be printed. On that campus? They'll have the ACLU on everybody's backs—"

"Then we got the other guy Harding claims was there," Reilly said. "Which no one including Harding apparently saw."

"I heard him," I said. "I told you, upstairs—"

"Him? You could tell it was a man? What, you could hear his balls banging back and forth?"

"He was on the stairs when I came in, probably on his way out. Then he was running across the hallway—"

"Well we need a little more than that before we go door to door," Reilly said, "rousting people out so's you can listen to them walking around, running up and down stairs. Keegan, do we have a positive ID on the girl?"

"Not yet," Keegan said. "The university won't confirm."

"Dr. Rosenberg and his wife?"

"They're downstairs now," Keegan said. "With some very fancy La Salle Street lawyer. Red suspenders."

"Whoop-de-do," Reilly said. "And Frost? Where are we with Frost?"

"I left messages," Keegan said, tugging at his pants; each tug revealed a wider crown of white leg above his socks. "That's what you do on this fucking shift—leave messages. Wake people up."

"Maybe we should send a unit. Where's he live?"

"Frost? Highland Park."

"Jesus, have we even got extradition out there?"

"I dunno," Keegan said. "I'm checking with INTERPOL."

I've been in this station before once or twice. It's a dead-end district on the South Side, full of uniforms eager to transfer, fringe detectives waiting on a pension. Keegan seemed right at home. Reilly's a different case. He's my age; about the same height, a little heavier. He looks like he played high school ball in the seventies, maybe had a few beers since then. His face has the weary mask homicide cops acquire after years of long shifts and unsolved cases. What he's doing down here in this district, pulling nights, I don't know. But he grew up nearby. For some guys leaving the South Side is like moving to Europe.

"Your girlfriend, Harding," Reilly said, breaking a bear claw in two, handing half to Keegan. Icing fell on both men's trousers like light snow. "How long you figure she was inside alone?"

"Two, three minutes."

"Why'd she go in first?" He looked around for a napkin, wiped his fingers on newspaper.

"I told you—she yelled for me to go back to the car, get a crowbar or something."

"A crowbar or something," he said nodding. "You mean a gun."

"I don't carry a gun."

"You don't carry a gun."

"No."

"You hear that Keegan?"

"I heard," Keegan said. "Maybe he's dumber than I thought."

"You go into a situation like that without a gun you're absolutely nuts. You didn't drop it somewheres? Tell me now, it's better than telling me later, believe me. 'Cause they'll find it. And if they have to hunt all night to do it they'll be very grumpy. Like Keegan here."

"I can't carry a gun. Not with my record."

"Something heavy, a .357, an old .44 maybe—"

"I told you—"

"Harding, if you're obeying gun laws you're the only one in the fucking state who is. I went hunting last fall? Even the deer are starting to pack."

"We know you've got a record," Keegan said, finishing his coffee. He banked the crumpled cup off the wall into the trash. My stats are on a smudged fax. "Man two involuntary pled down from murder, charges of possession thrown out, an eight-year sentence reduced to three, of which you served eighteen months, the rest suspended—what this says to me is you killed somebody and got away with it. Lucked out with a wimpy DA, some little hick town, fucking

Kentucky. What this says to me is maybe you thought you'd try it again."

"What Keegan means," Reilly said, "is when we get a statement from a witness to a double homicide that could fit on a baseball card—and that witness is an ex-PI hoping to get his license back now that he's rehabilitated himself—"

"Dream on," Keegan said.

"—we get *concerned*."

"Hasn't Lucy Williams told you anything?" I said.

"Not a hell of a lot."

"She didn't see who did it?"

"She says no," Reilly said. "She says she found Nora the same way you did—DOA. And that's all she remembers. Never saw your girlfriend. You gotta understand—we had radio contact with Lucy for about five minutes. Then she disappeared behind the moon. Last thing she said was she couldn't remember how she got to Kent. And could we send out for Chinese, hold the MSG."

"That's bullshit."

"This is what she said," Reilly said with a cop's shrug; one statement is like any other. "The lady has tracks six different places—behind her knees, under her feet, inside her mouth—enough for Metra to open a new line. She's in pretty bad shape, Harding. Close to an overdose. We nearly had another body bag up there."

"Wonderful," I said. When was this going to end?

"Yecch," Keegan said. "On her gums?"

"It keeps you in short sleeves," Reilly said, another shrug.

"Are you charging her?" I said.

"Not yet," Reilly said. "We're letting her complete her orbit first and return to planet Earth."

"Because I've been watching her for six weeks, Reilly. She did grass and X and pills and maybe even smoked but I never saw her shoot up."

"Well, you're the expert, aren't you," Keegan says. "Maybe *you* were fixing her up. You're the one with the possession charge—"

"Which they dropped. It was nothing, a plant, a frame."

"Sure, they usually are. It's unfortunate."

"We found needles," Reilly said. "The tracks are fresh. Maybe you haven't been watching so good. She had the combination plate. They emptied her stomach."

"They also emptied her pockets," Keegan said. "Ask him about the goddamn tape, will you? I'd like to get out of here sometime before June."

Reilly nodded but the phone rang before he could ask me much of anything.

"Don't tell me," Keegan said.

Reilly listened for a minute or so, one hand already reaching for a cigarette. "All right," he said. "Give me fifteen minutes." He hung up, staring at the phone as if it might ring again.

"We still have to swing past the morgue," Keegan said. "I thought we had another half hour. That's what they said, right? A half hour?"

"The sun's coming up. The Tac guys have to get back in their coffins before daybreak. At least we can smoke out there."

"I'm trying to quit," Keegan said, pulling on his old plaid coat.

"You'll never quit on this shift, believe me," Reilly

said. "Better get Harding some shoes and a coat; something out of lost-and-found. Maybe a sweater. It's
freezing out there by the water."

"Someone went swimming?" I said.

"We've got a floater," Reilly said, nodding. "Fifty-
seventh Street. A long walk off a short sidewalk."

"What size are you?" Keegan asked me. "Shoes,
coat."

"Eleven and a half; forty-two long," I said. "Anything but plaid."

"Let's go, Harding," Reilly said. "We're gonna
take a little field trip."

We drove across 11th Street to Pulaski. The heater
in Reilly's Plymouth didn't seem to be working but
at least I was indoors. Every doorway along West
Harrison was crowded with hookers, drunks, addicts.
Only the hookers made us; or maybe only they cared—
stepping quickly inside; disappearing into shadows.
Hookers have a great eye for detail.

Reilly pulled the tape out of his pocket as he drove
and held it in the air as if auctioning at Sotheby's.

"A TDK 90," Reilly said, "which you could buy
anywhere—Best Buy, Circuit City—am I right,
Harding?"

"I guess," I said, seeing for the first time a hiero-
glyphic I'd missed earlier—a black figure behind a
tripod and camera. Alison's store logo.

"You know what store I miss sometimes?" Keegan
said, unwrapping a cigar. "Polk Brothers. My old man
bought a Frigidaire there once, they delivered it, uncrated
it, there's a rat in the freezer. My mother faints. And the
old man gets another twenty-five percent knocked off.
Not from the rat. From the fainting."

"You didn't return it?" Reilly said.

"Why return it? It was perfectly good. A little Lysol." Keegan wound down his window; bit the end off his cigar and spit it outside. Then he turned to me as if we were out for a Sunday drive. "See Harding—we found the tape in Lucy's pocket. You tell us Lucy's been screwing Rosenberg—by the way, he insists they're quote unquote just fucking friends—maybe we've got us one of those meringue ah troys—"

"Something like that anyway," Reilly said, smiling.

"I didn't make the tape," I said. "I don't know who made the tape."

We pulled up behind a white limestone building; a squad across the lot blinked his lights to show he was awake.

"You and your girlfriend just got in the way, Harding," Keegan said, turning in his seat. He still hadn't lit the cigar. "At least your girlfriend did. You look all right. Don't he look all right, Reilly?"

"He looks fine," Reilly said. The Plymouth's doors opened stiffly, like arthritic limbs; bone rubbing bone. "Let's get this over with. I know it's February but Jesus fucking Christ it's cold."

"I thought you had a floater," I said.

"One stop first, Harding. To see a friend of yours. You've been asking for this all night, remember?" We walked single-file to the building's back door, squinting into the darkness from the bitter wind.

Out on the 57th Street Beach the wind is picking up, blowing snow into the water. Just to the north the land curls seaward; an area called the Point, a good spot for a picnic if it's daylight and summer and there's twenty or thirty in your group. There's no sand or beach, just rocks. The water's too deep for swimming but kids ignore faded warnings stenciled on the rocks and dive in anyway.

Reilly's Plymouth is littered with fast food; stray fries, calcified burritos. The heat's finally on but its one setting—full blast—is reviving years of leftovers buried in the seat cushions. The car smells like a 7-Eleven microwave. The radio is blasting a version of Chicago hip-hop with tough inner-city lyrics but no beat worth dancing to—emergency calls from all over the South Side. Nine hundred homicides in the city last year. The deaths at Kent join the hit parade.

Reilly finally motions for me to come out and join the carnival. Keegan's trip to lost-and-found produced mixed results—a brand-new hooded CPD sweatshirt, boots dotted with what I hope is paint, a ski jacket marked by grease and distressed down. Even without the grease you wouldn't want the jacket in Vail or Aspen—too much snow would blow through the bullet holes on any serious downhill.

I hang back but Reilly waves me forward. A uniform steps aside so I can have a good view. Keegan is off somewhere with the campus police. A sergeant stands with one foot on the tarp as though the whole mess might just blow away. The last temperature I heard was five degrees.

The body lying on the beach is gray and frostbitten but I don't think weather was a factor. Nature's indifferent and maybe cruel but doesn't require handguns to do its work.

"Do you know him?" Reilly says cupping his hands, lighting a cigarette. The smoke blows away like a lost kite.

I don't say anything at first. They have him lying

on his stomach, the way I saw him last night, when I thought he was Nora or some other girl. When he slid down Rosenberg's couch. Instead of the oxford blue shirt he's dressed in sweats so wet they're like a second skin on his small rear; peeled back to show the flesh-colored pantyhose keeping his genitals tucked neatly away; no coat or jacket, just a flayed cable-knit sweater that's unraveled with his life. He's been shot at close range.

Even with his arms at his sides you can see the frontal wounds curling around his rib cage; another wound, more like a scar with raised skin on his lower back. His head's turned sideways on the sand as though sunbathing. His face is gray, his lips light blue. His eyes stare unblinkingly at whoever—whatever—did this to him.

"Two shots, very high caliber, very close range," Reilly says, turning him over for me to see. The damage is terrible. "Maybe a .44. No wallet or ID. They left his clothes on, threw him in the lake. He got hung up on the ice. Who in the hell throws a body in the lake in February?"

It takes me a minute to realize the question's not rhetorical. Reilly's looking at me.

"This is why you asked if I had a gun?" I say.

Reilly nods. The others are looking at me, too, probably wondering who I am, what I'm doing out here.

But they must know I didn't shoot him. At this range I'd have blood all over me. Reilly wants me to play detective; that's why he held up removing the body. Why, I don't know.

"They wouldn't have tossed him here," I say, looking around. The dark water laps against the shore.

"Where then."

"Down there maybe, off the rocks. At the Point. The current pulled him here."

"What current," Reilly says. "Ten feet out in a fucking lake? Even a stiff could swim against that."

"Anyway we've got prints," the sergeant says. He's the oldest cop in the circle. "One set, right down the beach. We did impressions, stride tests, the works."

"Which means nothing unless you recover the shoes," I say. Still, if we're playing detective, they might have mentioned that up front. "One set? One guy carrying him all the way to the water? And what's he do then—wade into the water like he's baptizing him?"

"Doesn't make much sense, does it?" Reilly says. "Not a good way to hide a body. But that's the kind of night it's been. Busy, busy night."

"How'd you find the body?"

"Good hard-nosed police work, Harding. A lesson to guys like you."

"Meaning you were tipped. Somebody called the station? 911?" Reilly nods. "Can't you tell who made the call?"

"With the communications system downtown we got a better chance hearing Nixon's eighteen minutes. What else, Sergeant."

He hesitates, not knowing how much to say in front of me.

"Come on, come on," Reilly says.

"We got a possible ID. Just by chance—one of the campus cops knows him, from working in the hospital or something. It's not confirmed."

"What's his name?" I say.

"Like I say, it's not confirmed. The name we've got is Robin Connor. The cop thinks he was a senior."

"I wouldn't bet on him graduating," Reilly says.

The sergeant's blowing on his hands like a relief pitcher in late season. The sun's up now, edging above the lake but it hasn't warmed anything in this area code. Maybe Mars warms up in February. Not Chicago.

"Show Harding what the kid had on him," Reilly says.

"Oh yeah," the sergeant says. He holds up a watch. I try not to stare. Reilly doesn't hide how closely he's watching me. "Stuffed in his pocket. The time's stuck at midnight, which might be right. With a cheap Timex like this you can't tell. We dusted it."

"A school watch," Reilly says. "The kind they sell at the campus bookstore."

"Any prints?" I say.

"We pulled a partial. The water messed with it some. We were lucky it was in his pocket."

"Yeah, that was lucky."

"You think that's the kid's watch, Harding?" Reilly says. He holds the watch right before my face; it smells like fish and dark water and death. And the septic tank behind room nineteen. Then he holds it against the kid's wrist.

I shake my head.

"Why not?" the sergeant says. "Just because it's not a Swatch—"

"The marks on the leather band, where it was fastened. The kid's wrist is too thin."

"You see? I keep forgetting you're a detective. Then you stun me with reasoning like that." Reilly tosses his cigarette onto the snow. "Tell me if I'm wrong. It looked for a second like you knew him."

I shake my head. "I was looking at that mark on his back."

"That's part of the trauma from the gunshot."

"It's a scar," I say. "They call it branding."

I'm wondering if that's why he was shot in the chest; to cover up more scars like that. I'm thinking—Nora, Robin, Alison. I know Rosenberg's involved but there's no connection except me.

If I hadn't interfered would all three still be alive?

"Branding?" Reilly says doubtfully.

"That's what they do now. Like piercing, but a step further."

"You mean like a cow?" the sergeant says with disgust. "Jesus. That's fucking sick."

Reilly watches me for a second, waiting for some kind of reaction, then turns to the sergeant. "Cover him up," he says.

We went through four A.M. darkness to the morgue's rear door. Reilly used his badge to get past the guard and then we headed downstairs, our shoes clanging on hollow metal steps. The outer parts of the basement were dark; surrounding labs and support areas closed down; but the central part, the autopsy rooms, was brightly lit; the first circle, Limbo, the border of hell. Both troughs were occupied. Another seven or eight bodies slept silently under starched white sheets.

A transporter named Sharon silently pushed a metal gurney toward the morgue. She was wearing a white mask; red hightop gym shoes; she pointed to her stainless steel wagon, offering me a lift. "No thanks," I said. There was just one doctor working tonight; a young Asian pathologist I'd never met. The turnover's a little high down here at night, at both ends of the knife.

"Hello, Henry," Reilly said. The doctor looked up briefly; he wore plastic goggles with green Vicks inhalers stuck in each nostril. He looked like some kind of insect.

"You don't mind if we browse, do you Henry?" Keegan said.

"Are you looking for something in particular?"

"Black-haired bitch, real skinny, sliced across the front?"

I turned away, said nothing.

Henry scratched the inhalers with the back of his gloved hand. "Doesn't ring a bell."

"Came in with a Jane Doe whose chest looks like a fucking screen door."

"Jane's on deck," Henry said, indicating a metal gurney to his right. "But your other one could be any one of these. I'm running a little behind tonight."

"I thought our two had priority," Reilly said. "You promised. Are you breaking your promises, Henry?"

"This guy from Kenilworth got moved ahead," Henry said. "He's from a better zip code. Listen, I'm doing my best to get out of here on time. *They Saved Hitler's Brain* is on TV at five."

"What happened to Kenilworth?" Reilly said, looking closer.

"Shot him through a beautiful coat had to be worth two grand. Some Italian label. Rich black fur."

"You think you can save it?" Reilly said.

"I tried, believe me," Henry said, turning back to the body. "The coat was DOA."

Keegan walked around the room, hoping to find Alison; he was pulling sheets back with the flourish of a Vegas lounge magician. On the gurney closest to me an old man with thin white hair stared at the ceiling. The room didn't smell like death; just cold institutional processing. It reminded me of slaughterhouses in the stockyards, where the only place that really smelled like death was the killing floor.

All night I'd badgered them to let me come here, and now I was terrified of finding Alison; of what she would look like. Nora's body was horrible to look at. Knife wounds are always worse than gunshots. It isn't the damage. It's the intent, the passion, the way lives overlap when a knife is used. Pulling a trigger requires nothing but a steady grip and a decent aim. But stabbing someone—a woman—requires close proximity—you're close enough to look into her eyes, feel her breath. You're entering her body the way a mad lover would.

"Take a look at her at least, will you Henry?" Reilly said.

"Okay, okay." Henry stood over Nora's body, frowning, peeling off long yellow gloves so he could scratch his nose. "I thought you said this was a stabbing," Henry said. "Didn't they do a prelim at the scene?"

"I guess. Why?"

"What did they give you for time of death?"

"We had Sheldon out there tonight, Henry," Reilly said. "He never likes to be pinned down. 'Don't quote me on this,' Sheldon always says. He'd barely confirm she was dead."

"What did he say about this area around her lower face."

"Stab wounds," Reilly said. "But there was a lot of blood."

"Those don't look like stab wounds," Henry said. "Not around her face anyway. More like corrosion. And the stab wounds on her body look postmortem. Look at all the subdermal bruising. And look at the color of her skin, for God's sake. Did Sheldon do this over the phone?"

"You're saying she was stabbed after she was dead?"

"Can't say yet." He picks up Nora's hands. "No cuts. No defensive wounds."

"There was an awful lot of blood for it to be post-mortem, Henry."

"Are you sure it was hers?" Henry said doubtfully. "There's no blanching, her lividity's fixed—"

Reilly looked at Keegan.

"When will we find out?" Reilly said. "Sometime this century?"

Henry shrugged. "There's more than one knife involved, too," he said. "See the different angles of the incisions?" He smiled at Keegan. "Didn't any of you notice this at the scene?"

"Maybe the light's better here," Keegan said.

The campus cops are on the beach now; three squads lined like Tinker Toys in neat formation, mimicking the CPD. They're helping cover Robin's body with a heavy canvas tarp. Keegan's barking orders. At least with them he's in charge. One of the campus cops is running around like a Boy Scout, eager to help.

"Don't you bastards have anything for us?" Reilly says to him.

"We're still spinning our wheels over at Kent," the campus cop says. "That door's supposed to be locked that time of night. Buildings and Grounds is in deep shit. Wait until the president wakes up. College acceptance letters go out in another month—where would you send your daughter now?"

"I don't have a daughter," Reilly says, looking out at the water. "If I did, I'd tell her to be a nun."

"I picked up something on the campus scanner, Detective," a uniform is saying to Reilly. The EMT guys are sitting on their hands on the rear of the wagon, waiting for Reilly's signal. He's taking his time. "This was way afterwards but the dispatcher's chewing somebody out for not showing up earlier at a Code 99—"

"What the hell's a Code 99?"

"That's what they use in-house for big shots in trouble. You know, the dean's got a cat up in a tree— send all available units. Something went down around nine. Just false alarms but everybody got pulled, including the Midway patrol, right when the kid got snatched. The guy's a doctor in the med school named Rosenberg. South Greenwood."

"Why the hell didn't I hear about this sooner?" Reilly says. But he doesn't seem surprised.

"I guess he never filed anything with the district, just the campus police."

"And they're sitting on it?"

"Looks like."

Reilly thanks the uniform. Then he gives the EMT guys the nod they've been waiting for all night.

Reilly stares at me for a second. He looks older out here somehow. I feel like I've aged a bit myself tonight.

"Let's talk in the car," Reilly says to me. The techs roll Robin's body into an oily black plastic bag.

I'm as eager as the techs to get out of here but I measure my pace to Reilly's, walking slowly back up to the car.

"The Sherlock Holmes bit with the watch back there, Harding. I liked that."

"Glad I could help."

"Very impressive. Myself, I was noticing the class year engraved on the back of the watch—'76. I thought *that* was the key thing. Without you here, that leather band thing, I might've missed that altogether."

He opens his car door but doesn't get in, just lights another cigarette and then leans on the oxidized roof of the Plymouth; smoking, thinking, looking at me. He has too many lines under his eyes for sleep to erase. His ears are red from the cold.

"I got something I want you to read," Reilly says to me, unfolding a single sheet of paper, handing it across the car. "Something I don't know what to do with."

It's just a couple paragraphs; a robbery report from earlier tonight; an address I'm familiar with—Boone's. There isn't much there but I read it two or three times. I'm starting to feel a little dizzy.

"Is he all right?"

Reilly nods. "Normally I wouldn't even notice. Breaking and entering in this neighborhood's like some- body sneezing. Except the victim says he knows you. And the stuff that's missing is your stuff. Which he's been holding for you. He's kinda vague—something about acid, and videotapes and caulking guns? Does this make any sense to you?"

Now that the sun's up you can see a lighthouse miles to the south. There are one or two ships out there; lake freighters, heavy craft filled with ore. It seems miraculous they can float in the blue water.

"I need the rest of it, Harding," Reilly says. "Not because I care one way or the other, you understand. They're nice kids. Sweet kids. Wonderful kids. But you know what I'll have tomorrow? Another two. Then another two. I'm like Henry—I don't like getting backed up—"

"What makes you say two?" I say, stopping him. My heart stops too.

"What?"

"You said two—"

"I did?" Reilly spits on the ground. He looks at me silently, turns away, then sighs. "Shit, I'm sorry Harding—"

"She's all right? Alison?"

"It was a shitty thing to do. I apologize. Let me buy you a beer later. Rosenberg with his fancy lawyer stonewalled all night. We got nothing from him. She's in Recovery, doing fine. They closed her up hours ago. She's tough, Harding."

I feel a rush too good to be drugs. It sweeps away the numbness, overwhelms my anger at being toyed with in this way, my realization that Reilly has played it just right, kept Keegan away, waited for the perfect moment to tell me about Alison. I'm ready to talk.

The sun's up now; the fog burned from the skyline.

In the back of the car I tell Jimmy Reilly most of what I know.

EIGHT

They finally tire of me around six A.M., cut me loose on streets dark and slick with melting snow, empty of traffic. By then the evidence techs have relocated to Robin's room in Chamberlain. "Your boss, Wilson, called," Reilly says, "then *his* boss called. We're impressed, Harding." I never saw Stephen or Elenya Rosenberg, never heard from Frost. There's a row of cabs lined up in front of the station but no one eager to drive me further south. So I start walking. They say it's good exercise.

Two buses later I'm inside an El station, handing the clerk my transfer. "No return," I say, pushing through the turnstiles. Halfway up the stairs someone yanks at my sleeve. "You wanna go back?" he says. "Get me the transfer?" It's not really a question. He's fifteen or sixteen, wearing an old hooded sweatshirt, black wool gloves; no coat; I don't see any colors. I keep walking but he doesn't go away. "You must be deaf," he says. "Go back down the fucking stairs, get the transfer."

It's numbness or fatigue that makes me ignore him. By the time I reach the platform there are three of them, one with a malt liquor forty-ouncer smashed against the railing. I'm starting to consider taking the northbound train.

But we're not alone on the platform. "Police," a

man says in a firm voice, showing them the kind of
small automatic cops like to carry when off-duty.
"Early curfew, boys." There's a thirty-second pause to
save face, then they scatter.

"They thought you might need some baby-sitting,"
he says, smiling. He's tall and tired-looking, about my
age; my height but more solidly built. "Now I see why.
You're as stubborn as those three. Next time, carry a
few tokens with you. Maybe a Metra pass."

"You're tailing me?"

"Not exactly. I'm on my way home too. Helluva
night, huh?"

"I'm dead tired."

"Better wake up, Harding," he says.

I nod. I can see my face in his mirrored sunglasses.
He takes a seat in the middle car. I sit one back. He
must be Vice or Narcotics; he's wearing cowboy boots
that look like genuine rattlesnake. And he's good.
When I get off at Garfield I don't see him anywhere.

Alison's in SICU. The ward is quiet, lights dimmed like
a fancy French restaurant. The closest I've gotten to her
all morning is a brief glimpse through the glass cocoon
of her room. And I had to lie to get that far, signing in at
the nurse's station as a relative from out of town.

This time she's awake and drifting. She has a green
mask over her mouth, tubes down her nose and throat,
IVs tied to both arms. Above her head are monitors
with shaky green lines, flashing red and blue lights; her
life reduced to visual information. She has the pallor
and stillness of death. But the nurses tell me she's doing
fine. Reilly was right. She's tough.

I stand there for five minutes or so, gently holding

her hand—she has bandages on both palms and wrists—
talking enough for both of us in a librarian's whisper.
Her eyes open and close. I don't mention her injuries or
anything from last night but instead provide a running
commentary on the movie we were going to watch
together—*Dawn of the Dead*.

I'm not sure she's even awake—my babbling's
designed to reassure me as much as her—but when I
describe the scene where four zombies attack the
heroine in a shopping mall—I deconstruct this in a
lengthy Marxist commentary, throwing in Derrida,
Lacan, Walter Benjamin, Joe Bob Briggs—Alison, eyes
still closed, digs a nail into my skin hard enough to
draw blood, then slowly holds up five fingers. Five
zombies. "I stand corrected," I say. Her hands are cold.
But she's smiling now, a tiny half-moon beneath the
green mask. I would like to gather her up and hold her
but the way she's wired the monitor watchers would
think she'd gone into arrest. Or returned from the dead.

On the way out one of the nurses tells me that
Alison was a handful in the ER last night. "She told this
new intern, Rodriguez, not to administer any pain meds,
just give her a bullet to bite and a shot of rye. Then she
passed out."

"That's Alison," I say.

"You may as well come back later," she says.
"She'll be sleeping off the anesthetic for a while yet.
Even then she'll be a little loopy."

"That's Alison too," I say. "What happened to her
hands?"

"Just small cuts. Nothing serious."

In a crowded elevator I get a few looks for the
fashion statement I'm making with my grungy ski coat
and head bandage. Everyone else is facing Monday in

neatly starched uniforms and business suits. I face the wall and dig my hands protectively in my pockets and find another souvenir: in the lining of my coat there's a lump; not malignant, just my pager, which I'd forgotten about, inside a Baggie with some change and the marker for my coat and shirt; a present from Keegan. I switch it on and when it starts beeping the crowd reacts as one—digging, reaching, scratching—as though I'd tossed real bugs on them.

There are phones in the lobby but I need some coffee. On my way to the cafeteria I stop in the Department of Surgery. All the offices are dark, including the one Rosenberg shares with another doctor. Secretaries are still stuck in rush-hour traffic on the Stevenson and Calumet. The receptionist's desk is neat and clean and very locked. The Joke-a-Day calendar propped by the Tensor lamp still has Friday's date and last year's joke.

"You'd better repeat that," I tell an upset operator who's been trying to reach me for hours. I'm in the hospital cafeteria, a tray full of food I have no appetite for balanced on one knee, a greasy receiver jammed against my shoulder.

The noise level in the room is like a shooting gallery. But that's not why I need the message repeated.

"Are you sure about this?" I say. "It's *Doctor* Rosenberg who wants to see me? At his home?"

"Sir, I've been sure about it for the last two hours. Ten A.M., the doctor's residence on South Greenwood—do you need directions?"

"No, I think I can find it," I say. It's just past nine-thirty.

My truck is gone, impounded and towed to a lot

somewhere out in Blue Island. I'm told I can retrieve it in forty-eight hours—if I can fix the windshield and headlights and realign the front end. So it may sit there a few days longer. I can kiss the battery and tape deck and Patti Smith goodbye.

There are no cabs outside the hospital; not unusual for Hyde Park. I call everyone I know around campus who might give me a ride—Boone—and end up walking instead to 55th to catch an eastbound bus. A clerk at a rental agency reluctantly gives me the keys to the cheapest thing on the lot, a Ford Tempo that's clearly had a lot of body work. "You're lucky I give you that without a credit card," he says, taking fifty dollars.

My last fifty disappears at an overpriced men's store in the Hyde Park Shopping Center, buying a fake L.L. Bean flannel shirt. I feel very woodsy. It comes with a small cologne sample which the clerk assures me makes a real statement. Whether it's the right statement or not I can't tell. I save the cologne for a rainy day.

In the parking lot—the Tempo shimmying even in neutral—I remove eight pieces of cardboard and nineteen pins from the shirt. It's wrinkled but at least I can lose the damned sweatshirt, take the ski coat off. I remove the bandage too; it was starting to make me feel like a Civil War veteran on a postage stamp; all I needed was a crutch.

I make one final swing through the campus. At Kent the heavy front doors are closed off with yellow crime scene tape stretched like Christmas ribbon. A campus cop explains the situation to disbelieving lab students who would've slept in had they known. A unit from the CPD makes a lazy circle past me, the driver's face impassive behind reflective shades. Then he waves at me to move along. Already the area's changed, just traffic control now. Nighttime terror becomes daytime routine.

There's a single unmarked squad on Greenwood Avenue, not trying to disguise itself much; parked directly in front of the house. The white Buick's here too, guarding the crest of the drive. I'd like to look around the side yard for the Leica but after Sunday's bells and whistles I feel as if I'd need a map and a minesweeper. So I use the front door. My knees are a little wobbly; more from the motion of the Tempo than the prospect of this meeting. Getting out of that car is like getting off a boat.

A lock is thrown; the door squeaks free from rubber insulation.

"You're late," Stephen Rosenberg says, barely looking at me. He leaves the door open, his way of asking me to enter.

"Sorry—I seem to have lost my watch," I say but he doesn't react.

I follow him into a front parlor, the kind of room people furnish with expensive furniture but rarely use without the proper occasion. This must qualify. I've never been in a room like this where you were allowed to eat. The chairs are uncomfortable. He's looking at my nose with proprietary interest. I'm looking at his feet—below his expensive gray suit he's wearing beaded tan moccasins. I had a similar pair when I was ten, purchased on vacation at an authentic Indian trading post in Niagara Falls.

"I started in to work," he explains, "then realized I just wasn't up to it. Couldn't do that to my patients. The man holding the knife has to be razor sharp himself, you know."

"You should put that in your brochures," I say. "Maybe knit it on a sampler."

He stares at me for a second, wondering if I'm worth whatever he's after. I must be because he offers me coffee, which I accept, wondering if Elenya will bring it. Instead a servant appears with a silver tray and pitcher—the kind my mother left in the attic, wrapped in Saran Wrap—and tiny china cups too fragile to use with any ease of mind. Classical music shuts out the morning traffic; another layer of textured wallpaper. No Jethro Tull this morning.

"I thought we should meet," he says. "Since the police tell me you think I'm a murderer."

"It's what they think that counts, Rosenberg. And I see you're not exactly in leg irons. Where's your wife this morning?"

"In bed, asleep. This has taken a rather large toll on both of us. Whatever differences we have are nothing compared to the tragedy of these two deaths."

"I hope you've got a lot of room on that brochure," I say.

He stares at me. He's got a good stare. I'm not sure if he's upset or just looking at my bone structure, deciding where to make the first incision.

He's had a bit of work done on himself too; it's more obvious up close; an effort to keep time and gravity away from his blank good looks. There's something featureless, impassive about him. It's a look of boredom, the kind that takes years to grow into.

"I keep forgetting," he says. "You're not even a licensed investigator, are you? More like a Peeping Tom. Even the police said as much. My lawyer suggested filing invasion-of-privacy charges against you. Of course your pockets aren't very deep but a civil suit at least might put you out of business. Whatever business you think you're in. Tell me, is there anything private or confidential about me you didn't tell the police?"

"Just the biggest mystery of all, Stephen—why in the world Elenya married such a sad fuck like you. What were you doing to her last night? And that poor kid, Robin—"

"You had no business watching us."

"No? Try closing your drapes next time."

He rocks back and forth on the balls of his feet. The beaded tassels on his moccasins rock too. He hasn't sat down yet, which for some guys is an intimidation thing. Me, my legs get tired.

"What were you using on Nora?" I say. "Phenol acid in mustard?"

"That was lubricant. BananAppeal—something Lucy bought—I told the police—"

"Where's the bottle?" I say.

"We didn't keep it," he says, annoyed. "We threw it away."

"In the bathroom? The motel's Dumpster? Or the service corridor, hidden in the wall? I told the cops about your little love nest; they're probably down there now tearing the place apart. It's gonna lose another star in the *Mobil Guide*."

"This is ridiculous," he says. "We did nothing wrong. And you're making these outrageous statements—which is exactly why my lawyer's so insistent—"

"Look, if you invited me here to threaten me with lawsuits maybe we should just go our separate ways. The coffee's good but it's not worth that kind of aggravation."

"No, wait. That was my lawyer talking," he says, his tone changing somewhat. "You know how they are. I'm not suing you."

"Wonderful."

"In fact, I want your help. That's why I asked you here."

"What?"

"I want to hire you."

Well, the week has been full of surprises. And it's only Monday.

"Maybe we should back up a little—I thought I was a low-life Peeping Tom without any pockets."

"Exactly. That's why I want to hire you."

"And you thought what—you'd win me over with flattery?"

"We don't have to be friends. But I need your help. And I'll pay you."

"How much?"

"Whatever anyone pays you. I understand Warren Frost paid you six hundred dollars."

"That was to do something I wanted to do, for somebody I liked. For you the price would be different. Especially after what I saw last night."

"You don't know what you saw last night."

"I saw enough to know I'd want some answers before I took a dime of your money."

"I'll pay you ten thousand dollars," he says. "Up front. No strings attached." He takes out the check and drops it on the silver platter like a dirty napkin. It's upside down but my name's on it, next to more zeroes than I'm used to seeing.

I think they call it dollar diplomacy. There are other names for it: payoff; bribe. In Chicago, it's business as usual. Most of those questions have been plowed underground.

"I'll give you anything you need, Harding," he says. I'm touched. I can see the effort it takes him to say my name.

"Well, Stephen. I could use a little breakfast."

He puts his arm on my shoulder. For the first time I smell the alcohol on his breath.

"Let's go in the sun room," he says. "We can't eat in here."

His cook Giselle makes us omelets. The sun room's a hexagonal addition to the back of the house. I ran past it last evening. There's not a lot of sun here in February and the view is less than spectacular—a pine deck with covered furniture and gas grill; a neighbor's garage door with a bent basketball hoop.

"See, I feel I can talk to you," Rosenberg says, pushing his plate away. He ate even more than I did. "You don't like me. All right. You've seen me at my worst. I've no secrets from you. There's a wonderful release to that."

"Then you need a therapist. And ten grand buys a lot of fifty-minute hours."

"Elenya trusts you. She told me that. I value her opinion."

"Was that before or after you were hitting her?"

"No secrets," he says. "All right, yes. I have my problems in that area. I admit it. And I'm working on them."

"This isn't *Donahue*. Admitting isn't half the problem with me. All I care is that you stop."

"I've stopped already."

"I'm serious about this."

"So you'll take the job?"

"Fuck the job," I say, staring at him. It's my best stare. "I saw that bruise on her face the other night."

"Friday?" he says. "So that's where she was. With you—"

"You're quite a body puncher. I guess hitting her in the nose would be a breach of professional ethics."

"That wasn't me," he says. "Really, it wasn't. I didn't even know where she was that night—"

"And last night? Making like *Bonanza* with the fireplace tools?"

"What occurred last night is none of your business. And I didn't do that to Robin. He has other friends, believe me."

"You're the victim here, is that what you're saying?"

"No. But it's not just me that needs help. It's Elenya."

"You're concerned for your wife."

"I am, yes."

He offers me a cigar, which I decline.

Then, between puffs from a genuine Havana and sips of Starbucks Kenya blend—the same damn china, so thin I think the handles will break off the cups each time I take a sip—he tells me his version of last night's events.

"It was supposed to be a birthday party for my wife, Harding. I know I haven't paid enough attention to her lately so I set this evening aside, cleared the

deck so to speak, planned it just for her. We had a wonderful dinner courtesy of Giselle—game and roasted
mushrooms, Giselle's usually *nouvelle cuisine* but she
loosens up on special occasions—and then retired to the
den for after-dinner brandy and entertainment. Robin
stopped by after dinner. One thing led to another . . .
you saw the result. I hope you also saw that this was
three consenting adults enjoying themselves in the privacy of their home.

"Around nine the security alarms went off—we
now know why, don't we—and my wife panicked. We
heard sirens. I told the others to go upstairs, I'd deal
with the alarms and police, but Elenya must have
thought they'd be coming in—I don't know what she
thought. Before I could stop them she'd gone with
Robin out the back door.

"The police left. But an hour or so later they
returned, to tell me about Nora. Only then, while I was
dressing to return with them to Kent did Elenya return
to the house—quietly, through the back door. She came
up the kitchen stairs, changed her clothes, and then
came down to meet the police as though she'd just
gotten out of bed.

"Later, of course, I discovered Robin had been
shot, just after leaving here."

"What did Elenya say had taken her so long?"

Rosenberg paused, rolling the ash from his cigar on
the edge of his plate. "She said they'd just been sitting
in her car. They were talking, she said. They bought a
takeout coffee at the Starbucks on 53rd and just sat,
waiting for the police to go away."

"And you don't believe her?"

"I don't think it matters what I believe," he says.
"There's something else—"

"Are you saying you think Elenya killed Robin?"

"No, no. But I'm afraid the police may, if they find she was with him that late, and if she doesn't establish some sort of alibi—"

"Was Nora supposed to be there last night?"

"Nora?" He seems surprised. "No, of course not."

"What about Lucy?"

He shakes his head.

"Do you own a gun?"

"No."

"Does your wife?"

"No."

"Can I talk to her about all this?"

"Not now," he says. "As I said, she's sleeping."

"Wake her up."

"I don't want to wake her up. Someone is framing me. Someone is after me. They've been blackmailing me for months. Or trying to—I haven't paid. I wish to God now I had—maybe Nora would be alive. Now I'm afraid Elenya's in danger as well."

"Blackmailed how?" I say, and he excuses himself— he has perfect table manners—and returns a minute later with a greeting card similar to the one I found in Elenya's Porsche. Even the typeface is the same.

This one's not for a birthday, though.

"This is the latest," he says. "There's a dozen others."

A Get Well Message
For a Special Someone
Under the Weather
And Feeling Blue!

Dear prick: I know you killed them and I know how. Don't try to stay a step ahead. I'm right behind you.

There's no way to stop me.

"When did this come?"

"It was on my front porch a few hours ago. Ask Giselle."

"Can I see the others?"

"I destroyed them," he says.

"Not smart. What were they about?"

"Threats to expose me if I continued dating students. To show up at a faculty meeting and show a tape of me with a friend."

"You mean a boy like Robin. That would liven up the proceedings dramatically. There's nothing like sodomy to suspend Robert's Rules of Order. You never went to the police with any of this?"

"No."

"Not even after last night?"

"I'd rather handle it myself. Or rather, have *you* handle it. They said my wife would be in danger."

" 'They'?"

"There's two of them. At least, I think so—"

"You said you didn't pay—what were they asking?"

"One million cash."

"Do you have that kind of money?"

"Of course not."

I put down my coffee cup before I break it. "There isn't some little Swiss account you're temporarily forgetting?"

"What are you talking about?"

"Nothing. Forget it." I'm about to tell him the problems I have with this whole scenario—that it's an open murder case and I think he may be guilty; that even if he's innocent I've developed a genuine dislike for him—when Giselle appears, perfectly coiffed and attired, to see if the gentlemen will be needing anything further.

"No, Giselle," Rosenberg says, "it was wonderful as usual. Maybe a little more coffee, that's all."

She curtsies—I don't think I've ever seen that before outside a foreign film—and Rosenberg stands, holding his demitasse. It's clearly a message that the meeting is ending. I'm not sure what's been accomplished, on either side.

"Find out who's blackmailing me," he says. "Stop them any way you wish. Just keep the police out of it, and keep my name out of the papers. I'll make it worth your while. You'll be helping Elenya too."

"Right."

"I'm quite serious."

"Tell me—just how is she endangered by your indiscretions?"

"She's not entirely innocent in these affairs—"

"Let's drop this."

"Wait. I don't mean last night. You're right—she wasn't herself last night. Partly that's drugs—"

"Which you supply her with—"

"—one or two of the notes they sent me mentioned an affair she's been having. Threatening her as well. She's a very private person. She'd be devastated if any of this reached the newspapers."

"You've never talked to her about this?" I say.

"No."

Something must pass across my face. Like disbelief.

"We have boundaries," he says.

"I'd say they're breaking down. Did Lucy get any notes like the one you got?"

"Lucy? No, not that she told me—"

"Does she own a typewriter?"

"How would I know?"

"Do you?"

"No. Yes. An old portable Royal somewhere— what are all these questions about?"

"I told you I'd have a lot of questions. I suspect the police will have a few more. If I were you I'd find that typewriter. And check your outpatient surgery. Make sure all the phenol's accounted for."

"You can buy it anywhere—"

"If somebody's blackmailing you, Rosenberg, they might prefer using some of yours."

"You're taking the job?"

"I didn't say that. When did you leave the motel last Wednesday?"

"I don't know. Two or three."

"How was the room when you left it?"

"Not much better than when we checked in."

"Why go there?"

"Look, what difference does all this make?"

"None, I guess. Not now. But humor me."

"It was Nora's choice."

"Oh, come on."

"I'm serious. She liked those run-down places. We've been there before, as a matter of fact."

"Where did you pick her up?"

"Her dormitory."

"And afterward?"

"I took her back there, the same place—"

"And Thursday night? Where were you then?"

"In surgery, at the hospital—"

"How'd you know I was outside?"

"What?"

"Lucy said 'You forgot your camera.' When I found her in Kent. How did you know I'd been watching you?"

"I didn't. She said that?" Again, the surprise seems genuine. "I just found out from Detective Reilly this morning."

"One more question—how much did you pay Nora and Robin?"

"Pay? I've never paid them or anyone else—will you or won't you take the job?"

"You should just tell all this to the police."

He shakes his head.

"See, I can't help thinking the money's for something else. Not for stopping some mysterious blackmailers. Maybe it's my cynical nature."

"Like what?"

"Like staying out of your divorce, not helping your wife get the two million you've got stashed away."

"Now it's two million," he says, dropping his cigar in his coffee; it hisses like a snake. "I'm afraid ten thousand is as high as I can go."

He doesn't mention the blackmailers again. The check stays with Rosenberg, on the silver platter.

Giselle escorts me out a side door. I find myself on the driveway leading to the coach house. I pull the damn ski coat around me—the temperature's dropping again—and head toward the street.

I'm on the grass crossing the front yard when the front door opens; slowly, wood pulling free from rubber insulation. I'm preparing an excuse for Rosenberg when I see who it is watching me.

Elenya steps out on the front porch, wearing a long

terrycloth robe and slippers, her arms wrapped around her chest. It's a heavy robe but no match for this morning's windchill.

"Harding?" she says. "I thought that was you. I saw you through the upstairs window. I was upstairs, reading. I must have drifted off—"

"How are you?" I say, fumbling for something to say. There are too many questions she clearly is not prepared to answer. "Are you all right?"

"I'm fine," she says, giving me half a smile. "They'll be putting me in a nursing home. Who sleeps in the middle of the day?"

"People who were up all night," I say. But it doesn't look like I woke her. She still has stockings on below the robe. And earrings that dangle like question marks when she tilts her head.

She doesn't invite me in.

"You'll freeze," I say from the foot of the steps which is as far as I dare go.

"No, it feels good," she says. "The house gets too warm. Stuffy. And it's warming up a little, don't you think? At least I think so. They said it might even reach the twenties by the end of the week."

"Really," I say. "I hadn't heard that."

"I'm just so tired of this *snow*," she says.

We're talking about the weather.

We stand still and silent for a moment. Someone's lit a fire. The air smells like smoke. A flock of geese in chevron flight pass overhead. I hope they have a better idea of where they're going than I do.

"What happened last night, Elenya?" I finally say. She just shakes her head, pulls the robe tighter around her body. "Stephen told me it was a party for you."

"He did?" She rubs her eyes, red from crying. She's

not crying now. "It was Stephen's party, believe me. I heard noises. I should have stayed upstairs."

"The police—"

"They've been and gone," she says. "Been and gone." It sounds like a nursery rhyme. Her head is nodding gently to some internal rhythm.

I hear a noise. There's a glint of light in the crack behind the open door.

Something like fear crosses Elenya's face. It disappears quickly in the haze clouding her eyes. She doesn't seem to find it curious that I'm here, in her front yard. She has no questions for me. But drugs can do that, find a logic where none exists, drown the questions.

"I should go," she says, swaying a bit, a ship in rough water.

The door creaks behind her. She takes one hesitant step back.

"It was a terrible night, wasn't it?" she says again. I nod.

"You know about Nora, and Robin—"

"Been and gone," she says.

Elenya's hand is on the doorknob—she's about to go inside. But she hesitates for just a second. Her body is moving one way, her face and eyes another. For now all I get is the look she throws me.

I could be past her and inside in three or four steps but the expression on Elenya's face stops me more than any wall or door could. There's Halcion in her eyes but it doesn't completely erase the concern I see there.

Whether for me or her, I'm not sure.

She goes inside without saying goodbye. The lock is thrown. The blinds come down.

I sit on 47th Street warming up the Tempo a good five minutes. The Temptations are on the radio wishing it would rain. They've seen the five-day forecast. Then I drive north on Lake Shore Drive, fighting the morning sun.

"You have money for fancy new car, no money for rent?" Minas says, peeking out into the alley. He's chopping onions. I try never to argue with immigrants holding cutlery but I'm flat broke.

I retrieve the front section of his *Trib* from a fresh compost of feta cheese and potato peelings; zap cold black coffee in a microwave that beeps in counterpoint to my pager—yet another message, this one from Donnie Wilson. I turn the damn thing off. Now I remember why I buried it with my socks in the first place.

Details in the early editions are sketchy; there's a sidebar on the front page about a woman killed, another woman attacked inside a campus building in Hyde Park. Neither are identified. A university spin doctor won't confirm that either are students—"or have any ties whatsoever to the University of Chicago." Terrible tragedy; police uncertain of a motive. No comment. That's it. Nothing at all about Robin; he'll have to wait until the later editions.

Minas is reading over my shoulder, still holding the cleaver. "Police were here once already," he says. He has tiny pieces of onion like dandruff on his shirt. "Asking about you. They wake me up."

"Asking what?"

Minas shrugs. "How long you live here. Do I know Alison. Is Alison your girlfriend, does she stay overnight. Lots of questions. They show me pictures of other women; do they come here. Have I seen them."

"You make it sound like I'm Jack the Ripper. What did you tell them?"

"The truth," Minas says. "Whatever I know. I have building inspectors, health inspectors to pay off. Trouble with police I don't need." He motions to the refrigerator. "You want something? Leftover lamb? *Galactoburiko?*"

"No."

"Alison will be all right?"

"I think so." He's staring at my clothes. This stupid coat. I look like I spent the night on the sidewalk.

"This just came," he says, handing me an envelope. "Just arrived. Mr. Henderson brought it over himself." Minas is impressed. Henderson runs the tiny S&L down the street. It must be a slow day for foreclosures.

Inside I find a bank check for ten thousand dollars. The payer is Dr. Stephen Rosenberg. It's dated today. Payable to cash.

Minas, again reading over my shoulder, tells me not to worry so much about the back rent.

"I'm thinking of buying a bird," Minas says. He's fixing me a tray of food with a bottle of red wine—no leftovers since seeing that check. "Instead of an attack dog. A shrike."

"An attack bird? Can you have birds in a restaurant?"

"Let me read you," he says, finding a marked page in an old paperback dictionary: " 'The shrike is a carnivorous bird with a screeching call; a strong hooked bill with a toothlike projection, often impaling its prey on barbed wire.' "

"That might thin out your lunch crowd," I say.

The light's out at the top of the stairs. When I get to the landing wood chips and plaster crackle under my feet. I put the tray of food down on the floor.

I'm a distant second getting to my front door.

It's been kicked in, then ripped from its hinges; definitely overkill but if it was meant to impress me it's worked. My pulse is jumping as I walk through the rooms checking closets like a kid looking for the bogeyman in dark corners. The back door's standing open. I go outside and check the back steps. No one's here.

A file cabinet's overturned. The contents of my desk are scattered on the floor. As far as I can tell nothing is missing. It could have been an impatient client, bored with waiting. Maybe I should keep some magazines out.

Then I remember the crate of documents Frost gave me last Saturday. I'd shoved it under my dining room table, hidden by a plastic tablecloth two sizes too big. Not hidden well enough. It's gone.

I wonder if this is why Rosenberg made sure his service reached me; made sure I stayed as long as I did, stuffing my face with Giselle's omelets. I make a mental note: *eat fewer eggs*.

Minas says he'll fix the door. I can see he's picturing the shrike. So am I, possibly ten or twelve as watch birds flying in my living room. For now I nail the door to the frame then reinforce it with two-by-fours in diagonals. It looks like the house in *Night of the Living Dead*. I'll use the back door.

I call Boone. I haven't talked to him in days. He's reading *Scientific American*, waiting for his own door to be fixed. "They tore it off the fucking hinges," he says. "You wouldn't believe it, Harding." I assure him I can picture it. Just like me he was out at the time, pulling an all-nighter at one of his many jobs. All my stuff from Indiana—the caulking gun, the mustard bottle and syringes, the Beta video—all that's gone with the wind. As with the crate of papers, I'm not sure who'd want any of it except my good friend Dr. Rosenberg.

"Who knew you had it?" I ask Boone. No one; he doesn't know anyone.

I try to remember who I told. Donnie must have known. Did I tell Frost? Alison? I can't remember. It wasn't exactly a state secret. Now I owe Boone for both his lab work and his door. I tell him to put it on my tab.

The radio still works. What comes out is music with plenty of heartache and more than a few fiddles. It could be New Country, it could be Old Country. My brain's too feeble for such distinctions. I've lost my appetite for the food. I put it in the refrigerator, where it will have to fend for itself. The red wine is a recent vintage; the bottle has a twist-off cap. I pour it in a coffee cup. It looks like mouthwash.

The phone rings as I'm undressing. I answer it hopping on one foot, dragging my jeans on the floor; a new line dance for the country bars at closing. *Time please, gentlemen. Gather your ladies.*

"Harding?" It's Elenya, her voice a low murmur. "I'm sorry to bother you, I wanted to ask you—"

"It's no bother—"

"—but I wanted to ask you."

There's silence. I wait, listening to static. At first I think she's gone. There's a noise like Christmas wrapping paper. Ever since Illinois Bell became Ameritech my phone sounds like a party line.

"Elenya?"

"There's a man," she says finally.

"What man."

"Someone I met once, at the health club. Months and months ago. I only met him the one time. But I think, I mean now I wonder"—she's struggling to complete her thoughts—"he might be doing something—"

"Doing what?"

"—just he might be involved in this somehow."

"Involved in what? Nora's death? Robin's?"

She says yes.

"What's his name?"

"Gaelen."

"What makes you think he's involved?"

"You know, maybe he's not. God, Harding, I'm so sleepy—"

I picture her, head in hands. Perhaps Giselle watches from the wings.

Giselle, your mistress needs some coffee, please . . .

Or is the person watching from the wings the same person I sensed behind the door?

"Elenya, just tell me, please. What did he do?"

"He followed me," she says. "At least, I think so. No, I'm sure of it. He sent me things—flowers, these really expensive tiny white roses, with just a blank card. And sometimes I'd answer the phone and there'd be just this old song, from when I was in high school. It's not really creepy or anything but—"

"What song?"

" 'Cherish,' " she says. "The Association. Remember?"

"How long ago was this?"

"Oh, I don't know. Five, six months."

"How did you know he was following you?"

"Harding, I saw him sometimes, when I came out of the grocery—"

"Do you have a picture of him?"

"No, of course not—"

"What does he look like?"

"I don't know—"

"White? Black? Tall? Short?"

"White, tall, very tall, with dark hair, and a beard—"

"Did you ever see his car? Was it a red Grand Am?"

"His car? I don't know. I don't know much about cars—it might be red, dark red—"

"Is this the health club on 47th?"

"Yes," she says. Again I sense her drifting. "God, I don't know why I'm telling you this. But you've been so sweet. Maybe he's not involved, maybe it's nothing—I mean, it was months ago—"

"Elenya, listen to me. Okay?"

"—I haven't seen him in a long time—"

"I'm very glad you told me."

"You are?"

"Yes, I am. But now—what do you want me to do? Do you want me to find this guy? Talk to him? Tell the police about him?"

She's silent, I hear just her breathing like static on the line. I know something of how she feels, how the drugs pull at you. It's hard to concentrate. I'll talk to her again later, when she's straight. But without the drugs she may not want to say much.

"Maybe not the police," she says. "Maybe not now, not yet—"

"Did you tell Stephen about him?"

"God, no—"

"You met him once," I say, "talked to him, that's it?"

"Yes."

"There was nothing else?"

"What do you mean."

"Nothing, just—"

"Now you sound like Stephen," she says.

"I'm just trying to understand—"

"Forget it," she says, so quietly I can barely hear. I switch the radio off.

"It's this job, Elenya. I have to be nosy, ask dumb questions." The music's stopped but I'm still dancing.

"I thought I could talk to you."

"You can, you can."

"I met him once, Harding. At the health club. Not some motel in Indiana." She pauses. "All I seem to do lately is apologize. Only I don't know what I've done."

I tell her it's a feeling I know very well.

"So what now," she says. "What do we do?"

"We tell Reilly."

"Harding, please. No."

"Elenya—"

"No."

I don't understand her reluctance. If all they did was talk . . .

"Can't you do it?" she says. "Find him for me? Ask him all the dumb questions? That's your job, isn't it?"

"Except it's an open homicide case, Elenya. If you know anything you should tell Reilly. Or your lawyer."

"I've never told *anyone*."

"But why—"

"Harding, please. Believe me, it was hard enough even telling *you*."

I don't press her any further. Something in her voice says this is as far as she's willing to go.

When I finally get undressed everything but my new shirt gets tossed in the trash. I put the check in my sock drawer. Then I run the hottest shower my plumbing allows and stand in scalding water with my coffee cup.

Last night at the precinct house it was several hours

before anyone would let me wash up. A uniform went along as a chaperon. I scrubbed my hands with cheap pine soap, dried off with brown paper towels that smelled like glue. I scrubbed until the annoyed uniform nearly had to turn off the water and drag me from the sink but even now I think I see specks of Alison's blood beneath my nails.

Usually I hear phantom doorbells or phones in the shower. Today the rushing water seems filled with ringing pagers. The water provides a bottomless cup but I'm too tired to move. Red wine stains splash on the walls and shower curtain. It looks like Hitchock's *Marnie*. Inside the water I can also hear the whispered breathing of the respirators and ventilators in SICU; one final souvenir. *We fucked up Harding.* There are no messages on my machine.

NINE

I sleep until two A.M., when Warren Frost's disembodied voice wakes me from the living room. He talks right through the beep, a rambling monologue that takes two calls to inform me he's coming up, open the goddamn back door. I wash my face, stare at the clock. By the time I'm in the kitchen I hear him trudging up the steps.

"Don't you have a doorbell?" he says, brushing past me. He gets two juice tumblers from my kitchen and unwraps a bottle of Scotch. He slops as much as he pours but it's no great loss. One sip sends me to the freezer. There's no way to drink this without ice. It may be the worst Scotch I've ever had. There are tartan crests all over the label but it's bottled in Chile.

"Where have you been, Warren?"

"A bar on Diversey. J. Edgar's—you ever been there?"

"No."

"I don't recommend it. Not unless you like men in women's clothing."

"I mean all day. All last night. Since I sent you for that cop—remember that?"

He takes a large drink of the Scotch. "I didn't want to intrude."

"You fucking disappeared on me."

"And your fucking plan blew up in my face," he

says. "First you bring a girl instead of the man I paid
you for—"

"She's doing fine, Warren, thanks for asking."

"—we're supposed to be there helping Elenya, now
her husband's got her so scared—I don't know *what* to
do." He looks around the room for the first time.
"Doing a little spring cleaning?"

"Someone tossed the place this morning. Have you
talked to Elenya?"

"Of course I've talked to her."

"When?"

"This morning. Last night, she called me from the
police station—what's missing?"

"Nothing's missing. There was nothing here. She
called you? Really?"

"Why so surprised?" he says, giving me a funny
look.

"How did she find you? Reilly sure couldn't."

"I talked to Reilly too, Harding," he says. "Don't
believe everything they tell you down at the station. I
was there over an hour." He drains his Scotch and pours
another; I'm still laboring on my first, waiting for the
ice to melt. "You've got the old eleventh edition," he
says, seeing a row of battered Britannicas on my book-
shelf. He takes the first volume down and starts
thumbing through it. "They put these on CD-ROM
now, the whole thing on one little disk. Not the same
somehow, is it?"

"Don't spill your Scotch on the book, Warren,
okay? It looks like battery acid."

"Usually the binding's faded or watermarked—
you're lucky, these are in good shape—"

"What did you tell Reilly, Warren?"

"I mostly talked to Keegan," he says. "What did I

tell them? That we were outside Rosenberg's house around nine. That we set the alarms off and ran like hell. That while we were there we saw Rosenberg and someone we thought was a girl in the house. Then we drove to Kent. How much did this set cost you?"

"You didn't see Elenya?"

"No, Harding."

"You're sure you didn't see Elenya in that window?"

"I said no, didn't I? Do you think I like being an alibi for her husband but not for her?"

"Who's their lawyer?" I say.

"Kettering. He's Stephen's lawyer—I wouldn't trust him with anything regarding Elenya. I wouldn't trust him *period*."

"But he's representing them both?"

"He's advising them, Harding. They haven't been charged with anything—nobody has, not even Lucy Williams. The cops don't think Nora was killed last night, did you know that? Two, maybe three days ago. You know anybody with a big freezer?" Frost has taken over most of the couch. He's leaning back with his drink, the reflective barrister. He's fairly drunk, which for him is an accomplishment. His eyes are glazed like cheap pottery.

"The police had a team down at that motel of yours—"

"It's not my motel, Frost."

"No, but they keep calling it that. I don't think they were very pleased that you went through everything, destroying evidence."

"At the time, it wasn't evidence. It was just shit."

I tell him that his box of papers is gone. He frowns over his ice cubes. When I ask for reprints he drinks until the cubes fall against his face. "That's not so easy," he says. "You'd better ask Donnie. He can put his hands on anything—why are you still working for him, Harding? Running his errands, doing his dirty work—"

"Don't you like Donnie? Really? Because he thinks the world of you."

"He's a neighborhood thug who got lucky. Your luck wasn't so good. Who was your lawyer in Kentucky?"

"When?"

"You know when."

"Just a local. A name the PD's office gave me. I think it might have been his first trial, after moot court in law school. He probably lost that too."

"But you didn't lose, you took the plea."

"Yeah. I took the plea." I can never tell how much Frost knows of my past—or why he's interested. "You want something to eat?"

"No, I ate at this bar tonight—lots of finger food. Why is it transvestites have such tacky taste, do you think?" He kicks his shoes off, puts his feet on my coffee table. There are dime-sized holes in his Argyle socks.

"We can't all have your fashion sense, Frost."

"I mean, why all the glitter and sequins—why not opt for a nice conservative Peck and Peck ensemble, try to fit in." Frost's glasses are sliding down his nose. "Transsexuals don't dress like that. I have one for a client—works for the city running a road crew fixing potholes, believe it or not. Doesn't want anything special. Just wants to be a lady."

It must be getting late because the Scotch is starting to taste better. It still tastes more like tequila than Scotch. The lime I find in my refrigerator turns out to be a very old lemon. I pour myself a second over rocks and throw in some salt. "Is that a regular hangout of yours, Warren?"

"Harding, I swear to God just two weeks ago it was called O'Ryan's. I was in there drinking beer. Guys were playing darts, shooting pool. Tonight the pool tables are lined up as a runway for the fashion show." He's sinking; his head resting on the end of the cushion. "So how is your friend doing?"

"All right. Her name's Alison." I watch Frost rolling up his topcoat for a pillow, like a cowboy bunking down for the night. "She was sleeping after the surgery. I'm going in first thing in the morning."

"Buy her a card or something for me. And stop in at my office, okay? I'll buy you lunch. There must be somebody I can expense it to." He finishes his drink and puts the book and the glass on the floor.

I leave the lights on, carry Volume 25, *Shuvalov to Subliminal Self,* back to the shelf. First Reilly, now Frost; bringing up the Angela Martinez case. It always comes out in bits and pieces. Perhaps because it's spread over a number of years, and states . . .

It started here, of course, in Hyde Park the day Martinez attacked his daughter in front of me. When he jumped bail and ran south I ran too, leaving clients behind—I heard he had family in southern Kentucky and so I spent the summer in tobacco barns, church picnics, state fairs looking for one man, trying to forget a face.

His wife wouldn't talk to me about where he might have gone but from the money that supposedly disappeared with him I thought he'd end up in Argentina or Brazil—instead I got reports of him in the Daniel

Boone National Forest. They were third-party sightings as reliable as tales of Bigfoot but enough to keep me on Kentucky backroads the entire summer. I was out of my territory; in over my head—I was a city kid; never a Boy Scout; the nearest to this growing up was cutting through the rookery at the zoo to catch the #151 bus—but I moved from campsite to campsite; slept in the truck or pitched a tent, surrounded by wilderness. After a few months of this I looked a little like Bigfoot myself.

Then one night on a Lake Cumberland houseboat a stranger flashed a phony badge and suggested it was time for me to return home. It was a hot August night before a thunderstorm and the air smelled like rain. The man's name was Patner. He offered me a plug of Red Man and the wrong end of an eight-inch skinning knife; the kind with a curved point and notched handle that locals use cleaning game and rabbits. The offer was nonnegotiable. I had a gun but it went in the dark water. So did Patner. Both sank like the weighted bags of shit houseboaters drop from their portable toilets, into a bottomless well.

I got as far as Carbondale. The state police never found the gun. The knife turned up two days later, though, with Patner's body, facedown in a quiet slip near Wolf Creek Dam. They extradited me to a tiny courthouse near the Tennessee border, where a deal was cut. Patner had priors for assault and outstanding warrants in two states; no one was sorry to see him gone. I did eighteen months in state prison.

Eduardo Martinez disappeared. I never heard from him again. His daughter Angela, however, has never gone away.

"Is there anything I can do for you?" Frost says from the couch. One hand hangs down under the couch springs.

"Can you get me into the Hyde Park Athletic Club?"

"Not dressed like that," he says.

I explain very little but Frost agrees to help; he's too tired to argue. He'll have his secretary buy me a temporary membership. If I know Frost he'll get a refund out of it somehow. Maybe even turn a profit. With any luck I'll slip on some water, he can sue for negligence.

I put my glass in the sink. I have a feeling he snores, so I close my bedroom door. At least the check is in here with me.

The police are talking to Alison when I arrive so I curl up on a couch in the lounge. The nurses frown at me the way I frowned at Frost last night, with equal results. She's on a general floor now; her condition's been upgraded several times—it's either "good" or "stable," I can't remember which. The terms are like weather updates; meaningless, always changing.

At least I cleared a profit on Frost. After my hospitality he couldn't refuse my request for a loan, pulling three more fifties from a roll in his pocket. God only knows how much cash he carries around. I should have waited until he was asleep and mugged him. As it was he got his dollar's worth spending way too much time in my bathroom; leaving my toothbrush suspiciously damp.

I didn't sleep much. Every time I close my eyes now I drift off. A second ago I was at an ice skating party on the Midway, flooded and frozen like a man-made lake; Lucy was there doing figure-eights, silver chains dangling from her wrists. Even in my dreams now it's snowing.

I have a hangover from the Scotch or the red wine—maybe they're contraindicated. I should check with a nurse. One in a bright yellow pantsuit taps me on the shoulder. "Harding? She says she wants to see you."

Alison's door is propped open like a fifties sorority where everyone keeps one foot on the floor. Keegan has the only chair. He's watching morning cartoons; laughing at Bugs Bunny in *Treasure Island*; slurping Alison's lime Jell-O.

"Anything we should know?" he says, eyeing the bag I brought in case there's food he can pirate.

"About what?"

"We haven't seen you for a while. Any more of your girlfriends get run through with a sword? Made to walk the plank?"

"Go away, Keegan."

He laughs, slapping me on the shoulder with a folded newspaper, like a favorite pet. He has the same plaid jacket on but then I'm wearing the same flannel shirt. At least I've had a shower.

"Thanks for the backup yesterday, Keegan. At the El stop."

"What?"

"The tail you sent after me. I appreciate it."

"Right, right," he says. "Maybe we should wipe your ass for you too."

He heads for the door. "I'd better leave you love-birds alone. Try to keep casualties to a minimum, okay, Harding?" His footsteps die away. His body odor lingers.

A different nurse—older, actually wearing white—sticks her head in the door. She makes a disapproving noise with her lips you'd need a linguist or a field zoologist to identify. "She really doesn't need any more visitors right now."

"I'll just be a minute," I say. The nurse nods, frowning.

"Everybody loves you," Alison says, smiling. I drag a chair next to the bed and hold her hand. She squeezes back lightly. She's not wearing her glasses, which makes her eyes look even more tired. Her hair's matted against her face. Her face is paler than usual. Her hands are cold.

"You look good," I say, kissing her lightly.

"Never better," she says hoarsely, kissing me back. Her eyes flinch with pain. "I think major trauma agrees with me."

"The nurses said something about you moaning my name over and over—"

"You wish. I'm still a little zonked, though," she says. "My drugs of choice are Mountain Dew and Milk Duds. This stuff seems awfully strong. I think they had me on morphine for a while. You ever try that?"

"Once or twice. It gives me diarrhea."

"Well, you're the life of any party, Harding."

"It's working, though? You're not in any pain?"

"Just my throat," she says. "All the stupid tubes." She has a red water bottle with a twisting straw, the kind mountain bikers carry. She takes a long sip. She has trouble raising her head.

"What can I get you?"

"Do you see my glasses anywhere?" she says.

"Here."

"And my jewelry?"

"All here. Ring, Swatch, three earrings. Am I up to date? You didn't have anything else on your body pierced recently?"

"Just here," she says, raising her gown. The bandages are even whiter than her pale skin. "I can't show you the scars yet."

"That's okay," I say. "I didn't bring a camera."

She smiles, lies back for a second, watching TV. I get her some fresh water and a different helping of Jell-O off someone else's tray, closing the door on my way in.

"They said I was lucky," Alison says.

"Did they." I see now why she didn't eat the Jell-O. It hurts too much to sit up and she wasn't about to ask Keegan to feed her. She isn't so crazy about me feeding her either. My first attempt flops on her gown.

"Why are you lucky?" I say, giving her another spoonful.

"Abdominal surgery," she says, pointing down. "Interior bleeding."

"What about your arm?"

"Not so bad," she says, speaking in shorthand to save her voice.

"Is that all they said?"

She drinks some water, takes a long time to swallow.

"Gratuitous remarks," she says. "About my fabulous muscle tone, low body fat. What's in the bag?"

"Just a CARE package I threw together."

"Gimme, gimme." I open the paper bag and give her handfuls of bubblegum, Milk Duds, *Elle*, *Historical Photography*, *Black Belt*, cotton pajamas with feet, a new Discman and half a dozen CDs—Metallica, Bauhaus, Danzig, Motörhead, all the classics. She kisses me again. "Music for migraines," she says. I don't tell her it all comes out of her two hundred. Frost's money is gone too.

I have a million questions for her but she's already talked too much.

"Should I submit my questions in written form?" I say. "And you can write your replies?"

"I can talk," she says hoarsely.

"I just want to know how you ended up at Kent."

"Somebody inside said Nora just left her room. I saw someone I thought was her. She had a coat like you described. I followed her."

"And she went down 59th, and up Ellis, instead of cutting through the quads?"

She nods.

"And you followed her in your car?"

"Quietly, Harding. Even on wheels I'm like a panther."

"Well, we know it wasn't Nora."

"Obviously."

"You never saw a face."

She shakes her head. "I stayed almost a block away."

"But she went inside Kent?"

"I think so."

"You never saw her go inside?"

"She cut through the sidewalk, I was in my car—what happened to my car?"

"One of your employees—Dave?—Dave picked it up. They're using it at your store."

"Good."

"So why'd you go in? If you didn't see her?"

"I heard screaming. You must have heard it—"

"You heard screaming *before* you went inside?"

She nods.

"Harding, I told the police there was screaming. You really didn't hear it?"

"No."

I should go. She looks tired.

"Do you want me to talk to anybody? Do anything for you?"

She shakes her head.

"Don't be so damn self-reliant. Let me do something. What about your apartment? Do you have a cat these days?"

"No," she says. "Felicia took the cat. You could see how things are at the store, see if they need a hand. And I guess you could get my mail." She wants the water bottle again, then lies back on her pillow. "Check my plants. A little rhododendron in my bedroom needs some TLC."

"I'll water it, tell it bedtime stories." I lower the restraining bar on her bed and sit beside her, combing her hair back with my fingers, fitting her wire-rim glasses gently over her ears.

"My hair's a mess," she says, self-consciously, twisting the ends.

"No, it looks fine. Pretty wonderful, actually."

"Don't push it, Harding."

"Alison, I thought you were gone. I saw you lying there—I just couldn't believe it. And now I'm just so glad to see you're awake and talking and okay—"

"Hey, Harding," she says taking my hand. "You old softie. It's not your fault."

"Of course it is, Alison. I put you there, at risk, for no other reason than I needed your help. And you helped me. I'm responsible for you."

"I make my own decisions. I'm a big girl, remember?"

"How could I forget."

"So stop feeling guilty. I heal quickly. I've got insurance. If it makes you feel better you could clean my bathroom. And my oven."

"Don't push it, Alison."

"You know, I did exactly what you're not supposed to do. I reached for the knife. Counterpunch and run. Kick, for God's sake, don't go for the knife—"

"He hit you first with the gun?"

"He must have. I don't know why he didn't shoot me. And then he must have thought I'd stay down but it was dark and he hit me from behind and I wasn't about to just lie there and see what he did next."

"And he stabbed you how?"

"Whirled me around before I was even on my feet. And swung the knife, all in one motion. He was big, Harding. Really strong. You don't think I'd have ended up like this in a fair fight, do you?"

"I don't think it'll hurt your reputation any. No chance it was Lucy, some other woman?"

"Get real," she says.

An intern pushes open the door without knocking. He glares at me impatiently. His stethoscope's brand-new, with a shiny glint like a cheap chrome bumper. He has trouble taking Alison's blood pressure. But he's mastered the basic skills required of an experienced Health Care Professional. He's already an asshole.

"Family members only, pal," he says, barely looking at me. "Visiting hours don't start for another— let's see, ten minutes—so unless you're a family member you'd better scootsy-daisy—"

"My father," Alison says, smiling at me.

"Really," the doctor says, frowning. I don't think he's rotated through Geriatrics yet.

"I'd better get out of here." I kiss Alison on her cheek; she lifts herself to kiss me back, grimacing from the pain. Her lips are dry.

"Harding," she says.

"Yes."

"Remember what John Wayne would say to Ward Bond and the posse: I want him alive. He's mine."

"All right, Duke. I'll see what I can do."

"Wasn't that your father just now on the phone?" the doctor says to Alison. "Calling long-distance?"

"Stepfather," Alison says. "This is my real dad. Right, Dad?"

"I was just leaving," I say. "She gives you any trouble, Doctor, just let me know. She's not too old to put over my knee."

"Goodbye, Dad," Alison says. "Dad was just leaving."

TEN

Traffic on the Kennedy is slow. It's just past eleven when I park the Tempo in an outside lot, avoiding the outstretched hands of valet parking. Through several pages from his assistant Serena—Lake Forest College '94—Donnie has invited me to the Schaumburg Towers. We're doing brunch.

Despite Elenya's forecast the day has turned sunny and very cold; my breath looks like secondhand smoke. Every building for miles is colored glass—electric browns, golds, greens, blues—the Chicago School of Architecture reduced to Mies van der Rohe wearing iridescent aviator shades.

The hotel elevators are glass too, rising above a lobby of ferns and businessmen. I ride the express alone to the roof. The floors fall away below me.

Fifteen is so crowded with Elks I have to fight my way down the hall to the restaurant. The Ancient Mariner's tropical island promotion is in full swing today—the room is full of fake palms and driftwood, reggae Muzak, conventioneers full of complimentary banana coolers. I gave my name to a tanned woman in a grass skirt and wait by the bar. Through the picture windows I can just see the Mariner's nearest body of water—the hotel's outdoor pool—as frozen now as the smile on the hostess's face when she kisses me on both cheeks and drapes a pink lei around my neck. She smells like gardenias.

Donnie Wilson's sitting in a corner booth. A plate of food's pushed to one side to make room for his laptop. His hands are too big for the keyboard—his thumbs keep nudging the trackball, sending the cursor flying off to CyberSiberia. The glow from the screen is coloring his scrambled eggs light green.

"What a cold fucking day," Donnie says, typing with one finger. "As soon as my clock radio tells me it's five below I know I got problems. Even the locks on the 350 are frozen. And this is in the garage." He shifts his weight uncomfortably; the booth's not quite big enough for his frame. "So seven A.M. I'm breaking into my own car just to get to the fucking jumper cables, which do not fucking work. Then the auto club—which I pay two hundred a year for Executive Service—puts me on hold for half an hour with highlights from *South Pacific*. Somebody in that place has a sick sense of humor."

"The Broadway cast or the movie?"

"What?"

"Nothing—did you get it started?"

"I got it towed," Donnie says. "And this was *after* the cops rang my doorbell at six A.M., disturbing my breakfast companion and my granola. When your name comes up with the cops it's not exactly mail from home, Harding."

"Sorry, Donnie. I tried to keep your name out of it. It just wouldn't fly. I'm surprised they waited a day to talk to you."

"I was in Seattle, some seminar on computer crime. I caught up on my sleep. You need some lunch? I bet you haven't eaten." He waves his hand and a skinny waitress with a flower in her hair pours me fresh papaya juice and runs through items on the island buffet—Jamaican eggs, authentic Caribbean bacon.

"Caribbean bacon?"

"That's lizard," the waitress says. She taps her order pad with a pencil.

"Stay away from the lizard," Donnie says. "The conch I can recommend. And they do a good lungfish here. Blackened, broiled, whatever."

"We don't blacken the lungfish anymore," the waitress says.

"Trouble with the UMW?" I say.

"No, it's too good that way," the waitress says. "You know what happens? People literally beat down the doors to get the blackened lungfish. We can't get insurance. Try the Hawaiian poi. It's as fresh as you'll get in Illinois in the middle of February."

"Just coffee," I say. It's a little early for lungfish. Only when she walks away do I realize all the waitresses are essentially topless, wearing strategically placed leis as a halter. When they serve they have to bunny-dip to keep everything in place, the way Hef taught in 1962. Some things never change. No wonder the place is crowded with Elks.

"What are you typing?"

"Performance appraisals. End of the quarter. If you worked for me I could give you a raise. With one finger."

"You misspelled 'recommend,' " I say, reading the scrolling text.

Donnie frowns. "I did? Jesus, I've been spelling it that way for weeks. Are you sure?"

"It's easy to fix. Hit the Spellchecker. F4."

"How can you tell—"

"Here, let me do it." Computer criminals can rest easy in Schaumburg.

"How's Alison?" Donnie says. "She has a good doctor?"

"I guess." The computer grunts. "Now hit Replace. You see? Next time bring the manual."

"The cops said her wounds were superficial," Donnie says, downloading caviar on a Ritz. "The cuts on her abdomen were just slashes. Defensive wounds on her hands and wrists. Most of the blood was from a cut to her arm."

He always knows more than I know.

"Have you ever been stabbed like that, Donnie? I don't think there's anything *superficial* about knife wounds. She was in Surgical Intensive Care for God's sake."

"Easy, boy. Don't kill the messenger." Donnie pours us both more coffee from a carafe. "Nice shirt," he says. "Doing some forestry work later are we?"

"Go ahead, Donnie," I say.

"What?"

"Go ahead, say what you're dying to say. Get it over with."

He smiles. "You have to admit—I did warn you off this. I don't trust Frost, I don't like domestics, the whole thing smelled. I tried to warn you but you wouldn't listen."

"And?"

"And, well—"

"You told me so."

"I did, didn't I?" he says, pleased with himself. You'd think he'd predicted Mount Saint Helens or Black Friday.

"So how did you get involved to begin with?"

"Frost asked for help, practically begged me."

"And paid you something, I imagine, off the books."

"A small honorarium," Donnie says. "I have expenses."

"Like paying me."

"Exactly," Donnie says.

"What did the cops ask you?"

"Background, mostly. On you, Frost, the Rosenbergs."

"What'd you tell them?"

Donnie shrugs. "I'm a corporate executive these days, Harding." An extremely well-endowed wait-ress—seven leis—walks by. Donnie stares. "Which means I have to tell the truth or lie much more creatively."

"So what'd you say?"

"About you? Nothing. I stalled. It's the end of my fiscal quarter, Harding. I'm up to my ass in budget problems. Number-crunchers looking over my shoulder every time I authorize payment to someone not directly on the payroll."

"Like me."

He nods. "About Frost I told the truth—I don't trust him. The Rosenbergs I don't know all that well anyway. They also wanted me to supply an alibi for Sunday—that part I wasn't too thrilled with. It embar-rassed Serena, having to tell them about the bedroom in her condo and what I was doing in it."

"What *were* you doing in it?" I say.

"I had to tell the cops, Harding, I don't have to tell you," he says, smiling. "Which reminds me." He takes an envelope from his jacket pocket and hands it to me under the table. Either it's expensive onion-skin paper or it's been sitting near the Caribbean bacon.

Inside are crisp fifties and hundreds. It looks like nearly a thousand.

"What's this for?"

"I've got another job for you."

"I thought your number-crunchers were on your back."

He waves this thought away. "We'll put you on next quarter's books. That's the beauty of accounting. And this is a good job—you'll love this one, Harding."

"Just so it's inside. I'm running out of boots. What's the job?"

"A company in Elgin. Drug stuff. It's sneaky, you'll like it."

"You must have fifteen guys could do a job like that."

"More like fifty. No, Harding, actually, I don't. Most of my guys are more like specialists—"

"You mean they're goons."

"They have their limitations, that's all. This guy the CEO suspects is very sharp—Ivy League MBA with a Yale degree in art history. Real cocky. You know the type. He'll be surprised as hell running into somebody like you—just as educated and sneaky a low-life sleaze as him."

"I appreciate the compliment, Donnie."

"The nine hundred is just an advance, Harding. Nail the guy and it's worth two grand. Serena's got all the details. Okay?"

I hesitate for just a second. I'm tired but this will get my truck out of limbo. "Okay," I say.

"And look, if Alison needs a better doctor, just tell me, all right? I know a couple guys."

"Who know a couple guys? Thanks, Donnie. I'm not sure medicine works that way. I think she'll be all right. But there is something you can do for me."

Our waitress, Jayne, reappears to see if I need more coffee. "Bring me a decaf latte light would you, honey?" Donnie says. "Make sure it's skim milk. Are the beans fresh-ground?" She looks at him as though he's a five-year-old asking for Christmas to come early.

"What is it?" Donnie asks me.

"Those files Frost had on Rosenberg? Somebody lifted them from my apartment. Most of them weren't worth stealing. But if you could run off the banking records again—"

"All of them?"

"Just the last six months."

"I'll check," Donnie says. "I can't promise anything. This operation never officially existed to begin with. Doesn't Frost have copies?"

"He says no."

"Any other miracles you want me to perform?"

"A copy of the police report from Sunday would be nice."

"They won't release that, not on a double homicide."

"I'll settle for the report on Robin's room. What was missing."

A different waitress, Jenn, brings our coffee. Her name tag's pinned strategically to a single yellow lei, something that takes nerve and very good posture. I wonder if Jenn's really her name or if the other waitress stole her *y*.

"Do they make you dress this way all day?" I ask Jenn.

"No, honey," Jenn says. "Just days."

"The night shift's better?"

"The tips are better at night," she says. "Without the leis. But you can freeze your noogies off with just the G-string—we get a real draft from the elevator shaft. Even on fifteen. Go figure, huh."

We both watch her walk away.

"I must remember to come here for dinner," Donnie says. "You're sure you don't want something to eat?"

"No thanks."

"Forget the native crap—they'll make you anything you want. Waffles, pancakes, eggs and bacon—real bacon, Harding. Pig bacon."

"I'm not very hungry."

"Finish my eggs. I got eggs here I can't finish."

"No, really."

He nods, wiping his mouth with a heavy cotton napkin. An alarm on his pager goes off. "Jesus, I'm late," he says. "Walk with me, will you? I've gotta stop at the can." He backs down his computer, finishes his latte, then reaches for his coat, a sleek gray sealskin the gay busboys have been admiring with each circuit from the kitchen. No hat—Donnie doesn't wear hats—but a long white scarf, cashmere, imported from Lincolnshire, that hangs to his waist. He'd better keep the windows up driving the SL350.

From force of habit—we worked together for years—I watch Donnie's back as he threads a path through the crowded tables, steals a handful of mints from Jerry's Kids at the register, laughs at something the hostess says to him, one hand lightly on her back. I wait half a minute to see if anyone else in the restaurant moves in the same direction.

The bathroom's long and cool and quiet.

"What I'm worried about here is Frost," Donnie

says from the first stall. He uses the tip of one shiny black Italian loafer to kick the toilet seat up. "Because I don't think his hands are completely clean on this. I think he's after the Rosenberg woman and I know he's after the money. Don't get caught in the middle."

"He seems harmless," I say.

"The drinking? That's his cover. All those bastards drink. He's connected, Harding. He's not *made* but half his buddies are."

"Frost? Really?" I knew he had mob clients—it's hard not to in Chicago, working from the First Ward—but I saw him more as a hired hand. "Then why's he begging you for help with Elenya?"

" 'Cause you know the organization, Harding. That kind of shit's personal and they don't like personal. They don't *know* personal."

"They wouldn't want the money?"

"If the money was there they'd want it," Donnie says. "This is what convinces me the money doesn't exist. Because if it did and Frost's buddies caught wind of it do you think Frost would still be walking around without scuba gear? They'd be pulling him and both Rosenbergs from the Des Plaines River."

"Do you get mob intelligence stuff on your desk now?"

"Enough to know I'm glad I'm out of the city," Donnie says. "The wiseguys out by me are kind of different. They take their kids to Little League. They plant mums. They sign petitions for sidewalks. Course they're probably gonna *bury* somebody under the sidewalk."

"Still, it's more picturesque, isn't it?"

He must have had a few coolers before I arrived. This is turning into the world's longest piss.

"You remember my old man, Harding," he says.

"Sure I remember him."

"My old man used to say—this was his whole lecture on the facts of life, which he gave me when I was twelve, since he was afraid I was already fucking Mrs. Annastasio down the street—which I was—he says, 'There's only two ways to fuck, kid, whatever they tell you: in and out. No matter who they are, how much dough they got.'" Donnie's voice is hollow from the stall. "He had six kids, my old man, eight if you count the two that never made it past the front door at County. So he must have known what he was talking about."

The toilet finally flushes, a loud roar that echoes for several minutes against the tile.

"You must have given Serena a lovely evening," I say.

Donnie zips up his trousers, steps to the sink. "Look, I don't blame you one bit, Harding. Okay? No, really. She's a very attractive woman, completely different from Alison. Very classy. Exceptionally so. We both know how these things start."

"What things, Donnie?"

"Elenya Rosenberg. Jesus, Harding, aren't you listening?"

"Something got lost in the translation—what are you talking about?"

"She spent Friday night at your place, that's what."

"The cops told you that?"

"Not officially," he says.

"She was sick, Donnie. She stumbles in at three in the morning *and* I slept on the couch."

He nods, wiping his hands.

"Not that it's any of your motherfucking business," I say.

"Oh, it's my business, buddy," Donnie says. "And I

saw the way she was looking at you the other night. I wish to hell it *wasn't* my business but when they leave eighteen messages with my service and show up at my house and involve Serena it *becomes* my business. So I have to know what's going on."

"Nothing's going on," I say. "I barely know her."

He slicks back his hair, shakes the water from his comb and taps it on the chrome sink. "I ask only to be kept up to date on this, Harding, okay? Because it's not playing out as open and shut. They haven't charged Lucy with shit. They were holding her on some drug charge. She made bail first thing this morning."

"Who posted bail?"

"Some name that means nothing to me. I mean, it went through Manny's across the street from the courthouse but the deposit came from Nelson Bryars, RN. The address was South Drexel."

"You didn't check it out?"

"I could if it mattered to me but since it doesn't, why bother?"

"Lucy knows just how Rosenberg's involved, Donnie. And she knows who else was there too. She has to know. She was sitting in the room five feet from Nora with blood all over her."

"So was Alison," he says. "Come to think of it, so were you. Don't drag me into this any further, Harding. Okay?"

"Yeah."

"We're straight on this?"

"Like an arrow," I say.

Warren Frost's law firm is in the West Loop, close to city hall. I drive through town past gray snow and white sale displays. Ralph Lauren sheets and quilts on a four-poster in Field's main window start me yawning. I need some sleep. The window reminds me of the Red Lion Inn outside Boston, where Alison and I once stayed, sitting in huge rocking chairs on the front porch like an old married couple, drinking gin fizzes.

I create a parking space in an alley off Randolph. The garages are full and this way maybe someone will steal the Tempo. It's a strange part of town, the West Loop, government buildings funded for redevelopment beside run-down blocks where the money ran out. DA's and hookers warm bar stools side by side in the late afternoon. Maybe that's not so strange.

Frost's firm does a lot of city business and must like keeping a low profile. The building's exterior is blackened with grime. A large revolving door gives way reluctantly to my touch, wings of glass scraping the linoleum like fingers on a chalkboard. Other than the doorman the only person in the lobby is pushing retirement and a mop. There's a glass directory on the wall that's like a TV quiz show puzzle—missing white letters lying at the bottom of the black felt. The doorman tells me Partlow Lamb Andrews Frost is on twelve.

Well, Partlow Lamb and Andrews might be.

"I'm afraid Mr. Frost isn't in this morning," says the secretary in the outer office. She's petite and soft-spoken but her desk blocks the aisle like the concrete bunkers Rommel built at Normandy. "Did you happen to have an appointment?"

"No, I didn't."

"Because Mr. Frost is never in the office on Tuesdays."

"I see," I say, pausing. "Then why would I have an appointment?"

"Sometimes Mr. Frost gets his dates mixed up."

I bet he does.

I tell her I like her outfit, a purple miniskirt and swirling grape silk blouse that manages to be sexy while evoking childhood memories of Welch's jelly.

"Thanks," she says. "Fuchsia's one of my winter colors. Have you had your colors done?"

"Just last week. Battleship gray and off-white. Is Mr. Frost at home then?" I realize I don't know where that is. Highland Park somewhere. "Maybe I could reach him there?"

She shrugs.

"He promised me lunch," I say.

"I can validate your parking," she says. "I can't buy you lunch."

"Any way I can contact him?" I say, "Any way at all?"

"This is how it works," she says. "I can take your name. In case he calls in. Then I'd give him your name. He could call you back."

"Does he ever do that?"

"Not on Tuesdays," she says.

I thank her and leave. City hall secretaries are tough. You have to know your limits.

Activity in the lobby's picking up when I get off the elevator. The doorman's lost his chair to a kid reading *VideoGame* magazine, drinking a grape Slurpee. He's in his early twenties, with long hair tied back in a ponytail, wearing a Western jacket with fringe. The janitor's trying to mop but the kid isn't cooperating; just raising his feet a little, lazy leg lifts; that's it. The janitor rests his mop and stares at the kid. The doorman's watching him too. I'd guess he has about fifteen seconds more on that chair.

When I walk past, though, he climbs off and drops his Slurpee in the trash, then follows me outside, still carrying the magazine, which has a cartoonish pinball machine on the cover. He's about three steps behind me. It's not the best way to tail somebody but kids these days do things their own way.

I give him half a block, then stop before one of those $2.99 steak places. It smells like a cookout. A guy in a white chef's hat throws a ribeye on the grill and waves at me through the glass like a pitchman at a topless bar; another kind of meat market. The window's streaked with grease but I can still watch the crowd of white sale shoppers passing behind me. The kid stops at the very next building. Since it's a surgical supply store he's window-shopping trusses, colostomy bags, and adult diapers. I have to deduct ten points from his score.

To see how serious this is I make the chef happy and go inside. He points at the ribeye, which apparently has my name on it. But I sit at the counter and order only coffee. He plops down a cup of something black that has a hard metallic taste. I think it's been aged longer than the meat.

The kid comes right in and moves past me. I can smell cheap aftershave and damp cowhide—he's wearing leather boots and a large rodeo belt buckle. The jacket has a Midnight Cowboy look that's subtle as a sandwich board. I'm sandwiched in a bit myself— between the leather and the ribeye—both ends of the cow. He studies his menu, watching me in a security mirror. I give him points for that. The chef gives him my ribeye.

I pay for my coffee and leave quickly, reviewing what I have to offer: a little cash, no credit cards. A plastic watch. He's going to be disappointed. I'm in the alley near the Tempo, keys in my hand, when he steps toward me just a few feet away.

"I'm gonna need your wallet," he says, nervously wiping his hand across his mouth. "And your car keys. You hear? And keep your fucking mouth shut." He has a Southern accent but not from Virginia; his is more Appalachian—Uptown, Lawrence Avenue, via West Virginia. He doesn't look like a junkie.

The whole thing seems a little silly. A mugging, now? We're in broad daylight on a sidewalk crowded with city workers and shoppers. He still has the magazine and I see now he's dressed more formally than I realized, tattoos of gold chains around his neck and wrists; a surfer duck shirt under the buckskin jacket.

Silly or not, when he takes another step toward me I find myself all too happy to oblige him. Not with my wallet, though. I grab him by the arm and pull him past me—I like having the open street behind me—and then shove him up against a brick wall. He's shorter than me and I shove him harder than I need to not once but twice. It feels better than it should. His head smacks against a rusty drain pipe that rains dust the color of paprika. A part of me wants to hit him again. One or two people have stopped to watch. It beats pay-per-view wrestling.

"What do you want?" the kid says, surprised at being hit so hard, trying to twist free, as though I'm the one following him. He's frightened now, and breathing way too heavily for the little action that's gone down. His eyes are a little wild, too, which I should have noticed before now. I lose points for that. Speed freaks are the most unpredictable users. The drugs haven't helped his skin any, either—his face has acne scars and shiny red splotches like bruised strawberries. He's younger than I thought.

A crowd is gathering and I can see myself becoming the heavy in this so I let the kid go. But he has one final surprise, a move I hadn't expected. The magazine's been concealing a dirty steak knife, still covered with food and bits of meat—I step back, giving him plenty of space. Anything that can cut a $2.99 ribeye commands a certain respect. The next move's definitely his.

I can sense he wants to come straight at me. There's more anger in his eyes than the speed could call up. And it felt fine throwing him against the wall. After the past few days it's about time someone showed their face and came at me directly, even if it is the wrong someone. I take off my coat and wrap it around my left forearm, motioning him to come forward. For the second or third time lately I regret not having a gun.

But something holds him back—maybe the crowd, now growing larger. He backpedals slowly toward the sidewalk, then takes off through the crowd. In a second he's gone. One or two onlookers are knocked over for no reason, as if the kid's running up the score in a game of pinball. I help a lady up from the sidewalk. Her shopping bag has spilled enough green sheets to look like the Chicago River.

It's just as well—I was about to do something stupid. In fact I'm breathing now as heavily as he was. The knife goes with him. But he's left the magazine, complete with subscription label: South Side Associates, an address on the far South Side. I get a replay.

* * *

I've made several attempts at reaching Elenya, all unsuccessful. Either I get a machine or Giselle, who's even more curt. I try again from a pay phone in Hyde Park and get a busy signal—a good sign. I've also been trying to reach Nelson Bryars, the male nurse who posted Lucy's bail. There's been no answer at his home number but this time when I call the hospital the unit clerk on eight says he's due to work this evening.

Starbucks is just down the street on 53rd. I stop in there to ask who was working Sunday night. When I flash a Board of Health inspector's badge in the name of Dr. Marvin Winkler an assistant manager nervously produces two employees: Gayla and Brick; both in their teens. Neither of them remembers seeing Elenya or Robin. When I display photos I get blank stares.

"Were you busy then?" I say. "Too busy to remember just one or two people?"

"Not Sunday night," Gayla says.

"We were empty," Brick agrees. I'm using a photo of Robin from the front page of today's paper but since no one reads anymore it's like showing something from the Dead Sea Scrolls.

"What'd they do?" the manager whispers, pointing to the pictures. Bits of coffee are stuck between his teeth like poppy seeds.

"Don't worry," I say. "If they weren't here you're fine."

"Good, good."

"At this point, we're not even sure it's infectious."

While they grind up what's left of the Christmas blend I step outside to a pay phone and call Elenya. She picks up after one ring. "The police are here," she says, her voice flat.

* * *

Greenwood Avenue's a mess. There are half a dozen CPD squads, marked and plain, parked haphazardly on the street. The yard is full of cops. A campus cop guards the front gate, shut out, looking lonely.

"They won't let you inside?"

"I could if I wanted," he says with a shrug. Meaning he was notified as a courtesy but told to stay out of it. University business—a faculty member. Not university property.

"If they're searching the whole house it could take all day—"

"They're just doing the garage. That's all the paper's for anyway."

"What are they looking for?"

"Who the hell knows."

"How'd they get the warrant?"

Another shrug. Meaning they didn't tell him that either.

Reilly comes through the front door, followed by uniforms, Rosenberg, someone I don't know, Rosenberg's lawyer maybe. Everyone's talking at once. The wave he gives me is just enough to get me past the front gate.

"Not now, Harding," Reilly says, swinging around to the side yard, staring at the roof of the garage.

"Can I tag along?"

He shakes his head. The front door's open and Giselle's just inside, wrapped in a down coat, watching the mud everyone's tracking in. Elenya's in the next room, perched on a window seat, dressed in an over-sized sweater, tan slacks, watching Reilly and his men drag a ladder across the yard. "There's a gun," she says.

"In the coach house?"

"On the roof. At least that's what they say. I'm wondering which of our neighbors thought it would be amusing to tell them that." She turns to me, pulls the sweater back on her shoulders. "This is Reilly, the sensitive soul you wanted me to confide in? His men nearly broke the door down. They came in like stormtroopers. I mean, we have keys."

She's angry, a very good sign. Her tone reminds me of the night at Donnie's. I have nothing to report about Gaelen so I just sit beside her and watch the cops struggling with the ladder as Keegan pulls himself across the gutters, onto the roof. There's a chimney and five air ducts running from the old servants' quarters and by the time Keegan's checked the third one his sleeve is torn and covered with soot, flapping like a pirate's flag in the wind.

"They sent half the police force," Elenya says, massaging her left hand; once again the joints seem red and inflamed. "You'd think they had better things to do."

She catches my stare, and pulls her hands back into her lap.

"It's nothing," she says. "Nothing to do with anything—"

"If he's been hitting you—"

"No, no," she says quickly. She brings her hands back up, and holds them out for me. "Rheumatoid arthritis. I take prednisone and six different pills and usually it's all right. But it's gotten worse lately, I guess from the stress. Stephen hates it."

If something's not perfect . . .

"You should leave him," I say, getting up. My hand brushes her arm.

"It's not that simple. He'll be moving out soon anyway."

"When?"

"I don't know. Soon." She crosses her legs, tips one small shoe so it slides off her heel. "You don't really know him, Harding."

"Sure I do."

"He's changed, this last year. I don't know what happened. When you showed me those pictures, the Wednesday nights, I thought maybe I understood. Because it's usually Thursdays that he gets crazy. Thursday mornings. I bet his interns love him then. It's over by Friday. I stay out of his way."

Some of the patrol cars are leaving. Keegan's walking back to the ladder very carefully; I can hear the wooden supports creak and moan even here, through the window. There's so much snow and ice the uniforms have started a pool on which leg Keegan will break first.

A campus cop comes in from the kitchen, like hired help. "False alarm, Mrs. Rosenberg," he says. "They'll just have one or two questions for you, before they go. Shouldn't be much longer." She nods. I can see Keegan climbing down the ladder empty-handed. Reilly flicks his cigarette into the snow with disgust, waving the uniforms away. Rosenberg and his lawyer walk past us, barely looking up, mortician-like black coats and suits filling the window. They look like friends of Goodman Brown, heading for the forest.

"Harding," Elenya says.

"What?"

"I keep thinking of those two kids. Nora, and Robin."

"I know, so do I." Nora in particular shadows my thoughts; images of her from the motel; on the bed; on the floor. Marley's ghost, rattling a different kind of chain.

"You don't really think Stephen killed anyone. Or even had them killed. Not really."

"I think he's capable of it. Don't you?"

"No," she says, shaking her head. But she doesn't sound convinced.

I leave by the side door, following the route I took on Sunday night toward the rear of the house. The air seems raw and sharp, the afternoon sun pale, a million miles away. In a row of shaggy evergreens I find the Leica; its lens broken, film exposed. I gather up the pieces and put them in the Tempo, now jammed between two larger foreign cars; both graciously move when I slam my rented bumpers back and forth. On the way to Boone's apartment I stop at a corner newsstand off Hyde Park Boulevard. The wooden shack is crowded with stacks of late editions; skin rags clothes-pinned on a washline along the back wall. A kerosene heater supplies heat but the fumes have nowhere to go. The old man selling papers doesn't seem to notice. I lived under the El once; got used to the noise, had trouble sleeping after I moved. You can get used to almost anything.

ELEVEN

Tuesday afternoon Boone drops me off at a Toyota dealer where my truck is being patched together. We're meeting later for dinner. When I returned the Tempo clerks at the agency gathered like pallbearers in a Gorey drawing to watch me pull into the lot. They weren't happy to see the car returning. "I know how you feel," I said.

Repairing my 4Runner takes most of the afternoon, requiring serious evaluation of the Blue Island bar scene. The truck is being realigned, its frame stretched and straightened, and by five P.M. I could use some of that myself. Donnie's advance pays for a new windshield and battery and headlights. The stereo will have to wait. I stop at a record store anyway—Alison has a tape player—but the clerk tries to sell me the latest by Patty Smyth, insisting she's a Major Babe.

"Patti Smith," I say. "*Easter*. Accept no substitute." He needs a good rap across the knuckles. Driving north I reach in the glove compartment for my sunglasses and discover the mechanics' surcharge; my stash is gone. No more drugs. It's as good a day as any for a fresh start.

The Hyde Park Athletic Club is pleased to welcome me as a new member. There are forms to fill out and a fitness counselor named Elf to weigh me and measure my body fat with ice-cold calipers. Then Elf presents me to Raul, my personal trainer, who greets me with a very firm handshake. As we talk his eyes go to my stomach, my legs, my crotch. Raul may be taking this personal training thing a little too far.

"Do you have any specific fitness goals?" Raul asks me as we walk to the gym.

"Living through the week would be good," I say.

"What about problem body areas?"

"Yes."

"I mean, which ones—"

"I tend to think of my body as one large problem area, Raul. Head to toe. But I have problems with my back."

His face darkens. "Did you sign all the forms—"

"You mean the waivers, the disclaimers—don't worry, Raul, I signed everything. I won't sue. Maybe I could have a little tour?"

Raul shows me the lap pool; aerobic track; Nautilus machines; a cedarwood sauna full of steam. The air doesn't smell exactly like cedar. Old men stare at me like shades seeing Virgil. I give them a Virgil-like wave. No one waves back. No one's moving.

"Do you have free weights?" I say.

Raul says yes, taking me to a smaller room filled with wooden racks of barbells; mirrored walls; asexual grunts and groans. "Do you lift?" Raul says, looking at me doubtfully.

"I used to, at Bartlett Gym. A friend of mine said I should start up again. He comes here, maybe you know him—his name's Gaelen?"

"Oh sure," Raul says. "You're a friend of Gaelen's? He's in here all the time. In fact he was in here this morning doing some awesome reps on his del-toids. Just spectacular."

"This morning? Really?"

"Looks like he's bulking up, some kind of competi-tion maybe. He's really hitting the protein powder and B complexes lately."

"That's Gaelen," I say. "I guess he wouldn't be back today. He's probably home resting his delts. I could use a spotter."

"I'd wait until that back heals. Let me show you this lats machine we just got in—Elf really swears by it."

"He doesn't work Tuesday nights anymore, does he?"

"Who? Elf?"

"Gaelen."

"Well, you know Gaelen."

"Sure."

"A ministry like Gaelen's pretty near seven days a week."

"Ministry?"

"That's what he calls it now," Raul says. "He's a healer, Gaelen is. Hasn't he ever helped you with your back?"

"Not exactly," I say.

"You know, you look like your neck's a little stiff too."

"Just when I try to move it."

"See, you could use one of Gaelen's massages. Gaelen has magic fingers, magic hands. It's a damn shame what happened to him, with all the real criminals running around—hey, Elf, didn't you say this lats machine was awesome?"

"Absolutely," Elf says. "Your lats will pop like grapefruits."

"Is that good?" I say. Elf says it's good. We go through the locker room to the showers. I've seen showers before but Raul insists we disturb more naked men. I don't wave this time. Shower etiquette can have a sneaky subtext.

"Dual head with sixty pounds of thrust."

"You're talking about the showers," I say. Raul nods. Elf drops his towel; he's naked except for dogtags and a pair of hightop gym shoes. He wears the shoes into the shower.

"Ringworm," Raul says. "But the VA swears it's not contagious—just keep your feet moving. No more than five seconds on either foot. It actually makes showering kind of an aerobic exercise."

"Any idea when Gaelen might be in? I lost his home number—"

"Tomorrow. He does alternate sets. Wednesday is—let me think—chest and abs."

"Good—that's actually my day for abs too. Or ab, I think I have one ab here somewhere—I heard he was working out with somebody else, somebody new."

"Gaelen? Really? He's pretty much a loner. But you can't tell with old Gaelen."

"You really can't," I say. "With old Gaelen, you just can't tell."

Hyde Park Photo Supplies is busy with an afternoon rush. Felicia and I have an uneasy truce of a relationship; maybe that's why she picks my arrival as the moment to run some errands with Alison's Kharmann-Ghia. "Business is good?" I ask her as she pulls on her jacket, fluffs her hair over her collar. She dresses like Stevie Nicks—lots of frills and lace—but luckily for the business doesn't twirl around or sing like a chipmunk.

"You asked me that this morning," she says. "On the phone."

"I did? Sorry, I didn't remember. No changes since then?"

She gives me a Felicia look. "Don't burn the place down," she says.

Dave and Dave, the two part-timers who run the counter, are dealing with a steady wave of customers. I stay until Felicia returns, running the register, mischarging for everything. We have good traffic flow and I look good punching the keys but I cost the store ten or fifteen bucks easy. "Don't forget the sales tax," Dave or Dave tells me. "And don't give away so many plastic bags. You're eating up our margin."

I park my truck on Harper behind Alison's apartment and then walk across the street to the Co-op for groceries and beer. The apartment's cool, the way she likes it; the bathroom radiator turned off. I get the spare key she keeps under the sink and go back down for the mail; water the plants, take the garbage out—a downstairs neighbor, Mrs. Loomis, hears me moving around and brings up some newspapers. The kitchen's the way Alison left it Sunday afternoon; the *Trib* and *Times* stacked neatly on the table; her Braun coffeemaker clean, still smelling of vinegar. I make some coffee and then sit at the kitchen table, yawning, fighting to stay awake, with a packet Boone brought me from Donnie. The last sun of the day is making me sleepy.

At times like this Donnie's offer to join his firm almost sounds appealing. The money he gave me feels good in my pocket. My truck's fixed. And the background materials Serena assembled look interesting—the job might be too, for a week or so anyway. I wouldn't want to be Jack Hanson, the new marketing trainee, much longer than that.

The firm—Phoenix Rising, Inc.—does architectural renovation and "readaptation." It doesn't sound cutthroat but whatever the business someone's always stealing something. In this case it's a restoration process for murals and mosaics. I drink coffee and read about a railway station with WPA murals in Ohio—friezes and frescoes and tiles—and one Nicholas V. Leander, marketing VP, and his suspiciously long lunches, runny nose. They want him out but first they want to know who he's dealing with. They don't much care how I do it. So much for aesthetic distance.

I've done a dozen jobs like this for Donnie; none very dangerous; most of them legal, some not. The high point of my corporate career was the time I ran a microprocessing company for three days, while deciding which vice president was selling to the Japanese. Then as now I knew absolutely nothing about processors; micro, macro, food, whatever. But I found the bad guy and signed lots of forms and by the time I left as CEO the company's stock had climbed a half-point. Another week or two and *Forbes* would have been calling to do a profile.

I turn on Alison's Sony to catch the weather on the early news. It's snowing on the far North Side; a weatherman is doing a live remote from the Howard Street El platform. The combination of his happy-talk chatter with predictions of more snow doesn't sit well with the crowd. "It's getting ugly out here," he grins good-naturedly. "I'd better throw it back to Ron and Carol in the newsroom." A snowball packed hard with ice knocks his glasses off; a hand reaches for his black fur hat. Someone has his wallet. Ron and Carol, startled, turn to sports.

I rinse out the coffeepot and then root around for the only alcohol Alison keeps in her apartment, a bottle of 80 proof Absolute—she says it's the only thing that doesn't trigger a migraine—and sit with the bottle on a wobbly caned chair at her vanity. Her bed's made. A Man Ray monograph is turned upside down on her pillow. You can almost see the indentations of her body across the quilt. The marble top is crowded with bottles of perfume and lotion. I spray one or two in the air. None of them smells exactly like Alison.

Boone and I have dinner at a terrible Italian restaurant near South Shore Drive. He's good company because he works even longer hours for less money and has four or five different part-time jobs to complain about. For example, he spent most of today as a promotional bunny outside a furniture store, waving an oversized pink foam hand. His candy basket ran out early, the kind of thing to inspire drive-by shootings.

"Bunnies don't even have hands, do they?" I say. We're walking to my truck outside the restaurant. Both of us had too much Chianti. I brush something like cotton candy from Boone's hair. "Bunny fur. There's more in your beard and mustache."

It's a very clear night, very cold. The snow hasn't hit the South Side yet. "Remember how we laughed at Kopinski's job offer from the University of Panama?"

Boone says. "Doing black matter research in the tropics? Well, after today the Caribbean doesn't look so bad. Tenure track or not."

"Kopinski finished his dissertation," I say.

He is thinking of altering his dissertation in particle physics to a multimedia CD-ROM format. I picture an eighth-grade slide presentation featuring Mr. Molecule and Mr. Atom. I tell him about a friend of mine in English who switched his thesis on historical science fiction to an operatic production of *The Martian Chronicles* with disastrous results.

We drive across Hyde Park to 59th Street and try parking by International House but can't find a place. I end up back in the hospital garage. We hike the six blocks back. A Camry with a faculty sticker is backing into a campus bus stop, guided by two campus cops with orange flashlights and time on their hands. "They should just provide valet parking," Boone says. I'd planned on trying to find Esther at the front desk but the lobby's nearly deserted. The sidewalks and Midway are full of students walking toward Rockefeller Chapel.

"I can't stay long, Harding," Boone says to me. "If I don't get the bunny suit back by ten I lose the deposit."

"What's going on?" I ask a security guard outside I-House.

"Bulls by fifteen, last I heard," he says.

"No, this."

"Memorial service," he says. "For them two students."

"When, now?"

He nods.

"I didn't see anything in the paper."

"It's not official," he says. "This is just kids."

"The university won't be thrilled if the press gets wind of this," Boone says. We head west past the Lab School and Ida Noyes Hall. "They're in the middle of a special campaign to increase the endowment. The boys in fund-raising will have a coronary."

Rockefeller Chapel is more a cathedral than a chapel. Built to impress with oil money, it reminds you how Baroque drifted to Mannerism—every nook is filled with sculpture, inscriptions, carving, stained glass. On the east door that Boone and I go through are representations of Dante and Milton with the words "Blessed are the Pure in Heart." Processions of students pour in from every direction. Rockefeller isn't Canterbury but it might be tonight.

Boone sees friends of his near the front. I want to sit upstairs. A small loft like an opera box overhangs the center aisle. The pews are empty except for black hymnals and the smell of Lemon Pledge. Some music starts—power folk from WHPK. Bob Mould's on Hoover Dam, Richard Thompson's on the Wall of Death—I'm on a bit of a precipice here myself.

The speakers begin tentatively. The memorial was organized by the Women's Center and the student government and the first few speeches are more like announcements than eulogies. Then things become more focused. Someone puts up large grainy photographs of Nora and Robin. The pictures came from their college applications. They're high school yearbook pictures, making each student look impossibly young.

Roommates describe their pasts, their accomplishments. Robin was prelaw; Nora was headed for medical school. We hear the names of their sisters, brothers, parents but there are no family members here, of course. We're not their family; we barely know them, really. And both bodies are already on their way home to Yellow Springs, Ohio, to Timber Ridge, Minnesota. All we have are the pictures, which I study, looking for the Nora and Robin I met last week, trying to imagine them in a dorm late at night, discovering their lowest common denominator—Rosenberg—and plotting an extortion scheme worth a million dollars. It's good I'm in a church. The scenario requires a giant leap of faith.

By eleven o'clock there are several hundred people here and most of the nave is full. It would be easy tonight to get a good seat at the library. Amateur musicians overflow the choir lofts—guitars, violins, flutes, drums. Candles are passed out from Hyde Park Hardware bags. Instead of bread and wine the credence has bowls of punch and tofu dogs. People who knew Robin and Nora go to the microphone and offer remembrances. Some are sad, but most are funny. The air smells like grass. The punch is spiked. It begins to seem less like a votive mass, more like a Friars roast.

The music begins morbidly too, but gradually changes. Vaughan Williams's *Lark Ascending* is just too sad. The chamber group shifts to folk music and Morris dancing, then hip-hop and grunge. The front rows become a moshing pit. The last speaker—a woman from the Gay Rights Center—dives across the crowd like a seagull barely touching the water.

I'm in the balcony taking all this in when I see a familiar face in one of the side aisles. Lucy Williams is standing behind a group of students. She's alone, just watching, nodding to the music, still wearing her coat and hat. I think she's crying. Then someone's beside her with a hand on her shoulder; whispering in her ear—I'm confused for a minute, until I picture him the way he was on the train platform, saving my neck. Tonight he's not wearing the mirrored shades or the same jacket. Both hands are on Lucy's shoulders, as if rubbing her neck, though it doesn't seem to be relaxing her. Her purse is in her arms. She's holding it like a life-preserver.

I wish Alison was here—there's an earring code that I can never remember. There's one for handker-chiefs too, like the red one he's pulled out to wipe away Lucy's tears. His hands are huge. I think there's a code for that too. The crowd isn't just students—with staff, faculty, neighbors interspersed it could be a Saturday crowd at the Co-op grocery store—but this guy still looks out of place. He's sure not a cop. I look for Boone to tell him I'm leaving but I don't see him, and when I look again for Lucy she's gone. So is the guy.

I push through the crowd, go quickly downstairs and then out the front door. Lucy's headed west. When I call her name she stops, turns halfway, looks at me curiously. We've never really met, never spoken, but she knows who I am. She ignores me and keeps on walking. I'm a little out of breath when I catch up with her near Kimbark. It adds to the drama.

"Get away from me," she says.

"I just want to talk." We're near a streetlight. Snow is beginning to fall, dots of dust blown upward by the wind. She zips up her coat. "You asked me about the camera, Lucy, remember? Sunday night? How did you know I was outside each week?"

"You'd better go." She starts walking again. She looks a little strung-out. But she's not sick, in full with-drawal. She's running on nervous energy. I'm having trouble keeping up with her.

Finally I grab her arm.

"Let me go," she says, struggling. But when I remove my hand she doesn't leave. Instead she steps off the sidewalk, lights a cigarette near a huge elm tree. She keeps her back to the tree.

"Who are you working for?" she says. "Elenya?"

"Not exactly. I just want to know what happened Sunday night."

"Join the club."

"Didn't you see anything?"

"I've told the police what I'll tell you. Because it's the truth. I was on my way to see Nora, to talk to her, to find out what in the hell was going on. Someone grabbed me. He put something over my face. That's it. I don't remember anything until you came in. I barely remember that."

"Talk to her about what?"

"The tape I found in her purse Wednesday. Stephen has to be hit over the head with these things. 'She's so young,' he says. 'So innocent.' He thinks he's the master, she's the slave and it's the other way around—"

"Is that the kind of relationship you two have?"

She says nothing. We're walking again.

"I was wondering what made you switch specialties. You started out in Surgical OR, even worked in Stephen's unit—what made you change?"

"I got tired of the blood."

"Did you know Elenya then?" I ask a half dozen more questions. She won't answer any of them.

I grab her sleeve to slow her down.

"Let go," she says. "I'll scream. I mean it."

"Not yet."

"—I'm meeting somebody, damnit. I can't be late."

"Who? Stephen?"

"Let me go!"

"Who was that man inside tonight, Lucy?"

"No one," she says, tossing her cigarette away. But her other hand touches her throat.

"What's his name—?"

"Leave me alone," she says, loud enough that people stop and watch us. She wrenches her arm away and stumbles a few feet, her steps turning into a half-trot, then a run. I follow her, just close enough to see her turn north on Ellis, the same path Alison followed the other night.

The front doors of the hospital are locked this time of night. A security guard in the ER looks at me briefly, nods. I smile. The elevator door to the patient floors is just closing. I don't have any way of telling where Lucy's gone. But I can take a guess.

She usually works on eight. It's a locked psych ward but security isn't real tight. When I get off the elevator a male PA greets me and starts to ask me for my pass. I must look like a patient.

"Excuse me please, I'm Dr. Winkler," I say, moving past him. Physician assistants are trained to salivate at commands like that. "I'm looking for a nurse named Lucy Williams. Did she come up here?"

"Dr. Winkler?" he says, not wanting to offend. "I don't think she's supposed to—was that her? With the other doctor, going toward the rec room? I don't think we've met—my name's Bob—"

"Thanks, Bob. You're doing great work with the elevator." The floor's very quiet—every door wide open, every bed filled. It's unusually still for a psych floor. Maybe this is the day everyone gets those steel needles shoved through their prefrontal lobes.

The rec room isn't locked. There's a small window with a grid of wire mesh in the door. The exercise equipment looks secondhand; as battered as the patients who use it. The light's very bright. I can see Lucy pacing, smoking. It's probably the only place in the hospital you can smoke. Her hair is dirty blonde, pulled back as if she's working. A few strands escape, brush her cheek. Her eyes are narrow slits with too much mascara. When she hears me outside the door she rushes to the window, pressing her face to the glass like a child stuck inside on a rainy day.

"Not again," she says, not looking at me, trying to see out into the hall. Her movements are jittery, as if she doesn't have much time. In the harsh neon her features nearly disappear. Only her shaky hands seem alive. "What are you trying to do to me—?"

"Who's the doctor with you?" I say. "Rosenberg?"

"Get out," she says. "Please. Why are you here?"

"Why are *you* here, Lucy?"

"I work here," she says. And in fact, with her coat off she's dressed for work in the jeans and sweater that everyone wears on this floor as though that could make the patients relax. She even has her work ID clipped to her belt. The sweater's too tight across the breasts that contrast strangely with the rest of her nearly anorexic body. When she pushes her sweater up on her forearms—she's sweating as though we're in a sauna—I can see the hesitation marks etched on both her wrists.

"Not tonight," I say.

"I do, I do."

I'm blocking her way but she can see the tiny window in the door, the size of a sliding panel in a confessional. Behind her on the wall is a collage the patients must have made—pictures from day trips; photographs, crayon drawings; postcards—one from Disneyland; one from Sea World, a photo of a dolphin jumping high above the water—some trick to please the tourists—freezing him forever in midair, free of his watery cage.

I've never been up here before but psych floors, like psych patients, look the same wherever you go. The Clorox they throw on everything nearly works, nearly kills the stench of coffee and cigarettes, ruined lives, burnt synapses.

Lucy is a step closer to something. Her anxiety's growing.

"You're not allowed up here," Lucy says, "you have to go and I don't know what you're trying to do—"

"I'm trying to help."

"Then get out, right now, please, because you're absolutely—"

"I know it wasn't you, Lucy. You're a nurse, you couldn't kill her like that, with that much pain, torturing her—"

"—going to ruin *everything*—"

"Just a name, Lucy. Who was there? Who did you see—"

"No one!"

"Who was with you? Was it that man in the chapel—was that who killed Nora? Or the male nurse that bailed you out? Nelson?"

"Nelson! What—"

"If you're protecting Stephen for some reason—"

"You want me to say he's a murderer? Fine, he's a murderer. Will you leave now?"

Someone turns the doorknob behind me. There's a split-second hesitation before the knob snaps back, like the spring of a mousetrap.

"Oh no, Christ, wait," Lucy cries, bolting forward, and when I turn to see who's behind me Lucy comes at me with both fists. She hits me hard in the face with a strung-out fury. The attack surprises me enough that I take a step back and just like that she's out the door. This time it closes with a loud click.

I pound the tiny window, I pound the door; I pound the punching bag, which drops in my hands—on a locked ward everything—shower curtain rods, faucets, ceiling lights—has to break away like that. So you can't attach a rope. Doors open outward, so you can't barricade yourself in.

No one hears me for a couple of minutes.

Finally a nurse opens the door and looks at me curiously. Her eyes go to my wrist, looking for a patient's blue ID bracelet.

"Lucy?" she says. "You're not Lucy."

"No," I say but she doesn't hear my answer— neither do I. My words are swallowed up by a loud pulsing buzzer like a truck in reverse.

"Shit," the nurse says, pivoting like a point guard in her white sneakers. I barely catch the door before it closes behind her.

"What happened?" someone yells.

"The schizo in 8C—"

"Oh no—"

I'm in the hallway when I hear the glass shattering.

Three or four nurses run frantically past me, barking orders and directions—the nurse's station is a blur of flashing lights—even the intercom is calling for different doctors to come at once to eight—and then a nurse wanders out of 8C shaking her head, confused, her hands in her pockets, startled at the rush of people. She flattens herself against the wall to let us past.

The room's empty.

I duck into the bathrooms but they're both empty. So is the TV room.

At the far end of the hallway a fire door stands open, its metal security bar pushed in; a broken seal triggering yet another alarm. The male nurse I saw with Lucy steps from behind the door holding a candy bar and says simply, "I don't believe it. He jumped. He really jumped." He's dropping crumbs from the candy bar over his name tag—Nelson Bryars—and two lapel pins—a red ribbon and an American flag. What you might see at the VFW in San Francisco.

"Jumped? How?"

"Didn't the alarm go off in time?" someone says.

"He was just *gone*—I'm running down to ER," Bryars says. "Maybe—"

"Right! Eight fucking floors!"

They're like a mob pushing the fire door wide open, crowding around the shattered window. I lose my footing for a second and fall back against the wall. When I get back up I've lost sight of Bryars.

"It's supposed to give us time to get here *shit shit shit* how did he do it that fast—"

"Call downstairs," someone says. *"Now."*

"Where's ER?—somebody get *out* there—"

"He might still be alive for God's sake—"

"Where *are* they. Christ, what are they *doing* down there—?"

"Oh God."

"That door was *locked*—"

"Do you believe this?"

"I just *saw* him—"

"Me too—"

"I just *talked* to him—"

I'm standing behind the others. The narrow dark stairwell is like a tiny chapel, with a window ledge for an altar, and a stained-glass picture of terrible devotion framed above it.

Whatever was heaved first through the window—there's the outline of a missing fire extinguisher on the wall like a chalkmark of a body—it made a hole too small for a body. A carpenter's starting hole. The schizo from 8C must have cut himself terribly on the metal and glass, standing on the chair, crashing through the window, expanding the opening with just the force of his head and shoulders. It would have taken an awesome determination to do this.

There's glass on the floor—there's glass everywhere, crunching like ice—but the worst sight is the glass still left in the window's wire mesh—jagged edges flagged with torn bits of clothing, skin, blood.

As the nurses and staff crowd through the door I think I hear footsteps. A door slamming over my head in the stairwell. I take the steps quickly one floor up but the door's locked. There's only one more floor before the roof. All the exits are sealed.

We're fighting for the best position to view the poor schizo from 8C. A crowd eight floors below is doing much the same in the glow of the streetlights as doctors and ambulances finally arrive—when I turn and hear a quiet sobbing from a corner of the stairwell, half a flight down, where a figure is huddled, bare arms wrapped around a bare flabby stomach, a white hospital gown pulled over his head for protection. So he can't see.

When I touch his shoulder his sweaty hands unfold like a flower, trembling fingers clasped around a small bronze key. He offers it to me, and I palm it before anyone can notice.

Not that they're interested.

"Lucy," someone says, looking down.

"Oh God, Luce."

I check my watch: Midnight. So it's Wednesday.

The male nurse is nowhere to be seen.

"She's been exhausted."

"Working doubles all month—"

"She needed a rest—"

"She's off now," a voice says. "God, is she off."

They find the nursing chart for 8C beneath the chair, covered with drops of blood like sweat from a marathon runner. The notes for tonight's shift—neuro status, verbal response, restraints, mood/affect—are routine. But the last page is separate; the response typed. The name is signed in deep blue ink.

Psychiatric Observation:

> *I guess this is a confession.*
> *They were blackmailing Stephen. We had to do something. I know it doesn't make sense. I don't know why these things happen. They just do.*
> *We killed Nora Saturday night. On Sunday we dumped the body. We wanted you to think she did it. Then he'd be mine. And he'd be free.*
> *It's not really Nelson's fault, he was just trying to help me. Robin got caught in the middle . . .*
> *I'm very very tired. But it's over now.*
> *Stephen, I'm sorry.*

I love you forever.
Lucy

**If no further notation appears no unusual obser-
vations were made and no unusual activities or
incidents occurred.**

"That's that," someone says.

TWELVE

Geizel's Locksmith belongs to a guy I met on another case. His name's Eddie French. I don't know who Geizel was. I don't think Eddie knows either. But the sign's a fixture on Vincennes Avenue, so the name stays. I'm Geizel's first customer Wednesday morning.

"This is not easy," Eddie says, holding my key like a delicate piece of china. "This is not an easy thing." He leads me back through his workshop. It's jammed with pegboards holding nothing but keys, key masters, *Gallery* and *Hustler* centerfolds.

"You ever notice," Eddie says, digging through piles of blanks, "how a key looks like a woman's pussy?"

"Not really, Eddie. I think you've been staring at keys too long."

"Or pussy," Eddie says. "How's your friend Alison these days?"

"Nice segue, Eddie. You know Alison?"

"Naw. Saw her once in a Tough Woman bout over at the Y. She kicked the living daylights out of some Asian broad. Kicked her right off the canvas. Reminded me of Flying Fred Curry in the old days."

"That's Alison," I say.

"Hell of a woman," Eddie says. "How much does she bench-press you think?"

"I'm not sure—Eddie, I'm in kind of a hurry here."

"You said you found this where?" he says, pulling down dusty binders the size of phone books.

"A hospital. But I tried it on the only door that I thought it might fit." That was the fire door; I wanted to make sure the key was more than Lucy's way out of the hall. I didn't have time for much more. The cops were there very fast. Hurry up and wait. We finished at three-thirty A.M. Reilly drove me back to Hyde Park himself. "Cause of death shouldn't be hard to figure out," Reilly said. "Hit once by a blunt object. A fucking sidewalk." Lake Shore Drive was dark and silent. Reilly was in no hurry. He drove his Plymouth like a hearse. My truck had level C all to itself. I caught an hour's sleep in the back seat, a twenty-two-dollar parking charge when I left the garage.

Eddie turns up the radio, holds the key to the light. Kate Bush is cloudbusting, daddy; the only treatise on Reichian therapy I know of to be released as a twelve-inch dance EP. "This isn't a door key, Harding. Even you should have guessed that."

"It could be a key to a case or a cabinet, though, couldn't it?"

"Yes," he says. "I suppose. What did you do, steal the narcotics key off some poor student nurse?"

"Not exactly."

"No, of course you didn't," Eddie says. "Did you try this person's locker?"

I shake my head. The police got there first.

"Because that's the kind of key it is, Harding. Just a simple lock, too, the kind students put on lockers or bicycles. Pretty hard to trace. It's too common."

"So it's impossible? A dead end?"

"Did I say that?" Eddie says smiling. "Look, run

next door to the restaurant and get me some jasmine tea, will you? Here, you need exact change—the woman hates when you give her bills." He gives me a handful of quarters.

"I'll pay for the tea, Eddie," I say.

"No, you'll pay for the key and the labor finding the damned thing. I'll pay for the tea."

The Maywood Rental Storage Co. is located on a side street near the westbound Eisenhower. It shows up in the news as a favorite dumping ground for mob hits. I guess its location is convenient, halfway between the First Ward and Cicero.

I pull into its parking lot in early afternoon. I've been all over the city. It took Eddie a full pot of jasmine tea to find the key's manufacturer, a maker of garage door locks. "But industrial, not builders, not retail. Public storage, and different ones buy their doors different places. So we can narrow it down if you don't care making some calls."

Of course, given the logic of this case, I should have known it would be here, in Maywood. Of all the addresses Eddie came up with it's the closest to Hyde Park.

Todd the day manager is throwing salt on the driveway; he's listening to Van Halen on a Walkman, loud enough to drift across the parking lot. I show him my key and he nods, waving me through. I could have shown him my house key.

There are four rows of orange bays, like trees in a fruit orchard. A picture of a rabid dog says everything's protected by Sparky's Security. Sparky doesn't inspire confidence; he looks more like Cujo than McGruff the

Crime Dog. I park the truck around back and busy myself in the 4Runner until Todd runs out of salt to manage. When he goes inside I try my key on each lock.

It takes five or ten minutes. The numbering system doesn't make much sense; maybe that's part of Sparky's master plan. Finally an end unit, #1204 pops open.

Inside the small room I find boxes of thrift-store clothes; a cheap end table; the fake-brass headboard to a missing bed—enough clutter to discourage a casual intruder. It looks like leftovers from the previous tenant, like the floss and Mr. Tooth poster I inherited at my place. In the rear, behind a pine chest shaped like a pauper's coffin, are two cardboard grocery boxes.

The first carton holds seven or eight BASF reel-to-reel tapes. The tapes are in numbered cartons but I don't see any table of contents or the notebooks which must contain the logs. The boxes are new but the ends of the tapes are wrinkled and old-looking.

There are at least fifty TDK cassettes stacked in the second box.

These are identified better, with the type of initials that were on the tape found in Alison's pocket. They're stacked tightly, with double rubber bands around them in groups of five. I flip through them looking for familiar names and dates but nothing jumps out at me. The cold's beginning to seep through my jacket. I take two tapes—"Demo One"—the only one packed by itself; another one from further down in the box.

I pull the orange garage door down, and relock it, then lock the key in the glove compartment.

There's a tape player at Alison's but I don't feel like waiting. I go in the manager's office and ask Todd if I can borrow his Walkman for five minutes. He agrees but plants himself by the door so I can't run off with it. I don't turn it up very loud but the kid must hear it; he can't stop smiling.

The voice on "Demo One" is Rosenberg's again but this time he has a different partner. The tape itself isn't labeled but the index says "Manning $1/4$" printed in blurred red ink.

I fast-forward through the sex—Todd isn't happy with this—to a spot that sounds postcoital. Not through any sounds of tenderness but rather the murmured words of a doctor's devotion:

> "—twelve thousand five hundred minus three hundred. That's where we stand. Make sure you file the insurance forms yourself not through Sandra—follow-ups twice a week through, let's see, June 18, you'll be all set for summer—"
>
> "—does the numbness disappear?"
>
> "—the numbness disappears, always. Forget about the numbness. Do you have the check?"

I return the Walkman to Todd. He's got a tiny copper earring in one ear. I must be the only one on the planet without holes drilled in my body.

"You want a free calendar?" he says, giving me one before I can say no. Each page is a beautiful glossy picture of Maywood Storage from a slightly different angle or season, with typical customers in each shot—women in bikinis. July is a group shot; twelve bays filled with twelve different women smiling at the camera. I feel as if I have to feed another five bucks in the meter or the garage doors will come slamming down.

"Very classy," I tell him. I write the door number on the last page, near the flat stomach of Miss December.

"I'm in there too."

"In a bikini?"

"December," he says, flipping the pages. "That's me in the Santa suit." The boxes in the bay are wrapped in foil. Santa's helpers are sitting on his lap, wearing string bikinis.

"Good gig," I say.

I stop at a gas station with more space devoted to groceries and lottery machines than wiper blades or 10-40. The pay phone's by the refrigerator cases. A sign says they've overstocked on goat cheese. Their loss is my gain. A childish drawing of a stick-figure goat is taped to the glass. "Baaa. Buy my cheese," it says. Boone isn't much more civilized.

"Video Savages," Boone says answering the phone with a breathy voice. It makes him sound like he's got a cold. "What can I do you for?"

"Jesus, Boone. What year is this?"

"Harding? Is that you?"

"What have they got you doing, Boone, hosing off the walls?"

"New job, Harding. How'd you find me?"

"I was referred from the lab to the blood bank to the used-record store to here. Luckily I had enough quarters. Boone—have the police talked to you?"

"No," he says. "Why should they? Everything here's legal. I think."

Good old Boone. "What about Donnie? Have you seen him today?"

"Not yet. I'm due out there later. Listen, Harding, you should see this place. It's a sleaze superstore. Something for everyone."

"I've seen porno video stores before, Boone. What's all the noise? Are you in the back room with the Plexiglas booths and princess phones?"

"Outdated concept, Harding. Think multimedia. CD-ROMS; digital home theater—Tori Welles comes like an earthquake; six on the Richter. You better have reinforced concrete, steel I-beam construction."

"I like Ashlyn Gere."

"Oh we got her too—backwards, forwards. You name it."

"No men in raincoats? None of that heavy-grade Kleenex—"

"Well, yeah, that hasn't changed. With regular they're always repainting. Look, I can't take personal calls. They'll dock me."

"I've got another job for you. More tape; a lot of reel-to-reel. They'll be lots of different voices; one male, lots of females. You'll have to sort them out, give them names."

"Sounds like an animal research study. Miss Jane Goodall."

"You're not far off. But it should be perfect for a Video Savage like you. And don't tell anybody about it, okay?"

"You'll pay?"

"I'll pay."

"Last time, when you left me in that skiff in Belmont Harbor with my camera and a six pack of Stroh's—I sat out there for two fucking days waiting for some woman to take her top off and blow the guy on the deck instead of inside the cabin—"

"You got the shots. Everyone except the dentist and his gum specialist went home happy."

"Correction. I went home sunburned to an inch of

my life. For eighty bucks a day plus expenses. While you and Donnie Wilson probably blackmailed the guy for thousands. And remember that wife-beating Back of the Yards? I did all the photo work when Alison and you weren't getting along so well—"

"This case isn't like that."

"Meaning what?"

"Meaning it's not a common-law wife stabbing her husband with a dirty kitchen knife. Polaroids through the screen door."

"What was that guy's name? Grocer?"

"Grossman."

"Yeah it's the lemon merengue still on the blade I was thinking of—the DA should have gone for murder two, the guy could've died from food poisoning. I wired that kitchen for you, remember?"

"Sure."

"For fifty bucks and your Olivetti," he says. "Something tells me if plastic surgeons are involved this case is on a grander scale."

"Not really," I say. "I'm still using you, aren't I?"

I have another terrible dinner Wednesday—this one with Alison. Hospital food makes the airlines' seem four-star. It's a motivational problem. Both know a certain percentage are dying anyway; why bother?

The police are here when I arrive. Reilly is talking to Alison. Keegan seems more concerned about a late bulletin, a shooting at the White Castle on 79th. "I eat there every night," he tells me. He's wearing the same clothes he wore last Sunday. "If they closed the place down just for this I'll be very upset."

"A few bodies in the drive-through wouldn't bother you?" I say.

"Harding, the first call I ever had was a shooter that ate his own Smith and Wesson—"

"Here we go," Reilly says.

"My partner barfed the minute we walked in the kitchen and found the poor bastard—which was three days later, by the way; mid–July. And you know what I did? Finished the investigation, wrote up my report, then went straight to Bratislava and ate prazsky and rye bread and drank dark beer all night and you know what? It tasted great."

"Thus was the legend born," Reilly says.

We talk in the hall. Nuns walk past. It's not a Catholic hospital but there's no shortage of nuns.

"Why are you talking to Alison?"

"Routine," he says. "Unsolved homicides, the captain likes it if we ask a few questions. Funny, huh."

"Did Bryars turn up yet?"

"The male nurse? Nah, not yet. But we're sitting on his friends. And he's got family, here and Racine both. He'll turn up. He's too big to hide."

"What did you find in his apartment?"

"Enough," Reilly says. "Letters from Lucy. A typewriter matching the note and the birthday card both. Odds and ends. Syringes from the eighth floor, filled with phenol."

"But no gun."

He shakes his head. Keegan steps outside Alison's room.

"That was some performance on Rosenberg's roof," I say to him. "You must have really thought you had something to go up there yourself."

"I needed the exercise," Keegan says.

"Bryars made that call," Reilly says. "We pulled his phone records this afternoon. The details he gave us about Nora's body got us the warrant. He knew stuff that wasn't in the papers."

"Nelson's a bear losing his twinkie," Keegan says. "Lucy's a whore losing her main trick. It's a sad story, Harding. A real heartbreaker."

"What did you find in the motel?"

"Too much," Reilly says.

"Can I see the ME's report?"

"You know you can't."

"What did the schizo in 8C say?"

"That Lucy's an angel and she went to heaven. Come on Harding, don't spoil my mood. It's a beautiful night and I've got a confession. Nothing cheers me up like a good confession."

"A *typed* confession."

"With a signature. Devotions come to us in many forms," Reilly says. "We accept them all."

"Reilly, you should have been a priest."

"My mother would've been a lot happier," he says, agreeing.

A nun walks past, white Keds squeaking on the linoleum, her gold cross swinging like a referee's whistle. She smiles at Reilly.

"Go in peace," she says.

"Amen to that, Sister," Reilly says.

"I can't *believe* they're just closing this case," Alison says to me after they've gone. *"Fuck!"*

Her throat's much better.

She's even eating Cracker Jacks. She distributes

some in my cupped hands, some in hers; the communal wafer. I get the prize; a small tin angel. I think it's meant to be a Christmas ornament, which probably means the Cracker Jacks have been sitting since September.

Alison's wearing sweat pants and one of my blue work shirts. She pulls the faded blue cotton up to show me her bandages.

"You're saying a male nurse hurt me like this?" she says.

"I'm not, no."

"You saw him once, right? Was he big?"

"He was large," I say. "They found a lot of stuff, Alison, both in his place and Lucy's."

"A male nurse—"

"Look, a lot of them are army medics." I turn on the television. "Trained killers for the state. You've got nothing to apologize for."

I move the chair closer to her bed. We're drinking coffee from plastic cups and eating Cracker Jacks.

"Tell me something, Alison. You're around the campus a lot. Are there many like Rosenberg? With young kids I mean?"

"They're not kids, Harding," she says.

"You know what I mean."

"Robin and Nora? They were both twenty-one."

"And Stephen Rosenberg's forty-seven."

"So? You were thirty-four when we met. I was twenty."

"I was thirty-three, and that's different."

"You know how it was different? In that relationship *I* was the teacher, *you* were the student."

"You're lucky you're in a hospital," I say. "I'm compelled by the Geneva Convention not to retaliate."

"Oh, retaliate, Harding," she says. She gives me the last of the Cracker Jacks. "Did I tell you my dad called today?"

"How's Stan doing?"

"Stan seems happy. As happy as you can be in Fort Lauderdale."

She tells me about the Alinsky–styled tenants association he's formed in the Seniors Village; the miniature golf tournament he's won; the fruit he sends her each month UPS, as though you can't get grapefruit in Chicago. "I don't even like grapefruit," she says. "But he's sweet to send it." Alison has an easy relationship with her father, something I envy. She was the same way with her mother. When Sylvia died four years ago I went along to the funeral with Alison, coming out of retirement—we'd broken up months before. But funerals are rough when you're alone.

Not that I've been to many others. I was out of town on business when my own father died. I didn't come back. And I was in solitary when my mother died. No one told me for a week or so; a guard scribbled a note on toilet paper and included it with my dinner tray. Hallmark doesn't make a card for such occasions.

Alison is so bored tonight she's reading the packet of materials for my next job, studying quarterly reports and personnel profiles of Nicholas V. Leander; drawing a goatee and horns on his company portrait.

I put our trays out in the hall as if room service will pick them up, then get my shearling coat.

"You're leaving?" she says.

"I can stop back," I say. "I just need to check something out."

"Can't it wait until morning?"

"In the morning you're getting out of here, I'm

going back to the North Side. This is something down on 92nd. Won't take me more than an hour."

"Can you check my apartment again?"

"Sure."

"Bring me a frozen yogurt. Strawberry. And buy something for yourself so you don't steal mine. And don't be gone too long, Harding—the late movie is *Fists of Fury*. Chop-socky heaven."

I pick up a loose tail leaving Alison's apartment; not a car I've seen before, a tan Ford. It could be one of Reilly's but when I run a couple red lights he runs them too, which makes me nervous. It takes me ten minutes or so to lose him in South Shore, doubling back through Jackson Park. I never do see who's behind the wheel.

The address on the *VideoGame* magazine is ten minutes away, near where Pulaski turns into South Crawford. It turns out to be an Indian restaurant: Tandoori Grill. The red Grand Am is parked around back.

Inside there's a four-table restaurant with saris and Indian videos for sale; curling posters of Indian movie stars plastered on the walls. You can smell spices and curries and meat cooking in Tandoori ovens out on the sidewalk.

I ask the woman at the front counter if I have the right address.

"For Dr. Sawyer?" she says. I nod, paying for a cold Taj Mahal and something called a masala dosa, kind of an Indian crepe. It's delicious, I tell her, and she beams. "One more?" she says before I'm half done with this one; already returning from the kitchen with another.

"One more," I agree. I should have eaten dinner here instead of the hospital. "Is Dr.—"

"Sawyer," she says nodding, helping me. DC: doctor of chiropractic.

"Is Dr. Sawyer home now, do you know?"

"I don't think so," she says.

"But Dr. Sawyer lives here?"

"Yes," she says. "Upstairs."

"What about Dr. Swann?"

"Swann? I don't know him. You need treatment?"

"My back," I say, reaching behind me like an idiot or a method actor to show her; the motion sends a stab of pain through my spinal column. "Only I thought I saw his car in your driveway. The red Pontiac. So I thought he might be here. Perhaps he came home early?"

"I don't know," she says uncertainly, looking up as if for a sign; either from Shiva or Dr. Sawyer. "It may be houseguest. Dr. Sawyer drives other car. BMW." She turns down the sitar and table music and we both stand listening, heads tilted like songbirds. The sole customer in her dining room, an old Indian gentleman in a clean white shirt, puts down his can of Diet Coke and tilts his head too, listens with us.

"I hear something, I think," he says finally. The woman nods uncertainly.

"It sounds like a woman," I say.

"Television," she says firmly. "No woman."

"Is there a doorbell somewhere?" I say. "A separate entrance?"

"Around the side. One more masala dosa to go?"

"I can't. I'll spoil my breakfast."

"One more beer?"

"No, this is fine." I pay her and go back outside. There's just one floor above the restaurant. Tar paper covers the roof. The blinds are down on the front windows but I think I see a TV show's reflection in the glass on the other side. I ring the bell once, twice, hear nothing; try the door. It's locked.

The Grand Am's locked too, and sitting too near the street for me to try anything fancy. Or clumsy—I usually have better luck getting into cars with a brick than a slim-jim anyway.

The car's not new but must have just been washed and waxed; salt and weather stains removed from the tires and underside; the inside wiped down with Armor All. Even the ashtray's been scrubbed clean, though the sodium streetlamps give everything a yellow tint. A silver cross hangs from the rearview mirror in place of oversized dice. The engine's hot.

There's nothing on the bucket seats or dash except a radar detector and a CB radio. On the shelf above the back seat there's an odd selection of books; a Good News Bible, Plato's *Republic*, and a large paperback familiar to me from high school—Henry Miller's *Rosy Crucifixion*. I'm peering in the passenger window when a lunar eclipse covers the car in shadows. The eclipse taps me hard on the shoulder.

"Help you with something?" he says.

It's the guy I first thought was a cop; the one Lucy was talking to in Rockefeller Chapel. Up close he has a thin scar near his mouth that lengthens when he smiles. He's wearing narrow blue shades and a heavy black iron cross dangling over a bulky army jacket and he has my undivided attention.

"You must have been waiting for me," I say, wondering if he's annoyed at my slowness or amused at my stupidity. I walked right into this, but slowly. "I should have brought you a ribeye."

"Let's get in the car," he says, one heavy hand on

my arm. His hair is dark and smooth. He's chewing gum that smells like licorice. "We can talk better there."

"We'll discuss Henry Miller?"

"Why not," he says with a crooked grin. The scar extends about as far as it can go. His tongue is pierced too. "Though why I'd want to talk to a piece of shit like you, I'm not sure."

"That makes two of us," I say. "We have a lot in common already." I don't usually hit first but something tells me this is a good time to bend the rules. I'm sure not getting in the car with him.

I catch him across the mouth with the back of my hand. His head snaps back but his expression barely changes; his body barely moves.

I sense I have a long night ahead of me.

He pulls me roughly by the arm. I struggle free but there's nowhere to go. He grabs me by the jacket and swings me around, slamming me against the car. The side mirror jams in my kidney like a steel fist, doubling me over in pain. I'm not in shape for this.

I'm bent over, trying to catch my breath, when I see him raising both arms high over his head, hands locked together like an oil derrick—I don't have a gun and I can't see this headed anywhere good, so before he can bring his hands down on my back I reach out and grab his ankles, yanking his legs out from under him.

It's not a move most guys expect and it works well enough here; his arms are back far enough to leave him slightly off balance, his weight tilting back; he goes down like a Sequoia in a cloud of dust, giving me enough time to get to my truck. I assume he'll get the Grand Am and come after me but he just stands there in the street brushing himself off, a crazy grin on his face.

Any impartial judge would score it a draw. I'd lose points for unsportsmanlike conduct but earn a grudging respect for fighting above my weight class.

Unfortunately, my truck doesn't start. So I lose by TKO. Something tells me the official knockout is forthcoming.

"It works better with one of these," says the ribeye kid from the shadows, wires and a distributor cap swinging from his fist like ganglia, "don't it, Gaelen." The name lingers like a church bell in the cold night air. Under his other arm there's a deer rifle; a Mossberg pump, maybe 12-gauge. It could drop a rhino. He's also got a nickle Beretta tucked in his jeans. I'm flattered to have drawn this much firepower. I'm surprised they don't have mortars and antitank guns set up behind the chutney display.

The passenger door is unlocked but even as I'm reaching across to secure it an arm crashes through my window and grabs me by the throat, strong fingers like thick vines climb around my neck, dragging me out through the broken glass, onto the street. I'm not cut but Gaelen's face above me holding my head like a punching bag in his hands is the last thing I remember.

I'm semiconscious on the drive, tied with my hands and feet behind me, locked in the trunk. Gaelen pops it open. A heavy metal door is pulled shut. We're in an empty warehouse. It smells like animals, an old barn. It's a familiar smell. There are just the three of us here. I'm hauled out like a sack of grain and dropped on the concrete.

I'm hoping they don't know about my back.

"You're very tense," Gaelen says, feeling the

glands in my neck. His hands are cold, his breath smells like garlic. "Just like your little girlfriend."

I react to that but I don't get very far.

Surrender, surrender/But don't give yourself away . . .

It begins suddenly. They undo the ropes so they can have me flat on my stomach. The kid leans down hard on my back with the Beretta jammed against my neck; Gaelen, whistling—a happy worker—takes my right leg and examines it briefly—a specimen under glass—then twists it sharply. Pain shoots up my spinal cord like an electrical charge. But they ease up—clearly, they think they're dealing with an amateur here.

"Maybe you could tell me what you want," I say, my face flat against cold concrete, wet now with my saliva, "while I'm still conscious. Just for the hell of it."

"We want you to listen to your body."

Gaelen pushes down hard against my back, exactly at the fault line of my injury; the bastard must be looking at my X-rays. When the kid—his name's Oren; we're all on a first name basis here—grabs my left arm and wrenches it backward, dislocating the shoulder, I nearly pass out. My vision blurs; the colors in my mind swirl like a Fauvist painting. "Pain," says Gaelen, "is the body's way of saying something's wrong."

"What's wrong, Harding," says Oren. "Tell us what's wrong."

Then just as quickly the acid-like effect drops away. It becomes just the three of us in this dirty room. Gaelen knows what he's doing—how far to take me without losing me altogether. His hands are huge; they remind me of my grandfather's. Elenya's face hangs before me, a vision fanatics might see in an arrangement of clouds.

"She leaned on your *shoulder*," Gaelen says. "She slept in your *bed*."

"She did more than that, asshole," I say and Gaelen's on top of me again, leaping like a panther, slamming my head against the concrete floor.

There's blood in my mouth now, along with dirt and flecks of straw, and when I see Gaelen holding a syringe, flicking it with his finger so beads of water fly in slow motion I try to twist away but both men grab me, throwing me back down. Gaelen's knee is pressing against my back; his arm's around my throat as though he might just break me in two. I can't move. My pants are ripped to mid-calf. Stiff leather restraints are forced around my ankles, cutting deep into the skin. I'm distracted now by all the hands moving over my body and then a new, bright pain like a needle going deep into my back.

Gaelen's fingers twist my head to the right. For the first time I notice the spots of dried blood beneath his nails. There's a sensation of pressure, something being forced where it does not want to go. The pain runs parallel to my heartbeat, loud and irregular. When my heart skips a beat the next rush of blood causes sharp pounding. It's like spiking an exposed nerve with a high heel. Someone says my name. "Come on," I hear myself saying, in a curious blurred voice; a drunken bravado. "Come on come on."

The questions start then, along with a rush from the drug that intensifies the pain; makes it rawer, close to the bone. But they've miscalculated. Like most people they think distraction is the key to pain control; just the opposite's true. I've had a few years to think about it. You have to focus on pain, concentrate on it, make it your whole world, your whole life.

The tin angel from Alison's Cracker Jacks is in my right hand. The questions come from Gaelen. He starts by asking about the tapes but soon loses interest and switches to more personal topics—what the fuck am I doing with Elenya; how long have I known her; how long do I think my girlfriend's gonna live if I don't start talking.

"We know right where she is Harding. Right this fucking minute."

Have I met the Lord Jesus Christ my Savior.

When Oren talks his voice is elevated just a bit; trying to contain excitement or anticipation—he drops down to the dirty concrete floor; a boxing referee making the final count. His face is next to mine. His wild eyes are in my face.

"You'll end up at the bottom of the fucking lake! The worms are gonna eat your fucking heart out!"

"We can do anything we want," Gaelen says, the metal piercing splitting his tongue like a snake's. "Maybe we're through with you and your girlfriend. Maybe not. Maybe we'll come after you in the middle of the night. When you least expect it. So stay away from the Rosenbergs. Both of them."

"Let me gut the bastard, Gaelen!"

"It's not worth it. Play them some music. You like music?" he says to me. "Me, I love music. Can't get enough. This is our little house band."

Whatever composure I have left deserts me when Oren starts a tape recorder. The voices on the tape echo in the empty warehouse. They come from the back of the room, the back of my heart. They swirl in the air like ghosts.

A girl's face. A girl's long blonde hair swinging, barely touching the dirty floor.

The first voice is Eduardo Martinez, on tape talking not to me or the kid or Gaelen but his daughter Angela—teasing her in a different way than I'm being teased, smothering her protests. She sounds even younger than I remember her. I've never heard the tape before. I didn't know such a tape existed. And I have no idea what it has to do with the Rosenbergs.

At first the voices drift and fade, a couple in a cheap motel arguing in the next room. Then the kid brings the recorder closer, so the nuances of Angela's terror are unavoidable. Her voice cuts like a knife but I say nothing. They turn the volume up until it becomes distortion. Something inside me moves very far away.

The kid's wearing blue headphones now; the cord dangles at his side. Gaelen steps forward. I begin to lose track of time.

By the time the tape runs out and their frustration with my silence translates into fiercer, less scientific beatings I have the tin angel pushed nearly through my palm. The pain from its broken edge is sharper and brighter than anything these two are doing. I home in on that like a beacon.

I come to on the ground in a narrow alley. Religious tracts from the Universal World Church are frozen so close I can read the sales pitch. Right now they seem comforting. My legs feel a little numb and I'm so sleepy that I nearly give in and close my eyes. Then something brown and very fast scurries beneath a Dumpster just in front of my face. I get to my feet fairly quickly.

For five or ten minutes I lean against a red brick wall, waiting for a heavy, sick dizziness to pass; it won't. A pasty film covers my mouth and lips, and my left shoulder and lower back burn with a fierce white pain. My right hand throbs. I need a drink very badly. A morphine drip even more. I hear Angela's voice repeating words and phrases I've spent years forgetting. Her copper bracelet's in free fall in the torn lining of my coat.

There's a streetlight at the end of the alley. It takes me a good five minutes to reach it. When I do I discover I'm no longer in Oak Lawn. They've dumped me on East 63rd behind a row of abandoned tenements. My coat's torn and my wallet's gone but a black dry cleaner on Stony Island pulling a security gate across his front window lets me come inside to use his phone and warm up.

I dial a number I've never used before, one Donnie had me memorize months ago in case my back was to the wall. I think this qualifies.

"Yes?" An unfamiliar voice answers on the first ring; he sounds young and a little unsure. I can almost hear the pencil scribbling.

"We'll be right there," he says.

"Wait—how long," I say but the connection's dead.

My ring and watch are gone. There's blood on my shirt and trousers, clumps of dirt matted in my hair. My fingers smell like dog shit. None of it seems to surprise the dry cleaner, working his way through a pack of Kools in the dark. It's just another night in Woodlawn.

He turns on the radio; Marvin Gaye's *What's Going On*. I think it's a legitimate question.

"How they supposed to find you?" he says finally.

"What?" There's a stack of dirty laundry on the floor I feel like curling up on.

"You didn't tell them where you was," he says and I'm thinking—good point, very good point—when just at that minute a horn beeps outside. I think I see two familiar shadows in the car but it's dark; I can't be sure. The car could be the beige Ford, it could be the Grand Am.

Mother, mother, there's too many of you crying sings Marvin.

"Do you have a back door?" I say.

The dry cleaner's name is Purdy—he tells me this three times—just call him Purdy, everyone does including his wife. Purdy's Sunshine Cleaners I repeat it several times; it begins to sound like a kind of mantra.

His car's parked alongside the pawn shop next to his store, easily visible to anyone on the street, so I have to walk down to 61st Street, two very long blocks. A Jackson-Howard B train swings around overhead throwing sparks; last stop, end of the line. I don't know how long it takes me but Purdy is waiting patiently. He's driven around Woodlawn to throw them off. There's no better place in America at night to lose a car full of white guys than South Woodlawn.

"What kind of car was it, did you see?" I say, hobbling up to him.

He shakes his head. "Ford maybe. I don't keep up with them new models so much anymore." He's staring at me, wondering what sort of trouble I've brought him. "Coulda been a Chevy."

"Can you drive me to the hospital?"

"Jackson Park Hospital's right down the block."

"Not Jackson Park—the university hospital. The night entrance, the ER—I'll pay you."

"This ain't no cab," he says but then relents. "Come on, get in."

His car smells like cigarettes and dry cleaning solvent. We stop at a Walgreens so I can buy two bottles of Canadian Club—on special—and a bottle of Advil but it's difficult moving down the aisles and it's even harder paying without a wallet. So Purdy buys, then tells me he doesn't drink. A clerk tries to interest us in vodka or gin; clear beverages are hip these days. By the time I get back to the car I'm having trouble moving my left arm.

I give Purdy my name and address and an IOU I'm sure he never expects to collect on. He actually waits to see I get inside all right. He's right; he's no cab driver; more like a saint.

A resident watches me stutter-step through the sliding glass doors and calls for a nurse to take me to a back cubicle. The admitting clerk finds my name in the computer. I'm an alumnus; they like that. It may be the only place in the city where it counts.

The resident is reluctant to shoot me full of painkillers without a full workup. I'm reluctant to stay that long with Alison upstairs alone. Meanwhile the drug Gaelen gave me withdraws in fits and starts— something about the hospital's bright neon is triggering small explosions behind my eyes, flashes of light like tracer rounds arcing across my retina. The ER staff watches me as though they can see it too. I hope they've got a good seat. From this side it's like a small-town Fourth of July.

"Did you fall?" the resident says, trying to rotate my arms. A nurse is working on my hand. I have no idea how I got my coat off.

"Something like that."

"Your left shoulder's in bad shape," he says. "I've never seen this shade of purple before. What would you say this is, Doris, grape?"

"More like magenta," says the nurse; the resident Crayola expert.

Thank God he's not as choosy as Purdy. When the nurse leaves we work out a trade: one bottle of CC for two ccs of cortisone and a tetanus shot. No painkillers though; it's going to be a long night. The resident wraps my hand in gauze.

Alison's asleep when I come in; the TV's still on. I pull the chair next to the bed and put my legs up next to hers. She's wearing the pajamas I bought her with the feet sewn in. She stirs slightly but doesn't speak. I have the bottle open and a cup the resident gave me; I suspect it's for other uses. The whiskey tastes good, though cuts in my mouth burn with each sip. The cortisone eases the stiffness in my shoulder. I swallow three Advil. My chair faces the door, which doesn't lock. There's nothing else I can do.

I must be too late for *Fist of Fury*, on TV anyway. The late late movie is *Funny Face*. Astaire's aged a bit since he and Ginger flew down to Rio last Wednesday night but then so have I. Audrey Hepburn however looks sensational.

When I reach for the TV remote I brush Alison's hand and she wakes up very briefly; a little confused. She says my name in a whisper. The sweet heaviness of her body brings a flood of memories. "It's all right," I say, turning off the TV. She nods and falls asleep again and after half the bottle's gone I eventually do too, listening to Alison's soft breathing and the muffled sounds of the hospital running at night, distant small-craft warnings.

PART THREE
GAELEN

THIRTEEN

Leon Chang's warehouse runs behind a dying business district on the edges of Chinatown. The boarded storefronts along this stretch of 23rd Street are weathered folk art, a display of every brown that plywood turns in bad weather. A currency exchange is the only business left on the block. In the gloom of the street and a morning this overcast the bright yellow signs for *Welfare Checks Cashed/Gas Bills Paid* begin to look cheerful.

Chang deals in illegals—people, hardware, software. He's a last resort. That's where I am right now.

"It's all ready," Chang says. "Moy has the paperwork."

Chang is nothing if not organized. Mr. Moy sits behind a haze of cigarette smoke, in a cage of cinder block and chicken wire. Moy himself cannot make change or accept cash; I think he married into the family. So you pay Chang's brother in the currency exchange. He places a neat rubber stamp on your hand, as though you're leaving a high school dance.

The money is laundered through gas bills and money orders and then comes back to Chang, to the strongbox on his desk, the old Boston Co. safe hidden behind more concrete, more chicken wire. "Family

owned and operated since 1947" is stamped on a tin
plate above Chang's cage. I think he found the plate at a
scrap yard.

"Business is good?" I say.

Chang says he can't complain. He's wearing a duck
hunter's cap, clipping an article from *Reader's Digest*.
"My Most Unforgettable Fence."

I did a favor once for Chang, removing a lid from
a can of heavy-syrup Del Monte peaches from his
brother's neck, wrapping the carotid with a sweatband.
Somehow the kid survived. I was in turnaround before
moving south; Chang's brother was on his way to some
very hard time on a rape charge. The girl was twelve, and
wearing the black and white robes and veil for Saturday
services. I think he did the whole two years in solitary.

"Very good first quarter," Chang says. "And the
more things they ban, the better. The latest is these little
inhalants. See?" He hands me the latest China White,
this time mentholated. "You boil the crystals inside,
soak a cigarette in the chemicals—better than mushrooms. Before that it was glue."

"What about spray paint?"

"Very good for us," Chang says. "Also markers.
There's always something new. It's recession-proof.
Next I think will be butane." There's a steady stream of
kids outside Chang's window. It must be recess. From
the street it looks like a TicketMaster.

"You made a good purchase," Chang says. "I
always say, buy quality."

"Where did it come from." I take the gun out of a
Cermak Currency Exchange money bag and sight it
with my left hand. My right still has the bandage. An
old man working a digital powder scale and reloader
throws up his hands in mock surrender.

"A good home," Chang says. "Not to worry. Very clean. Very cold."

"It feels kind of thin," I say, testing its weight. I haven't shot a gun in years. The type of cases I've been on don't usually require a Browning 9mm automatic.

"That's how they make them these days, Harding. You're out of touch. Don't worry, you could put an elephant down."

"I may have to," I say, thinking of Gaelen. "What kind of ammo do you have for this?"

"For you only—no extra charge, nylon-coated hollow points. Two boxes. Fifteen-shot magazines. Okay? And I have something else that might interest you."

Chang turns his back briefly to get another small box. Whenever Chang turns his back his guards scan the exits. There are three if you count the garage door. One of the guards is casually watching me, his right hand lightly touching his sidearm. There are three other weapons I can spot right off, including a kid in a "Love Sucks" T-shirt with a Remington pump. There are probably others. The closest exit is the rear door and it would be five or six very long steps to reach it. Especially the way my back feels today. I'm limping just a bit too, from the leather restraints and Gaelen's laying on of hands.

Chang takes out a glint of steel and polished chrome no bigger than his fist.

"You see? Very light, very tiny. Easy to hide. But still .32 caliber."

"I don't think so. What would it stop, a squirrel? A rabid chipmunk?"

"Not for you, Harding. For your girlfriend," he says. "For her personal safety."

"You've heard about that too, have you?"

"Newspapers reach us even here. Pony express stops at Cermak once, twice week." He moves around to the front of the desk and puts the small gun in my hands.

"It's spotless, Harding. That's why I thought of you."

"You mean you filed down the numbers. That doesn't mean so much anymore. The FBI labs have gotten better at dealing with that."

"No, I mean it's clean, guaranteed, one hundred percent. Completely untraceable. A virgin. The Browning they can trace to someone—don't worry, not you, and not me. But this no one can trace. This gun does not exist."

"How much?"

"For you? Five hundred. Anyone else I would hold out for at least eight."

"Better hold out." I open Chang's door. One of his goons is a little too close. He's holding a baseball bat. I don't think he's getting in shape for 16-inch softball. Everyone in Chang's family makes me very nervous.

"I'm on a budget here," I say. "What you're advancing is generous enough." Too generous; I have no idea how I'll pay Chang back. On the other hand, without the Browning the question may be irrelevant. And I need the money he's advancing almost as much as the gun.

This morning, for the hell of it I dug Rosenberg's check out of my socks drawer and walked it to the S&L, where an embarrassed teller informed me the check was really a line of credit, since withdrawn.

"Withdrawn when."

"Let me see—last Wednesday." After Lucy died, and the police focused on her and Nelson Bryars.

Chang is watching me sympathetically.

"Why don't I loan it to you. Since you're buying the Browning. Let her try it out for a few days. Get the feel of it. Sort of a test drive."

"Chang, you should be selling used cars."

"We have those too," he says. "Very low mileage." There's a pause of just a split second. Chang leans forward. "Are you by chance expecting trouble today? Something I should know about?"

"No, why? Just because I'm buying guns? Most of those kids buying glue are probably carrying Uzis."

"You look like you've been in a fight. Bruise on your face. And you're wearing a vest."

I smile. "Is that what it looks like?" I doubt if the back brace I'm strapped into today would stop a .22.

"Just a little trouble with my back," I say. "A bad disc. How's your brother doing?"

"Very busy. New franchise in Lake County. What else can I can do for you?" Chang has no time for small talk. He's like a commission clerk completing a sale. "Perhaps jewelry, a new wristwatch?" He brings out an ice bucket full of rings, pendants, bracelets, digs out a gold Rolex, a black Movado. If they're fake they're good enough to fool me, which is basically all I ask of anything in life.

"I have cousins in hotel maid service," Chang explains. "The benefits of an extended family."

"Twenty?" I say, taking a Movado. I should bring Alison here. Chang's Outlet Mall. "I'm having trouble with my watch lately."

"Twenty-five. Pay me when you can. Okay? And Harding—let me know how she likes the gun."

* * *

Chang's warehouse and curio emporium is one of my last stops. The day begins too early—five A.M. Alison's still sleeping but the hospital's wide awake and full of noise—nurses prepping patients for seven A.M. surgery, emptying Foley bags, talking and laughing, pushing rattling carts like stewardesses on a short flight.

The same resident's on duty in the ER. He sends me to Hematology and X-ray. Nothing's broken but a spirited discussion ensues regarding discs and tendons and the various hues coloring my shoulder. A three-doctor consult and the sixty-four-Crayola box from a pediatrics ward are required to complete the diagnosis. The resident straps me into a Victorian brace worthy of De Sade, pumps me full of codeine and cortisone, and writes me prescriptions for Fiorinal, Flexeril, Finklestein—an orthopedic guy who works wonders. "Otherwise we're sending you to Lourdes," he says. His rotation over, he's going home to drink Canadian Club and watch *Jeopardy!*.

Boone meets me at the hospital with his Escort. He agrees to stay with Alison. Plus he'll drive me to the cops if I buy him breakfast. Since the reason I've called him in the first place is to borrow money our plans do not quite mesh. He's brought a paratrooper coat that weighs ten pounds, with enough hidden pockets to satisfy a magician. We have pancakes at the Wheel Cafe on 35th Street. Boone pays. The food is good but I have trouble getting into the booth and the coat.

"You're grimacing with each bite, did you know that?" Boone says.

"Don't watch me eat then."

"It's very entertaining," he says. "Quite a floor show."

The police are equally sympathetic.

"You were mugged," Reilly says when I corner him coming out of Interrogation. "Congratulations. The desk sergeant will find someone to talk to you."

"You can't do it?"

"I'm working Homicide, Harding. You seem to be mostly alive. For now, anyway. If you turn up dead later maybe I can talk to you."

"Can't you give me ten minutes? There were two of them. The one named Gaelen—I saw him with Lucy. And he's been following Elenya Rosenberg—he was following me, too, last week—"

"Did he confess and leave us a murder weapon? If not, he'll have to take a number. Goodbye, Harding."

A uniform named Hernandez takes my statement, then shows me some mug books. The name Gaelen rings no bells in the police computer.

I tell Hernandez about Oren but he loses interest midway so I cut it short. He does however get a squad car and drive me to the Tandoori Grill, just opening for lunch. The woman remembers me but that's about it. Nobody saw anything. Nobody heard anything. "We have the music playing very loud all the time," she tells us, meaning the Ravi Shankar Blues Band. She sells Hernandez two masala dosas.

My truck is still parked around the corner. A kid in greasy overalls at the corner Shell helps me replace the distributor. Since fixing the window takes three hundred—more than the windshield—I buy a roll of clear plastic at a hardware store and tape on a temporary bandage. It's a simple robbery so they won't come out and dust for prints. Hernandez leaves after reminding me not to drive without a license. When he's gone I take

95th to the Ryan and then head north, windchill whistling through the Saran Wrap, tugging at its corners like a child picking at a Band-Aid. I sense I'm being followed but I can't find the precise car pursuing me.

The state DMV is on the West Side. The lines are long, snaking through the foyer, doubling back and intersecting to create odd pockets of discussion, like crossed phone lines. Long haulers with suspended permits bump into old ladies memorizing the eye exam. Nervous kids trying to get their temps have all the copies of "Rules of the Road" and most of the chairs. The rest of us stand and commiserate. Most of the guys in line lost wallets filled with credit cards, a problem I don't have. Each of us has a story.

"You got mugged outside an Indian restaurant?" the guy in front of me says. "No kidding. Me, I got mugged outside a Thai place."

"Szechwan-Hunan," says another.

"Armenian."

"Czech."

"Mexican."

"I'm eating at home now, man."

"Fucking' A."

The last guy in line has dyed blond hair; his roots are showing. So is his navel.

"Fusion," he says. "Eclectic contemporary." He points to his belly button. "They ripped off my stone, man."

"No shit," the Czech guy says. We give the fusion guy plenty of space.

* * *

They give me a ten-day permit until the police paper-work sorts itself out, then I drive east on Roosevelt Road to Maywood Storage. Since everything in the glove compartment's gone I'd guessed the tapes were too, and sure enough, as soon as I pull into the lot my back starts hurting—the door to bay 1204 is hanging from a single chain. It's been ripped right off its tracks. Sparky the Rabid Security Dog must have taken the night off.

Todd's in the manager's office again. It takes me a minute to remember the stupid calendar, Miss December's flat stomach. I left the calendar in the truck. I may as well have drawn them a map.

He slides open his window.

"Is everything gone?" I say.

"Cleaned out," Todd says from his tollbooth of an office. "Last night, sometime. Hey, it happens. Nobody got hurt, that's all that matters, right?"

"Right."

"You a friend of hers?" He's wearing a Rollerblade helmet and a spandex jumpsuit, auditioning for *American Gladiators*. "The girl who rented 1204?"

"Why?"

"We've been trying to reach her, that's why. She don't answer her phone. And she needs to file insurance forms for reimbursement."

"I know her. I'm not sure I can reach her. Not anymore."

Todd says it's a shame, and I agree.

I tell him thanks, put the truck in gear. If I leave now I can beat the afternoon rush hour. Or is there another rush hour the other way? I'm trying to figure out suburban traffic patterns when Todd interrupts.

"I'm thinking," Todd says. "You think she left school or something?"

I put the truck in neutral, set the hand brake. "What do you mean?"

"Nothing, just—I know a girl went to school down there. She transferred out after one quarter—too cold, you know? All those gray buildings—"

I leave the engine on, jump down from the truck.

"Can I see the paperwork? Maybe her writing's smudged, sometimes her threes look like fives. Maybe you're just reading it wrong."

"All right." He hands me a rental agreement, made out not by Lucy but by Nora Taylor. She used her real name and address. The date on the form is December 24. Merry Christmas. I'd just assumed the key belonged to Lucy.

"Don't they have to leave some kind of deposit?"

"Sure. Most people use your major credit card."

"And Nora?"

"On the back there. Should be a Xerox." There is, a photostat of Nora's receipt. Or rather Robin's—five hundred dollars, paid in cash.

"Everything all right?" Todd says.

I nod.

"How often did she come here?"

"Who knows? I only saw her once or twice."

"Was she alone?"

He nods. "No. Wait. One time a friend drove her. A guy. They were both talking about classes. Listen, are you really a friend of hers?"

"Of course."

"Well, you tell her to call us, right away."

"I'll tell her."

"And tell her we're sorry."

I nod, putting the truck in gear.

"You want another calendar?" he says.

I tell him no. One was enough.

I eat dinner alone in a Mexican place—the same one the DMV guy was robbed in—drinking frozen margaritas, keeping my eye out for muggers. Donnie finally answers my page, apologizes, gives me an address in Hoffman Estates. He's been in budget meetings all day, moving decimal points around, juggling imaginary numbers. He's spending the evening hitting imaginary golf balls.

VirtualLinks is a computerized golf center. Outside the wind's howling but Donnie's wearing Dockers shorts and an Izod shirt and golf shoes, standing on AstroTurf with a four-iron, teeing up at an imaginary ball. His head's covered with what looks like a toaster. There are fifteen other men above him wired the same way, standing in cubicles like the set of *Hollywood Squares*.

I start to pull at his sleeve but the attendant, Skip, stops me.

"Don't interrupt him," Skip says to me. "He's in another world. It can be jarring coming out of a VR sand trap too quickly."

"What's he looking at?"

"Right now?" Skip checks his monitor. "Right now he's playing the fourteenth hole at St. Johns, outside Glasgow. It doglegs to the right. A very tricky shot. He's just got to avoid that sand—there, he's done it. Well done. Good show." I think Skip's affecting an English accent. It sounds like dinner-theater *Pygmalion*.

Donnie removes his VR helmet.

"Good shot, sir," Skip says.

"Harding—you should try this. Out of season—short of flying to Hilton Head—you can't beat it."

"You're sweating," I tell Donnie. "And you haven't moved an inch. Is that imaginary sweat? Do you use imaginary RightGuard?"

"Of course I'm sweating—I just played eighteen of the toughest holes in the world. What was my score, Flip?"

"Skip, sir. One-forty-four."

"A nice round number," I say. "Above your bowling average, I think. Since when do you play golf?"

"Since now. Since my boss does," Donnie says. "And half my board. It's all the old geezers talk about sometimes. What a stupid fucking game, huh?"

"I've never been a fan," I admit. "I like the shoes, though."

The old Donnie played darts in bars. The new Donnie plays golf. He unplugs himself and dumps the toaster into Skip's hands—we walk over to VirtualLinks's nineteenth hole where luckily the whiskey is not virtual but very real. Donnie orders mineral water from Brazil. It's made from "authentic rain forest rain" and there's a cheerful aborigine on the green label. I order a SimCity Cocktail, made from authentic Kentucky sour mash. There's a drunken hillbilly on its label. A computer monitor—probably made for high-tech video games—is showing the Blackhawks game.

"I owe you an apology," Donnie says. "About last night. The kid forgot to ask where you were." Donnie shakes his head. "He's a new hire, right out of DePaul. Has a degree in criminology, which should tell you what that's worth. We're like the godamned FBI now, we only hire college grads." He pours himself more water. "You're all right? You're walking a little like Walter Brennan."

"I'll live." It's not wise to drink like this with muscle relaxants as a chaser but when the bartender gives me a refill I don't object. At least Donnie's paying: I tell him what happened last night. He's sympathetic but loses interest even quicker than Hernandez. Getting mugged's very low on a victim's status sheet.

"Because if you need a back guy my sister Janice uses some midget in Humboldt Park. He takes off his shoes, walks on her back with these steel balls between his toes. Straight from Bangkok, I could get his number."

"I appreciate the thought."

"No way you can find them?" he says. "No idea who they are?"

"They weren't real forthcoming."

"So what do you do? Just wait for them to hit you again?"

"I have one or two ideas."

He nods, waits until the bartender leaves, his fingers drumming on the green glass bottle.

"One of them's just a kid," I say. "The other guy's name is Gaelen. He's the one I want."

"First or last?"

"I don't know. Can you run it through your mainframe?"

"Sure but if the police don't have anything I doubt we will."

"You never know. Run the name Sawyer too. He's some kind of doctor."

"How is he connected to this?"

"I have no idea. I'm flying blind, Donnie. As usual."

He nods, writing this down on a napkin.

"What was weird was this tape they played me."

"Of what."

I pause. "You won't believe me."

"Sure I will. I'm gullible as hell."

"Eduardo Martinez. And Angela."

Donnie says nothing. He's looking for the bartender.

"I swear to God, Donnie—"

"Harding . . ." he says finally, shaking his head.

"You think I'm making this up?"

"So what's the connection?"

"I don't know. How the fuck would I know?"

"They kidnap you, beat you up, play you a ten-year-old tape—"

"Maybe Martinez is back," I say.

"Drop it, Harding."

"Well somebody sure is fucking with me, Donnie."

He thinks about this, doesn't argue.

"What are you gonna do?" he says.

"I don't know. Go after Rosenberg somehow."

"I thought you were after this Gaelen—"

"Somebody's running him."

"You don't know it's Rosenberg. Are you after him or his wife?"

I say nothing. The drugs and the alcohol are making me talk too much. I ask about the banking records—the ones stolen from my apartment but he shakes his head, says Frost must have them.

"He says no, he got them from you."

"He's wrong. His brain's pickled from all that booze. But this might interest you," Donnie says, taking a neatly folded piece of cream-colored paper from his wallet. Expensive paper, with two watermarks: the onion-skin seal of the manufacturer; the circular impression from a sealed condom.

It's nothing official, just a note from a contact of Donnie's. It says fifty thousand dollars entered Rosenberg's checking account last Wednesday, left the same day for points unknown. The bartender's trying to tell me about the Blackhawks' lack of scoring in recent games. I'm more interested in this latest power play of Rosenberg's.

"My guy says there wasn't anything overseas, just domestic, moving some liquid mutuals into his local account. And it's his business account, Harding."

"So?"

"So it proves nothing. Maybe he needs a new stethoscope. He's low this week on gauze or those little rubber hammers. This Gaelen—you know nothing about him?"

"He makes a strong first impression. Other than that, no, not much."

Donnie knows I'm holding something back—he's too smart to think differently—but he doesn't push it. The new Donnie. He's now a Concerned Guy. The Good Friend.

I should tell him more. But I don't know who to trust anymore.

"You wanted the police report from this kid Robin's room? I couldn't get a hard copy. But there was eight or nine hundred in his account at the Bursar's. And nothing much missing from his room. They left the heavy stuff—a TV, a new computer. So it wasn't much of a robbery."

"What kind of computer?"

"You gotta be kidding, Harding."

"They still don't know where he was shot?"

"Off the record, they've got a spot in Jackson Park, by the lagoon. They're running a lot of stuff out of town, different labs."

"What kind of stuff?"

"Jesus, I don't know Harding. It's a fucking lagoon. Ferns maybe, or lichen, moss. Pond scum. You get your truck fixed okay?"

"Yeah."

He waits half a beat.

"I have people," he says. He's sucking on the lime from his drink like a sugar cube.

"I know."

"They can be discreet. And they listen to me."

"Thanks, Donnie. What I need is information. The rest of it I'd rather do myself."

Donnie wipes his hands with his napkin.

"What about a gun?" he says quietly.

"I'm all right."

"Do you need money?"

I shake my head.

"And you're ready for this job Monday?" he says.

"I will be by then."

"Call me once you're inside." He finishes his water. "Let me know if you need anything. At least you'll be around architects and art history bozos. Nobody's gonna break your arm in there." He motions for the bartender so he can sign his tab. "I have to get going—I've got another eighteen holes and I don't want some bastard playing through. And the back nine's in Asia somewhere, Geisha girls watching and applauding. Maybe they drop their kimonos if you break par. You wanta play?"

"I don't think so."

"They've got a back room, Harding, in this place, just like a porno shop. VR sex, total immersion. And the girls never say no."

I'm on the hospital elevator, on my way to see Alison, when I decide to make a slight detour to the OR. A nurse in green scrubs says Dr. Rosenberg's in the middle suite. She makes it sound like we're at the Four Seasons. "But you can't go in there," she says, much like Skip. "Didn't you hear me? I said no—"

"Isn't the surgery gift shop back here? Because I wanted to buy one of those cute little hats," I say, pushing through the swinging doors.

Two doctors are washing up, hands in the air, assisted by white-gowned nurses; some sort of religious ritual. The high priests turn to view this interloper in their sanctuary. I smile, head bowed in penance.

"Just passing through," I say. "So sorry. *Mea culpa.*"

"You can't—" say a choir of voices.

It's surprisingly easy to get right to the heart of the operating room. I was expecting armed guards or some kind of elaborate security system of vacuum-sealed doors and double-keyed locks like in *Andromeda Strain*. These doors are more like the screen doors on my Uncle Bud's back porch. Bud never locked his doors either.

There are six green figures hovering around the body. Rosenberg sees me first. He removes his fancy microglasses, stares at me across a vast expanse of exposed nose. Bach's Goldberg Variations, one of the Glenn Gould transcriptions, are playing on a portable stereo. Glenn hums along as though he expects the patient to join in. Rosenberg's eyes don't blink. He doesn't seem surprised to see me.

"I forgot you liked Bach," I say. "I'm used to hearing Jethro Tull when you're around naked bodies."

"Will you take over, please, Dr. Lewis?" he says to an assistant.

"Should I get Security, Doctor?"

"No—tend to the patient. Please." He leaves through another set of doors, loose green pants flapping like a sheik's robe. When I catch up with him he's standing before a shiny metal sink. The others in the room leave like townspeople clearing the street at high noon.

"What do you want?" he says. "You've interrupted my septectomy."

"Is that what that is? It sounds so scientific, doesn't it? And here I thought it was just another overpriced vanity rip-off—"

"Is there a point to this?"

"I haven't heard from you," I say. I'm talking to his back, which I don't appreciate. "I've thought it over and decided I'd like the job."

"What job?"

"Working for you. Finding the bad guys, the black-mailers. Ten thousand dollars. You still want me, don't you?"

"Well, yes," he says, turning, drying his hands. "But I'm not sure you're worth that much money anymore."

"How much would you say I'm worth?"

"I was thinking of a trade. You tell me what you've found out. I don't press charges for invasion of privacy."

"I've dropped a bit in value."

He smiles.

"That's always a risk when you're speculating. You have to know when to buy, when to sell. The check was yours. You could have cashed it."

"And now?"

He tosses his rubber gloves in the trash. "Now someone else has the check. It's a business decision."

"And the fifty thousand? What kind of business is that?"

"What—"

"You've withdrawn a lot of money. And you cashed in a lot of stocks, went to a lot of trouble to get it quickly—was that because of Lucy? Was she going to say something you didn't want the police to hear?"

"I think you'd better leave."

"See, the cops are buying the typed confession now—they've got the typewriter and the signature's kosher—but you and me, we know it's not real hard for a doctor to get a nurse to sign something, is it? Especially if she needs a fix and you're holding the needle—"

Someone asks again about getting Security. After a beat, Stephen nods. His hands are long since dry but he's still rubbing them.

"Who got the money, Stephen? Was it Gaelen?"

"I don't know anyone by that name."

But the fear that darts across his face says otherwise. It's the first time I've touched a nerve. Security arrives to escort me to the front door. Rosenberg watches me silently. He'd be a hell of a poker player. I understand better now. He's not fearless. But it's not me he's afraid of.

The surgeon's steady hands are trembling just a bit.

"Tell me, Stephen—when you tried to hire me— were you sending me after the tapes? Or after Gaelen?"

"Our business is over," he says, his face impassive. This time they lock the doors.

I stay with Alison until midnight. Her stitches are starting to itch. I don't think my back can take another night in this chair. We're both tired and grumpy. I give the nurse my phone number and go to Alison's apartment for a few hours sleep. I sleep in her bed.

She calls me at two to tell me quick, turn on the TV. I think the Chinese or the Southern Baptists are invading but it's just Don "the Dragon" Wilson kick-boxing, saving the world. We watch together over the phone with Alison providing a running commentary on the Dragon's freestyle moves. When I start to snore at a crucial moment Alison yells in the phone, waking me up.

FOURTEEN

On Friday morning Lucy Williams is buried quietly in a small cemetery on the far South Side. I go mostly out of curiosity, wondering who'll show but the turnout's sadly small, mostly family. A gray day. The nurse I saw in the rec room Tuesday night is standing off to one side. She's dressed in black with an art deco scarf that looks like stained glass, her hands folded in front of her waist, as Lucy's probably are now. When the service ends I walk to the gravesite.

It's snowing lightly. We're standing under a canopy as though waiting for a cab.

"Did you know her well?" I say.

"You're not a cop," she says, recognizing me but not placing me.

I shake my head. "Just a friend."

She looks around. The few mourners have already scattered. Even the minister's back in his car, lighting a cigarette.

"Lucy didn't have many," she says. "Not from the looks of this."

She digs through her purse for a Kleenex. I give her one that's wrinkled but clean.

"Thanks."

"How well did you know her?"

"Not that well," she says, blowing her nose. "But

I'm head nurse. Somebody from the unit needed to come. She was a good nurse, whatever her problems were. We've all got problems, right?"

"Right."

"Have you known her long?"

"No, just the last few months. I met her at a party. At the Rosenbergs'."

She starts to say something, then thinks better of it. We walk across the slick grass toward her car, one of a half dozen parked along the drive as though it were a scenic outlook.

"You'd think a few more people could have come, that's all," she says.

"I don't see Nelson Bryars, that male nurse on your unit—"

"He's on vacation. The police talk about him as though he's a suspect."

"And?"

"He didn't kill anyone. Those two kids, and Lucy? Are the police nuts? He's not that kind of guy. Half the nurses on the floor use him as a baby-sitter."

"He seemed upset that night, running down to the ER."

"We were all upset. Nelson might even think it's his fault, since he was the first one there. It all happened so fast."

"There was a physician's assistant around too—"

"Bob's just an agency guy. He doesn't work for us." She looks at me closer, trying to place me. We're nearly to her car, the last ones in the cemetery. I'm in *Night of the Living Dead* territory again, the opening scene. Any old man who approaches me will get a rock in the forehead.

"Did you see anyone else that night, someone who didn't belong—"

"You're not really a friend of hers, are you?"

"Not exactly," I admit. "But I did know her. And I liked her. I just never got the chance to know her better."

"What were you doing on the floor that night?" She takes off her scarf, folding it in triangles like a flag. Her hair is blonde.

"Trying to help. But my batting average isn't real good lately."

"Don't you think she jumped?"

"Through a closed window? You're a psych nurse—don't you think that's pretty unusual?"

"It happens," she says. "Some of them would go through a brick wall to get out."

She gets in her car, which sits in a gully. The door barely closes, dragging mud and grass. "I don't know your name," she says, winding down the window.

"Harding."

"Harding, I'm Jesse," she says, extending a hand. I'm always surprised when someone's friendly with no angle. She has a very firm handshake.

"I didn't see any doctors here today," I say, and her smile hardens.

"That's always the way. But they were very friendly with her up till now, believe me."

"Like Dr. Rosenberg?"

She nods, starting the engine.

"He's married though, isn't he?" I say.

"Oh sure," she says. "They're all married."

* * *

From one South Side graveyard to another—the Union Stockyards closed years ago but there are still a couple of meat-packing plants in the neighborhood. I see signs for Personnel but I don't really need a job. A foreman asks me what I'm doing. "Just admiring the buildings," I say. He looks at me like I'm from Mars. As long as I'm not from Oscar Mayer, trying to steal company secrets, make a better hot dog. He has one bucket of fat hanging over his belt; another vat or two inside to render. I walk around the neighborhood, trying to feel nostalgic. I grew up in the next ward, had relatives here, the remnants of Packingtown. The river no longer runs blood-red from the slaughter but the smell—ground into the dirt and the trees and the concrete—lingers.

That's what I recognized Wednesday night, boxed in the trunk of Gaelen's car—that smell. And on South Racine—not far from the old Armour plant—I find what I'm looking for, a large abandoned warehouse, big enough to land jets. You could drive a car right inside, pull the sliding metal door shut, and do about anything you want. There's nothing and no one around for blocks. I test it out by screaming, then wish I hadn't.

The memories of childhood are strong. The memories of Wednesday night—the grainy texture of the concrete floor, the stuffy closeness of the air, the straw that clung to my face and neck—are stronger. There are footprints and body marks in the dust; rusty Mountain Dew cans; a crumpled pack of Beeman's Blackjack beside a metal trash barrel, the kind used for street-corner space heaters. I walk around in circles, waiting for God knows what, hearing only a distant train and the echoes of my boots on the concrete. Gaelen's words still echo too—exhortations, prayers. No one comes down here by accident, looking for a good time. Either Gaelen or Oren must have memories much like mine.

I ask around at the nearest thing to a shopping district; a string of run-down stores—Hi-Lo Foods, Sally's Hair Spa, a pool hall, two laundromats. There's not much retail left. A cabbie dropping off a fare points me to the nearest bar, two blocks south, Biff's Chop House. A hostess offers me a power seat, booth one, but I just need a spot at the bar and a word with the bartender. I don't think Biff's here. He's probably out getting more chops, a longer drive since the stockyards closed. No one knows anyone called Gaelen. But after I buy a second round, then a third—conducting a key word search through very soggy memory banks—the name Oren flutters onto the screen, along with its mate. "I think his last name was Bauer," says Leo, a retired shoe salesman. "Played softball in the summer league. Needed a haircut then too." The phone's in the back, near a cigarette machine the luncheon crowd is punching like a slot machine. My luck runs out. There are too many Bauers to check on a pay phone. A waitress brings me a double bourbon and a menu shaped like a horseshoe. I thank her. I thank the hostess, standing in for Biff.

The Oriental Institute at 58th and University is quiet as a tomb. Warren Frost is bent over a glass case reading the inscription on a folded card, a place setting for the mummy resting comfortably there. "Hasn't moved in three thousand years," Frost says. "Not a bad life."

"I thought you were taking me to lunch."

"I am, I am." He's bought a necklace at the

giftshop—Egyptian, gold, very expensive. "For Elenya," he explains.

"Really."

"I quit drinking—did I tell you that?"

"Frost, you're full of surprises."

I wait for him to finish his tour. Old pottery doesn't do much for me and I've seen enough dead bodies for one week.

Since lunch is on Frost no expense is spared. I should have eaten at Biff's. We walk the two blocks to the campus bookstore and clear newspapers and flyers off a ledge in the lobby. A student in ripped Levi's gets me to sign a petition—I don't even know what for. Frost buys a whole bag of food from the deli just to our right. He's wearing a wrinkled suit that looked better earlier in the day.

"My kind of place," Frost says. "A Jew deli run by eighteen Koreans."

Frost has a triple-decker he can barely fit in his mouth; pastrami, corn beef, tongue, all kinds of cheese, and Russian dressing. He may as well just mainline cholesterol right into his arteries.

"I hope you're hungry," he says. "I got chicken salad on wheat, tuna on white, I got plain tongue on rye."

"Give me the chicken salad. Who do you suppose it was ate the first tongue."

"Some epileptic maybe," Frost says. He hands me a sandwich and a coffee. "You need some creamer? Sugar? Brown sugar?"

"Give me one sugar." Frost is drinking orange juice without the vodka. He probably just found out it comes that way. "To what do I owe this repast, Warren?"

"I heard what happened to you," he says, munching like a grasshopper. "I was worried."

"Rushed right down here, did you."

Frost moves to his second sandwich. A girl sitting next to him is watching him eat. I catch her eye and shrug. She sticks a finger down her throat.

"I'm allowed," Frost says. "That's the program. Anything I want to eat during the first two weeks. Just so I don't drink."

"How long since you had one?"

"Since that Scotch we drank the other night."

"Now I understand. That Scotch would make anyone stop drinking. They should pass the stuff out at AA meetings."

"It was time to quit," he says.

"Just like that?"

"A man can change, can't he?"

"I guess." The new Frost. He must have had a very rough week. Frost never ceases to impress me.

"Are you working?" Frost says.

"A job for Donnie that starts Monday. Why. What do you want?"

"What makes you think I want something?"

"You're buying me food. Not especially good food but nevertheless I feel I'm being fattened up for something. What is it?"

"Did you get the banking records from Donnie?"

I shake my head. "He says you have them."

"He does? How strange. I wonder why he won't give them to you—"

"That's not exactly what I said—"

"The effect's the same. He's sitting on them. But why?" Frost ponders this but doesn't let deep thoughts interfere with his lunch. "Let me see who I can call. I know someone at Hyde Park Federal."

"Then I'll owe you for that too, won't I? In addition to lunch. What is it you have in mind, Warren?"

"First of all," he says. "Before you say anything about it, before you say no, I want you to understand that it's not for me—"

"Just tell me what it is."

"An act of generosity. Helping a friend. I'd do it myself but I'm a lawyer, Harding. I deal in litigation, civil proceedings—"

"Can we be more specific?"

"There's an office," Frost says. "And a desk. And something I need that's inside the desk—"

"I take it the office, and the desk, are locked?"

He nods.

"With alarms?"

"There might be one or two."

So much for litigation and civil proceedings.

"You want me to break in? Is that the kind of legal advice you give your clients? It's a wonder they never made you a judge." I give him what's left of my sandwich. "Thanks for lunch. You can have my pickle."

"Wait. It's for Elenya. He has letters of hers—"

"What kind of letters?"

"You know the kind," Frost says. "And recordings."

"And he keeps these in his office?"

"That's right."

"How do you know that?"

"He tells Elenya. He taunts her with them. 'Just try to divorce me,' he says. 'I'll put you all over the tabloids.' "

Putting himself there too I think, but say nothing—

in divorce cases people do crazy things. But letters? So what?

"She can't get into her own husband's desk?"

Frost shakes his head. "When this divorce thing surfaced he changed all the locks. And told his staff to stay away from Elenya. He pays their salaries, Harding, not her. They listen to him."

"This is the office building on Woodlawn?"

"Yes."

"You sure you don't want me to break into the Department of Surgery in the hospital too?"

"I hadn't thought of that," Frost says.

We walk through the bookstore. I pass the philosophy section quickly. Just seeing the *Republic* makes me reach for the Fiorinal. It's the same translation as Gaelen's. Frost loiters by the magazines.

"I like Elenya, Warren. I want to help. But the answer's no."

"I didn't mention the payment."

"It's not the money."

"That's good," he says. "Because there isn't any."

"Put the *Penthouse* down, Warren. You're getting pickle juice on Miss March."

I use the phone in General Books to call Alison. She's still grumpy. Luckily I have something for her to do and all she needs is a phone. I'm going after Rosenberg but not quite the way Frost planned. I give her Bauer's name too. "What's it worth," she says. "Fifty?"

"Forty," I say. You have to admire her, bargaining from a hospital bed. I buy a stack of magazines for her, the kind you can't get in the hospital gift shop—*Tattoo*, *Reps and Abs*, *Gothick Sex*, *Off Our Backs*, and two

UFO zines for me—I find the idea of space aliens conquering the world very comforting; maybe because all my money problems would vanish. The cashier gives Frost a dirty look when he grabs a handful of free bookmarks and four campus maps.

"I do have something to offer you," he says. "Kind of an incentive."

"What? More sandwiches?"

"Do you remember Michaels, the fellow on the license appeals board who turned your application down?"

"He wasn't the only one," I say. Internal alarms begin going off. "The vote was four-zip."

"But his vote counts for a lot. Especially now—he's vice chairman. Lots of pull. Lots of influence."

"So?"

"So I can't pay you. But I can deliver Michaels."

"You're joking," I say, staring. "He's squeaky clean. He's a Republican—he's a fucking Methodist. You can't deliver Michaels."

"It's done. He's delivered."

"Just like that?"

"Just like that."

"And how are you doing this?"

"You know how these things work," he says. "I have to tell you how these things work?"

"If it's that easy," I say, "maybe I should go see him myself."

"What, like during office hours you go in, you make an appointment?" Frost says, smiling. "I don't think so."

"Why would the governor sign it?"

Frost laughs. "You think he cares about you? Listen, some assistant signs it. They slip it in, some

Friday afternoon when the office is half-empty. Everybody's leaving early, they're thinking of Old Style, not Harding. Signing this, signing that. What's one more paper to sign? You worry too much."

"I like worrying," I say. Why this offer surprises me I don't know. In this city everything but potholes can be fixed. Nothing's final. Look at Rosenberg, fixing nature's little flaws. Nothing's final in his world either. He's pocketing millions. Look at his wife trying to fix that by filing for divorce.

I'm thinking of my business reopened, my license framed and back on my wall, a second chance, even as I hear a favorite phrase of my old man's; basic Chicago philosophy, echoing as loudly as my boots did on that warehouse concrete floor: the easiest cons are always the ones you pull on yourself.

"See Elenya," Frost says. "Talk to Elenya. Before you say no."

FIFTEEN

When I get to Greenwood Elenya answers the door dressed in jeans and a cashmere sweater, more casual than I'm used to seeing her. But she looks terrific—no makeup, her eyes clear. She takes me to a family room and offers me coffee. I say yes, wondering if Giselle will bring it but Elenya makes it herself. I follow her into the kitchen.

"I have to grind the beans," she says. "Stephen's obsession. When I get my own place I'm buying nothing but Folgers. And plain tea bags, not what Stephen insists on—loose Lapsang Souchong kept perfectly dry, cold spring water boiled in a separate pot. I'm dunking a tea bag in a cup of tap water and microwaving it."

There's something very erotic about the way she says "Lapsang Souchong" but I doubt it comes up in conversation much. "You're moving out?"

She nods. "I have a sister in Galena. She paints. I haven't gone there before because she's got five kids, troubles of her own. And because I don't like running—"

"You're not running."

"No?" she says, not convinced. "It feels that way. For months now I've pictured kicking Stephen out of the house. Instead I'm moving in with a sister I see once a year. Who has a husband even worse than mine, if you can believe that. But I just don't know where else to go."

"Galena's a little extreme."

"I know."

I pause. "You're welcome to stay with me. Until you can find someplace better—"

"Thanks, I don't think that would—"

"Unlimited tap water, unlimited aspirin. Tea bags too. Not even Lipton. Tetley."

"I appreciate it," she says. "But Warren thinks it would be better—until the divorce is settled—for me to stay with a neutral third party, like Sandy. No matter how crowded we are in quaint little Galena."

"Warren's probably right," I say. "But what a spoil-sport, being right all the time." We're both a bit relieved, I think, after this exchange. She'd rather find her own place. As for me—all I know is I want to help her. For some reason it's easier to do that if I keep my distance.

Besides, as Keegan would point out: the people near me tend to get hurt.

The green Krups is bubbling like a steam locomotive. There's a kitchen table but it's not the kind of house where it ever gets used. We take our coffee to the family room.

Elenya sits with her legs together, balancing her coffee mug on her knees. The rug is a large Early American shag complete with a large bald eagle. The last room we went through looked like French Provincial. Just as the exterior's a hodgepodge of designs every part of the interior seems to have suffered through a different decorator.

Elenya sees me looking at a row of pewter cups lined up on a mantel.

"Stephen's major flaw," she says. "Well, one of them. He refuses to throw anything away. Especially his trophies. Those are for golf. Or bridge. I forget which."

"Do you have much to pack?" I say.

"No."

"Stephen knows you're going?"

She nods.

"If I were him I'd be here trying to talk you out of it."

"You're not him," she says sadly. "But I do need to keep packing. I promised Sandy I'd pick up her kids from band practice. Do you mind coming upstairs?"

Well, no. I'm thinking that the way she looks in jeans Stephen should be nailing two-by-fours across the doors and windows.

Her bedroom is Laura Ashley with a dash of Crate and Barrel and an imposing queen-sized bed. There's one dresser and only one set of clothes in the closet. It's clear she moved Stephen out as best she could some time ago. She resumes packing, neatly folding clothes that she arranges in a large soft Samsonite.

"One of everything," she says. "That's what I keep telling myself. I only want one suitcase. Travel light. I'm sharing bunkbeds with a twelve-year-old, so it's not exactly a *pied-à-terre*."

"What about furs and jewelry? And money?"

"I have money. Not two million dollars but enough to tide me over. The furs I'm leaving. I don't even wear them anymore. Some jewelry, though, the really valuable pieces Stephen gave me early in our marriage. Things like this." She holds up a gold necklace with a heart-shaped pendant, large enough for a tiny picture, though this one's empty inside. "I really can't bear to look at them anymore."

"Melt them down," I say. Looking out the bedroom window I can see the path I took around the side of the house Sunday night. From here it looks like an obstacle course of trees and lawn furniture. Keegan's footprints are still visible on the garage roof. "Did the police ever apologize for that mess last Tuesday?"

"I don't know."

"What about Stephen—what's he said to you, since last week? Since you saw the pictures of him with Lucy."

"Nothing much."

"He hasn't denied it or explained or apologized or anything?"

"He said, 'You see? Now we're even.' Balancing the books, he says. For psychic pain I've apparently caused him over the years. God only knows what he's talking about. I don't think it matters much anymore." She takes a dress from her closet, compares it to another. "Hand me that garment bag will you?"

"He told me he thought you were having an affair."

"He did? When?" She doesn't seem surprised.

"That Monday."

"You didn't mention it before."

"I didn't think it was important. Supposedly that was part of the blackmailers' leverage. Besmirching your reputation."

She keeps packing, says nothing. I think she's rearranging the same clothes over and over. "He called me a whore once," she says. "One of those Thursday mornings. It took two Bloody Marys to get it out of him. And then he looked remorseful, and terribly guilty. 'I'm sorry, I'm sorry, please forgive me.' And then he hit me. That was the first time." She's avoiding my eyes. "Did Warren talk to you? He said he was going to talk to you."

"We had lunch, yes. I'm still digesting it. The food and the offer. He asked me to do something I'm not crazy about doing—"

"You don't have to. If you don't want to, I understand perfectly—"

"But that's Warren," I say. "If *you* ask—if you tell me something about it—"

This bothers her. "What's the difference who asks you?"

"In my business—all the difference, believe me. What is Stephen hiding?"

She says nothing for a while. I sit down on the bed beside her. She has a beautiful cashmere sweater in her lap. Her fingers slowly start kneading it like dough, twisting and stretching the fabric until I put my hands on top of hers, and she stops.

"Help me, Elenya. I'm in the dark."

"Last Friday," she says. "When I came to your apartment. I didn't come straight from home. I drove to that motel in Indiana—"

"Really? Why did you do that?"

"Someone called me—a man. I didn't recognize the voice. Not Gaelen. A younger voice. Said he was a motel manager and that my husband was there and needed help. I called the hospital and Stephen wasn't there."

"Why didn't you call me? Or Frost?"

"I tried calling Warren. I couldn't get through. And I didn't know you well enough."

She knew me well enough a hour or so later to sleep in my bed. But I don't say anything.

"The motel was dark. I nearly turned around. There was no one in the manager's office. But the door to room nineteen was standing open. The window was open too. And someone was in the bed."

"The lights were on?"

"No, but I could see—"

"It was just the bedclothes, Elenya."

"No, Harding—there was moonlight. It was Nora. And she was dead in a horrible way. Parts of her face were gone." She stops. "Why is this happening?" she says. "Do you know? Is it just because I want a divorce that all these people have to die—"

"No." It reminds me of Lucy's suicide note: *These things just happen.*

"Someone hit me. I must have blacked out. And when I woke up the body was gone. There was no one there. But it *felt* like someone was there. I had blood on my hands. The curtains were blowing—it was like a ghost story. I drove around for a while. Then I came to you."

"The bruise on your face was from him hitting you?"

"Yes."

"But you didn't see anyone, hear anyone's voice?" She shakes her head.

"Elenya. How did he hit you on the face, and remain unseen?"

"I don't know. Do you think I'm lying?"

"No, of course not. Did you leave your car unlocked at the motel?"

"I don't think so."

"What in the motel do you remember touching?"

"I don't know—"

"Where was your husband that night?"

"I'm not sure. He didn't sleep here."

"Does that happen often?"

"Enough," she says.

"What do you think the point of it all was?"

"The point? This is the point." She gets a small clasp purse from a bureau drawer, removes a key. The key unlocks a jewelry box. Inside is a single VHS cassette. It's a brand I've never heard of, from Taiwan. She feeds it into a Sony VCR and finds the remote for the television.

At first I think we're just watching TV, an old French movie, Robert Bresson maybe, on PBS—black and white; a donkey loaded with packs climbing a hill. Then I realize the movie's on the tape; subtitled in shaky letters. The screen goes blue, then refocuses— someone dubbed over the movie. This part's still in black and white. It looks like a cheap camcorder; the kind of surveillance film you see from a convenience store murder.

We see room nineteen of the Hoosier BudgetCourts from a corner angle. Nora lies in the bed, still alive. A woman enters from the side wearing a black fur. You can see Elenya's face fairly clearly. She walks to the bed and raises her arm and then there must be an edit but it's very skillfully done—the woman has a knife now, a letter opener, and she stabs Nora repeatedly. You can't see her face during the stabbing. You can't really see if Nora's alive or dead.

The woman leaves, her back to the camera.

The screen turns blue; the movie struggles back into focus. The pack donkey climbs down the hill.

"Can I see it again?" I say, and Elenya nods. She leaves the room to get a glass of wine while I run the tape back and forth. I can't see the cuts on this machine but any kind of decent equipment would show them. No one could hope to prove anything with a tape like this.

Unless they just wanted to frighten Elenya, make her stop fighting for the divorce money. They might have succeeded at that—she's leaning against the door frame, nervously downing Chablis. I turn the TV off, eject the tape. It's prerecorded, cheaply reproduced.

"It's an obvious frame," I say. "You shouldn't be afraid of it."

She nods, biting her nails.

"I got a phone call afterwards," she says. "That there are other copies of the tape—better copies, ones the police would spend months trying to figure out. That all the time I'd be in jail for murder. And lots of details about what would happen to me in jail."

"Unless you did what?"

"I don't know. They never called again. But now you see why I didn't go to the police about Gaelen—"

"You're sure it wasn't his voice on the phone either time?"

"No," she says. "I know his voice."

"Elenya, stealing a single copy of a tape like that from your husband's desk—if that's where it is—wouldn't help very much."

"Warren didn't explain this very well, did he?"

"Warren didn't explain anything, Elenya."

"I don't want you to steal the tape back. I know they might have tons of copies. But Stephen keeps a disk in his office desk. It's full of pictures—ones he took over the years. Of his little dates. He's put them all on one disk."

"You mean like a CD-ROM?"

"No, it's a computer disk. I don't know how they do it. But he can look at his favorite photos any time of the day. If he gets bored cutting people up. And I guess it's safer—there's no negatives around. It's easy for him to make copies."

"He told you about this?"

"I know about it," she says without expression.

"Frost mentioned letters—"

"They're mine," she says. "Warren wants the disk—he says it will be good self-defense. But I want the letters. Stephen had no right taking them."

"Elenya, this videotape—how was it delivered?"

"It wasn't," she says, finishing her wine. "That's why it frightens me. It was here waiting for me. As soon as I came in the room Saturday morning. It turned on all by itself. After the night at your house. All by itself."

She tells me briefly how she found it that morning—the TV and VCR plugged into a single power box; probably controlled by an exterior remote control. You can buy them anywhere. Remotes are just like pagers— with enough power you can go through walls, around corners. Since the tape was commercial it started as soon as the power went on. The equipment's in the basement now. She doesn't want to look at it anymore.

"That was nearly a week ago," she says. "What are they waiting for?"

"I don't know. Maybe they already got what they wanted. Let me check out the stuff in the basement."

I go down there by myself, turning on lights as I go. It's chilly and a little damp, the way cellars are in old houses. There are cracks in the foundation and spiders wintering in the masonry. Overhead fluorescents flicker uncertainly; the ballasts in half of them must be shot. They blink on and off, buzzing like locusts. The furnace is gas, located near a boarded-up coal chute. I wonder how many years it took to get rid of the coal dust.

The wiring and power box Elenya mentioned are in a bushel basket near the laundry room. They might have come from Radio Shack; there's no way to trace any of it. I lean against a warped closet door, near the fuse box, thinking that I'm in a familiar position— having more questions than answers. I'm getting used to it. There are piles of clothes all around my feet— mostly Stephen's—socks, underwear, shirts I recognize from past Wednesday nights. From now on he'll have to do his own dirty laundry.

Maybe it's the sight of the coal chute or the laundry smells haunting this little room—bleach, detergent, starch, the rusty drain in the cold concrete floor—that remind me of my own house and the way my mother spent her Saturdays—washing, ironing, folding my father's clothes—staying longer than she needed to in a basement much damper and darker than this. Our coal chute still worked—the last one on the block—emptying into a tiny room that couldn't quite contain the black dust. It spread like fallout through the house, covering my Little League trophies, taking the shine from my Schwinn if I left it down there more than a few weeks.

My father worked for a roofing company. He spent his days climbing across the tops of buildings, running up there like a child, tied down by black tar and gravel shingles. He was paid on Fridays, in cash, in a corner bar on Ashland that closed at six just for my father's company. Crews drove in from all over the Midwest. The beer was free. This was as close as the firm got to any kind of fringe benefit—insurance that wives like my mother actually saw some of the paycheck, before the men could drink it away.

Sometime after midnight Friday night the axis of my parents' world tilted. Being a roofer is a miserable job—climbing across rotting rafters, falling through soft spots or skylights, freezing in the winter or getting no work at all. Back on the ground the free beer raised dissatisfaction and frustration in the roofers like knots raised above the grain of the pine or ash they used to repair rotten wood. More than once I found my father dead drunk on the front lawn. More than once I helped him inside to the downstairs bathroom and held his head while he was sick, then wiped his face and put him to bed on an army cot. More than once I noticed those lightly amber bruises on my mother's arms. I learned to rise early on Saturdays, eat breakfast alone, finish my chores, and leave the house as early as possible.

"Someone was inside my house," Elenya says coming halfway down the stairs. Her arms are crossed against the chill. And then something in one of the ballasts pops, shorting the fuses, and we're really in the dark. There are no windows on this side of the basement. The only light's from the kitchen. That door swings slowly shut.

"Harding," Elenya says, sounding frightened.

"Don't worry, just go upstairs—"

I'm not sure which I hear first—the kitchen door being locked, Elenya crying from the stairs, or the closet door swinging open behind me. It doesn't much matter. When Gaelen's arm sweeps down across the back of my neck it drops me to one knee. I start to get up but he hits me a second time, even harder, an animal's feral fury. Despite the cool air he's sweating, probably from hiding in that closet, and his perspiration drips on my neck. Elenya screams something, asking him to stop but he's not listening. When he hits me again it feels like he wants to pound me right into the ground.

It's dark when I come to. The power's off. I wish now the Browning was closer than the truck. The house is silent.

"Elenya," I say. "Are you here?"

There's no answer, but I hear something on the steps.

"Yes," she whispers to my right.

"Are you all right?"

Again, no answer.

I bang my knee on a wooden support, feeling along the wall until I come upon the metal fuse box. When I flip the circuit breakers a bit of light comes from the kitchen. The door's open again.

Elenya hasn't moved. Her arms are wrapped around herself protectively. She's crouched on the stairs, her arms around her knees. She's pressed against the wall as far as she can go.

"Where did he go?" I say.

"Past me," she says trembling. "Upstairs."

"Did he touch you?"

"No, he just brushed my cheek. I didn't even really see him—"

"Did you hear him leave?"

"No," she whispers.

I take the stairs two at a time. I'm not armed but I'm dumb enough to hope he's still here. The first floor's empty and seems warm after the basement. Since Elenya's still downstairs I move quickly through the rooms to the upper floors. The house is too big to check every closet and look under the beds but I don't think he'd hide again. Anyway, he got what he came for: the videotape's gone and the bushel basket's now empty in the basement. Gaelen's cleaning up. As I return through the kitchen I realize I should have grabbed a knife. But I don't like knives much.

"Harding?" Elenya says, a strange emptiness in her voice. She's still on the stairs, half in darkness. I shouldn't have left her alone.

"He's gone, Elenya. I'd better call the police—"

"Just come down," she says, and so I do.

We sit for several minutes without speaking. My back hurts like hell, as does my neck and left shoulder. I listen to the house adjusting to the cold weather. Elenya's holding one hand lightly over her mouth, rocking back and forth like an autistic child. I don't know how to comfort her. I don't know much of anything.

"Let's go upstairs," I say. "This time you can give me the aspirin. And I could use another coffee."

"That's how this started," she says. "We had coffee. I was sitting alone and he offered—I don't know why I said yes. Except there's lots of faculty and grad students there. He seemed all right. He seemed normal. Whatever that is."

"You went out together?"

"No, this was in the gym. The coffee. They have a little restaurant, a health food bar. We talked about tennis. I was having trouble returning serve, because of my arthritis. And he looked at my hands, my wrists, and massaged them a little bit, very gently. That's why I thought he was nice. He seemed concerned. And gentle. I thought he *worked* there or something. Like a trainer." She shivers. "Only—then the gifts started arriving, and the phone calls and the flowers, and I came out of the Co-op to find him waiting to carry my bags—waiting the whole time in a pouring rain, just standing in the parking lot—"

"Let's go upstairs."

"—maybe I should buy a gun. Why doesn't he just go *away*—"

"It's cold down here," I say. "You'll feel better upstairs. And out of this house. I'll help you finish packing."

"Yes, all right," she says.

But she doesn't move. I have more questions about Gaelen but two things tell me this is not the time to ask them: the look on Elenya's face; the sliced wire I notice for the first time running from the main phone jack. Telling Elenya her phone's been tapped will just frighten her more.

"Why won't he go away?" she says again.

"He's going away, Elenya. I promise."

When I reach out my hand I'm not sure she even sees it. My fingers brush her sleeve.

Finally, she looks up and slowly extends her hand and I lead her upstairs.

SIXTEEN

"I don't need a gun," Alison says. I'm pushing her through the hall in a wheelchair, which she just loves. Hospital rules, I tell her. I'm lying. Her Nike bag's on her lap, the pajama feet stuck in the zipper. "I appreciate the gesture, Harding, but I can take care of myself. And my stomach hurts when I laugh so don't make me laugh, okay? No giggling, no chuckling, nothing. I mean it. No dumb jokes."

"Knock-knock."

"Don't try it, Harding. Don't even think about it."

In the elevator I begin a story about a horse in a bar but Alison quickly puts her Discman on and cranks up MC5. "Kick out the jams," she says loudly, playing air drums. A nun standing next to me shakes her head, fingers her rosary.

"Brain disease," I say. "Four, maybe five weeks."

"Oh dear."

The glass doors of the ER open with a gentle whoosh and we're outside in the cold. Under her black wool coat Alison's wearing a long red dress—something easy to slip on and off. I found it buried in her closet behind a dozen pairs of black jeans. I think the dress was designed to be tight but she's lost weight on the Jell-O diet. It hangs on her like a caftan.

I get the truck from the hospital garage; we drive

north on Cottage Grove toward 57th. I give her two hundred from the checkbook I'm using as a wallet.

"Where are we going with this?" she says pocketing the money.

"Your place."

"I mean this—this—" she says, holding up a sheaf of yellow pages torn from her notebook; the project I gave her on the phone. "And what about lunch? I never even had breakfast. You promised me hamburgers—"

"Tell me what you found out."

"Her name's Elizabeth Manning. North State Parkway, very classy digs not far from the old Playboy mansion. Speaking of implants—and I thought you said Rosenberg only did noses—these were silicone. But you must know all this already or you wouldn't have had me call."

"Tell me anyway," I say.

"She's still listed as a patient of his, her account's still open. And the account at Medical Records says paid in full. Like you thought. Everything's covered as 'medically necessary.' "

"What about the HMO?"

"At Reese? I told you—"

"At Mitchell."

"They're cool. Zero balance. I'm no CPA Harding but I frankly don't see where this is headed. The transfer payments are routine. I mean, if you're hoping to prove insurance fraud you'll have to do way better than this."

"And Rosenberg's office? What's the status of her account there?"

"What's the difference?"

"Humor me."

She sighs. "I never got through. Listen, as it was,

the nurses thought I was working a telemarketing scam—I was on the phone for an hour."

I make a quick U-turn right in front of the Medici. Alison can't believe it, seeing her MediciBurger vanishing right before her eyes.

"My lunch," she says. "My french fries, my malted—"

"We have to finish this today, Alison. Before everything closes for the weekend. At midnight Sunday my truck becomes a pumpkin and I become an art historian."

I'm either getting careful or paranoid. There's no one in the lot behind the Hyde Park Shopping Center but I have to circle twice before feeling comfortable with the spot. And I park the truck crossways to shield Alison from the wind and the gaze of southbound traffic.

"I have a phone in my bedroom," she says.

"I know. I like this one better."

She drops a quarter in the slot.

"You used to like my bedroom."

"I know but . . ."

"What?"

"It's gotten a little crowded in there."

She jabs me in the ribs. "You want me to apologize for something?"

"Absolutely not—I want you to use the phone before we freeze."

"What's the secretary's first name?"

"Sandra."

"Small office?"

"One or two nurses—" but she holds up her hand.

"Humana HMO," Alison says, her voice becoming low and gruff; she winks at me, "trying to close the file on Elizabeth something; computer's down, I'm looking at this really muddy carbon—Is this Sandy? Sandy, this is Dottie West again in Medical Records—"

"I like the low voice," I whisper. "Very butch."

"Shut up, asshole," Alison says. "No, Sandy, not you, I'm sorry—we have this kid interning from IIT—"

I open the passenger door of the truck and reach under the driver's seat. The Browning is taped to the springs. I undo the duct tape, check the gun's chamber and safety, then open my coat and tuck it in my belt. You could hide a small arsenal under this coat.

Alison is watching me from the pay phone. She doesn't like seeing the gun.

"How are we doing?" I say.

"We're on hold," she says. "You understand that to prove insurance fraud you'd have to access charts in the hospital and office both—short of breaking in I don't think there's any way you can do that, unless you know the passwords for both systems—"

"We're not proving insurance fraud. Is she still seeing Rosenberg?"

"One more time this Saturday. Routine follow-up. Here. Listen to this." She hands me the phone so she can find some gum. She's standing right next to me. "The two hundred you promised was for last Sunday, Harding. You still owe me for the darkroom, plus another fifty for today, right?"

"Forty."

"I thought we said fifty." Her fingers slide down my pants leg to my crotch. "You're still ticklish," she says.

"No, I'm not."

So she grabs harder.

"Shit, Alison, don't do that in this weather. You call that tickling?"

"I can do worse."

"Forty, fifty, what's the difference. It's negotiable."

Instead of Muzak, Cosmetic Procedures Inc. uses a tape loop of Dr. Stephen Rosenberg recommending facial and body sculpturing to achieve the ideal classical form. Implementation is less than Hellenistic—tummy-tucks, spider vein treatment, liposuction, abdominoplasty, breast enhancements. Microrhinoplastic enhancements.

"The problem," Alison murmers, "is the enhancements tend to wind up scattered through your immune system. Or down here, around your knees, or here, under your arms, or maybe here—"

"Stop it, will you?" I'm having trouble concentrating on the recording with my face this close to Alison's. "This is a public place."

"Your jeans are getting tighter," she says, amused.

"Fatty cells," Rosenberg says in a droning voice, "vacuumed from your corrugator cutis ani are said by some to resemble Tapioca or caviar or even small-curd cottage cheese—"

"I think it's lunchtime," Alison says, smiling.

The Medici's not a favorite spot of mine—it's crowded and overpriced and this stretch of 57th Street is dry. It's Alison's request. We're in a booth just past the open kitchen. I'm sitting so I can watch the door.

"God, that looks good," Alison says when the waitress brings the food—huge hamburgers on black bread, greasy french fries. "I'm going straight into a food coma."

"You're going to miss hospital food, Alison. Don't

come knocking on my cellar door when you need that Jell-O fix. What did you find out about the Bauers?"

"Nothing from them, not directly. Are you gonna eat all your fries?" I shake my head. "But the parish priest was very helpful. Mr. and Mrs. Bauer lived there fifteen years or so. Mr. Bauer—Max—had a problem with his heart and a problem with the bottle, the Mrs. came to mass very regular."

"Lived where?"

"Sorry—North Lincoln. Not far from your place, the dump you sublet coming out of prison. Where you first entertained *moi*. Hand me the ketchup, will you?"

"You have an address or phone?"

"They're dead, Harding. Deceased. Anyway they're not Oren's real parents. The Bauers were foster parents—and the place was like Grand Central with kids coming and going. Father Pat—don't you love it?—doesn't remember the kids' names and since I was Sister Teresa from Child Welfare I couldn't really ask—I supposedly *had* their names."

"That's all?"

"Not quite. Father Pat remembers young Oren very well. Because he worked at the church, don't you see. Oh, the boy was a wonder—"

"Your Irish accent is worse than mine."

"Sorry. Father Pat was a little vague at times. I think his arteries are narrowing a bit. Oren ran away. He thinks."

"How old was he then?"

"Fifteen, sixteen? Who knows, Harding."

"Why would he take the Bauers' name?"

"I don't know."

I write this down in my detective's notebook,

impressing Alison tremendously. *I don't know.* She takes what's left of my sandwich. "If you're not going to eat it."

I can get the rest from Child Welfare, I'm not really interested in the details of Oren's childhood. I just want to find Gaelen, tie him to Stephen Rosenberg. The rest is history.

"Elizabeth Manning's account is paid in full everywhere except Rosenberg's office," Alison says. "She had your basic thirty-thousand-mile tuneup. Spread out over three or four visits. She's paying it off in installments."

"I bet she is." I look around, disoriented for a second. The restaurant's a mirror image of the one I remember. But the furnishings and wooden booths look exactly the same. "Didn't this place used to be across the street?"

She nods. "Can you remember the last time we were in there?"

"A long, long time ago." The music was the same, though: Dylan. "Visions of Johanna." "Why?"

"The night of the Lascivious Costume Ball," Alison says. "Remember? The first of many stops before we went to Ida Noyes. You said you couldn't drink on an empty stomach."

"I did?" That's no longer a problem.

"You really don't remember?"

"That night's kind of hazy," I say. I do recall trash cans full of punch just inside the door, made from grain alcohol and food coloring.

"You don't remember dressing up like Superman and Lois Lane?"

"Which was I?"

"Superman," she says.

"Good, good."

"What about the nude Greco-Roman wrestling where you started a grape fight?"

"You're making this up."

"Remember how the night ended?" she says, stealing what's left of my french fries.

"Something romantic?"

"You tell me."

"At the Point?" I say, guessing. "Watching the sunrise?"

"Close," Alison says. "Very close. Billings emergency room, the nurses holding your cape, watching your stomach getting pumped."

"We had some great times," I say.

At the door to Alison's apartment I ask her to wait in the hall.

"Are you carrying me over the threshold?" she says, a bit impatient with my concern but she indulges me, she waits. I go through each room, open the closets, check the locks for any signs of tampering. Everything looks secure.

I put her Nike bag on her bed, and then I show her the gun.

"I know you can shoot," I say. "But if you want some target practice there's a place in Riverdale we can drive to. I'm as rusty as you are."

"Harding, really," she says. "I don't like guns."

"Take it. Please. Until this is over with. And you know the rest: don't go out tonight by yourself—"

"I have to go back to work—"

"Stay here. Don't let anyone in. And page me if anything happens. *Anything*. I'll be back in a couple of hours." I show her how the safety works, check to see she has a full chamber. It's only a .32 but I had Chang load it with devastators; full metal jackets. Gaelen's big but if the bastard's not wearing body armor he'll go down.

I just hope she'll use it. She likes to kick. With someone like Gaelen you need more than concentration and a good sense of balance.

"If anyone asks, the gun belongs to me," I say. "Tell them I've got the registration, the papers, everything."

"Who would ask?" she says.

I don't answer, unlocking the back door, going down the steps; I want to check the alley. The building's well maintained front and back and the rear steps face a row of stores so there's usually foot traffic even after dark. The back door is solid core with a heavy dead bolt. If I were coming in I'd come in through the front.

Alison waters her plants, sorts through her mail. I use the kitchen sink to wash my hands and face with cold water. I take two more Fiorinal, put a couple in my pocket, leave the bottles with Alison. My back's okay as long as I keep moving but my left shoulder aches and aches.

"How close are you to Felicia?"

Alison takes a breath. "Is this official police business or just deep background for *People* Magazine?"

"All I care about is your safety, Alison," I say. "Can you trust Felicia? That's all I want to know."

"Trust her?"

"If your life was on the line could you trust her?"

"I think so," she says.

"Good."

"Is my life on the life?" she says, watching me carefully.

"It could be. I want you to have somewhere else to go. In case something happens. Someplace I know you'll be safe."

"He wouldn't come after me—"

"He already has, Alison. Both of us. And I don't think he's through with us."

She takes this in. I'm upsetting her on purpose. Alison's one flaw is underestimating her opponents. On a day like this a little paranoia is very healthy.

"If you're going out to look for him, I'll come with you," she says.

"No. Not tonight."

"Then you should have the gun—"

"I have one," I say. "Lock your doors. I'll be back. Or I'll call."

I go out into her hallway, go upstairs and look around, then come back down. She's waiting at her door.

"Put the chain on too," I say.

"Harding—what I said the other day about bringing him back alive?"

I nod.

"Fuck it," she says.

SEVENTEEN

t's late Friday afternoon when I get to what passes for an office park on the South Side; a cluster of squat low-rise buildings in Calumet City. Out here the windows aren't tinted bronze or gold but covered instead with peeling green paint and thick black security bars.

Dr. Sawyer works on the third floor for something called Midwest Sports Medicine. Reilly was understandably cautious about nosing around in a doctor's office without good cause.

But I don't need good cause to do much of anything.

The waiting room's not exactly SRO. There's one old-timer with a walker, a mother with her daughter, a little girl with a sprained ankle reading *Highlights*. MRIs of famous torn rotator cuffs are framed like Monet's haystacks. A secretary in a white uniform asks if I have an appointment; I say no.

"Are you a new patient?" she says.

"I think so. I've been referred by Dr. Rosenberg." She nods. "Dr. Stephen Rosenberg." The name doesn't seem to mean anything to her.

"If you'll just fill out these insurance forms—"

"Is Gaelen here today?" I say.

"Who?"

"Gaelen? Doesn't he work here?" She shakes her head; again, no reaction. I have to fill out the forms standing at the counter; a nub of a pencil's leashed there with a string. I invent insurance and Social Security numbers and have to restrain myself from using favorite names from the third grade—I.P. Daley; Dick Hertz. And just in from the Orient—Hu Flung Poo, his good friend Dung Flung Hi. These are the kinds of jokes that get a yawn from Alison.

I go through most of the magazines, looking at the address labels. Some say South Side Associates, the name that was on the kid's video magazine. Some say Sawyer; some say Swann. Some say Midwest Sports Med. All of them have this address.

A nurse calls my name before I'm halfway through the latest *Bones and Health*. "You can take that with you," she says cheerfully.

Everyone seems glad to see me.

One mystery is soon solved. I wasn't sure why a doctor was living above an Indian restaurant. Sawyer's a chiropractor, borderline at best; both his diploma from a trade school in Grenada and his license look like photocopies. He's at least fifty or fifty-five but with the ruddy good health that comes from a tanning bed and too many vitamins. His blue jumpsuit's open at the neck and the skin there is thick and leathery, like a turtle's. Gold chains are in danger of disappearing in the furrows.

"I was hoping to see Gaelen," I say.

"Gaelen?" he says, surprised. "I haven't seen him in a while—why don't you take off your shirt."

"I thought he worked here—"

"Not really," Sawyer says. "Just for referrals. When someone needs a special massage."

"I've heard he has good hands," I say.

"He does, he does." Sawyer smiles at me brightly. "What can we do for you?"

I tell him I'm there for my back but when I take off my shirt it's my shoulder that gets his attention. "Oh my," he says. It must have changed color again. Sawyer's face changes color too, turning white; his eyes go to the ceiling and then somewhere behind his forehead. The nurse gets the smelling salts.

When he comes to he apologizes but he clearly smells a lawsuit. I'm given a quick light-fingered exam, pamphlets on reflexology, shiatsu massage, modality therapy, and cheerfully shown the front door. "Stay off that shoulder, you hear?" he says, as though I've been deliberately injuring myself. Well, maybe I have been.

The office closes at seven. There's a well-advertised ADT alarm system on the window in Sawyer's office; at least three doors and four locks between it and the front door. A determined thief would either know just what he wanted and go in fast, ignoring the alarms, or go in slowly through the ceiling.

I came prepared to do neither but I'm not quite ready to leave. Instead I move the 4Runner to a lot by a bar called the Dixie Chicken where it can sit comfortably among the friendly minivans and pickups. Inside there's a noisy Friday night crowd. I sit near a crowd of guys clearly in for the night, hang my paratrooper coat over a chair, and drink Budweiser. No one pays me much attention. No one notices when I pick up a blue denim jacket from the coatrack and head out the door. It's my lucky night. There's a ski hat in the pocket. Everything but gloves.

When I walk through a back alley to Sawyer's it's nearly seven. Since I don't feel like fooling with the outer door I go inside now and wait in the shadows on three. The only other tenant on this floor's a refinancing company whose office is stripped bare to the wallboard. They must have lost their lease.

The nurse comes out first but doesn't wait to try the handle. Sawyer must still be inside. I tap the single spot that lights the hallway, just enough to shut it off without shattering the glass, then wait next to the door. It's dark enough now that when Sawyer comes out and turns to lock the door I can catch the door with my foot before it closes, press one hand against his neck to keep him looking forward, and press the Browning against his back to keep him quiet. There's usually sixty seconds to turn off the alarm.

"Take my wallet—" he says. "Please don't hurt me."

"Are there motion sensors?"

"No, no—"

"Is the main alarm set?"

He nods. I push him back into the office with the Browning. The lights are off but with my encouragement he finds the alarm and switches it off. Then I tap him about the way I tapped the spotlight, just enough to knock him out. I assume he has health insurance.

I take off the ski hat—it smells like cheap fabric softener—and use Sawyer's keys to get through the other doors. Then I drag him back with me to his office. I get scared being in the dark alone.

Sawyer's office is pitch black but I only bang my knees once or twice before finding a coat tree by the window. Most doctors have penlights around and quacks like Sawyer overcompensate. His lab coat has three of them along with a heavy stethoscope, reflex hammer, tongue depressors; a pocket full of rectal thermometers imprinted with an alderman's name—great giveaways, I would think, at political rallies. There's a Kleenex-shaped box of surgical gloves in an examining room so I snap on a tight pair.

The penlight produces a narrow beam of light. The filing cabinet is next to Sawyer's desk, and there's a curious display across its metal top; plaster casts of spinal cords. If they're real we're dangerously close to Ed Gein or Jeffrey Dahmer territory. When I pick one up it bends and cracks. I put it down. It looks like a dusty crawfish—if Jonnie dropped one in my pants at the Belmont Cove I'd jump halfway across the room. As fetish material the collection's fairly powerful. Primitive Zuni figures, Hopi Kachina dolls look like Precious Moments in comparison.

The cabinet's locked but very old and these locks are easy to pop—you just yank the drawer far enough off its tracks. Of course, that involves prying the metal around the faceplate loose; luckily Sawyer's office is filled with helpful tools—metal splints, rongeur pliers, long forceps to pull the manila folders out. I think what finally pries the cabinet open is a tuning fork.

The files themselves are interesting, if not particularly relevant—lots of tax data the IRS would love to see, letters to other doctors about political health care issues, medical PACs, insurance kickbacks. Toward the back there's an unmarked file of nude photos, mostly men, but shot from behind; backbones and spinal cords in sharp focus. Some of them are postmortem. Some look like official autopsy photos. Some look homemade.

None of this is very helpful and may be more than I wanted to know. It isn't the skeletons in Sawyer's closet or the ones on his filing cabinet that interest me—I want something that ties him to Stephen Rosenberg. I want to know something about Gaelen.

I hunt for twenty minutes, through every file. If there's something here I don't see it. Even a ledger of consulting doctors with dollar amounts by each name—kickbacks for referrals—is missing Rosenberg's name. He isn't even on Sawyer's mailing list for Hanukkah cards. The best I can do is an AMA list of Chicago physicians, listed by specialty. Rosenberg's name is on here, of course. There's a black mark near his name. It could be an asterisk. It could be a dead bug.

I pour myself a drink. Sawyer's desk has two bottles: Old Grand-dad and Metamucil—a mix for an old-fashioned I don't really want to try. There's a tiny shot glass being used as a paperweight which I clean out with my shirt. This woodsy shirt is paying for itself.

On the desk top Sawyer has a handmade variation on those idiotic executive toys with four balls that knock back and forth. Sawyer's adaptation is less high-tech, more Fred Flintstone. I don't really want to think about where the balls came from. My eyes are getting used to the darkness now, and I can see what the shot glass was holding down—a faded black address book.

I get my trusty penlight; the beam's so tiny I have to read line by line like a portable scanner. I turn first to the Rs but Rosenberg's name isn't there. Then I go through the whole book checking first names, looking for Gaelen. No luck. No Gaelen.

But in the Ws I run across Wilson, Donald. What's even more surprising is the address that's listed—his home address with his unlisted home phone. I don't know what to make of this. But I don't have a lot of time for reflection.

Something moves at the edge of my peripheral vision. I turn off the penlight. There's someone moving in the hallway. It's not Sawyer; he's still down for the count. My eyes have adjusted to the dark so I sit and wait, something I've honed to perfection over the years.

He's moving now toward the front door. If I'm smart I'll just let him go, catch him in the hall or the lobby, even follow him out to the street, but I'm as dumb as ever. A sudden flush of anger seizes me thinking it might be Gaelen. Or even Martinez. I think of Angela. I put the penlight in my pocket and follow the shadowy form toward the waiting room.

My memory of that room isn't quite as sharp from this direction. I trip on an end table, not enough to make me fall, but since the figure is turning and I can see well enough to recognize Oren's face and the large revolver in his hand I hit the floor and roll over once—my back hurts like hell but it's surprising how fast you can move when somebody's shooting at you. A shot ricochets over me, tearing pressed wood from the prefab door frame. It takes me half a second to remember where the safety is on the Browning, enough time for the kid to turn and fire another shot wildly in the air, enough time for more plaster and wood chips to rain down on me. Not enough time for him to get out the door.

"Drop the gun," I yell once—some Amnesty International rule, I think. He's not doing well with the handgun; I bet he wishes he had the Mossberg pump. The thought that he might keeps me down, hidden and quiet. I assume this is the end of it.

But he turns toward me, not toward the door, raising the gun, not lowering it.

"I mean it, Oren—drop it now—"

I should have test-fired the Browning. My first shot is high but catches him in the shoulder. It throws him against the wall, pinning him there for a split second, like a butterfly under glass. My second shot puts him down. I don't need a third.

He's spread-eagled across the cushions of a vinyl couch. Instead of a surfer duck shirt he's wearing one from the Marine Corps that's now properly baptized. He's dead before I reach him. Semper Fi.

The gun must have fallen behind the couch. I don't bother looking for it. Better the cops find it where it fell. I reach inside his pocket for his wallet. There's no driver's license, no ID, just a picture of Cindy Crawford in a bikini and a fifty dollar bill he took off me the other night in the warehouse. I take it back. I take the picture too.

There's a key on the floor—it fits the front door. I put it back by the kid's outstretched hand. Who gave him a key? And the alarm code, which I see written on his wrist like a crib sheet—who gave him that? My heart's still pounding but not from seeing Cindy in fishnet. It's been a while since I've killed anyone. It's not something I enjoy doing. Still, I'm glad I'm on my feet instead of on the floor.

There isn't time for a drink, which I could badly use. I go quickly through the office wiping down places I was dumb enough to touch before I got the gloves. Sawyer's still out but he seems to be sleeping just fine, his nose twitching like a rabbit's, eyes in REM. He's probably dreaming of a waiting room filled with shin splints, multiple fractures, contusions. I wish I could sleep like that.

I'm on my way out when I decide to check the room the kid came from. It's not locked. There's not much in the room—an examining table, a sink, glass bottles with cotton balls and rubbing alcohol. But there's a small office-furniture desk, again not locked. On the top there's a stack of papers—the kid must have set these down when he heard me, because one or two are on the floor, another's outside the door. They're Illinois physical therapist license applications filled out neatly in black ink, all stamped "Denied," all for a Gaelen and all with different last names—Hughes, Hackett, Henry. One for each six-month period the last three years. The work address listed is Sawyer's. So is the home address. Maybe Gaelen was sleeping on the table, bathing in the sink. The rest of the desk is filled with a weird selection of pamphlets—gnosis, Taoist qi gong, meridian therapy, theosophy, tai chi, Young Republicans.

On my way out I grab the patient list and thumb through a box of diskettes sitting by Sawyer's Macintosh. They're labeled in a typical doctor's illegible handwriting—Sawyer's even mimicking that—so I just grab a handful and stuff them in my pocket. Then I leave, ducking out a back door into an alley. The crowd at the Dixie Chicken is even noisier now than before. The house band's playing Little Feat. I drop the blue denim coat and get my own, then walk through the darkness to my Toyota. A familiar light blue pickup is parked by a hydrant but there are too many people around for me to mess with it now. I dismantle the gun, wipe the pieces clean, then litter side streets all the way home.

The bar at O'Halligan's in Bridgeport is crowded with kids instead of the usual neighborhood drunks. A rock band is playing on what passes for a stage—a platform made of wooden pallets. With everyone dancing there are plenty of empty tables. Boone is drinking Singapore

Slings from a Collins glass. I'm drinking Killian's. It's one A.M.

"What do you call this shit they're playing?" I shout to Wes, the bartender. He has a towel over his shoulder, as though he's headed for the showers.

"Celtic-rave," he says. "The white kids like it. You need another beer?"

"And a shot, Wes."

Boone is watching the girls dance. Most of these kids don't go to college. This is a blue-collar bar. Friday night is when they let loose a little, the way they used to in high school. Most of them probably miss high school.

I picked up Boone at Video Savages at midnight. I don't feel like going home yet. Gaelen's application is in my back pocket with Cindy Crawford. I don't feel like pursuing either right now.

"It's just an idea," Boone is saying. He's a little drunk. "Just a way to make a little extra money. I'm not exactly getting rich as a promotional bunny. And this thing you want me to help you with tomorrow is just for spec—"

"It might turn into something. You never know."

"That's what I said, Harding. You want me to work all day for nothing, for some woman I don't even know—"

"What do you mean—make a little extra money? How?"

"Think phone sex," Boone says. "They get fifty bucks a cover and then five bucks a minute for stuff that's either canned or so scripted you might as well be watching the Playboy Channel."

"How can you afford cable on a promotional bunny's salary?"

"I ran a line from Mr. Gronski's basement down-stairs—that's not the point, Harding. Computer sex, phone sex is big business these days. A lot of it's done around here. Porn's illegal in these little towns. Farm boys need someone to talk to after they've put the cows to bed."

"I bet you've got some phone bill."

"Not exactly," he says. "I've got this other box I built with mail-order parts. And I ran another line through the basement."

Boone's undergrad major at Chicago was physics, not all of it theoretical.

"What does computerized sex and phone phreaks have to do with Rosenberg?" I say.

"Nothing. It was just an idea."

"What idea?"

"Forget it."

"Don't pout," I say. I'm in no mood to go home. "What was your idea?"

He pulls his chair closer. "This thing we're doing at Rosenberg's office. We could leave the camera and taps in for months. And we could sell everything to Janie's cousin Richie when we're finished."

"Janie your ex-girlfriend? Richie her cousin the seminary student at St. Rita's?"

"That's Father Richards, Harding, her other cousin. I'm talking about Richie Dugan."

"I thought Richie Dugan was selling tires."

"You're still thinking of the deal Father Richards got me on those four Michelins," Boone says. "That was Father Richards, Harding, he's out of the seminary now. He's assistant at St. Boniface."

"I remember the priest delivering the tires," I say. "But those weren't Michelins. He had a warehouse of them behind the parish. You were stiffed. It's like a cookie sale or a bake sale. You made a donation."

"Father Richards said they had to scrape the label off to sell them below market price."

"They were retreads from Bolivia or Panama; they sure as hell weren't Michelins."

"So how come you can still see the outline of the little Michelin cartoon guy on the inseam?"

"The fucking priest drew that on with a magic marker," I say, downing the shot and then the rest of my beer. "You should stay in Temple, Boone. Messing with a Chicago priest is the big leagues. What does this have to do with Rosenberg—did he got stiffed on some tires too?"

The band is playing *She Moved Through the Fair* in a loud, power-chord arrangment. It sounds like the Chieftains jamming with the Ramones. Wes the bartender brings me another beer and yet another shot.

"Richie Dugan," Boone says, sipping his drink, "is a part-owner of Video Savages. That's how I got the job. He runs a 900 service out of the back. And a couple of sex bulletin boards on the Net. The people who join spend big bucks to download binaries and gifs—"

"Speak English, Boone."

"Dirty pictures. They get tired of professionals. They love amateurs. They transfer these pictures to their computers; trade them back and forth like baseball cards. Richie's always looking for fresh material. Like what we'd pull off that camera. Even if there's no sex, just naked women. I know he'd be interested if we asked him."

"But did we actually ask him? Tell me we didn't ask him."

"No," Boone says. "Of course not."

"How lucky for us."

"It was just a silly little idea I had."

"Don't sell yourself short," I say, finishing my beer. "It's one of the silliest fucking ideas I've ever heard."

The band is playing *Sir Patrick Spens* with feedback and a reggae beat; the crowd is skanking as much as white kids can skank. A banner over the door says it's "Island Music Night"—I guess Britain and Ireland are islands just as much as Jamaica. I find a pay phone next to the bar.

Overhead there's a television showing Australian rules football; very boring. No one's watching. There's probably a bar in New South Wales right now showing American Seniors Tour golf. I turn the channel to a movie.

Alison answers on the first ring.

"Whatcha doing?"

"Nothing, Harding. Watching TV, flat on my back. My stitches are driving me crazy. I was just thinking of you—there's a telethon on Lifetime for male menopause."

"Thank you," I say. "I was going to watch the movie on eleven."

"We can do that," she says and I wait while she switches her set. Gene Kelly, in striped shirt and beret, is dancing with a cartoon mouse. Leslie Caron sits somewhere nearby.

"Oh God, this is one of my favorites," Alison says. "I always wanted to be a dancer. Did I tell you that?"

"I believe you did, yes. Did I ever tell you my idea for remaking old movies with zombies? Right here, for instance, all these kids dancing with Gene could turn into flesh-eating zombies. Gene would have to lay down a suppressing round of automatic gunfire to get back to his studio and paint. Or you could have cartoon zombies chasing the cartoon mouse."

"Harding are you drinking?"

"Not anymore," I say. "I quit a good ten minutes ago."

"And so you called me. How sweet."

"I called," I say, "to see if I could get you anything, do anything for you." Gene is swinging around bannisters, leaping flowerbeds. I have always felt that Gene is unnaturally brawny for a dancer. But that's just the kind of thing that could save your ass if confronted with zombies.

"Are we on for tomorrow?" she says.

"If you feel up to it." I can tell she's tired but I don't feel like hanging up. "Can you get the truck?"

"I think so. You don't want to rent something?"

"We're on kind of a budget here, Alison."

Searching for topics I tell her about Richie Dugan, gray-market Michelins, Father Richards, shrike attack birds, Boone's job at Video Savages. Anything except what happened tonight, which I'm doing my best to forget. The alcohol helps some, especially combined with drugs. In situations like this, drugs are underrated.

"Are you following this?" I ask her.

"Not really," she says. "Though I did have a Princess phone when I was fifteen. Isn't Kelly terrific? Did you see that extension?"

"I bet you were a handful at fifteen."

"Oh, I was a real wildcat," she says, laughing. "You would have been no match for me."

"I'm no match for you now," I say, aware that my

voice sounds funny and wishing now I hadn't called her. Jesus, I can be goofy sometimes. Wes has my tab. I point him toward Boone and accept a final beer.

When I pull out money for a tip Cindy's picture floats to the floor. A woman in heels and a tube dress hands it to me, smirking slightly; I don't blame her. "It came with the wallet," I say. There are numbers on the back—R34-L62-R27—and a name—"Bev Lans"—I hadn't noticed, written in soft pencil. I don't think the numbers are Cindy's measurements; I hope they're not Bev's.

"I just wish you'd have waited for me last Sunday. And let me go in first."

"I know, Harding."

"I worry about you, that's all."

"I know, Harding, I know. Jesus, you're a sweet drunk."

"Astaire or Kelly, who's the better dancer?"

"Astaire," she says. "But my money would be on Kelly in kickboxing. In a fair fight anyway."

"You're saying Fred Astaire would cheat?"

"Those metal taps on his shoes, Harding. They could be deadly."

"Gotta go," I say.

"Gotta dance," she says.

EIGHTEEN

eilly can talk to me now because he has a homicide. Technically it's not his case but when Sawyer mentions Gaelen as a "disgruntled former employee" bells go off in Reilly's head and that means my pager goes off in O'Halligan's men's room. Everyone around me checks their beepers before zipping, not a pretty sight. There's pager panic in the stalls too—a loud splash announces that someone has slippery fingers.

They're treating it as a robbery, probably the first piece of luck I've caught on this case. I have Sawyer to thank for that. He told Reilly there were two men, one of them a real big guy wearing a denim jacket. The big guy must have killed the kid and kept everything.

I'm not sure why Sawyer invented this scenario—a box of diskettes doesn't seem like grand larceny—until Reilly shows me Sawyer's list of missing items: a fax; CD-ROM; laser printer; portable X-ray unit; assorted medical equipment. The estimated inventory loss is over fifty thousand. "Luckily, he's insured," Reilly says with a wry smile.

They're having trouble putting a name on the kid I shot, though. Sawyer claims not to know him. His prints don't match anything local. They're sending his picture around the country. "White trash," Reilly says. A runaway with track marks to rival Lucy's. "If we're lucky he's got something more than rehab for a record." No one but his mother's mourning. A parole officer somewhere gets his caseload lightened. Sawyer gets a new office.

I confirm that the kid's the one who helped Gaelen work me over. I don't tell them that he might have lived with the Bauers. I don't want them thinking I know more than they do, that I've been after this kid. Reilly says that Gaelen was a physical therapist who lost his license years ago and disappeared. "Sawyer said he tended to get a little too physical. I guess you could attest to that, right, Harding?" Sawyer felt sorry for him so he gave him space in his office when he came back to town last summer. Last names are a problem—Sawyer knew him as Gaelen Hughes but someone else says his last name was Henry. Addresses for Gaelen are years out of date. The probation officer has him living at 4700 East 63rd. That would put him in a very exclusive neighborhood with a wonderful view of the lake, though humidity might be a problem. He'd be twenty or thirty feet underwater. The Social Security number is faked.

A uniform will talk to some other chiropractors and physical therapists. When the state office opens, Reilly will check Gaelen's old license and get a photo—until then I should stay out of it. I agree I look terrible, I should get some sleep. Where was I last night? At Alison's apartment. Reilly calls and Alison backs up my alibi. I have no doubt that this will cost me money.

Since it's Saturday I'm not confident about the state office finding Gaelen's records—not today. I make a few calls of my own, borrowing the White Pages from the desk sergeant. "Landsburg, B; Landsbury, B; Lans-comb, B"—I run through every permutation, annoying one and all by asking for Beverly at five A.M.

When I trade in the White Pages for the Yellow I annoy the desk sergeant but it's worth the aggravation. There's a quarter-page ad for Beverly Landscaping. I drive out there through a steady snowfall and find the front door locked—it's still pretty early—but someone's home; syrupy violin music seeping underneath the garage door. An old man fixing lawn mowers opens up. Gasoline fumes and semiclassical Muzak pour over me in equal amounts.

He regards me suspiciously until I ask which he prefers—101 Strings or Paul Weston's *Music for Dreaming*. His face brightens. We discuss how the Boston Pops went downhill under Williams, classic recordings by the Jackie Gleason Orchestra, and mourn together the loss of Lester Lanin and Guy Lombardo.

"Tunes had melodies then," he says.

"Tunes had tunes," I agree.

"And I don't like this *jazz*. Where in hell's the melody?"

"I bet you're a Ferrante & Teicher man. Les Baxter."

"Oh, we think alike, my friend," he says, then remembers we're in a room full of Toros and Cub Cadets. "Didja leave a snow blower to be fixed? Or a mower? We're running that off-season special again this year." He looks around his shop as though mine could be recognized by its easy listening attitude. What kind of mower does Floyd Cramer use?

"A hedger—I left one to be sharpened with a kid a while back but I must have lost the receipt. And I can't remember the kid's name. Owen, maybe? Or Oren? He was wearing this Daniel Boone jacket and I think he had gold tattoos around his throat, like a choker—"

"That sounds like Oren," he says nodding. "Haven't seen him in months. Sure it wasn't a power rake—I seen a power rake go through here a week or so ago—"

"Could we call him and see? Would you have an address or phone number for him?"

"Over in Personnel," he says, and I think he means another building but instead he holds the door open for me and I follow him to a back room connected by a long wooden hallway; it creaks and bends like a gangplank.

Personnel is a cardboard filing cabinet. Oren's application lists his last name as Miller but I wonder about that, since the address on East Congress he's given would put him in the middle of Monroe Harbor. Oren clearly has fun with his forms. The Social Security number's bogus and I'm surprised I.P. Daley isn't listed as a credit reference. But something jumps out at me. In a spot for "closest relative" Oren's written, then scratched out Gaelen's name, and an address that's definitely above sea level. It's just readable, when I hold it to the light.

"You have to understand, we mostly hired Oren to cut lawns. Last summer he worked some on the crews doing tree and stump removal. Winters we don't hardly see him. But if he's misplaced your hedger we can probably find you another one just as good."

"Oren had a friend with him named Gaelen—a real big guy with short dark hair, an earring, lots of jewelry—"

"Sure."

"Does Gaelen ever come around here?"

"Yeah, he worked here some too," he says. "Part-time, not on the payroll. Sort of a big brother. And I believe he got Oren back to the church."

"Gaelen's religous?"

"My yes. Born-again."

"I guess he used to be a physical therapist."

"Really?" the old man says. "Seems to me he had some kind of job at a butcher's or a meat packer's. Used to kid everybody at lunch, which part of the cow they was eating that day. Which reminds me—this one time out in Park Ridge?" He pushes his baseball cap back on his head. "Oren and me were working for this fella wants a ground mole captured alive, taken to a forest preserve or a zoo or something—won't let us use poison or traps, nothing. 'Don't hurt the little mole,' he says. Like it's a poodle or a cat or something. So we spend all day digging the guy's yard up till it looks worse than what the mole did to it. Finally we corner the sucker, flush him toward Gaelen with water hoses, and then—and this was a thing of beauty, you really had to see it—Gaelen scoops the mole right out of the tunnel with his shovel, flips it up in the air and then *wham*—slams it with the shovel like he's hitting a baseball. All in one motion. Well, the other guys on the crew just applauded. It was a work of art." He laughs. "He knocked the living bejesus out of that mole too."

"That sounds like Gaelen," I say.

There's a safe sitting behind a white laminate desk; I assume the numbers on Cindy's picture must open it. Oren must have been planning a small-time robbery; helping himself to seed money.

"You see Oren, you tell him to stop by," the old man says. "Let me hear what he's doing with himself."

"You know Oren," I say. "Probably not a hell of a lot. Lying around somewhere."

"You got that right," the old man says.

On the way out I notice two things—Lawrence Welk's *Tribute to Cole Porter* album on the stereo; and Schaumburg Associates' We Protect sticker on the window glass. I don't know which I find more unsettling.

The address Oren scratched out is an old railroad flat in Harvey. There are places to park in front but I leave my truck around the corner. There's no name on the mailbox. I go first around back to see if the Grand Am's at home, and find a narrow staircase leading to the cellar and a slatted wood door with a forgiving lock. I walk in darkness for a few feet until the string from a sixty-watt bulb glances off my cheek like a snake in a carnival haunted house. There's just enough light to reveal a room crowded with storage; flimsy cardboard boxes, newspapers tied with string, old *Life* and *Look* magazines, 45s, a pink record player. There are two other tenants in the building and their names are everywhere in plastic lettering. Clearly somebody got an embosser for Christmas.

Over to one side—behind cast iron barbells and a weight bench—I see the junk taken from Maywood Storage—boxes, end table, headboard. A box of basement tapes. There's a Xeroxed list, in Nora's hand, the same handwriting that was on the storage application. The list displays an academic's fondness for detail. Described are dates with Lucy, Stephen, and Robin in various combinations, tapes and sexual acts compiled like footnotes in a thesis. The Wednesday night sessions sound vaguely familiar but there are others—

mostly Tuesdays and Fridays—that definitely break new ground. Also here—in another hand—are notes someone's made on Nora and Robin—campus addresses, phone numbers, class schedules, clothing, hairstyle. Surveillance notes.

Other than the home gym nothing else down here seems to be Gaelen's. I fight with a lopsided closet door for a few moments before it opens on an ancient burial ground; there are gray metal shelves full of abandoned pickles and preserves, old-fashioned mason jars with thick white wax at the top, like specimens in a medical museum.

Upstairs the only lock's a bicycle lock shoved through a cheap metal hoop, like you might find on a barn door. I'm wearing gloves and I don't want to break in but when I pull on the lock it falls off. No one turned the combination.

There's a large front room with very little furniture; a kitchen and dining nook; two rear bedrooms. One I sense is Gaelen's, only because it's freshly painted, white on white; with two ornamentations—a large wooden cruciform, relic-like in its realism, and a framed picture of Elenya Rosenberg. Gaelen must be struggling, trying to serve two gods. There's a spartan-like bed and stiff-backed chair that look purposely uncomfortable. A few clothes hang in the closet; I don't see a hair shirt. Instead of a door there's a white muslin curtain more like a veil.

The other room is Oren's, and looks more secular. A mattress is on the floor, covered with a dirty sheet, surrounded by magazines—*Topheavy*, *Adult Video News*, *Outlaw Biker*, *Skin & Tattoo*. The dresser is unfinished pine with an ashtray full of Marlboros and clipped roach ends. A collection of beer cans is stacked in the window.

They weren't rinsed very well; a line of ants is picnicking on the pop-tops. Wine bottles are topped with candles and melted wax.

A sketch book and drawing pencil are on the far side of the mattress. The book's filled with Frazetta-like women riding winged horses; the stuff of heroic-fantasy comics, bad tattoos. On one of the pages—with yet another Amazon astride Pegasus—there's a curious drawing of a rectangular box. The horse and woman are lushly drawn; the box is like an exercise from mechanical drawing school. The numbers "75-15-10" are written on the horse. Another safe, another combination? The horse doesn't look like something Brinks would use. The box looks more like a refrigerator. Or a coffin.

Once again I'm looking for some connection to Stephen Rosenberg. I find one but it's not the one I was hoping for.

Hanging with the grunge uniforms of a twenty-four-year-old male in Oren's closet are some women's clothes. There are just one or two outfits—a sweater, coat and hat, no shoes. Oren's not cross-dressing. The clothes are Nora's. The coat's the one I described to Alison; the one she followed from I-House to Kent. Most of the stuff still has Nora's name sewn on the labels, a mother's way of making sure the clothes could be easily identified. It worked.

With Oren's long hair and short stature and Nora's coat it's not hard to see how Alison was fooled. Lucy said she was going to I-House at the same time—that's when she was knocked out. Maybe they were afraid she'd seen him, or would remember something. For me at least this ties Oren and Gaelen to Nora's death. So does a tape I find in Nora's coat. I pop it into Oren's cheap rack stereo and have to scramble for the volume control. It's a tape of a woman screaming, and yes, it sounds like Nora. But not the way she screamed when I heard her on Wednesday. These are clearly screams of pain, and terror, and they're very difficult to listen to.

I back up the tape and find a familiar spot.

"All right all right I'm doing it— Hello my name is Robin and I really need to see you tonight at Chamberlain House—"

The call that led me to Robin's room, made by Nora. No wonder the fear was so real in her voice. There are other tapes—Rush, Kentucky Headhunters, Molly Hatchet. Oren must be in a band. Some of the tapes are plodding roadhouse covers of Clint Black and Alabama. There's a Gibson six-string in the closet. I'm looking around the living room when the music breaks off into a performance piece by Gaelen that scares the shit out of me. It's a cappella. Gaelen doesn't need any backup.

I am one I am one I am one I am the one . . .

I'd like to let Reilly just find this. But with Gaelen's shrine to Elenya the police might get the wrong idea. Especially if they see what else I find in Oren's closet—a pair of expensive leather gloves, with a fur hat that matches the coat Elenya wore to my apartment. The gloves are badly damaged. The leather is creased and burned, with yellow stains that were scrubbed but wouldn't come clean. Something similar was tried with the hat—it's pinned to a dry cleaner's hanger. An attached tag has a picture of a very sad owl. "Hooty the Owl Says—We're Sorry! Not Every Item Could Be Restored." A box marked "irreversible damage" has an emphatic check mark, right by Hooty's beak.

I start to leave through the front door but there's a CPD squad pulling slowly to the curb up the street. So I leave like a thief, taking the sketchbook, noticing as I hurry down the back stairs that the book has my name written on the cover, several hundred times, the way teenage girls do for their latest crush. I need my sunglasses; the morning sun grows brighter, even as the temperature drops. The alley is littered with garbage.

When I finally get home from my all-night odyssey Minas stops me on the stairs. He smells like green peppers. Saturdays are big money for him; tourists lose their way, think Lakeview is Greektown. I steal a cup of coffee. I'm too tired to bother with the microwave.

"You do this again, you lose your lease," he says.

"What lease?"

I think he's overreacting—the coffee's from last night for God's sake—until I get to the top of the stairs; once again I'm walking on wood chips and plaster. I should have come home sooner. My front door's sitting in my living room.

The apartment's much worse this time; Gaelen's frustration at not getting what he wanted. What he wanted was me. Deep grooves are cut in the furniture like wood worked over with a bowie knife. The thick vinyl on the recliner has been flensed like animal skin. The drapes have been yanked from their metal rods. He's tied the cord into a hangman's noose and it's dangling over a director's chair whose arms have been ripped off and tossed aside. They're a poor substitute for the arms Gaelen was hunting for. He's even left marks on my walls, probably a comment on my color scheme; I should switch to white on white.

He left my books alone, though, which gives you some idea of his value system. He wouldn't hurt my hardcover *Iliad* but would probably have killed Minas if he'd gotten in his way. Modern Greek, Ancient Greek.

"Dr. Winkler—he said he was a city inspector," Minas says. "He even showed me a badge. It looked very official. A very shiny badge."

"Yeah, it's very effective," I say.

"I'm buying the bird," Minas says.

The bedroom's the worst.

No chance of me creating any cozy New England-ish effect with that Ralph Lauren four-poster in here now. Gaelen's marked his territory, just like room nineteen at the Hoosier BudgetCourts. He must have had a few coolers too before arriving. I open the windows, then close them back up; there's not much point. I'm not staying here tonight. The apartment no longer seems to belong to me.

The contrast between his room and mine is unsettling. So is Gaelen's selectivity. My stereo's in pieces, but only some of my records have been broken: Patti Smith, the James Gang, The Who. A Louisville Slugger signed by Ron Santo I keep for summer softball and midnight prowlers has been snapped in two—over Gaelen's leg, I imagine. And a daguerreotype Alison refinished and gave me still hangs on my bedroom wall, frame intact, perfectly straight, with a single slash mark through it like a cut that didn't bleed. My closet's full of surveillance electronics, untouched, but it takes me ten minutes to figure out what's different about my desk—he didn't take the portable CB sitting there since last Sunday, just dropped it on the couch on his way out. It's still set to channel seven.

On top of the bed, smelling the worst, is an old suitcase of mine; the only luggage I own. I don't travel
much. I may travel less now. Some of my clothes
are folded inside, covered with excrement. There's no
note anywhere, nothing written in blood on the walls
but the message couldn't be clearer if he'd sent me a
greeting card.

My phone's tangled under my couch but it still works;
so does my answering machine. I punch Rewind; the
machine whirrs backing up. There are three messages.
The first two are diatribes from Donnie and Frost, both
pissed at being called in by the cops concerning some
kid neither one knows—Oren something—they want to
talk. They want to know what in the hell's going on.

The third one's longer. It's from Reilly, sounding
relieved at finding a machine to talk to. They found lots
of stuff at a place in Harvey. They have prints from a
truck they towed that match prints found in both Kent
and the motel. And blood samples from the back of the
truck. Small world—the truck belongs to Oren—his last
name's Bauer—and both of them lived in the place in
Harvey. So they're picking up Gaelen, as soon as they
can find him. And they're bringing in Elenya Rosenberg too—somebody set this up, paid Gaelen and Oren,
and she's got motive to her eyeballs. Robin, Nora,
Lucy—they were all doing her husband. And isn't she
filing for divorce? And isn't there some Swiss account
Stephen might be persuaded to share if he was facing
prison and a murder charge and she could get him off?

*He'd have to be persuaded. Gently persuaded. That
it was in his best interest to do this thing. Everybody's
best interest, really—*

Did I know Elenya was having an affair with this Gaelen? Some mad passionate affair that Rosenberg's told everybody at the hospital about—am I the only one who didn't know?

Did I really think the case was closed? Did I think the police were that stupid?

The phone rings, layering chimes over Reilly's goodbyes. I press pause.

"You need to come downtown, Harding," Reilly says. Hello and Goodbye. "So we can have a little talk. Have you ever considered working for the city? Because you're down here more than I am."

"Look, I got your message, Reilly. I'll come down but I have no idea why you're arresting Elenya Rosenberg, and anyway what she needs is a good lawyer—"

"That's not why I called. We found your prints in Robin's room—you know that, don't you? And all over the motel and Kent—and on the watch. It's your watch, isn't it?"

"Yeah, it's my watch. And that's just what I'd do after shooting somebody—stuff it in his pocket."

"Hey, we don't know. Maybe you wanted to see if it was waterproof. Test the warranty or something. Reason I called—the gun the kid used in Sawyer's office. The .44. It's the gun that killed Robin."

"Small world."

"Oh it's getting even smaller. We found your prints in that office too. And this .44—are you listening?"

"I'm listening."

"Because I hate talking to myself. The number's gone but the lab pulled up enough for us to check the old records. It's registered to you."

"What?"

"It's your gun, Harding. Or it was, ten years ago,

when you were licensed. I think you said you lost it somewheres in Kentucky? A lake?"

The third message is very brief.
     "Don't give up on me, Harding," Elenya says. Then she's gone.

NINETEEN

Sleep will have to wait. So will Donnie and Frost.

The job I have planned normally takes a week or so to set up. I have one day. Frost doesn't care when I go inside but I do; Elizabeth Manning is due at Rosenberg's office at eight P.M. tonight. I want to be there—electronically at least. It may be nothing but I don't know what else to do. Boone will help me and so will Alison. Until the cops bring Gaelen in I'd rather have Alison uncomfortable in the truck than alone at home.

Rosenberg's medical office on Woodlawn is a converted brownstone. It's too close to campus for us to try anything after dark. And it's secured like a fortress. After the alarm systems at Greenwood that shouldn't surprise me but this place is even worse. Sitting on Woodlawn Avenue in my truck I can count at least three lines piggybacked on phone wires. They're ID sensors that are usually hooked to exterior motion detectors, overkill in an office building.

The sky is clouding; there's a storm due in later tonight. Right now there's a little wind but no snow. The temperature's fifteen degrees.

Boone goes inside for a brief look. "You're a fresh face," I tell him. "So to speak."

"You're right—those are motion detectors," he

says. "Some German brand I've never heard of. Lots of umlauts. The place is bigger than it looks. And something's wrong."

"What do you mean?"

"Some of the stuff's real new. Other stuff looks disconnected that shouldn't be. And there's way too many wires around back and in the lobby."

"Maybe they're remodeling. What's the floor plan look like?"

"There's doctor's offices on all four levels. A basement door off the lobby. The back doors look sealed, so one must be a fire exit. A tiny elevator they must have built just for federal standards—it's just a fucking brownstone, Harding. The others on this block probably weren't thrilled having it rezoned. And see that fence around the backyard? Inverted barbed wire, real heavy-grade, five-inch hooks you could hang meat from."

"What floor is Rosenberg on?" I say.

"Three. There's a shrink across the hall, the rest of the building is lousy with ophthalmologists." He folds up the little map he's drawn. "I couldn't get past the receptionist, Harding. Somebody has to get into the back office."

"I know."

"Somebody has to go inside."

"I know, Boone." A horn beeps behind us. Alison waves from the cab of a borrowed truck.

"Your muscle's here," Boone says, adjusting the rear mirror. "Will you look at that. She got her hair cut."

"Yeah, she did, didn't she." It's shorter, more stylish, combed to the side in a boyish part. Alison pulls alongside in her truck.

"What are we doing?" Alison says, smiling at me.

"Park it," I say. "We're going in."

*   *   *

Chang is very proud of the equipment he loans me. Most of it's state-of-the-art circa 1975—heavy oversized analog receivers and amps. "Everything still with original warranties, Harding," he says. As though I could mail all the paperwork in twenty years later. Chang also supplies me with a different gun, a 9mm Glock that's even lighter than the Browning. It feels like a toy but Chang tells me it's a favorite of drug dealers, terrorists, the NRA—the holy trinity of firearms approval.

Alison drives to Chang's with me and comes inside this time. She's walking slowly but then neither of us would win a marathon. The smell from the illegal chemicals has her wearing a handkerchief over her face.

"Will you take that off," I say. "You look like Jesse James. You're making the hired help very nervous."

"They're destroying the ozone layer in here," she says.

"How do you like the .32," Chang says to her politely.

"I don't like guns," Alison says.

"She likes it. She's keeping it," I say. "Don't mind her. She's grumpy."

The VW bus comes from Nina, a friend of Alison's who runs a sushi restaurant. The first time we fire up the space heater fish oil drips from the metal ribs of the truck like resin and cats appear from nowhere, clawing at our tires. We leave the heat off, work in our coats.

Boone brings a few things he's borrowed from WHPK, where he's a part-time DJ and engineer. He covers the windows of the VW bus with brown paper; hangs a blanket on clothesline behind the front seats.

"They don't make 'em like this anymore," Boone says, admiring the '68 microbus.

"There's a reason for that," I say. "It handles like a milk truck." I'm hoping I don't have to use it in a high-speed chase.

Alison brings brochures and sales literature from her store—flashy cameras and computerized video equipment she doesn't sell but gets mail about from manufacturers. I have props left over from other jobs; a wired briefcase, a business card that says "Missy Evans," a name Alison isn't thrilled with. Missy represents Advanced VidTek. She sells photo-imaging hardware to cosmetic surgeons so people can try on different noses before making a purchase.

"All we want is the inside layout," I tell her. "We need Rosenberg's private office and examining rooms. You're a sales rep. Open a few doors by mistake, apologize, get out. Make a map for Boone. He's like any academic. He works better with something in print. Okay?"

"You don't like the hair," she says.

"What?"

"The jacket then. Or the blouse. Something's bothering you."

"I think you look great."

"The blouse is pure silk and the suit's Armani. I practically had to leave the mortgage on my shop as collateral. The shoes alone must have cost Nina two hundred. Italian pumps."

"Don't lose them."

"Thanks, I'll try to keep them on. If you don't like the way I look just say so. Is it the haircut? You like my hair longer?"

"It isn't the hair. I like it short. It was shorter when we first met."

"I know. What then."

"Nothing. The blouse is a little sheer, that's all."

"I made the bandages as flesh-colored as possible. Do they show that badly?"

"No, no."

"I figured if nothing else it's an ice-breaker, a conversation piece."

"But am I supposed to see your nipples?"

"You are today," she says. "Maybe Rosenberg won't notice I don't know what in the hell I'm talking about."

She's in there nearly an hour. I can hear some of what's happening through the briefcase. When she comes out she has an elaborate revision of Boone's little map in her Kodak notebook; now in four colors with a key in a corner box. While we're reviewing it Rosenberg's white Buick backs down the drive. He'll be gone at least an hour making rounds at the hospital.

Boone goes in next with an old mailman's uniform we customized and some of Chang's special bug spray. It comes highly recommended, since it was banned by Reagan's EPA, guys who thought lead was a natural substance, like sunlight.

By the time I make my way into the building it looks like a fire drill. Nurses, secretaries, doctors are out on the yard, the front porch. Someone on the third floor's even opened the window and stepped onto the ledge of the balcony. Since he's holding his nose he looks less like a jumper, more like a swimmer at summer camp attempting a cannonball. I think it's the shrink.

Boone was right—it's just a brownstone, remodeled to within an inch of its life. The elevator's out of order. Everyone's on the stairs. Boone's inside Rosenberg's suite, now empty. People left in a hurry. There are half-finished cups of coffee; a sweet roll with two bites gone. It reminds me of nuclear holocaust films like *On the Beach*. The chemicals in Boone's spray probably have a similar half-life.

"We're lucky the secretary's got a phobia about cockroaches—"

"I thought you were spraying for termites," I say. "Your uniform says termites. The contract we typed up for you says termites. The cap you're wearing has a fucking iridescent termite painted on it."

"I know Harding, but then his secretary started calling the management company so I had to improvise. They renovate these old places with this exposed brick—it's like building the bugs a hundred new front doors."

I stop what I'm doing and look around my feet.

"You let some loose, didn't you?"

"Not in here," Boone says. He's standing on a chair, placing Chang's small video cameras in the ceiling tiles. "Just a dozen or so but real big ones—project roaches, a friend of mine in Social Services brings them home in his clothes when he visits Robert Taylor. These are the flying kind. They look like they have teeth."

"I'm glad you kept this low profile." It's my own fault. I hired Boone. I search for someone else to blame, but no one immediately comes to mind. "We've got maybe half an hour."

He nods, moving to the examining rooms. The place is huge. I move to Rosenberg's private office.

There's a TV/VCR combination, a computer with CD-ROM. Rosenberg's gone multimedia. The desk—rich cherry wood, gold handles—is large and expensive-looking. It's locked but the money was spent on the wood, not the locks, which are rudimentary. I pick the one on the middle top drawer, pull that out, and then reach behind the others to undo the catch. Both bottom drawers are now open.

One drawer is filled with medical records; I flip through them but on first glance don't see anything worth taking. The other has a wooden inlaid tray, and below that, a handful of letters. The envelopes are addressed to Elenya at different locations—Hyde Park, Lake Forest, New Buffalo. But I'm confused; they're from Stephen, and when I read one or two they seem harmless. And they're old—from the first years of their marriage. Maybe Stephen has a sentimental side. I don't see any disk. The Macintosh on a side table is turned off but I don't see a floppy in the slot.

Then Boone sticks his head inside the door.

"Lock and load, Private," he says. "We gotta move." I start replacing everything, and when I accidentally brush the medical files the alphabetical headers shift direction.

Everything changes.

There are other files, facedown and backward. There's a copy of the same tape list I saw in the basement in Harvey; this one has a yellow Post-it with "Found this in Nora's purse—LW" written on it. A passbook business account—the same one with the fifty-thousand withdrawal—that also shows a ten-thousand withdrawal from October. Two patient histories, the name Martinez everywhere, the name Donnie Wilson listed on payment receipts. Pages and pages of typed gibberish. Phone bills that include numbers I remember even now, ten years later—Rosenberg to Donnie, Rosenberg to Eduardo Martinez. Two sides of a triangle. A strange portfolio of handwritten pages tied with a red ribbon. Business documents, carbons, other letters. *One of Stephen's worst flaws—he won't throw anything away.* Everything but a disk.

Boone is yelling again. I turn on the fax and the copier, dial Hyde Park Photo Supplies, fax what I can, copy or steal the rest.

I look hurriedly for a wall safe, check one last time for the disk, then lock everything back up, leaving separately from Boone through a side door. We're in and out in twenty minutes.

Elenya is waiting for me in her Porsche. The motor's running. She's parked on 60th near Cottage Grove. We walk to the fountain and sit on the edge of the concrete rim. The huge figure of Time shields us from the wind. Across the empty pool the hundred figures he's watching are crushed together. Some are happy—a child held aloft by his father. Others look like a Bergman movie. My eyes are drawn to a man and woman swirled together on the far right corner. The man's arms are outstretched. The woman's hand is on her breast. Features on the concrete faces have worn away. They're linked forever in a drama only they understand.

I made one stop on the way, picked up the faxes at Alison's store. Everything's on the floor of my truck. I haven't had time to sort it out.

Elenya huddles in her black fur. "Thanks for coming," she says. "I wasn't sure you'd be here."

"They don't really believe you're a suspect? It's crazy."

"They want my lawyer to bring me in," she says. "They don't want a fuss. Tonight or tomorrow. I don't think they want the university trustees upset." She shakes her head. Her short red hair barely stirs in the wind. "They think Gaelen's the killer—I hired him to do it, I was in love with him, I couldn't have Stephen killed or there'd be no money. Do you understand it? Because I don't understand any of it."

She's wearing small red shoes that she tucks against the concrete wall. I think she'd like to just tap them and be in Kansas.

"Do you have a good lawyer?" I say.

"Someone Warren recommended," she says. I recognize the name she gives me—a LaSalle Street attorney, from a higher caste than Frost. "He does criminal law. That's what I am now, I guess. A criminal."

"Not for long. Stephen can't get away with this."

"No?"

"I have something left to try—"

"They said you're a suspect now too. For killing Robin."

"That shows you how nuts they are. I saw Reilly, made a statement. I may need your lawyer. Have you talked to your husband at all today?"

She shakes her head.

"What does he usually do Saturday nights?"

"Why? Don't you have a date?" she says with a little smile. "I don't know. He works sometimes."

"At his office?"

She nods.

"Does he keep a safe there, do you know? A combination safe?"

"Not that I know of."

"Have you ever heard him talk about a patient named Elizabeth Manning?"

"He never talks about his patients. I think they bore him."

"But you never overheard anything—about her, about other patients that made you wonder?"

"What are you saying? That there's others?"

"I think so."

"At this point I think it's a little academic, don't you. Next to murder. You're hoping to catch him screwing his patients? So what?"

"It's not much. But it might be all we have. Without that disk, we don't have much to bargain with."

"But you got the letters?"

"Yes," I say, giving her the paper bag. It doesn't seem like much. A handful of old letters, something from your attic. Old technology. I don't ask her what they're for. I'm embarrassed to have read them. "There's one or two other things in there too."

"You can still get paper bags at your grocery?" she says, opening it as though it's a lunch I've packed.

"You have to ask. They hide them under the counter, like *Penthouse*."

She looks at the hat and gloves and picture from the flat in Harvey. She doesn't say anything right away. I look up at Time. He's not moving.

"Where did you get these?" she says. I tell her.

"I must have dropped them Friday night. Or they took them—"

"I know. I mean, that's what I assumed."

Neither of us mentions the picture from Gaelen's wall. I don't know why I gave it to her. I could have kept it or just thrown it away. But it seemed to belong with these other things.

"They'll find Gaelen, Elenya. If Stephen's involved one or both will talk. You can still get your divorce. Move away from here."

"Yes?" she says. "Why is it I don't think that will be enough?"

The first bells of the afternoon ring across the Midway from the seminary tower. Kids wander out of Washington Park, heading home for dinner, trying to beat the storm. It's the kind of winter day where afternoon disappears too early into dusk.

"You grew up around here, didn't you?" Elenya says, looking around.

"Not Hyde Park. Closer to Bridgeport."

She's from back east somewhere, isn't she?

I realize I don't know her very well. It doesn't matter much.

"I went to school here too," she says.

"What? Really?"

"Just one quarter. I couldn't stand it. Too cold."

"That happens," I say. "But you ended up back here anyway?"

"My husband dragged me back," she says. "For his residency. And we just stayed. My family's gone now anyway. Just my sister. Are your parents still alive?"

I shake my head.

"What about your house? Is it still standing?"

"Long gone. Just an empty lot."

"And you never married."

"No."

"You're single the way I'm married," she says.

She looks at the letters, undoes the rubber band, and flips through them. She pulls one or two out and stares at the lettering.

"Are they all right?" I say.

"They're fine," she says. "They're just what I need somehow."

"Elenya, did you ever hear Stephen talk about Eduardo Martinez or his daughter—"

"The girl that was hurt. No, I don't think so. Why?"

"I found something in his desk with their name on it."

The Martinez case has come back with a mad rush this week. And it happened just five blocks north of here, 55th and Cottage Grove. That was a much warmer day than today, full of sunshine and promise. Sometimes those are the worst.

"Are you still looking for him? The father?"

"Everyone tells me he's dead. I'm supposed to move on."

"Yes, that's what they say," she says, smiling. "What if he wasn't dead. What if he were here right now, right in front of us. Right here." She draws her shoe across the brown grass. Instantly that spot of frozen mud is different from all others.

"He's not."

"But if he were—what would you do?"

"Why do you ask?"

"I don't know. I guess I'm curious. To see if it—whatever it is—hate, obsession—how long it lasts. Is it over?"

"I think so."

She nods; I don't think she believes me. I don't blame her.

"What did he do to her?"

"Elenya—"

"Tell me. Please. Then I'll shut up. Frost wouldn't say. His damned lawyer's reserve."

"He raped her," I say. There's more but it seems pointless to describe it. Everyone says it helps to talk about it. It never does.

"Was it worth it, do you think?" Elenya says, a question that catches me off guard. "What you did. What you tried to do."

"I don't know. How do you measure something like that? It cost me years, my license, my work—"

"Not to you," she says, her breath like smoke. "To the girl, Angela. Was it worth it to her, what you did—"

"Elenya, he molested her for years—"

"But is that what she wanted, do you think, to have people killed like that?"

"I don't know, Elenya."

"Did she really want her father killed?"

"I don't know."

"You never asked her."

"No, I never did."

She nods, folding the bag. We both stand. My legs feel stiff. The cold from the pebblestone concrete has chilled me to the bone. I can feel my back tightening up, the familiar crease of pain across my shoulder.

"I wish I could have gotten you that disk," I say. "The letters aren't much."

"They mean a lot to me. Really. I appreciate what you've done. Maybe it's sentimental."

"Nothing wrong with that."

Traffic rushes by us on the Plaisance.

"He won't leave me alone, you see," she says. "He won't let go." I nod, even as I realize I don't know who she means—Gaelen? Stephen?

She turns from the Midway to the stream of frozen concrete.

"Isn't this just the most depressing fountain?" she says.

TWENTY

don't have time to drive all the way to Schaumburg. I do it anyway.

The weekend guard in Donnie's building
makes me wait in the lobby while he sends my
name upstairs. Decorators routinely sweep through this
building like Delta Force commandos looking for anything remotely comfortable. I'm sitting in a little room
ringed with airport lounge chairs, my boots propped on
a large purple coffee table next to stacks of unread
*Architectural Digest*s. By the time the guard wakes me
small lakes are forming under my boots from melting
snow. The guard moves the magazines.

I take the maintenance elevator with two guys in
blue uniforms. They're escorting a green toilet crated in
wood and sprayed foam, like a piece of sculpture. I
have the files from Rosenberg's office.

A receptionist outside Donnie's office tells me I'm
late.

"Across the hall," she nods, "at the Bijou. They
almost gave up on you. There was some talk of sending
out the dogs with a search party."

I ask her if there's any coffee and she answers no,
sniffing. Everybody in the city has a cold. Even people
without colds are faking it. Her Garfield mug smells
like mint. Donnie must be on his herbal tea kick again.

When I slip into the media room Donnie barely

turns his head. He's watching a surveillance video I made of Lucy Williams the first night I followed her and Stephen.

"I thought you threw this out," I say.

"Are you kidding? This is a classic," Donnie says. "Some film institute gets this when I die."

"Does your boss like you watching amateur porn on company time?"

"My boss is in Japan," Donnie says. "And you should see the collection of stuff he's got. He's hooked up with these computer sex bulletin boards—you know about them?"

"A little." There's no sound, since he's advancing the film frame by frame with the remote's jog-shuttle. Occasionally he'll freeze the picture at a favorite spot— a particular look in Lucy's eye, a close-up of her tongue licking something, disappearing somewhere. The way her breasts overflow her tight suit.

"Do we have to watch this?" I say.

"It's kinda like ballet, don't you think?" Donnie says.

It's a highlights tape, what's known in porno as a compilation, and I don't see Balanchine's influence anywhere. A very long afternoon at the South Bend Holidome has been condensed to a single reel, making the sex more frantic, more desperate, something I wouldn't have thought possible at the time.

"What made you get this out?"

"I dunno. Nostalgia? But I want to show you another one." He changes tapes. "This one's just Lucy—same place, same dumb Holidome but two, three years ago, before you started watching them."

"I knew they went back that far. I didn't know you were filming them."

"We weren't. This isn't ours."

"What?"

"Frost gave me this when he asked me to take the case. As an example of what we'd find."

"Why didn't you show it to me then?"

"Because Rosenberg's not in it. I showed you stills, remember? Of Lucy's face, so you could ID her. Maybe you don't remember. You were doing a lot of shit then, Harding. I was holding your hand each time you crossed the fucking street."

"Who made the tape?"

"Frost never said. I kind of think he might have made it himself."

The tape's badly made but what's remarkable isn't the deterioration of the film stock but the way Lucy Williams has changed. In recent films she's like a scarecrow—thin, gaunt. Here she has a swimmer's back, brown skin, fine light hairs on her neck and arms. No needle marks. She's on a StairMaster. The camera leaves her bent head in a blur of motion and zooms to the tiny digital dials set in the crossbar between her legs. Her breathing and heart rate accelerate even as her foot motion slows to a stop, confusing a computer chip not programmed for high-impact workouts. Her thigh muscles lengthen and tighten as the dials crash in EE. The sound, in real time, is the same agonized climaxing I sometimes hear in my sleep.

"Warren told me about the job," Donnie says, turning to me. "You going in Rosenberg's office for the disk and the letters. His idea but with you taking all the risk. I'm not sure it's such a good idea. Not so soon after this kid getting killed."

"The kid's name is Oren Miller, Donnie. Since

you're so concerned. He worked for a landscaping company you do security for."

"Really? Which one?"

I give him the name. Maybe he sounds surprised, maybe not. You can't tell with Donnie.

"This Dr. Sawyer, Donnie—you ever hear of him?"

"Not until the cops called me—"

"Did they ask you why you're in his phone book?"

"What? No."

"I'm asking you, Donnie."

"That's gotta be a mistake. I'm on all kinds of mailing lists—"

"It's his personal address book. With your name in it. And while I'm in there reading it little Oren shows up with a gun to blow me away—"

"That was you did that?" Donnie says. "I don't know him, I don't know either of them—what the fuck are you inferring here?"

"Implying, Donnie. I just want to know if we're straight."

"You've got the nerve to ask me that? After all we've been through?"

"I do, yeah."

"And you want me to fix your door and your locks," he says.

"Yeah."

Donnie cuts the sound and picture and turns on the lights. I take the Martinez medical file and drop it on the chair beside him.

"What the fuck is this, Donnie?"

"Where'd you get this?"

"I want to know about this—"

"Back off, Harding. I asked where'd you get it."

"Rosenberg's office."

"You already went in? Does Frost know?"

"No. And don't tell him—"

"You read it?"

"Of course I read it."

"Let me get us a drink."

"I don't want a drink."

"I've got the Dewar's out, Harding. Don't turn me down so fast."

He pours us each a neat tumbler, and waits for me to sit down. We're in red velvet theater seats Donnie bought when they tore down the Michael Todd. With all the herbal tea Donnie's been drinking in here the room smells like mint juleps.

"The chiropractor and this kid I know nothing about," he says. "You tell me I'm in his book. I believe you. The kid cuts grass for some company where we watch the payroll or run a simple alarm system—I believe that too. But it's coincidence, Harding."

"You never used to believe in coincidence, Donnie."

"Yeah?" He nods. "Maybe I still don't. You can be sure I'll be checking up on both these things."

"Do you know this fellow Gaelen?"

"No, I do not. Nobody by that name. Now that's the fucking truth, Harding."

"All right."

"You believe me."

"Yeah. All right." I don't believe anybody anymore.

Donnie's intercom buzzes. "Not now," he says.

"You better take it, Donnie," a secretary says.

"All right," he says, picking up, then says, "Wait a minute, I got him here. I'm putting you on the speakerphone."

It's Reilly.

"Harding? You there? I'm just telling your boss we had your buddy Gaelen. Down by that motel, heading south—the locals picked him up. Two state troopers."

"What happened."

"One of them's okay, multiple fractures. The other's on a respirator. He might not make it."

"Jesus. Next time just shoot the bastard."

"Yeah, well, every cop in Indiana's looking for him now. I doubt he'll come back this way without a personal invitation from the state's attorney."

"Thanks, Reilly," Donnie says, about to switch off.

"Wait—that's not why I called. We found something about this kid that should interest you—his name's not Miller. It's Patner, late of Louisville, Kentucky. Now very late. Since you killed his old man nine years ago I thought you'd be interested. This family's dropping like flies. Let's hope Allstate's got a good rep in southern Kentucky."

Donnie's listening with his ear close to the speakerphone, as if it was an old radio playing some crime melodrama from the forties. I don't think they were ever quite this violent.

"Oren lived here, in Chicago, with a foster family," I say, my mouth dry despite the whiskey. "Their name was Bauer."

"Right, right. DCFS faxed me some shit—"

"Who put him there, with the Bauers?"

"It doesn't say."

"Those files aren't sealed like adoptions."

"I know, Harding. But it's blank. Just a date—somebody dumped him there eight years ago."

"Martinez," I say to Donnie, who frowns. But I can tell from his eyes he believes it too. "The bastard put Patner's son in a foster home three blocks from my house. He even waited until I got of jail, just to make sure I was coming back to Chicago."

"Like planting a bomb with a real slow fuse," Donnie says.

Oren is Patner's son. No wonder he was reluctant to drop that steak knife the other day and play his little part in the drama. Somebody must have paid him a lot for his restraint.

How long had he been following me?

"We still haven't gotten Gaelen's files," Reilly says. "We'll get them Monday when he's in jail. Oh, and Nelson Bryars turned up last night in south Woodlawn. Shot with your .44. You might consider doing some sort of ad campaign for the NRA."

"Reilly—listen. In Indiana—did Gaelen get away in his own car? The Grand Am?"

"Yeah, why. You concerned about his gas mileage?"

"I just want to know, that's all. If I see the car."

"He's headed south again, Harding. Don't worry about it."

"I like to worry," I say.

Donnie punches a button; the speakerphone shuts off.

"You okay?" he says to me.

"Yeah."

"So let's talk about Angela Martinez," Donnie says.

We finish that bottle of Dewar's and start another. Dewar's tastes smoky compared to Chivas but I'm not complaining. Donnie's appointments must have given up on him long ago. I go out to look around and find the hallways filled with suits. Donnie and I are in our stocking feet, sitting on the floor, drinking. "I'm in conference," he tells Serena. He locks us in.

"I never knew he had a kid," Donnie says. "Patner."

"I didn't either."

"That was you that iced him?"

"What are you gonna do, call the Mounties?"

"Shit, Harding. I'm your friend."

I say nothing.

"Do you know how old this is?" Donnie says. At first I think he means the whiskey.

"Like yesterday, Donnie." Like last night's nightmare.

"Nine, ten years. Fucking Kentucky," he says, angry now. I don't know if he's mad at me or the commonwealth. "I should have come down there and helped you. But what the hell do I know about Kentucky?"

"What do you know about Patner?"

"The old man? Nothing. An ex-cop with priors, working out of Frankfort. Just local color. Martinez must have hired him when you started getting too close."

"I never got close, Donnie."

"He was probably getting tired of looking over his shoulder," Donnie says. "That can make anybody a little nuts."

"What about the phone logs. You talked to Martinez—"

"Early on, yeah," Donnie says. "Before I knew he was nuts. I never dreamed he'd come after you both like that—"

"You told him where we were?"

"Not intentionally, Harding. I swear to God. But something I said must have tipped him off. Because he attacked you two days later. So I'm as responsible for her getting cut as you are. And I've lived with that, just like you. But it's getting real real old—"

"And these checks in her file, with your name on them, made out to Rosenberg?"

"Those were the payments I made for Angela. Rosenberg did three operations on her. He was the best, so that's who I bought." Donnie finishes his drink. I haven't seen him drink like this in years. "What'd you say that doctor's name was, the guy who had my name?"

"Sawyer."

"That might be why I'm in that guy's book. If he doesn't keep real current records. Angela did some rehab shit, remember? At RIC?"

"Sawyer's a chiropractor, Donnie, not orthopedics."

"They do referrals, Harding. Pain control, shit like that."

I suddenly feel short of breath. "The police said Gaelen lost his license around then."

"So?"

"Do you have a Mac?"

"Serena's got one—I'm strictly a Unix man now, Harding."

I run back down to my truck. The disks I swiped at Sawyer's have been bouncing around in my glove compartment all day. I use Serena's desk and Mac and scan through Sawyer's old business records, patient histories, the kind of stuff they used to put on microfilm. I look for Angela everywhere. Ten years of records. It takes two minutes to find her.

*Angela Martinez, one year post-op pain assoc.
with movement in arms and wrists, referred from
RIC . . .*

"Have you seen this before?" I ask Donnie. He
shakes his head.

I haven't either. It wasn't in Rosenberg's files,
because it occurred after she was his patient.

Sawyer's notes are neat, precise. He did what he
could to help her.

Then he recommended she see a specialist, a
physical therapist he knew. Someone with good hands.
The name isn't there. Something else is; a cross-listing,
another document. A letter of reference from Sawyer to the State Medical Board pleading Gaelen's
case.

> *. . . little to be gained suspending such a qualified
> therapist . . . have referred patients to him many
> times . . . complete confidence in his judgment . . .
> caring professional concerned with his patients . . .
> unfortunate accusations of Ms. Martinez cannot be
> proven . . .*

"What the fuck did Gaelen do to her?" I say.
"Donnie?"

"I don't know, Harding."

"You were here, weren't you—"

"Let's go back in my office."

"Those state records must show what he did."

"We'll get them. Slow down, Harding. It's Saturday night, remember? We'll call the state offices
Monday."

"Monday's too late. How can we find out now?"

"We can't. Even Reilly can't, you just heard him say so. It's ten years, Harding. It'll keep till Monday."

My heart is racing. I'm pacing Donnie's office, an animal chasing its tail.

"How could you not know this?"

"I was just paying off her bills, Harding. I paid Rosenberg, told him that's as far as it went."

"You never talked to her?"

"No. Come on, Harding. You better sit down, you look like you're gonna tear somebody's head off. And I'm the only one here." He gives me another drink. The Dewar's doesn't taste so good now. "It's probably the best I've seen you look in years."

"Why didn't you ever tell me you paid her bills like that?"

"I don't know. You were in prison. Things changed."

"It's been eating away at me for years—"

"So what," Donnie says. "We're both at fault. But I did something about it. I helped her. What the fuck did you ever do for her?"

"Nothing," I say, thinking: the new Donnie.

It occurs to me that Donnie's been sending me money as well—in the form of work. He must feel guilty about me losing my license. Nine, almost ten years, and not a word said. We're not much better than the Rosenbergs.

"Where's Angela now?"

"I don't know. Really. I looked once, five or six years ago. Maybe she changed her name. She was real good at hiding. You remember that."

"Yeah." I know who she learned that from too. "Who's in your computer lab tonight?"

"Henderson's the manager. I can page him."

"Not the manager. Somebody younger."

A kid in his twenties responds to Donnie's call. Donnie looks skeptical but Kevin comes in without knocking; untied gym shoes, a cup of Gatorade, a *2600* T-shirt. I feel we have the right man for the job.

"Ten minutes," Kevin says when he sees the assignment, the pages of gibberish I found with the medical files. "Maybe less." I thought they were fax transmission errors. I know what they are now.

Donnie asks what else I found and so I tell him about Gaelen's basement, about the list of recordings made by Nora and Robin and how I figure Gaelen and Oren must have stumbled on their operation—Gaelen was following the Rosenbergs, Oren was following me—and taken it over, killing the students when they became expendable. Lucy died because she might remember something she'd seen, like Oren coming out of Nora's room that night with I don't know what. A souvenir.

I show him the bankbook. "I think the money went to Gaelen," I say. "Stephen paid him to approach Elenya, have an affair with her and get it on tape. I don't think Stephen wanted a divorce. He doesn't like giving things up." *Especially his trophies.*

"The ten set it up," Donnie says. "What was the fifty for?"

I pause. "There was a portfolio, a diary Gaelen supposedly kept—like Nora's lists of tapes—of his nights with Elenya. Remember the Hitler Diaries? This was just as genuine. I doubt Rosenberg even saw it before handing over the money. And who knows, maybe he believed it. Maybe he wanted to believe it."

"I take it you don't."

"No," I say. "I don't."

Donnie nods, a Donnie nod that means maybe yes, maybe no.

Kevin's back in five minutes.

"They're double-encoded," he says. "Kind of a nifty program. The pictures are kinda weird, though. Who's the girl?"

"You wouldn't have made any copies," Donnie says to him.

"No, sir—"

"We're adding a new position in your department," Donnie says, sifting through the pictures, handing them to me. "Information manager."

"We've got one of those."

"Good. Now we'll have two. The job's yours," Donnie says, "if you can keep your mouth shut."

"About what?"

"The pictures."

"What pictures?"

It's always rewarding to see initiative rewarded.

They don't shake hands but Donnie gives him fifty bucks. Donnie's not very religious. But it's always appropriate to end a business agreement with a benediction.

The first batch of pictures are of Angela and her father. They're bad enough to justify money changing hands. But two million seems a little excessive. Until we get the second group.

There are ten altogether, black and white portraits of a male face. In the first two pictures he's as I remember him. When the others are put in sequence the aging process speeds up, like plants in time-motion photography.

"Jesus," Donnie says. "For two million you'd think they could make him younger."

"No, this is smart. You wouldn't expect it, so it would be the best way to hide. Martinez was always smart." My eyes stay focused on the man in the first picture. The other, older man doesn't exist for me. "How do you know he's dead?"

"Some report I got."

"But how do you *know*—"

"You mean did I drive a stake through his heart?" He holds the whiskey bottle upside down, letting the last drop fall in his glass. If it was a bottle of ketchup he'd be pounding it with his hand. "I know because I got an obit of his ex from the Springfield paper. And it says she told a reporter he was dead. Right before she died."

"He could have fixed that," I say.

"Harding, he's dead."

"Do you know how easy it would be to plant a story like that?"

Donnie sighs, opening another bottle. "The bottom line, Harding, is this. He's dead. Do you want him alive? If you want him alive, he'll be fucking alive forever. Is that what you want?"

I say nothing.

"There's no point now, Harding, doing this thing tonight at Rosenberg's office. You're aware of that."

I shrug.

"You just said yourself he didn't kill anybody, he maybe hired Gaelen for—well, for the kind of shit people hire *us* for—but that's it. So there's nothing to be gained doing this."

"You're right," I say. What I don't tell him is that Gaelen's diary mentioned videotaping those evenings—Wednesday evenings, nine of them—with Elenya. Stephen wouldn't have paid without proof.

What I don't tell him is how obsessive the diary is, cream-colored paper inside a folder of marbleized cardboard, tied with a red ribbon. It looks like a small press chapbook of poetry. What I don't tell him is how detailed the descriptions are.

I read it in my truck, in Donnie's parking lot. I would read a bit, then put it down, then pick it up again; the pull of pornography. After a while the words all ran together.

anal angel

rimmed Elenya reverse cowgirl fisting makes her
come the hardest
suck my dick she's screaming
Gaelen Gaelen Gaelen

everything I dreamed of . . .

What I don't tell him is I burned the portfolio. And how much I want the tapes.

"They know it's Gaelen," Donnie says. "They'll get the rest of it out of him. He'll squeal. It'll be a helluva juicy press story—can you imagine Gaelen's trial, if they bring all his shit in? The tabloids get ahold of it?" He shakes his head. "Rosenberg will be screaming bloody murder."

"So will Elenya. She'll be screaming too."

"You'll call it off?"

I nod. I can't nod like Donnie but I'm working on it.

" 'Cause there's no reason to do it."

"You're right, Donnie. Absolutely."

"Good," he says. "That's settled, at least." He checks his watch, then the liquor supply. "What are we doing here, getting drunk?"

"Not with half a bottle left."

"Hell, this is the suburbs," he says. "They deliver."

But when Serena comes in with more Dewar's I ask for coffee, black. I go down the hall to use Donnie's executive bathroom, stopping first to find a phone. Alison's in the truck with a cheap cellular.

"Everything okay?" I say.

"Everything's fine," she says. "I'm trapped in a four by ten room with a man who wheezes and sniffs like a terminal asthmatic. I think he breathed too much bug spray."

"Give him a handkerchief. Gaelen's out and on the prowl so we're shutting down early. Wait for me, okay? Keep your doors locked. Keep your gun out. And change the radio to channel twenty. Not seven. Twenty."

"Piece of cake," she says.

"Change the radio now, will you?"

"It's done."

"Everything works out okay, maybe we'll stop at Jimmy's later."

"S'mores and kamikazes at my place," Alison says.

I wash my face with cold water, stare at my eyes in the mirror. Donnie's headed for a late dinner. I'm headed for a party in the city—east on the Eisenhower; straight down the 90-94 pipeline. Halfway there I turn my CB radio on, switch to channel seven, boost the power to the max, spend five minutes talking to myself. The roads are full of Saturday night fever. Everyone's pushing the limit, trying to beat the storm.

TWENTY-ONE

The pictures coming in look like something from the moon landing—pixels of dots, lines, and gray shadows. Two phones are tapped; another three bugs have been scattered throughout the offices. Everything's bouncing off an antique receiver we've stashed on the fourth floor. The system's so primitive it would probably be laughed out of a high school science fair.

But it works. And Elizabeth Manning's apparently just the Main Event. There's a precard I hadn't counted on: Rosenberg's seven o'clock—Gretchen—arrives early with heavy wet snow. She's wearing a long coat, carrying a wicker basket large enough for a Ravinia picnic dinner. The nurses have all gone home.

Rosenberg welcomes her into his private office, closes the door. The picnic starts almost at once.

They're very noisy eaters.

"It's not really that loud," Boone explains. "The damn microphone's right under her butt." She comes out at seven-forty, the basket swinging under her arm like Little Red Riding Hood just as Rosenberg's eight o'clock pulls in the drive.

"What kind of coat is that?" I say, wiping steam from the windshield.

"Knockoff Lagerfeld," Alison says. "Who wears the real thing in this weather?"

"Someone who can afford another."

The two women briefly cross paths. Gretchen opens Elizabeth's tote bag and they talk a minute, laughing. Maybe they're comparing recipes. Then Elizabeth goes inside. Gretchen backs a Civic down the drive.

"What's in the basket you think?" Boone says.

"I doubt if it's fried chicken and potato salad."

"A little wine, a little latex?"

"Something like that."

"Can you surrey?" Alison sings. "Can you picnic?"

The Radio Shack mike in the lobby reports Elizabeth's progress. Her steps on the limestone floor throw echoes like waves in a pond, fluttering the VU needles. The signal isn't very clear.

"We could boost it," Alison says.

"I don't want to boost it. Everybody's got a scanner these days. You never know who else is listening."

"Like us," Alison says.

Elizabeth goes upstairs, enters the office. Most of the building's dark now. The shrink and his nurse are outside warming up their cars, heading home. We have a tiny Watchman courtesy of Chang—"still in original box, Harding. All the original paperwork." It's like seeing a movie on a wristwatch.

It's just past eight o'clock.

"This is disgusting, Boone," Alison says. "Turn it up just a bit."

"Can you tell for sure what they're doing?" I say.

Alison shakes her head. "They're not talking much. But I don't think he's just giving her a second opinion. You've got the video."

"The video's from the Voyager probe. Give me the Sennheisers. And the field glasses." I like the way

Alison's dressed tonight: black sweats, a black nylon flight jacket, heavy black boots that look like they're made for climbing telephone poles. Modern Gothick. For once she's dressed for the cold—even brought gloves and a hat. Granted the gloves are ripped at the knuckles and the hat's a Riot Grrrl cap turned backward, but since she usually just jams her hands down in her jeans like a latino boy waiting for the El, it's a major concession.

"This is illegal, right?" Alison says. She's chewing Black Black Japanese gum. It smells like evergreen trees.

"It's sort of a gray area." I'm watching the front, trying not to look yet again at my watch. The Glock is tucked in my belt with a full clip.

"It's not gray," Boone says. "It's pretty goddamn black and white."

"Maroon and white," Alison says, pointing out the rear window. A campus patrol car cruises past us slowly. "It's just a routine patrol. He comes every eighteen minutes."

"Just like Rosenberg," Boone says.

"Is that how you're timing him?"

"That's how they set the atomic clock," Boone says. "Alison, just so you know—the phone taps alone are federal. That's two or three years in Marion. Just for the phones. When you add state and local—"

"Is that the only patrol?" I say. "None from CPD?"

Boone shakes his head.

But then all the needles start bouncing into the red. "What the hell," Alison says, jiggling an A/B switch patched with duct tape to the input jack. Nothing calms it.

"A short circuit?" Boone says, puzzled.

"It's worked fine all afternoon."

"Do a test on another line."

All three of us have phones on now, listening to static.

"I hear it," Alison says, tuning in. "I don't think it's in-house. More like background noise boosted somehow, nonspecific. We need Dolby S."

"Somebody's jamming us?"

"Maybe not on purpose," Boone says. "It could just be somebody's ham radio misfiring. With this equipment anything's possible. It could be a kid with a toy train."

To me it sounds like distant, muffled thumping; underwater. Voices not quite human, dolphins crying out. Then, it stops. The line becomes clear again.

"Ghosts in the machine," Alison says, shrugging. "Boone, tell Harding your brilliant idea for security."

"Will you forget that."

"He thinks we need a password. For getting in and out of the truck."

"Like what? Swordfish?"

Just then a Yellow Cab makes a U-turn on Woodlawn and slides into the driveway. The door on the far side opens; the interior light turns on briefly but I can't see much. Someone gets out and hurries up the stairs. It's not Gaelen.

"That's odd," Alison says, flipping through her notes.

"Why?"

"Rosenberg's eight-thirty? He hasn't got one."

My damn pager goes off. I don't recognize the number. When I answer with the truck's cellular I'm surprised to hear Reilly, distant on a bad connection.

"You'll have to speak up, Reilly—"

"Can you hear me, Harding? Because you sound like you're in fucking Finland. Listen, let me speak to McKenzie, will you?"

"Who's McKenzie?"

"Should be a tan Ford, the one you've been losing all week."

I motion to Alison to check the other window; she nods, surprised.

"How'd you know we'd be here—"

"We should have taken out an ad," Boone says, muttering. "Sent up flares."

"Just let me talk to him, all right? Put him on."

"She's leaving," Alison says, grabbing my arm, pointing to the brownstone, "look, the side door. Why is she using that door when her car's on the street—?"

"You know, Harding, Dispatch picked up your broadcast, your ten o'clock with Elenya and Stephen tonight—aren't there obscenity rules on CBs? I mean Jesus—the FCC or something should take away your license, if you've got one—you won't be able to get a dog license in this town—"

"Tell Harding your password, Boone. This is great," Alison says.

"Password," Boone says.

"That's it?" I say. "The password is password?"

"Isn't that great?" Alison says.

And then it starts. Something rocks the van like a grenade, sending all three of us flying. Boone crashes against the tape recorders. Blank reels of tape unspool like garden hose. Alison's glasses come off; her headphones bounce off the wall.

"What the fuck—"

"Somebody hit us? A car?"

"More like a truck—"

"From the side?"

The van's rocking back and forth like a cradle.

The phone's overturned like a cheap paperback, its spine broken. Reilly's gone.

"Someone's out there, Harding," Boone says.

"Good guess." I climb into the front but the passenger door's jammed shut.

"What's he trying to do, tip us over?" Boone says.

"Harding, the back door's jammed—"

Now it feels like a demolition derby. The front windshield cracks.

The momentum of the rocking begins to send us into each other; the equipment tears loose, wires flying everywhere; we're like a patient on life-support, IVs and tubes ripped out all in one motion.

"Jesus Christ!" Alison says when she slams into the wall. She's holding her stomach. "That crazy fucker!"

The driver's door is jammed too. I turn in the seat so I can use my right shoulder and hit it once, twice, three times. Finally the lock comes free and the door springs open. I tumble outside into the street just as another explosion rocks the van. There's smoke everywhere. Except for two blown tires, there's not much damage. Percussion grenades. Smoke bombs. Gaelen's car is blocking the street, its front grille locked on the VW's side trim in a death grip.

I cross the street to the Ford, cold and quiet. McKenzie sits in the driver's seat, both hands on the wheel, as though ready to leave for vacation. Part of the rear antenna's been snapped off, jammed through his throat. The radio cord's wrapped around his neck. I feel for a pulse but there's nothing. The gun is missing from his holster.

"Harding," Alison says, calling to me from the

truck—when I climb beside her in the front seat she shows me the tiny picture on the Watchman. It's Gaelen, in Rosenberg's office, but I already knew that.

That's when the screaming begins, on all our speakers, from all our damn microphones—so loud you'd think the street would finally awaken. But there are no sirens, just the sound of Elenya calling my name.

The door to the brownstone is unlocked. I take out my Glock. Boone's in the truck with the radio. "Keep it on whisper, okay?" I tell him. "So the whole neighborhood doesn't hear me coming." Alison is on the welcome mat, the .32 cupped in her left hand. "Will you stay behind me this time at least?" I say, and she nods. I don't believe her. Her cuts have reopened—the black cotton sweats sticking to her stomach as though she's come from a workout. "Take the safety off," I say, and as she fumbles with the gun I step inside and shut the door. And then I lock it.

The lobby is sleek, modern, and way too bright. I wish there was another way to do this but there's only the one staircase. I'm sure not taking the elevator. I was just here a few hours ago but everything feels different, the way school changes when you're there at night for a basketball game, when the halls are quiet and your homeroom and locker seem like someone else's.

The steps are white with a narrow runner and they creak like the hull of an icecutter. I hear something above, to my right. That's the shrink's office. If he's here he picked the wrong night for group.

I turn to the wall; cup my hands over the radio. "Boone—is there someone else up there, across the hall?"

"The light's on," he says. "I don't see anyone moving around. But the shade's down." I hear it again, this noise. It could be the wind. It sounds like someone walking on the roof. "Should I say over? Over."

At the top of the stairs I test the shrink's door—unlocked—and then go inside, very fast and low, expecting to draw some kind of fire. Nothing happens. I fumble with the radio in the low light. There's some kind of noise coming from the back like forced heat; the hiss of automatic door springs. "Boone, can you see anything? In the shrink's—"

"Nothing, Harding. Not a damn thing."

Before I cross the threshold I check the stairwell again, up and down—the steps to three and four are on a separate frame, across the hall, like a store that wants you walking through Ladies Wear to find the escalator. Everything's locked down tight. When I get near the storage room I turn off the radio, to avoid feedback—Boone's planted mikes and a camera around here somewhere, keeping watch on our receiver, hidden behind paint cans and Hoover Quik-Brooms.

The steps squeak more on the way down. Outside Rosenberg's polished rosewood door—with his name etched in bronze and gold—there's an antique hall tree with a small mirror; old-fashioned English umbrellas propped in the plant stands. I switch the radio back on. There's a slight hum, then quiet. Time slows. The world shrinks to this building, this hallway. I remember what I found here earlier today. It seems like another lifetime. When I look at the figure in the mirror it's a face I don't recognize. His eyes are set.

"He's behind you," Boone cries, not bothering to whisper—his voice lost in submachine-gun fire. Bullets rip past me through glass, wood, plaster—I kick the

door open and roll inside. One round grazes my shoulder, another whizzes by my ear like an angry yellowjacket. I'm as close to the floor as I can get and still get off two rounds, enough for one glimpse of Gaelen in the shrink's doorway, his face lit up by the firefight. I think he was smiling. I might have hit him but that Glock isn't going to stop him, not in this lifetime.

There's not much of a crowd in Rosenberg's waiting room, just a couch; plastic tables and chairs I could hide behind—cover that might work against an old Colt on *Gunsmoke*. The gun I saw Gaelen holding looked like a Cobray, a fucking dangerous weapon, shaped like a T square; not much larger than a handgun but capable of hundreds of rounds. Gripped hard in his hand it seemed an extension of his arm.

The next door leads to a hallway. I try the doorknob gently. It's open. I hear the noises again, above somewhere. Someone running on the roof. They distract me so much I barely notice the figure half-hidden by the drapes, crouching beneath the window.

When he moves I nearly shoot him.

"Frost, my God, what are you doing here—"

"I was with Elenya, he just grabbed her—"

"Where is she now? Have you seen her?" Frost shakes his head. A bit of moonlight comes in through the window, showing the streak of sweat on his forehead. He's wearing a suit again. I think he wears suits to the beach, like Nixon.

The radio comes to life. Frost jumps.

"Harding? Are you there?"

"No, Boone. I'm in the fourth dimension."

"—he's moving again—"

"Moving where, Boone?"

"We should get out of here—" Frost says. He's drinking from the silver flask, filled once again with rum. So much for the new Frost.

"Boone? Talk to me."

"He's *moving* for Christ's sake," says Boone, fear in his voice despite the five hundred yards between us. "—wait, there's *two* of them—"

"That's Elenya," Frost says. "I told you she was up here."

"Boone, slow down. Where is he? In the hallway? Where?"

"—just ahead of you, Harding. It's all shadows back there but he's moving *toward* you—"

"We should get out of here," Frost says, back-pedaling. He trips over a chair, stumbles briefly; loses the flask. He doesn't stop to pick it up. I hear the beginnings of sirens finally, twisting in the night air. They seem miles, worlds away.

"Get out *now*," Boone says, "do you hear? He's got some kind of gym bag he's messing with—Harding, are you even listening? Go back—"

"Not without Elenya," I say. Frost is gone now, on his way downstairs.

Gaelen's shadow crosses the dark glass black on black.

The sirens grow stronger, more distinct.

The first thing I see when the door swings open is Gaelen at Rosenberg's black desk like a CEO or a father at Christmas dinner. He has Elenya on the floor tied very loosely, just enough to keep her from running off. A dog on a short leash. The Cobray's short shaft is near her face. She looks very frightened. I put down my gun. I did get him earlier with the Glock—there's a shade of red like fresh cranberries seeping into the fabric of his shirt—but he barely favors it.

"I came a little early," he says.

His coat must be back at the police station. He's wearing a heavy Indiana sweatshirt, the kind sold as a souvenir at gas stations; the '76 sales tag is attached with a safety pin. He has two other piercings as well, in both eyebrows. His earring tonight is polished silver. His black hair is cut short but still very thick.

He kicks my Glock across the floor, examines my radio before tossing it on the couch.

"This is how we're doing it," Gaelen says. "It's very simple. Elenya and I are staying. You're going. Now. I want you to turn around, walk outside to the elevator, go back down to the first floor."

"Don't do it, Harding," Elenya says. "He's got some kind of bomb out there, and remote control—"

"I told the police the lobby was wired to explode," Gaelen explains patiently. "It's not. I don't know anything about bombs. Turn around, Harding, and walk out of here. I won't shoot you in the back."

His eyes are very bright, on anyone else a crystal meth alertness but Gaelen doesn't need drugs. He's high on life. His jeans have blood on the legs and crotch. His hair has a sheen to it like a stallion that's been run till it dropped.

The gym bag Boone mentioned is on a glass end table. Gaelen holds a remote in one hand, cradles the Cobray in his lap. Elenya sits on the floor, her legs tucked back, pale and slender. She tugs at her dress each time Gaelen looks at her. And he looks at her a lot.

I'm wondering if he'd hurt her. How many rounds I

could take at this distance and still get my hands around his throat.

"Get in the fucking elevator, Harding."

"I'd rather not—"

But he's nudging Elenya to her feet with the tip of the gun, herding both of us through the door. The phone rings and rings.

There are patches of light on the landing. Gaelen doesn't press the button, instead pries the door open with his bare hands. The veins bulge on his wrists like restless snakes.

"Plenty of room," he says. What he wants us to see is the figure huddled in the corner, knees against his chin, black service mask tied around his face. What I focus on is another gym bag a foot or so away from Stephen Rosenberg, just out of reach.

Gaelen drags a shiny chrome trash can over to prop open the doors. He pulls his sweatshirt up to wipe his face, exposing a navel ring below rows of thick abdominals, a blue computer disk hanging from his neck like high-tech dogtags.

"You're still hoping to blackmail him? After this?"

"The account numbers are on here," Gaelen says, more to Elenya than to me. "Two million dollars."

"You killed a Chicago cop, Gaelen. Two Indiana troopers are on life support. There's probably fifty cops out there right now arguing about who gets first shot. And who gets to play with you afterward. You won't get fifty yards."

"They won't shoot. I have a hostage. Hell, I've got three."

"Let them go," Elenya says suddenly. "If I have to stay—you may as well let them go. They don't matter. Untie Stephen. He can't breathe in that thing."

"Why would you ask that?" Gaelen says quietly. "After all he's done—"

"Just do it, will you?"

"But why?"

"I don't want anyone dying," she says. "Not for me."

We're standing on the landing, halfway between the staircases. The cops must be out there somewhere but there's very little sound coming in, even less light. The book on this situation is keep the guy talking, keep everyone alive. Gaelen may have read that book.

Right now he's staring at Stephen Rosenberg.

"He's not worth killing," I say.

"What the hell do you know."

"He's not worth your time."

"Time? That's all the bastard left me. Do you know how long ten years is? He took away my work, my life—"

"What do you mean? The medical board took away your license."

"He wrote the fucking letter that convinced them. I just found out last year it was him—he wasn't even on the fucking board. I don't think he even knew who I was—not then, not last fall, when he saw me at the gym and asked me to screw his wife. He knows now. I'm taking his money, I'm taking his wife—"

"What did you do to Angela?" I say softly.

"Who?"

It takes a great deal of restraint not to respond to that the way I'd like.

"Gaelen," I say slowly, "don't tell me you don't even remember her name."

"I did nothing to her. She was crazy."

"What did you do, Gaelen?"

"I helped her. Like I was helping Elenya. That day in the gym"—he takes Elenya's arm—"remember Elenya? When your wrist hurt?"

"No," Elenya says.

"You were dressed all in yellow, like a sunflower—"

"No," she says. "I don't remember."

She doesn't look frightened anymore. Just angry. When she shakes off Gaelen's hand her eyes flash in the dark. We're both awake. Time to leave my corner.

"Have you looked at that disk?" I say.

"What?"

"The disk, Gaelen," I say. "Have you looked at the fucking disk? Because it needs a code word. You won't get the money. This is all for nothing."

"Don't fuck with me," Gaelen says. "I'm warning you, do not fuck with me now."

"I can fix it," I say. "Just let Elenya go. Take me instead."

"Rosenberg gave me the disk, Harding. He would have given me some fucking code—he would have given me his grandmother."

"He doesn't know Donnie Wilson and I installed it—it's a security code, Gaelen. That's what we do, remember? You need it to get the numbers, otherwise all you get is Stephen playing with himself. And the Swiss aren't going to give you two cents for that, much less two million."

"Why would you fix it?"

"I told you why. Let Elenya go."

"I'm not stupid, Harding."

"Of course not."

"If you're fucking with me I'll shove the computer sideways up your ass."

"I'd expect no less."

He glares at me, trying to read my face. There's nothing there.

"You might want to look at it, that's all," I say softly. "Before you fade into your fucking sunset."

There's a Mac in the receptionist's small cubicle. I'd rather use one in a larger room but the Cobray's jammed in my ribs.

I'm amazed we still have electricity. The computer's an old LCIII; out of date, underpowered, much like me. My fingers run over the surface of the blue disk as though reading Braille, searching for a small plastic switch. It's been broken off.

"Where's the bomb, Gaelen? In the elevator? In that gym bag?" I'm treading water, trying to think of something to do. The disk is still coated with Gaelen's sweat.

"Hurry up."

"Just dynamite? Something easy—maybe something Oren learned blowing tree stumps for that developer—like that combination he wrote in his book—75-15-10—I thought it was a safe—"

"Are you gonna turn it on or do you want your shoulder broken?"

The monitor snaps on. When I get the first menu I pop in the disk, then use the mouse to punch it up. Gaelen frowns a bit when the blue disk disappears, so I get something on the screen right away.

It's a Quicktime or Photoshop program, about as it was described; lots of pictures; boys and girls. A surprising amount seems to be solo. Rosenberg's favorite body image must be his own. The quality's not very good—faces are grainy; body parts out of proportion—

but it would satisfy the hunger of a middle-aged doctor bored with his marriage; the lust of a local news team.

But I don't see any numbers.

"They must be just after this," Gaelen says. "In the next reel." You'd think he was showing vacation movies. He's leaning over my shoulder now, a little worried. The screen's fairly distracting; the pull of pornography. From the corner of my eye I can see Elenya take a step toward the door.

"What's the fucking password?" Gaelen says, turning. A siren starts somewhere far away. It feels like we're at the end of the world.

"Password," I say. "'Isn't that great?'"

"Erase it, Harding," Elenya says behind us, an edge to her words that seems to cut Gaelen as he turns toward her and I do the only thing I can think of, hitting the margin at the bottom. The screen goes blank. The text has just moved off-screen but Gaelen doesn't know that.

He panics, reaching for the keyboard, pushing me aside. And he lowers the gun. I throw myself against him with my whole body, slamming him against the wall, knocking the wind from him. I hit him hard in the face but he doesn't go down. We're too close for him to shoot. He shoves me across the desk and holds the Cobray against my throat. His weight's on me and I can't breathe until finally my hand clutches a bottle vase—I feel like Beowulf fighting Grendel with a chalice instead of a sword—it shatters against Gaelen's cheek, sending shards of glass into his eyes. His cheekbone gives way like soft spackle. When he backs up I hit him hard and low, in the knees—an illegal clip. His legs are locked. I hear something crack. We both tumble into Rosenberg's office. Despite his pain Gaelen grips me around the waist. His head slams a metal cabinet but he won't release me.

I don't have any weapons except the gunshot wound in Gaelen's side. My shoulder throbs but I ignore it and jack my elbow hard into the red raw flesh. He grunts. His grip loosens and so I hit him there again even harder. It's the only Achilles heel he has. I dig at the fleshy wound like a corkscrew, my fingers clawing and gouging as if trying to rip his heart out. Finally he screams, releasing me.

The Cobray's lost in the next room but there's a glint of black steel now in Gaelen's right hand. I'm not sure how he can see me. One eye is bleeding. The other's just as red, as red as the beam of light from a SIG Saur's laser sight, crawling up and down my leg like a skittish spider.

I'm in motion as he shoots. The bullet strikes me in the lower side; it twists me around but a rush of adrenaline and the grace of shock carry me forward, pushing him to the wall. This time it's me who won't let go—I hold his arm overhead with both my hands, find his wrist and twist it back until the SIG finally drops to the floor. Then I keep twisting. His hands turn over. So does his wrist. The bones snap in two places.

I pick up the gun. I hope to God he keeps the damn thing fully loaded. He backs around the room to the window, in retreat for the first time. He's breathing hard, holding his wrist, blood dripping from his face. I could stop now—I finally hear people outside—but I don't even think about it.

"What did you do to her?" I say. "To Angela?"

Despite the blood on his face and mouth he's trying to frame a smile.

"Nothing her daddy didn't do," he says.

The first two bullets send him to the glass. The rest of the clip sends him through it. The open window's like a black hole. It swallows him up. He falls back through the window, arms outstretched. I hear him scream. I don't hear him land.

Cold winter air rushes in through the window. Parts of the outside world rush in too—sirens; men's voices; shouts from outside the building. I can hear my own heart pounding. My side begins to burn. Gaelen hangs below me on the barbed wire fence like a scarecrow. His earring gleams like a fallen star. He could be anyone down there, especially if I concentrate on that face—that older face—of Martinez.

The phone's buzzing constantly with an annoying electronic beep. When I finally pick it up I realize Elenya's gone.

The voice is Reilly's—"Harding? Jesus Christ is that you?"

"Reilly, don't come up yet—the elevator's wired—"

There are voices in the lobby now, someone running down the stairs.

The elevator lurches to life. And then there's an explosion that throws me backward, into the air. I'm dreaming of childhood before I land.

When I come to someone's coughing much too loudly, an annoying rusty hack. That's me, I discover, breathing the dust and insulation flying everywhere. The phone's now untethered but still gripped in my hand. I must have thought I was hanging on to something secure.

The front wall of the office is completely gone

now—in fact there's a clear sight line out onto 57th Street. With better weather you could see the lake, maybe Michigan, the East Coast, Europe. The stairs have torn away from the building. The elevator's on the thirteenth floor. I don't see Elenya anywhere.

"Sit tight, Harding," Reilly says, his voice barely audible on the radio. I'm in no hurry. There's a little housekeeping to attend to in the back room. I find a sink that still works and drink some water. I rinse Gaelen's blood and tissue from my hands.

Lights flicker on and off. When I turn on the TV in Stephen's office a demo tape starts automatically in the VCR; just like the cosmetics counter at Bloomie's or Field's. The skin on a woman's face is being surgically sliced, then pulled back by anonymous white-gloved fingers. A familiar voice is calmly detailing the procedures. Stephen Rosenberg's in the room with me now.

Gaelen's gym bag is on the floor, covered with dust. Inside are seven tapes labeled "Elenya Rosenberg." Seven's my lucky number. The first six are blank; the digital counter stays at zero—they weren't erased; they were never used. The seventh is the tape I watched at Elenya's, with a second part I haven't seen—voyeuristic shots of Elenya walking or driving, coming out of the health club, shots of her bedroom filmed through the window. Most are from far away, sometimes a block or more. Sometimes she's just one of a dozen women in the picture. The ones of her house are from across the street. That's as close as he got.

In the examining room I find a large bottle of phenol acid, high-concentrate. I pour it into a pan. Then I sit and wait by the TV, the hiss of the acid defacing the tape, the white noise of the blank screen filling the room. The gunshot wound in my side is like a motor slowly accelerating.

"We got it all, Harding," Boone says, when I finally come down the ladder. Alison's already left for the hospital. "Everything but the window and the elevator—didn't I tell you those cameras were good?"

I'd forgotten all about the cameras and the tapes. No wonder there's so many news trucks outside. The whole thing was on closed-circuit TV.

"That's why nobody came up?" I say. "You were watching?"

"We were waiting for a commercial," Keegan says.

"You're a hero, Harding," Reilly says. "Except I couldn't see what happened to Gaelen at the end, at the window."

"He slipped on a banana."

"Yeah, that's about what I thought," Reilly says. "Could you see Elenya going back to the elevator?"

"What do you mean?"

"We saw the elevator blow, from this side," Keegan says. "Her husband got out. We didn't see her in it. Your camera didn't show the hallway until the fucking wall blew down."

"Sorry, Keegan. I was on a limited budget. Next time we'll try for better coverage."

"But she was in it, right?" Reilly says.

"Where else would she be?"

Reilly sees a fireman who's just come from the elevator shaft.

"Anything left?" Reilly says. "Anyone in there?"

"Cockroaches the size of hummingbirds," the fireman says. "Nothing else."

Reilly pulls up his socks, tightens his shoelaces.

We walk outside. The police are keeping reporters and neighbors far away. It's a busy night now up the block at 57th Street Books. The free coffee runs out early. Frost is giving an interview to Action News. Rosenberg pushes through the police line—next of kin; building tenant; victim.

"This is your fault," he says. His face is red and still lined with indentations from the leather, covered with sweat.

"You look grief-stricken," I say to him. "How did you get out of there tonight?"

"He ran like a scared rabbit," Reilly says. "Says Elenya was right behind him. But she never came down."

"This man's a thief—he took valuable property from my office," Rosenberg says to Reilly. "Private letters—"

"You gotta be kidding," Reilly says. "Back off, will you? Half your fucking building's down on 58th Street, your wife's blown to smithereens, and you're worried about some letters?"

A paramedic brings me a blanket. My jacket's gone but I don't feel cold. They get a stretcher out for me, back up another ambulance.

Rosenberg won't go away. His attention's split between his brownstone and me. Every once in a while the aftershocks cause another part of the facade to slip. Years of renovation fall to dust.

"I'll pay you ten thousand dollars," he says. "Fifteen."

"Excuse me, Stephen, but I've been shot. Could this wait?"

"Twenty-five thousand."

"Everything's gone. Your little disk included. Bye-bye."

"Where are the letters?" he says. "I don't care about the fucking disk—it's the letters I want. Thirty thousand—"

"I'll trade you," I say. "You operated on a man named Eduardo Martinez ten years ago. What name did he take. Where is he."

"Who?"

"Don't play dumb—Eduardo Martinez." I say the name slowly. "You helped his daughter Angela. You gave him a new face. For two million dollars."

"I don't know him."

"You can't still be afraid of him, after ten years—"

"Not exactly." He waits until a cop walks past, leaving us alone. "He's dead, Harding. Let's leave it at that."

"What name did he take?"

"None."

"Do you want the fucking letters or not?"

"He died on the table." He sees my look of disbelief. "It happens, it can happen anytime you use a general. There's a risk. Respiratory failure, circulatory failure. We did seven operations on him—outpatient, in my office—and on the seventh he just didn't wake up."

"What'd you do, bury him in your garden?"

"There's a funeral home—this really isn't your business—"

"And you just kept the money?"

"He wasn't paying me two million for the surgery, Harding. My fees aren't quite that high. I helped him set up a Swiss account, it was supposed to be temporary—his wife was trying to get him declared dead so she could seize his assets. She wanted the money. Now will you please tell me where my letters are?"

Remnants of the last explosion are still suspended in the air; bits of wood and ash and paper floating down on us like snow. I swat at some to show him where his letters went. "Elenya had them," I say. "And I believe she took them with her."

He stares at his building, his elevator, his wall, what remains of his property.

His property's gone.

"I don't believe it," he says.

"Believe it."

"The numbers were on them," he says. "That's where I kept my bank numbers. On the outside of the envelopes—"

"Not the disk?"

"No, of course not—what disk? You had my disk, the blue one?"

"For just a second. I wouldn't worry about your money. The Swiss are very understanding. You'll get your money eventually."

"But not for days, maybe a week—"

"So? Who else would take it in the meantime?"

He stares at me.

"I'll see you in court," he says. The ultimate threat.

"I don't think so. Now that I know what you do with your patients in your own office—do you want that on the local news? You and Elizabeth Manning, for example? Or Gretchen? And listen, I was wondering: when the liposuction tubes come flying off right in the middle is that like some sixties Wesson oil party where anyone can join in?"

"Fuck you," he says.

"Sure, get in line."

He hasn't said a word about Elenya, or what she went through tonight. Or the money he paid Gaelen—what he paid it for. Not a single word. Or the fact that Lucy worked in his office around that time. *I got tired of the blood.*

You want me to say he's a murderer? Fine, he's a murderer.

He walks away to stare at his building.

The cops won't go after Rosenberg for anything. They'll pin it all on Gaelen. The university won't want it going any further.

I pull the blue disk from my pocket and toss it to Boone.

"Put this on the Net, will you? Richie Dugan's sex BBS, the bondage newsgroups. Maybe the university's Web page. Let people have a good look at the real Rosenberg. Let 'em download that sucker."

Boone pockets the disk, grinning.

They put me on a stretcher; it feels wonderful to lie down. Maybe getting shot means I can finally get some sleep. The ambulance attendant is checking his watch—he's got a late date. He's closing the rear door when Reilly stops him.

"Couple of things," Reilly says, "before you die. I see Elenya's coat up there. I don't see your jacket."

"I'll buy another."

"Back there, by the window? We found a rope ladder. Real good one, too—Sears. A Craftsman."

"Bob Villa will be thrilled to have your endorsement."

"What do you suppose it was doing up there?"

"I'd guess it's Rosenberg's. In case of fire break glass, drop ladder."

"Funny thing, though—it wasn't in a closet, just

shoved under some crap, like somebody was trying to hide it. And the top of the damned thing has broken glass in the rope."

"There's glass everywhere."

"No but this is glass stuck down in the fibers. Like it was used already. Tonight."

Reilly's not looking at me. He's lighting a cigarette. The ambulance attendant is waiting to close the back door.

"Well, I guess he used it before," I say. "Somewhere else. Where there was glass."

"That would be one explanation," Reilly says, nodding. "A fucking *stupid* one, but shit, I guess Forensics can match glass samples. And there's spots of blood on there too we could match if we wanted to—"

"My side hurts, Reilly," I say. "I'd really like to go to the hospital and sleep for a week or so."

"You're right, I'm keeping you," he says.

I'm not sure why Elenya left her coat. But she can afford to buy another. When I pulled in that ladder I could feel the weather changing; growing even colder. The moon peeked from behind a cloud. A heavy snow was covering Gaelen.

I saw her just as she climbed off the last step. I couldn't think of anything to say. But she was shivering. What she needed was my coat. It drifted down to her like a lost parachute. Minus fifteen windchill tonight. More snow tomorrow. But if she goes far enough she'll stumble on daybreak. It must be warmer somewhere.

"Are you sending the ladder to Forensics?"

"I don't see the point," Reilly says. "Let the dead stay dead, am I right?"

"You would've made a good priest after all, Reilly," I say.

He nods to the attendant, slaps the back of the ambulance.

I can unclench my fist now. Elenya's wedding ring—I'd found it inside her coat—falls to the stretcher near my leg. Later tonight or tomorrow I'll seal it in an envelope and slip it through the mail slot at Purdy's Sunshine Cleaners, in Woodlawn one last debt to pay. He can walk right next door to pawn it.

And maybe Elenya will find some use for Angela's copper bracelet, when her hands stumble upon it, in the pocket of my jacket. They say copper has healing properties.

The ambulance grumbles to life.

The door slams, shutting out the night and the cold.

EPILOGUE

Friday night I'm in my apartment with a full pot of coffee and Patti Smith on my stereo—she's dancing barefoot, loud enough to make Minas pound my floor with his mop handle. I'm too sore to dance. I still have stitches from my surgery. A book on mosaic tiles is putting me to sleep when the phone rings, and I turn down the music.

"It's me," Alison says. "I'm at the Knotty Pine on South Shore Drive, do you know it?"

"The Knotty Pine? That's a gay bar, Alison."

"No kidding. Maybe that's why nobody's buying me a drink. How soon can you get here?"

"I thought I'd stay in, eat some dinner, maybe rearrange my record collection—"

"Now, Harding. And don't worry—it's like riding the El; just don't make eye contact. No jewelry, no handkerchiefs. And leave the L.L. Bean look at home." She hangs up. I turn the coffee off and change my clothes.

It's closer now to Easter but the Knotty Pine still has its Christmas decorations up—two sagging strands of lights taped to the front door; a crudely drawn cross-dressing Santa stenciled on the window. Alison's in a back booth with two of her friends. The dance floor's full of guys in VFW windbreakers and bowling shirts. It must be league night.

"This is Patti," Alison says, scooting over, "and this is Lisa. We suffered through lab school together. Patti's studying ruthlessness in B-school. Lisa's a prelaw."

"As opposed to pre-op," Lisa says, smiling. Roy the waiter brings their drinks. I order a beer and ask for a menu. If nothing else the ache in both shoulders gives me an excuse to drink.

"The food's at the bar," Roy says. "Karaoke buffet. The specials tonight are pickled eggs at the bar and stallion guards in the back."

"We'll pass, Roy," Alison says. "On both, I think."

"That's it?" I say. "No sandwiches, nothing?"

"There's a Wendy's two doors down, honey," he says, bringing me an Old style. "You enjoy the show."

The bar's blue-collar, mostly men; a few women. Patti and Lisa are wearing dresses and heels. Alison's wearing black jeans and a black turtleneck; a leather vest; black Doc Martens; no makeup. She's the sexiest of the three.

"Why'd you call?" I ask her as the house lights dim. "Sssh," she says, touching my lips with her finger. A blue spot follows a Donna Summer clone named Nikki on stage; she starts lip-synching a disco *Mac-Arthur Park*. It's not a very good performance but Nikki's outfit and makeup are good enough to fool me until the cake's nearly melted in the rain. "Nikki" is Nicholas Leander, vice president of marketing; my latest assignment for Donnie. He's exchanged his nine-hundred-dollar Italian suit for a sequined blazer and a curly black wig.

The music turns into a medly of *MacArthur Parks*—Gloria Gaynor, Sinatra, Tanya Tucker. The poor guy's changing costumes like crazy. It's the hardest I've seen him work all week.

"Would you like to dance?" I ask Alison.

"I'd love to. But I'm not sure I can move."

"I know, I'm wrapped like a mummy under this shirt. Come on."

We ignore the changing tempos, slow dance to everything. Alison puts her cheek next to mine. I put my arm lightly around her. We touch each other as though we're made of glass.

"It's been a few years, Harding," she says. Her body sways gently. "I was beginning to think you'd made some close friends in prison."

"Like Rocco, you mean? It's hard keeping in touch."

"Are you wearing cologne?"

"It came with the shirt."

"The new Harding," she says. "I like it."

When Nikki finishes he follows a tall blonde in spiked heels to the T-room; I look inside the curtain long enough to see Nikki doing coke with the blonde. He doesn't see me. Bodies shift in silence. "Are you in or out?" someone says. "I'm out," I say. "Maybe later." They've got a real humidity problem in there. I've got Nikki on drugs, sex, disco.

John Cale comes on the jukebox. *You know more than I know . . .*

Alison returns from the bathroom. "No doors," she says, frowning.

"In the women's? Tough crowd."

We get our coats and say goodbye to Patti and Lisa. I offer them a lift but Lisa says no.

"Thanks, we'd better stay," Lisa says. "They give prizes later, and the guys in ABBA are buddies of ours. We should stick around and give them our vote."

"You have our proxy," I say, looking around the

room. I've lost Nikki but the blonde is easy to spot; she must be six-two in heels.

The streets are deserted down here this time of night. We're waiting on the curb while a taxi slows, looking for a fare, when Nikki and the blonde come up behind us; both of them are sniffing, that coke afterburn in their eyes.

I start to turn away but Alison reaches up and pulls the hood on my parka up over my head and wraps her arms around me in a kiss. Her mouth is warm. She smells wonderful. Her body fits tight against mine, as if completing a puzzle. They walk around us talking softly and laughing. We kiss until we hear their car doors closing.

The cab pulls away. We're alone on the street. I kiss her again.

"I saw Cary Grant do that once," Alison says, her green eyes shining. "Did it work?"

"Perfectly," I say. "It worked perfectly."